Series: Sanity & Tallulah

Title: *Sanity & Tallulah*

Author: Molly Brooks

Imprint: Disney • Hyperion

In-store date: 10/23/2018

Hardcover ISBN: 978-1-368-00844-0

Hardcover Price: US $21.99 / CAN $21.99

Paperback ISBN: 978-1-368-02280-4

Paperback Price: US $12.99 / CAN $13.99

E-book ISBN: 978-1-368-02737-3

Trim size: 5 ¾ x 8 ¼

Page count: 240

Ages: 8–12

Grades: 3–7

ATTENTION, READER:

This is an uncorrected galley proof. It is not a finished book and is not expected to look like one. Errors in spelling, page length, format, etc., will be corrected when the book is published several months from now. Direct quotes should be checked against the final printed book.

We are pleased to send this book for review.

Please send two copies of any review or mention to:

Disney Book Group

Attn: Children's Publicity Department

125 West End Avenue, 3rd Floor

New York, NY 10023

dpw.publicity@disney.com

SANITY & TALLULAH

Sanity &

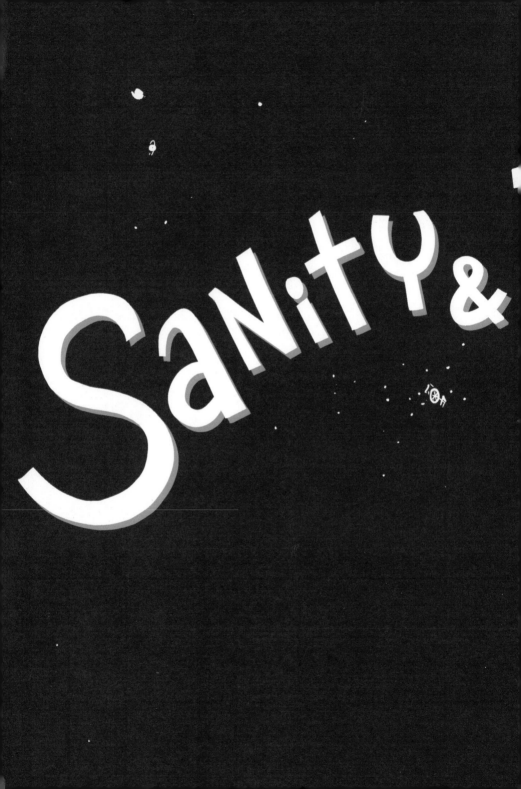

TALLULAH

MOLLY BROOKS

Disney • Hyperion

LOS ANGELES   NEW YORK

First Edition, October 2018

10 9 8 7 6 5 4 3 2 1

FAC-008598-18250

Printed in the United States of America

This book is set in 9-pt Gargle/Fonstpring

Designed by Maria Elias

Library of Congress Cataloging-in-Publication Data TK

ISBN 978-1-368-00844-0

Reinforced binding

Visit www.DisneyBooks.com

dedication tk

SANITY & TALLULAH

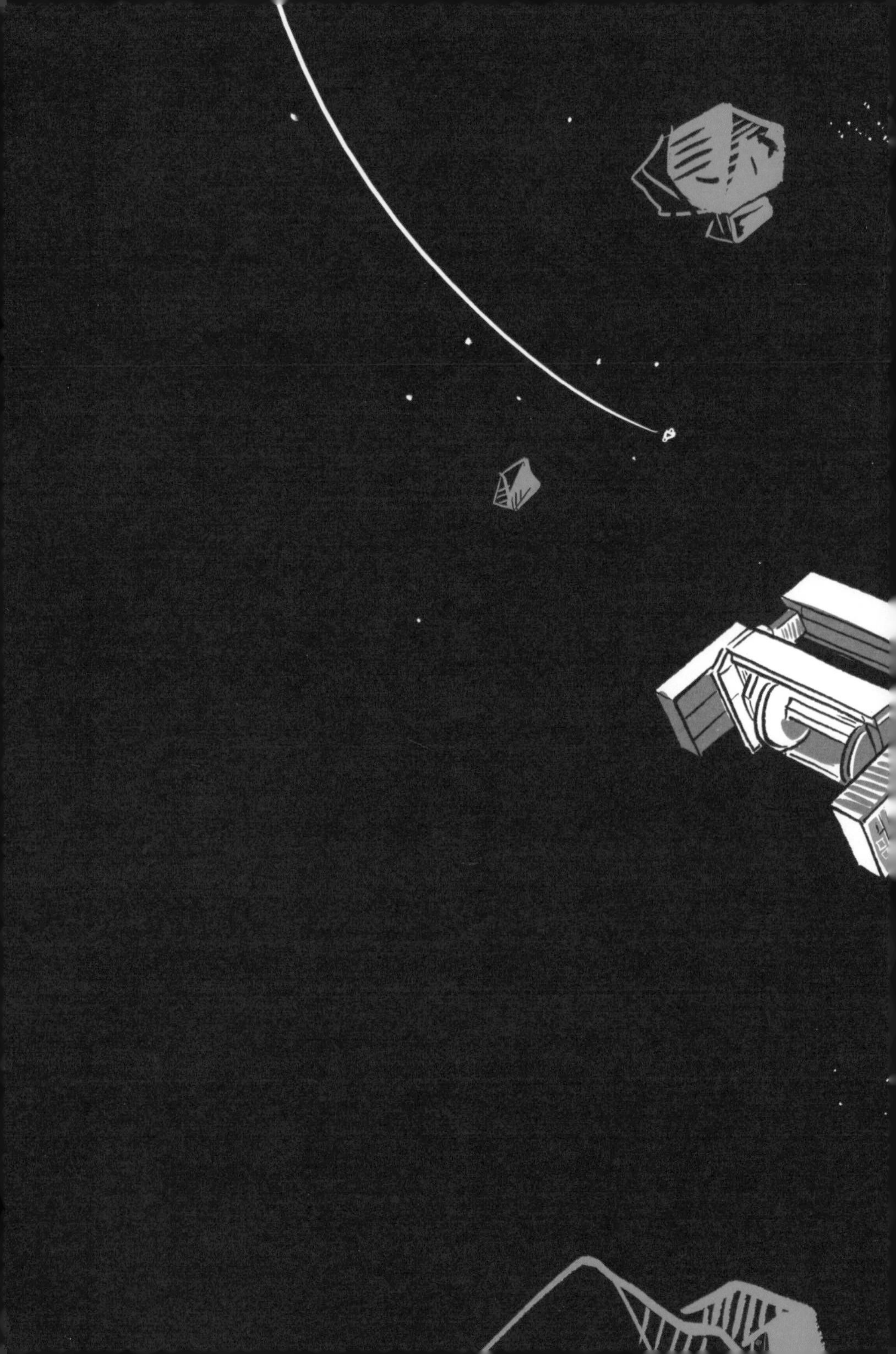

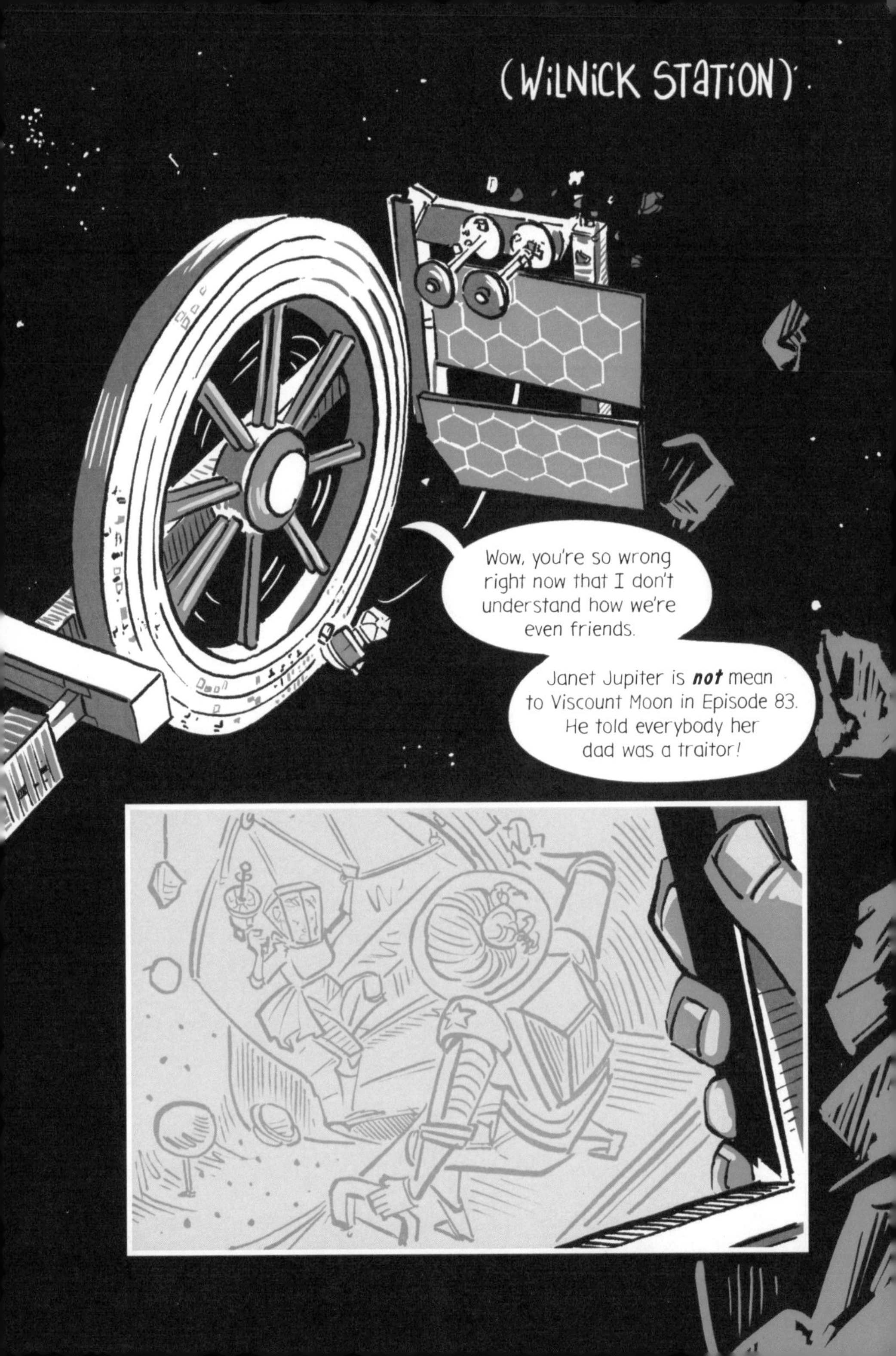
(WILNICK STATION)
Wow, you're so wrong right now that I don't understand how we're even friends.
Janet Jupiter is ***not*** mean to Viscount Moon in Episode 83. He told everybody her dad was a traitor!

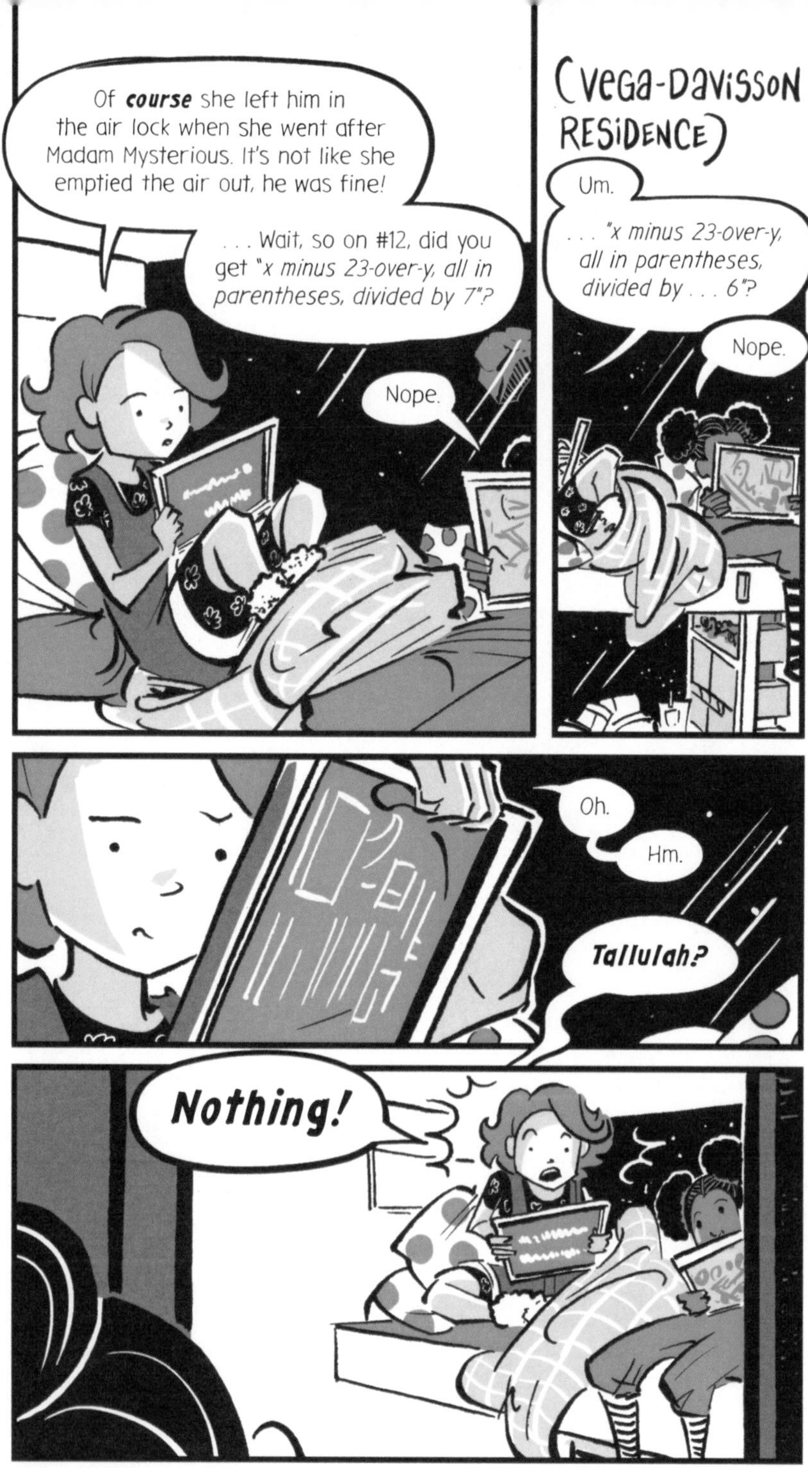
Of *course* she left him in the air lock when she went after Madam Mysterious. It's not like she emptied the air out, he was fine!
. . . Wait, so on #12, did you get *"x minus 23-over-y, all in parentheses, divided by 7"?*
Nope.
(VEGA-DAVISSON RESIDENCE)
Um.
. . . *"x minus 23-over-y, all in parentheses, divided by . . . 6"?*
Nope.
Oh.
Hm.
Tallulah?
Nothing!

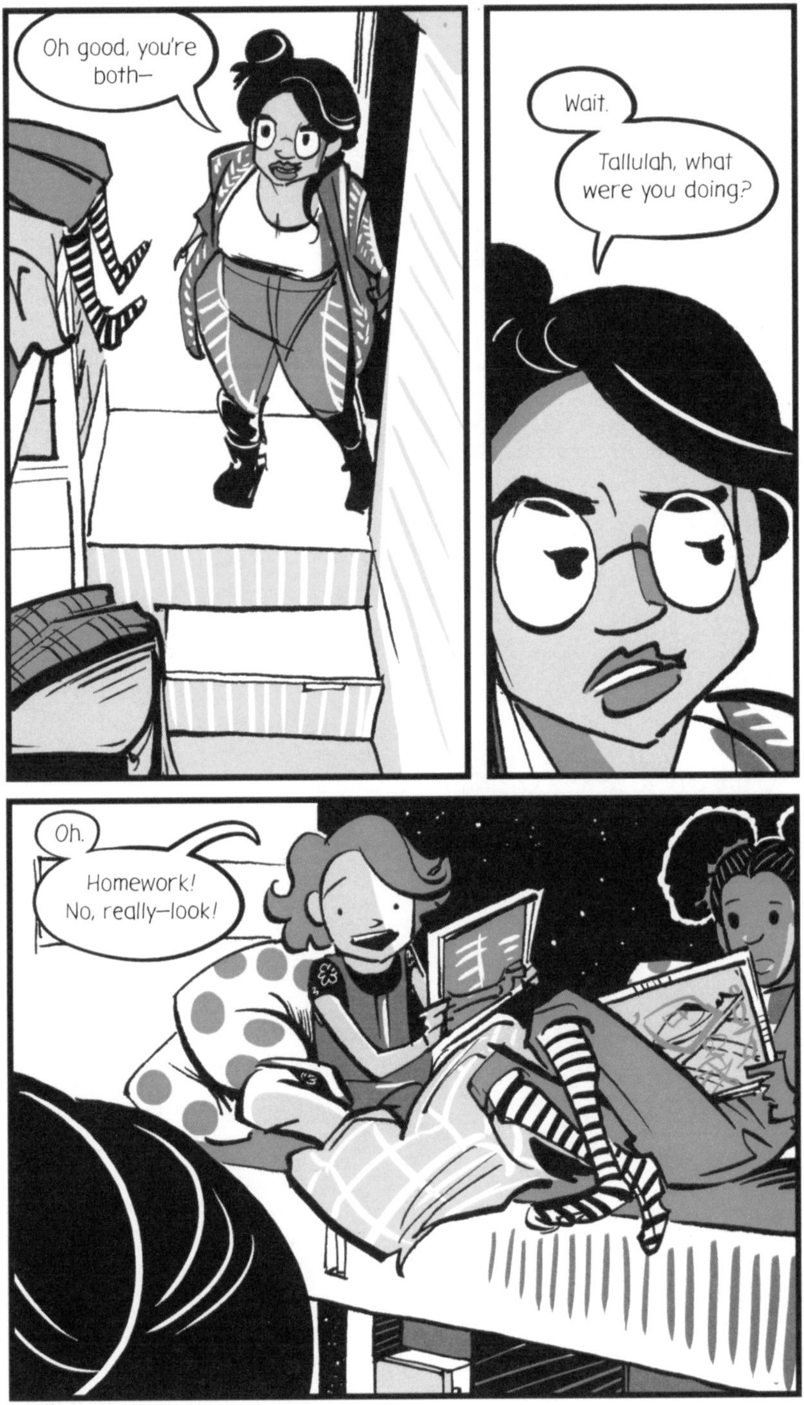
Oh good, you're both–
Wait.
Tallulah, what were you doing?
Oh.
Homework! No, really–look!

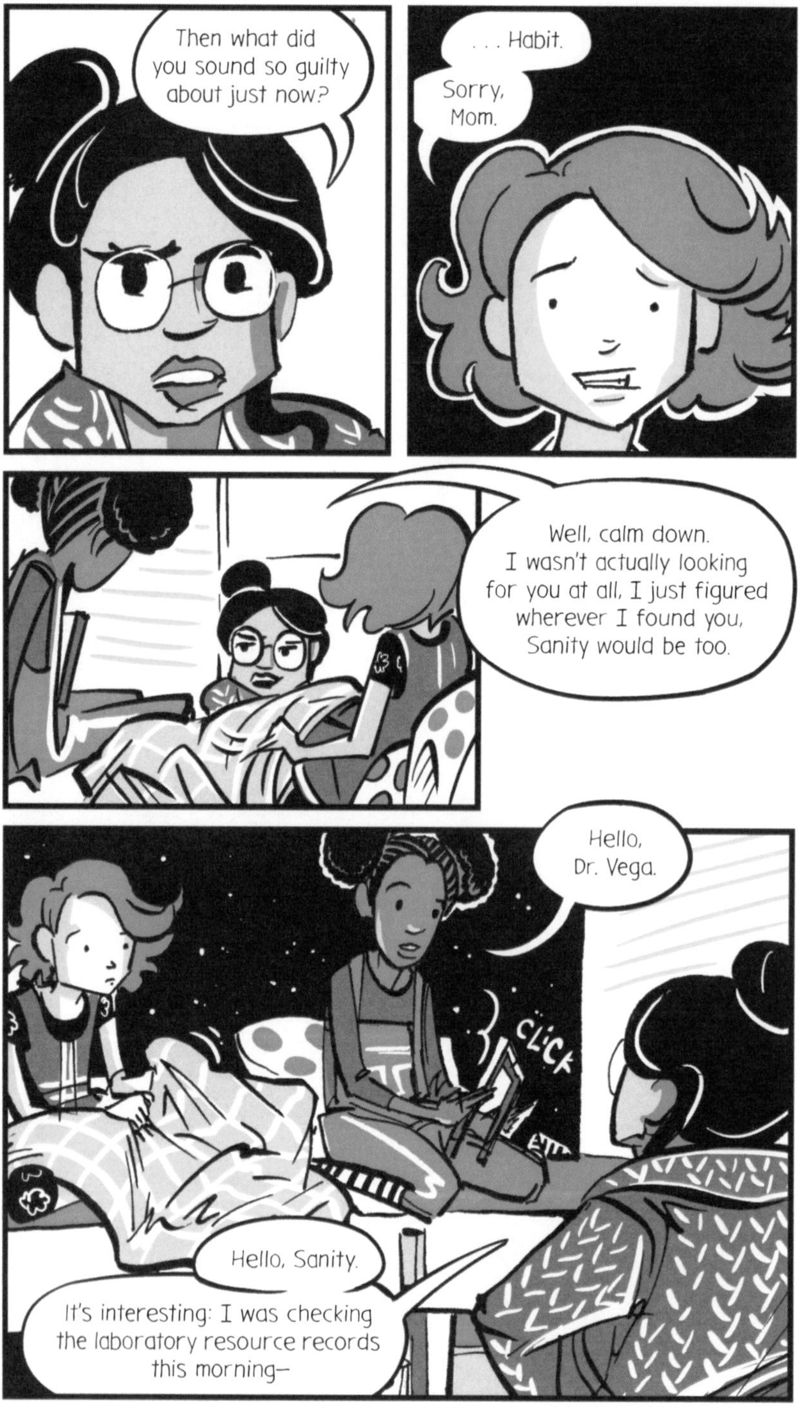
Then what did you sound so guilty about just now?
. . . Habit.
Sorry, Mom.
Well, calm down. I wasn't actually looking for you at all, I just figured wherever I found you, Sanity would be too.
Hello, Dr. Vega.
CLICK
Hello, Sanity.
It's interesting: I was checking the laboratory resource records this morning—

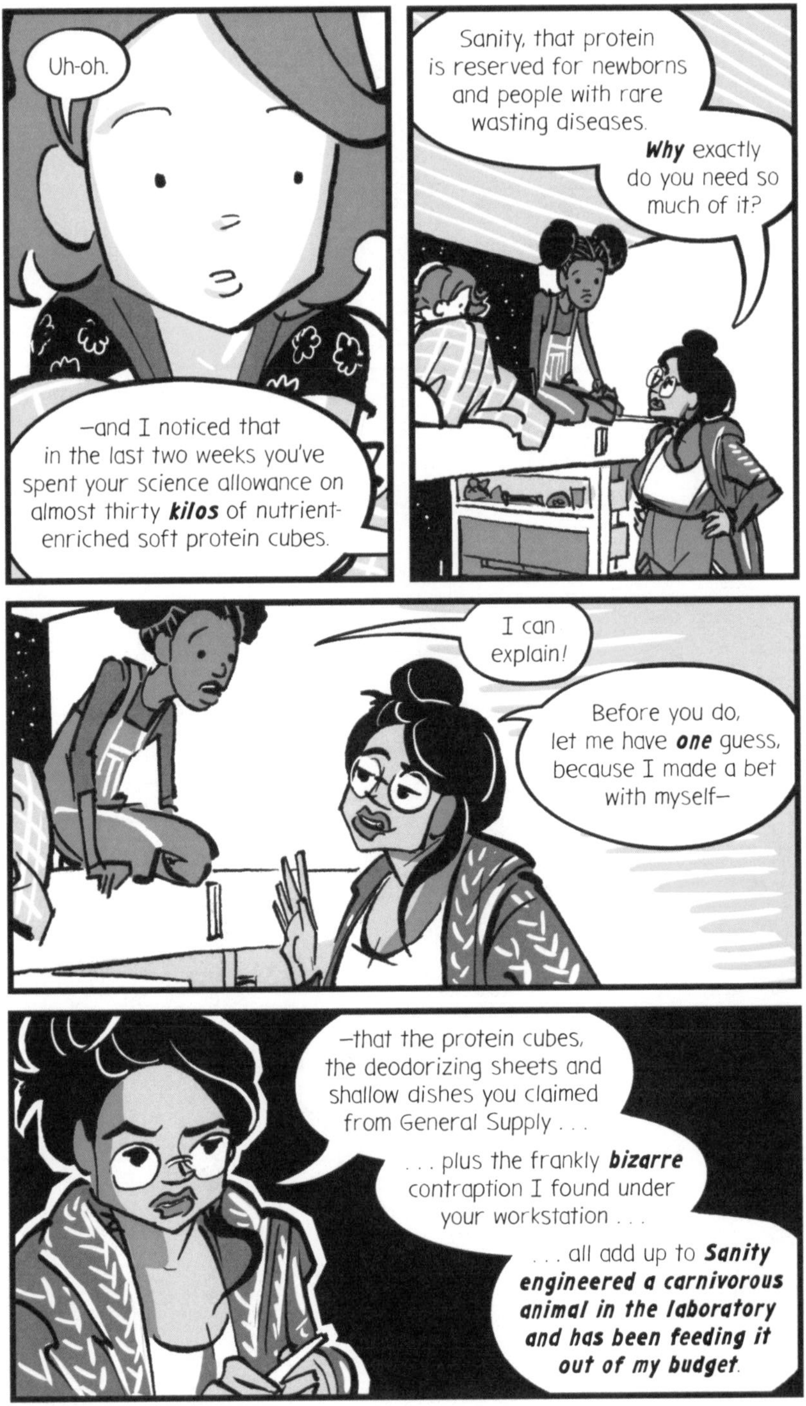
Uh-oh.
—and I noticed that in the last two weeks you've spent your science allowance on almost thirty **kilos** of nutrient-enriched soft protein cubes.
Sanity, that protein is reserved for newborns and people with rare wasting diseases.
Why exactly do you need so much of it?
I can explain!
Before you do, let me have **one** guess, because I made a bet with myself—
—that the protein cubes, the deodorizing sheets and shallow dishes you claimed from General Supply . . .
. . . plus the frankly **bizarre** contraption I found under your workstation . . .
. . . all add up to **Sanity engineered a carnivorous animal in the laboratory and has been feeding it out of my budget**.

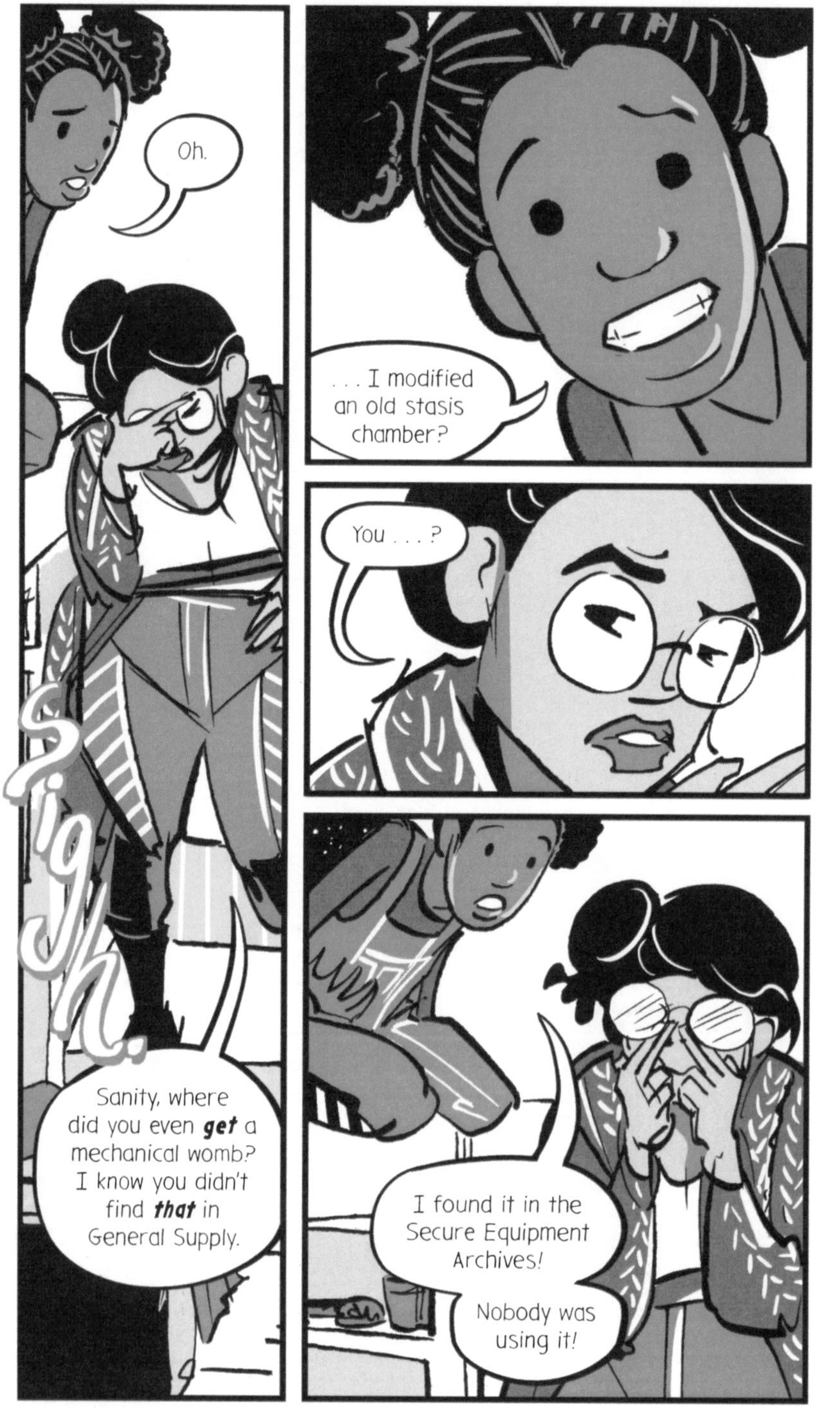
Oh.
. . . I modified an old stasis chamber?
You . . . ?
Sigh . . .
Sanity, where did you even **get** a mechanical womb? I know you didn't find **that** in General Supply.
I found it in the Secure Equipment Archives!
Nobody was using it!

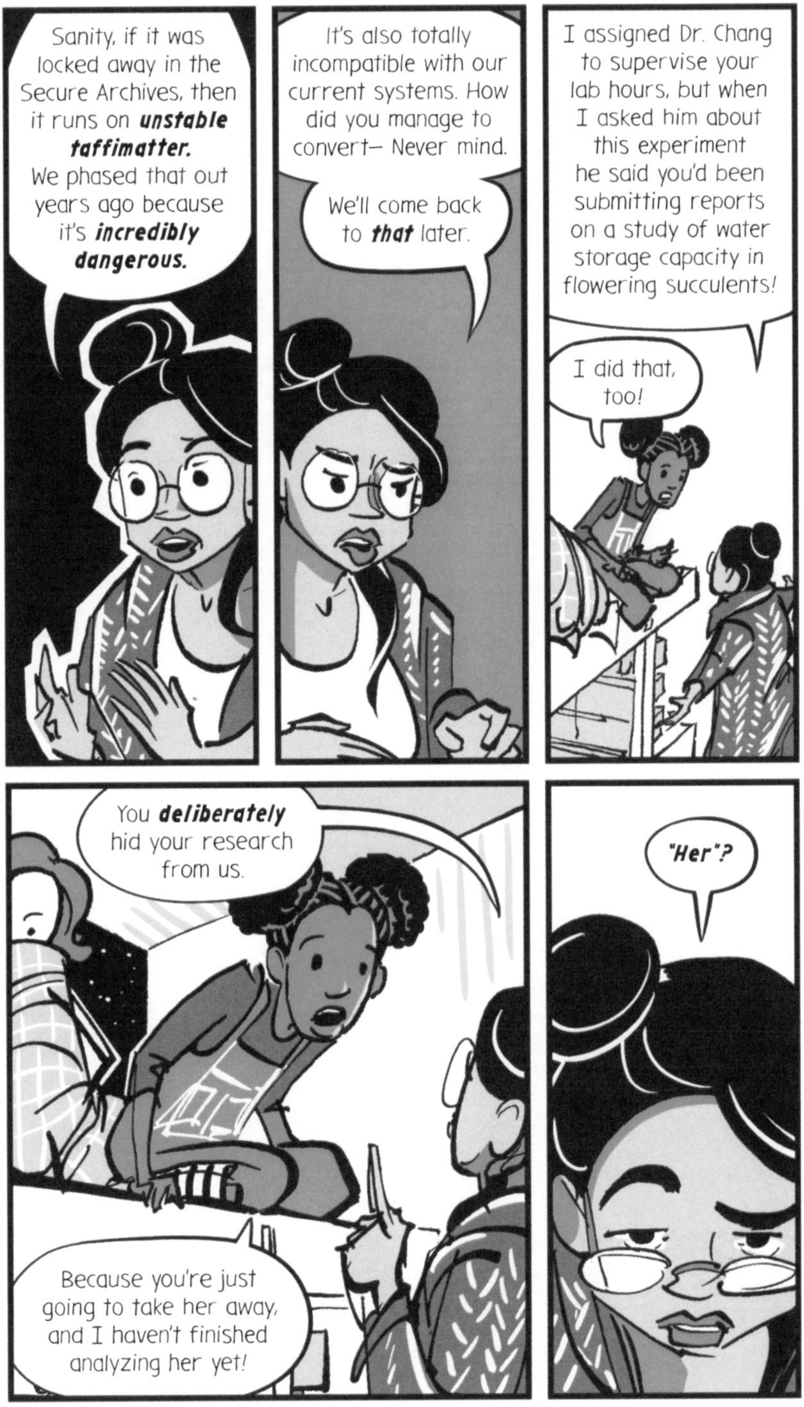
Sanity, if it was locked away in the Secure Archives, then it runs on **unstable taffimatter.** We phased that out years ago because it's **incredibly dangerous.**
It's also totally incompatible with our current systems. How did you manage to convert— Never mind.
We'll come back to **that** later.
I assigned Dr. Chang to supervise your lab hours, but when I asked him about this experiment he said you'd been submitting reports on a study of water storage capacity in flowering succulents!
I did that, too!
You **deliberately** hid your research from us.
Because you're just going to take her away, and I haven't finished analyzing her yet!
"Her"?

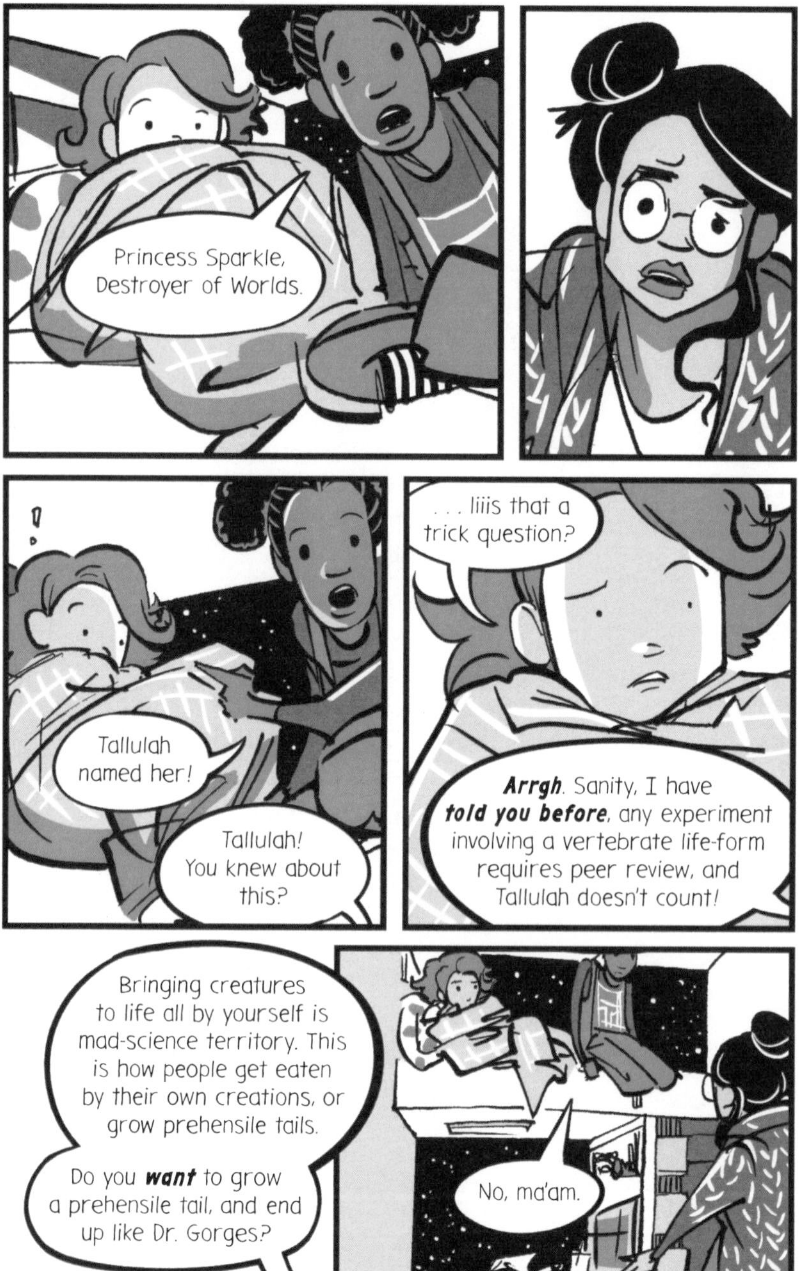

Princess Sparkle, Destroyer of Worlds.
!
Tallulah named her!
Tallulah! You knew about this?
. . . liiis that a trick question?
Arrgh. Sanity, I have ***told you before***, any experiment involving a vertebrate life-form requires peer review, and Tallulah doesn't count!
Bringing creatures to life all by yourself is mad-science territory. This is how people get eaten by their own creations, or grow prehensile tails.
Do you ***want*** to grow a prehensile tail, and end up like Dr. Gorges?
No, ma'am.

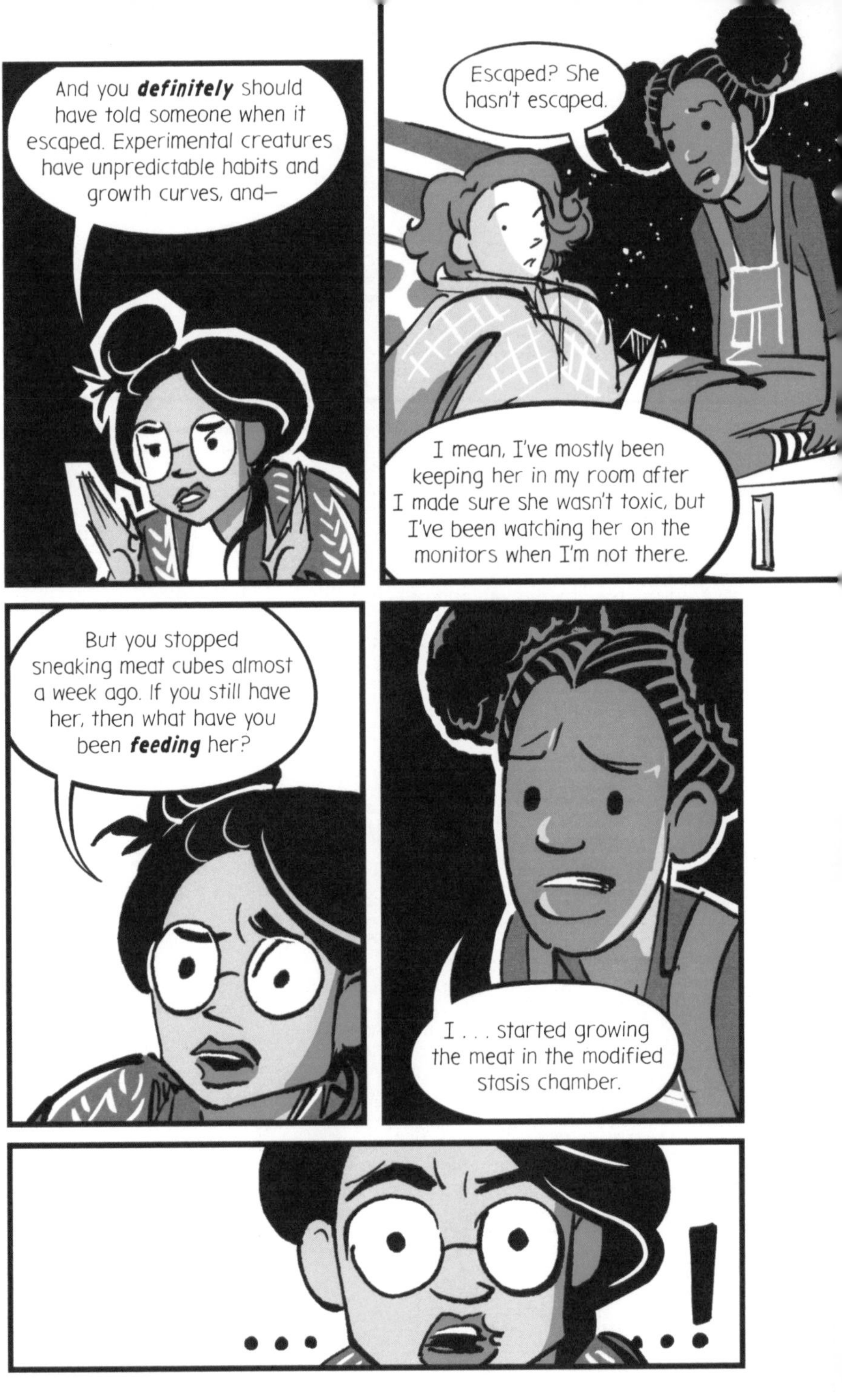
And you *definitely* should have told someone when it escaped. Experimental creatures have unpredictable habits and growth curves, and—
Escaped? She hasn't escaped.
I mean, I've mostly been keeping her in my room after I made sure she wasn't toxic, but I've been watching her on the monitors when I'm not there.
But you stopped sneaking meat cubes almost a week ago. If you still have her, then what have you been *feeding* her?
I . . . started growing the meat in the modified stasis chamber.
. . .
. . !

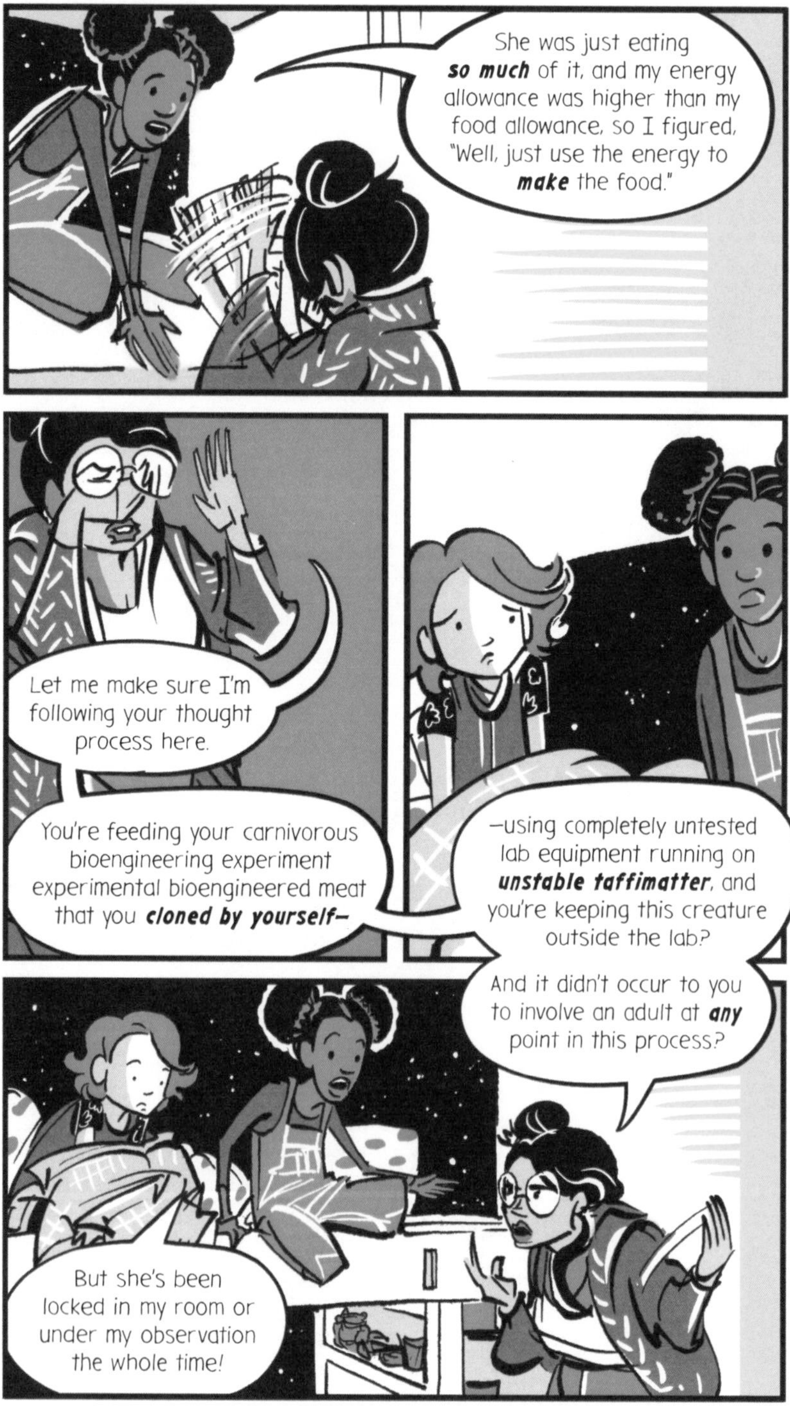
She was just eating **so much** of it, and my energy allowance was higher than my food allowance, so I figured, "Well, just use the energy to **make** the food."
Let me make sure I'm following your thought process here.
You're feeding your carnivorous bioengineering experiment experimental bioengineered meat that you **cloned by yourself—**
—using completely untested lab equipment running on **unstable taffimatter**, and you're keeping this creature outside the lab?
And it didn't occur to you to involve an adult at **any** point in this process?
But she's been locked in my room or under my observation the whole time!

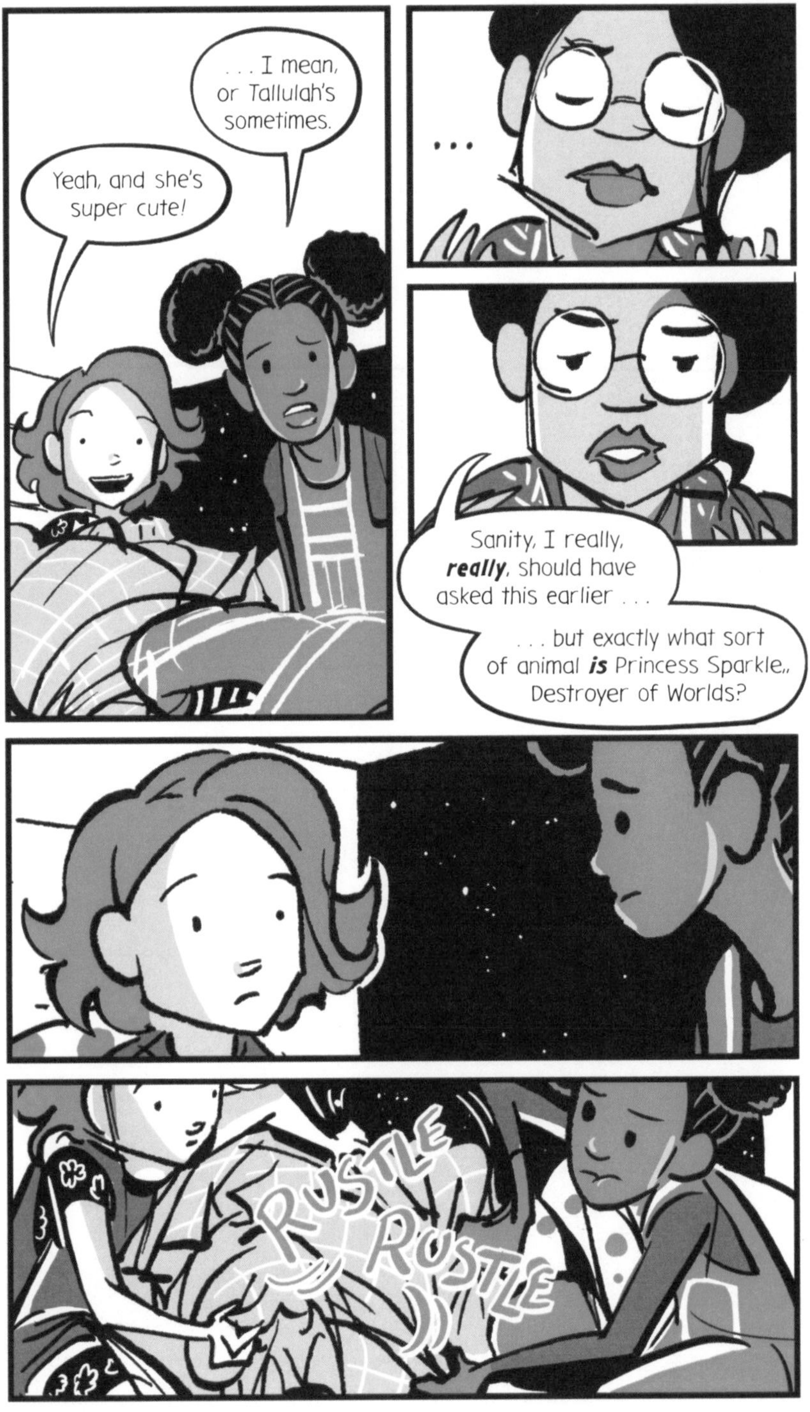
Yeah, and she's super cute!
. . . I mean, or Tallulah's sometimes.
. . .
Sanity, I really, **really**, should have asked this earlier . . .
. . . but exactly what sort of animal ***is*** Princess Sparkle,, Destroyer of Worlds?
RUSTLE
RUSTLE

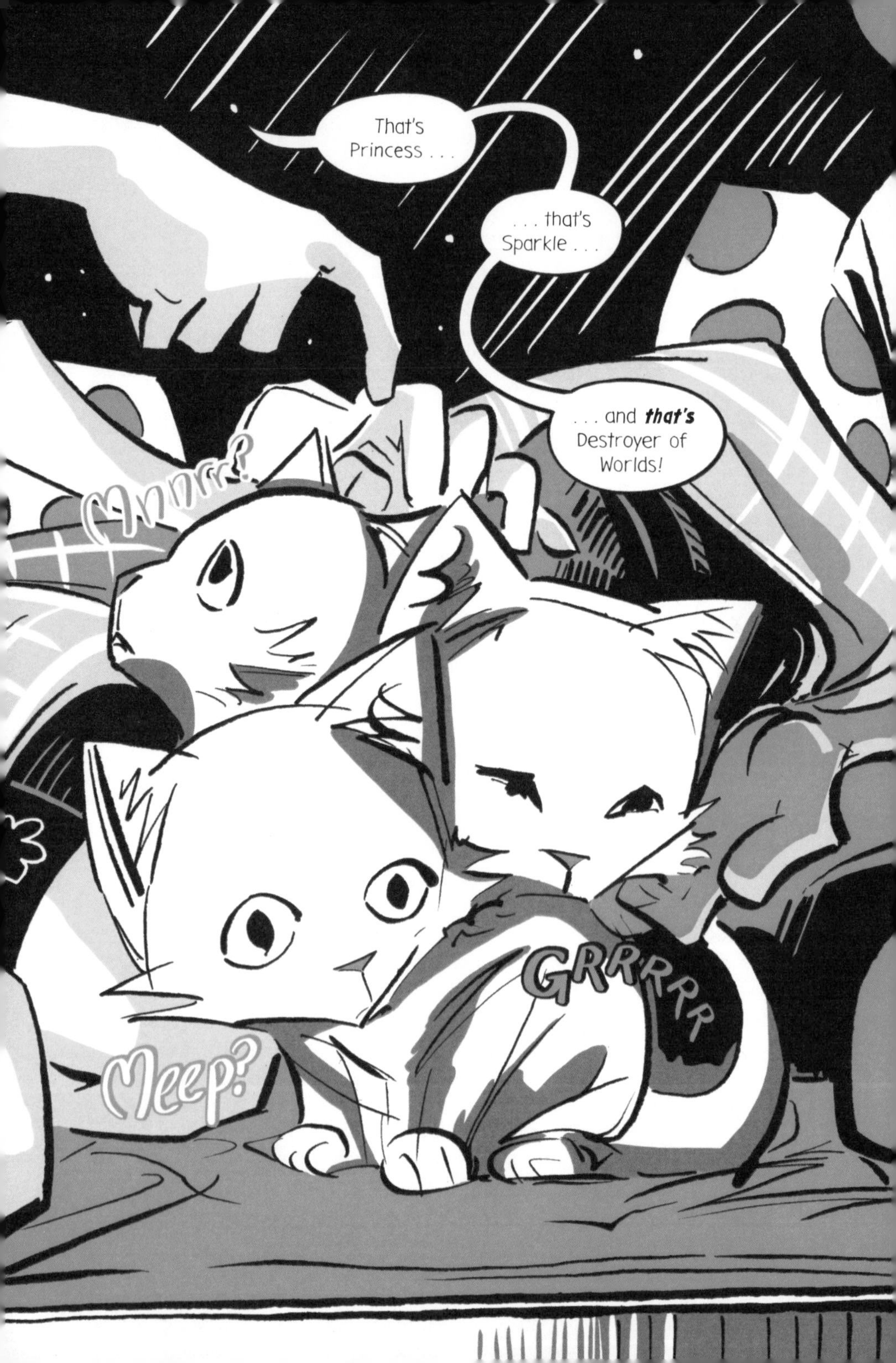

That's Princess . . .
. . . that's Sparkle . . .
. . . and ***that's*** Destroyer of Worlds!
Mmrrr?
GRRRRR
Meep?

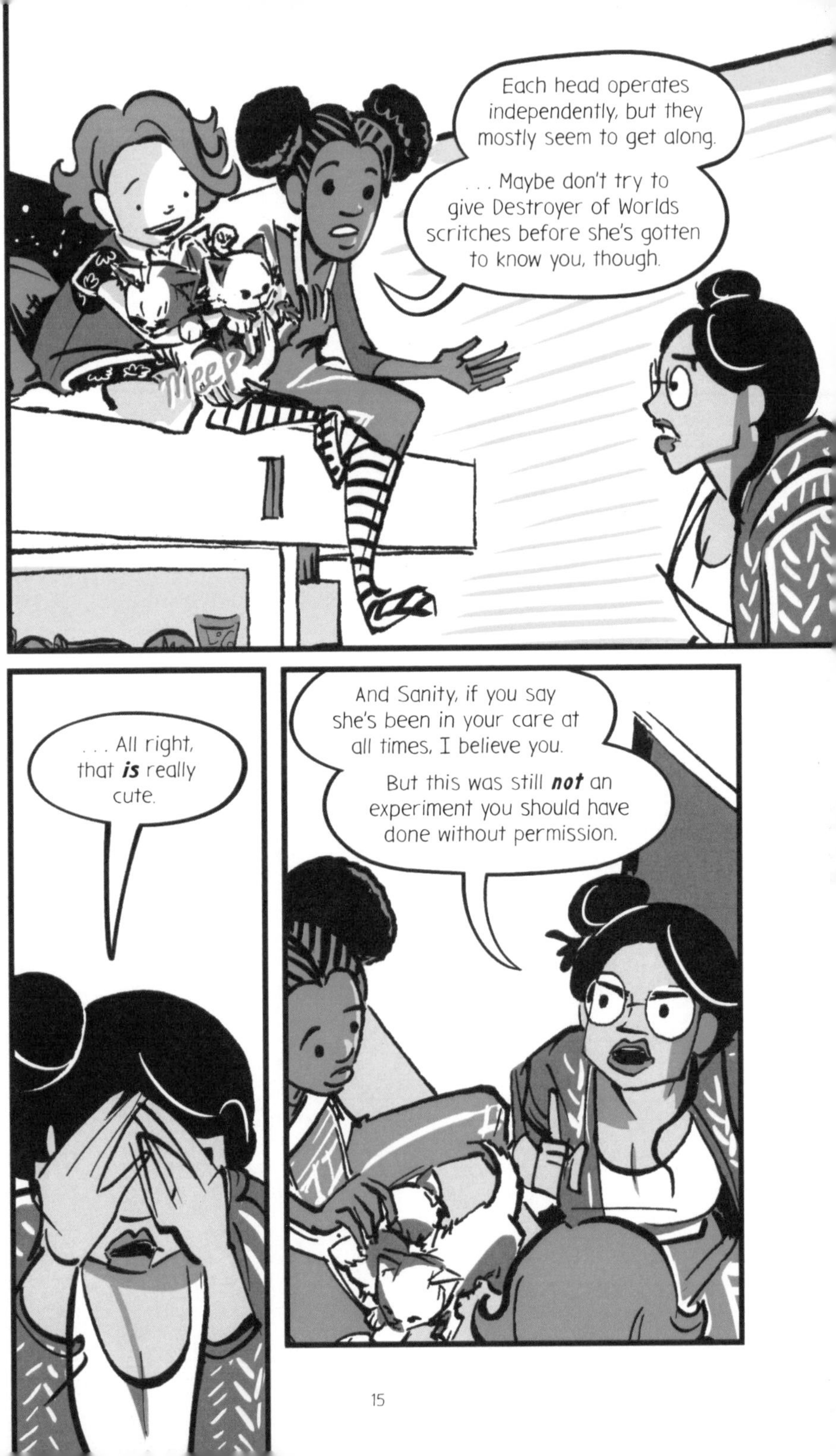
Each head operates independently, but they mostly seem to get along.
. . . Maybe don't try to give Destroyer of Worlds scritches before she's gotten to know you, though.
Meep
. . . All right, that *is* really cute.
And Sanity, if you say she's been in your care at all times, I believe you.
But this was still ***not*** an experiment you should have done without permission.

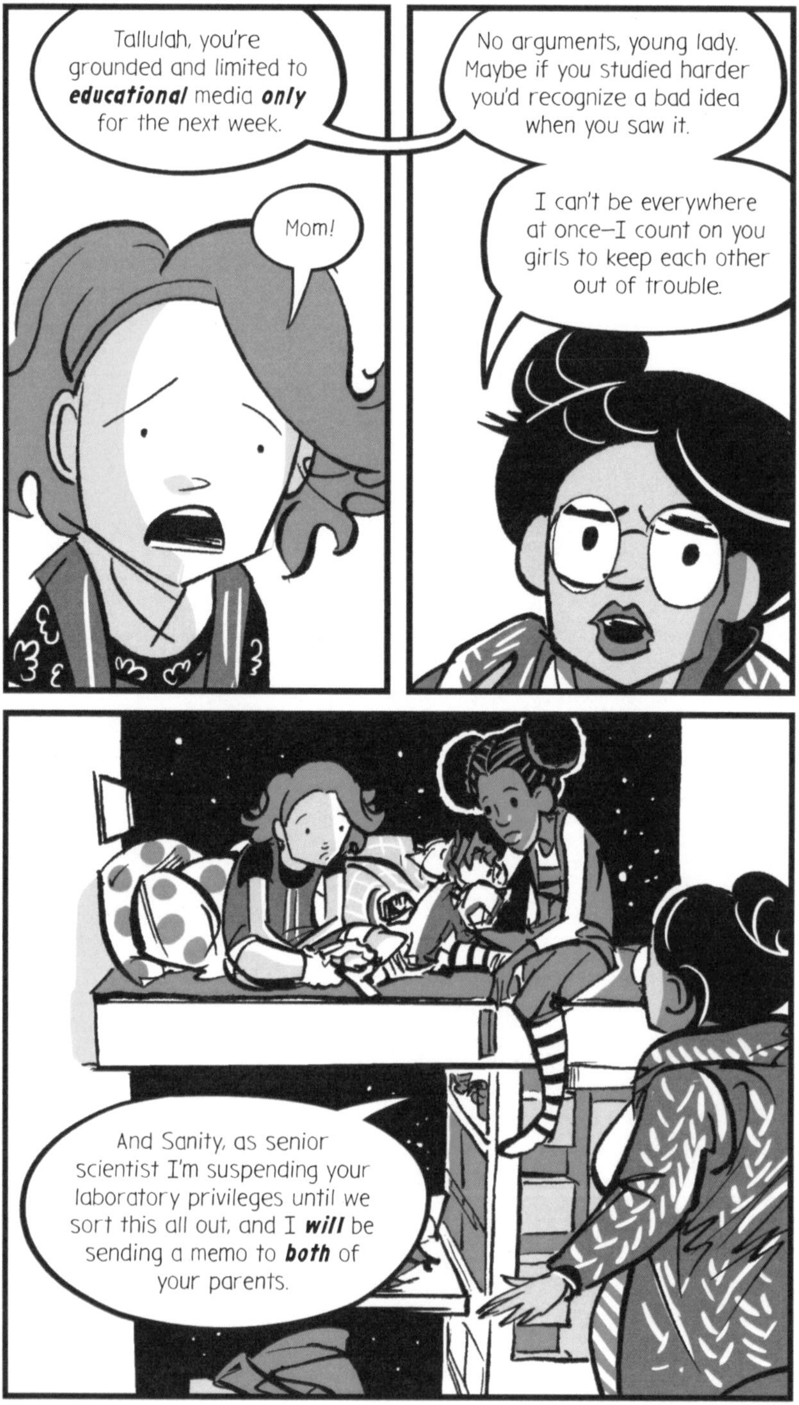
Tallulah, you're grounded and limited to **educational** media **only** for the next week.
Mom!
No arguments, young lady. Maybe if you studied harder you'd recognize a bad idea when you saw it.
I can't be everywhere at once—I count on you girls to keep each other out of trouble.
And Sanity, as senior scientist I'm suspending your laboratory privileges until we sort this all out, and I **will** be sending a memo to **both** of your parents.

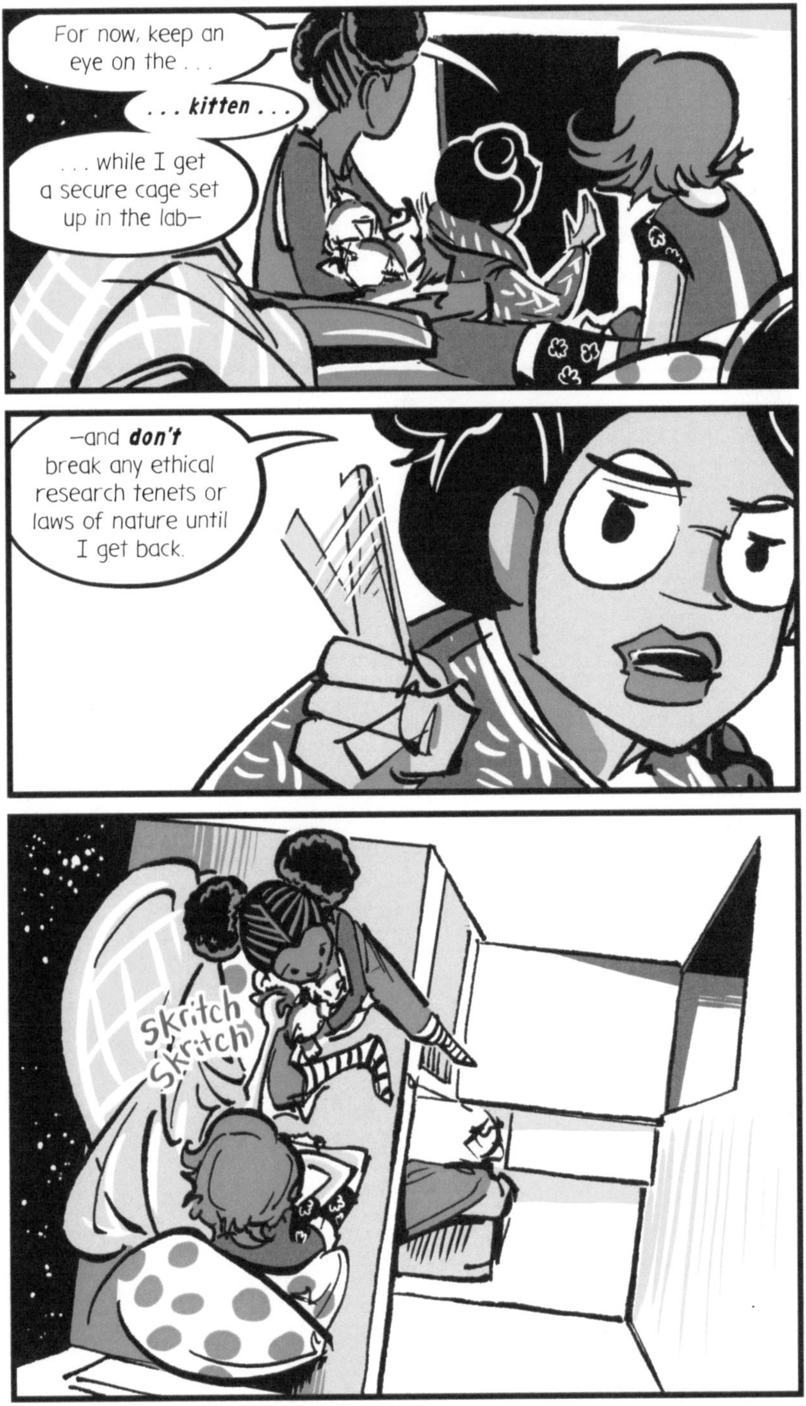
For now, keep an eye on the . . .
. . . **kitten** . . .
. . . while I get a secure cage set up in the lab—
—and **don't** break any ethical research tenets or laws of nature until I get back.
Skritch
Skritch

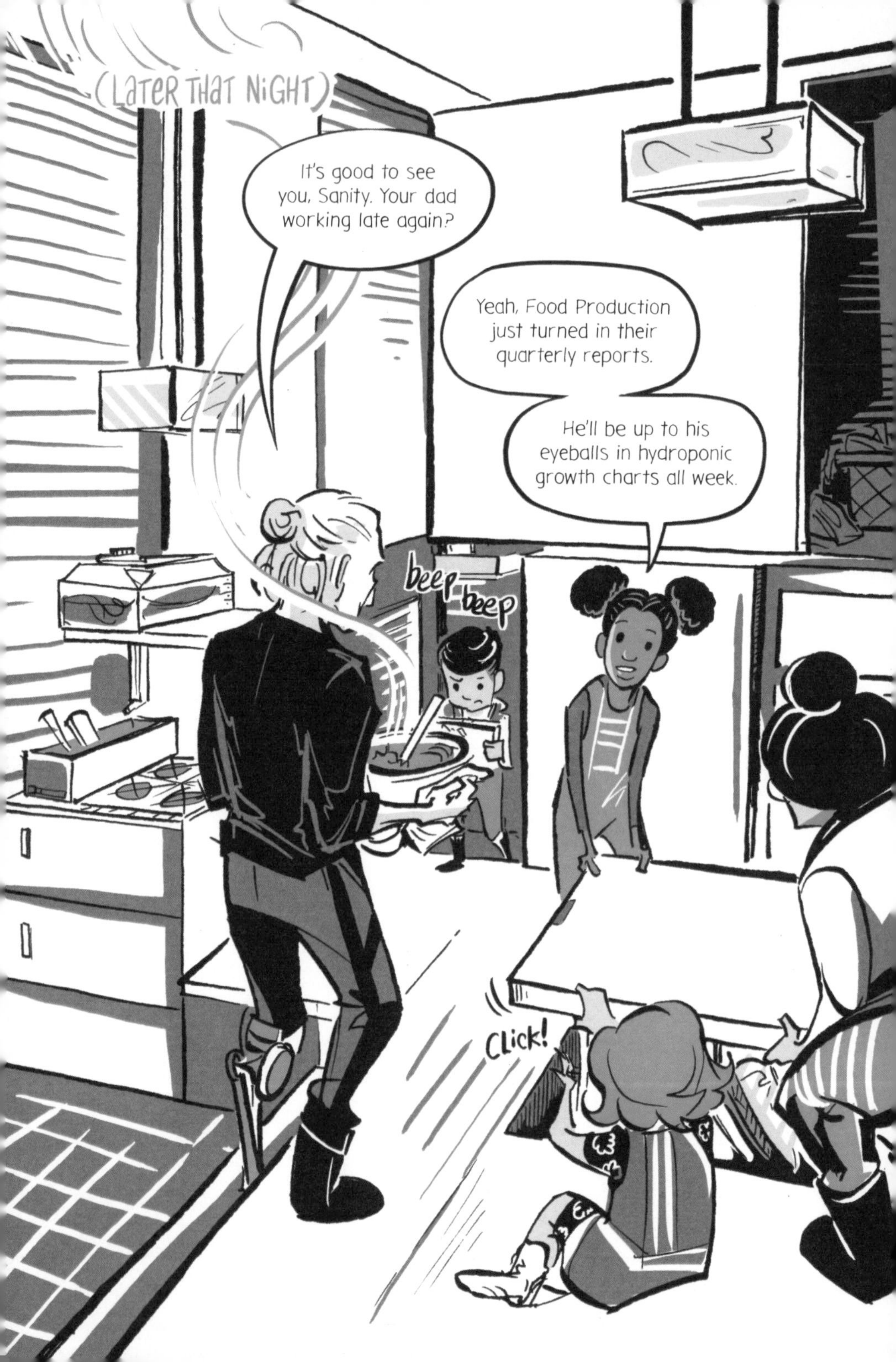
(LATER THAT NIGHT)
It's good to see you, Sanity. Your dad working late again?
Yeah, Food Production just turned in their quarterly reports.
He'll be up to his eyeballs in hydroponic growth charts all week.
beep beep
CLICK!

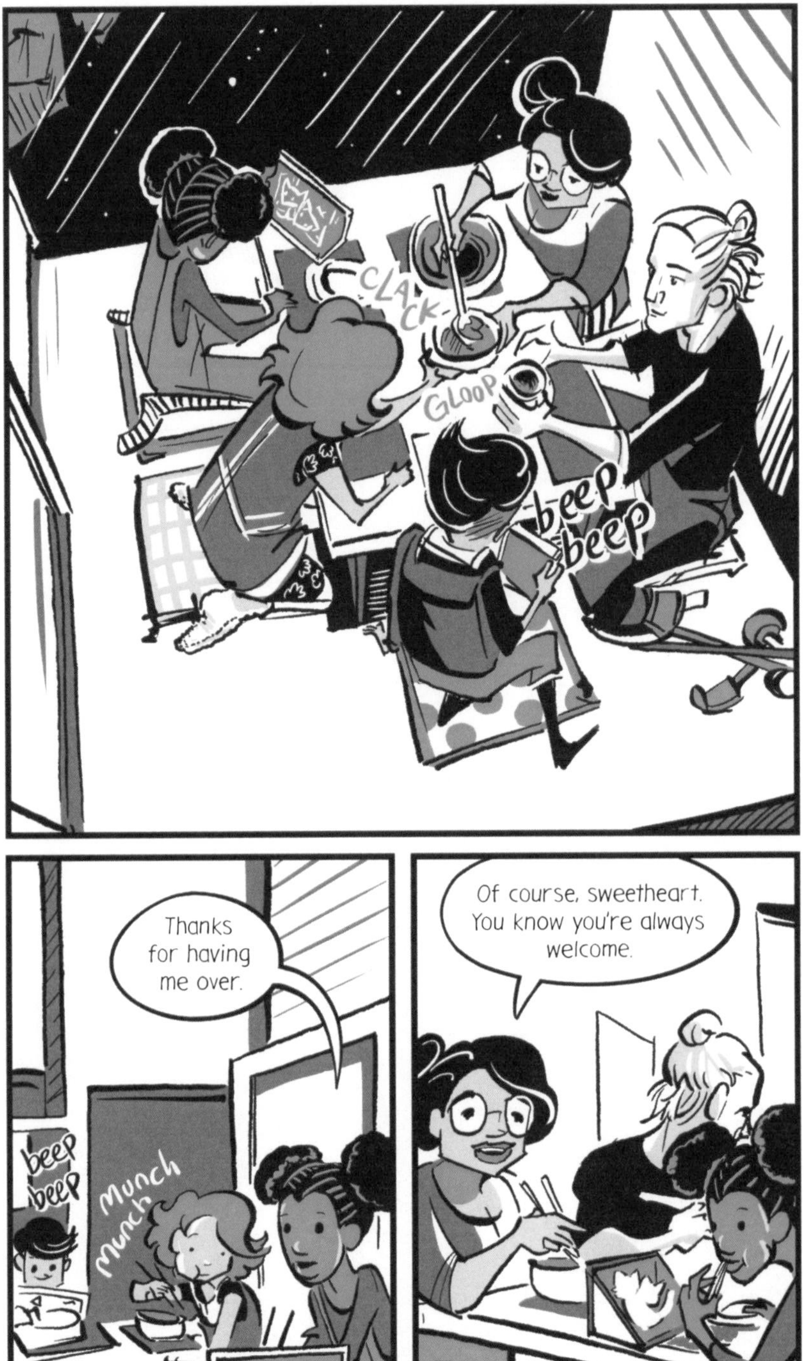
CLACK
GLOOP
beep beep
Thanks for having me over.
beep beep
Munch Munch
Of course, sweetheart. You know you're always welcome.

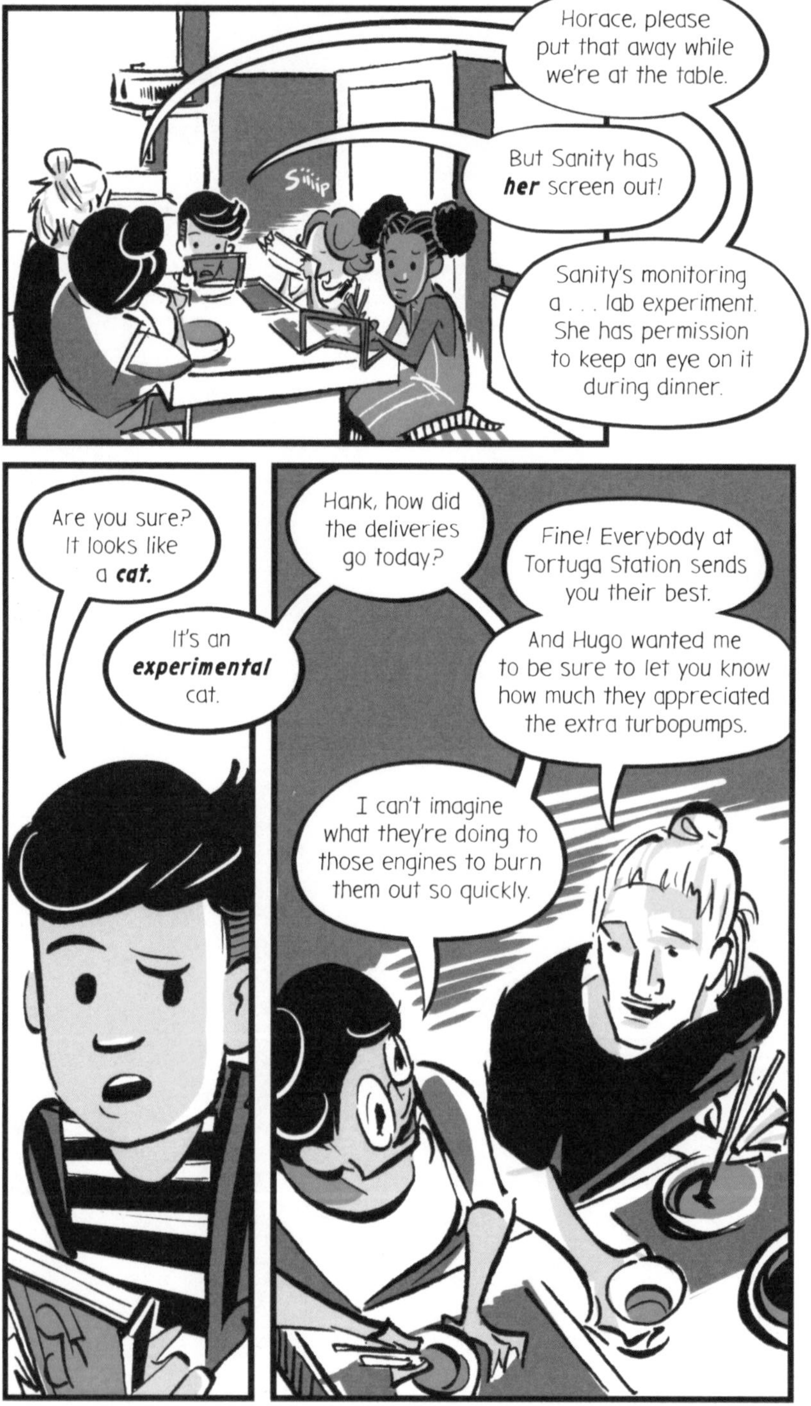
Horace, please put that away while we're at the table.
Siiiip
But Sanity has **her** screen out!
Sanity's monitoring a . . . lab experiment. She has permission to keep an eye on it during dinner.
Are you sure? It looks like a **cat.**
It's an **experimental** cat.
Hank, how did the deliveries go today?
Fine! Everybody at Tortuga Station sends you their best.
And Hugo wanted me to be sure to let you know how much they appreciated the extra turbopumps.
I can't imagine what they're doing to those engines to burn them out so quickly.

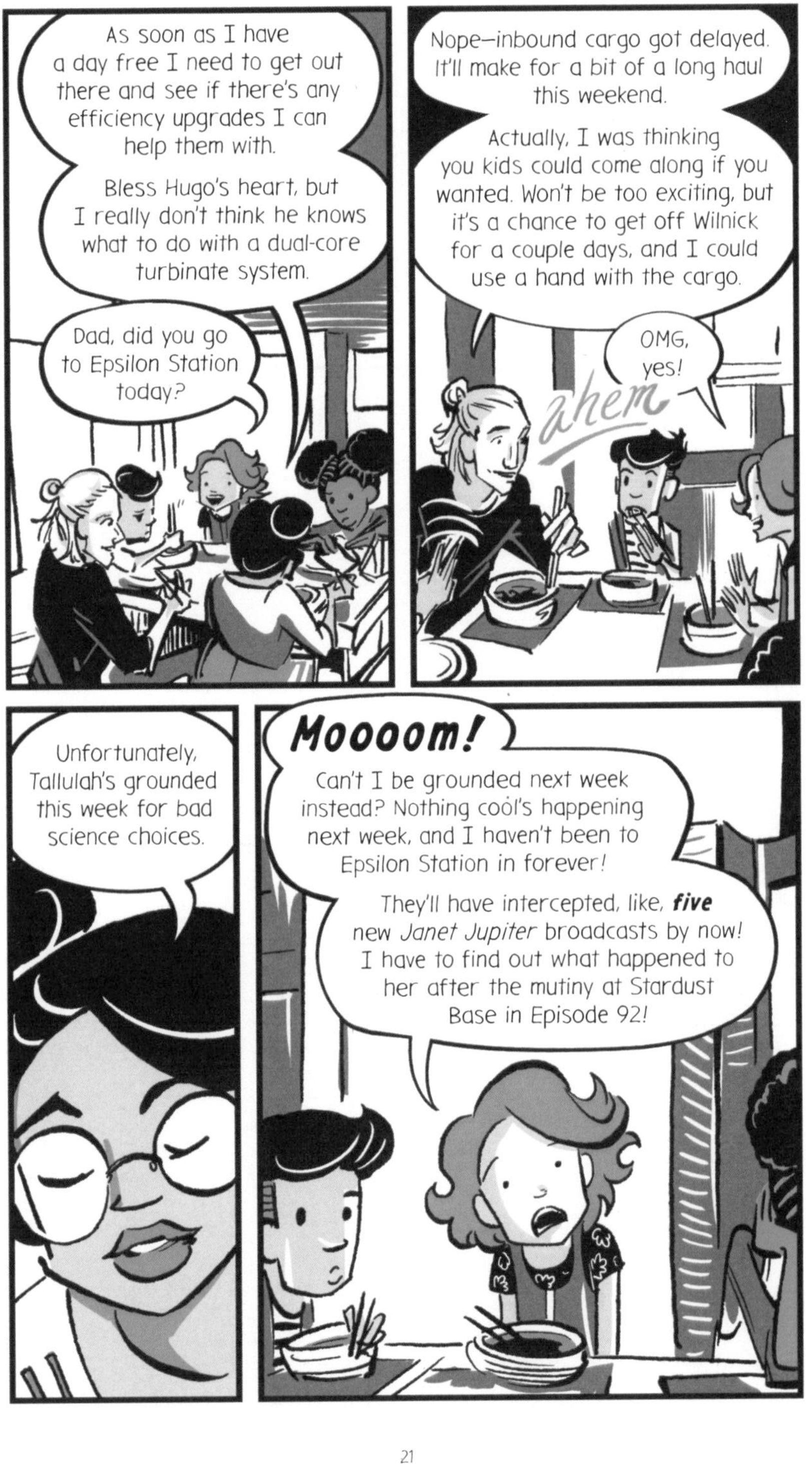
As soon as I have a day free I need to get out there and see if there's any efficiency upgrades I can help them with.
Bless Hugo's heart, but I really don't think he knows what to do with a dual-core turbinate system.
Dad, did you go to Epsilon Station today?
Nope—inbound cargo got delayed. It'll make for a bit of a long haul this weekend.
Actually, I was thinking you kids could come along if you wanted. Won't be too exciting, but it's a chance to get off Wilnick for a couple days, and I could use a hand with the cargo.
ahem
OMG, yes!
Unfortunately, Tallulah's grounded this week for bad science choices.
Moooom!
Can't I be grounded next week instead? Nothing cool's happening next week, and I haven't been to Epsilon Station in forever!
They'll have intercepted, like, five new Janet Jupiter broadcasts by now! I have to find out what happened to her after the mutiny at Stardust Base in Episode 92!

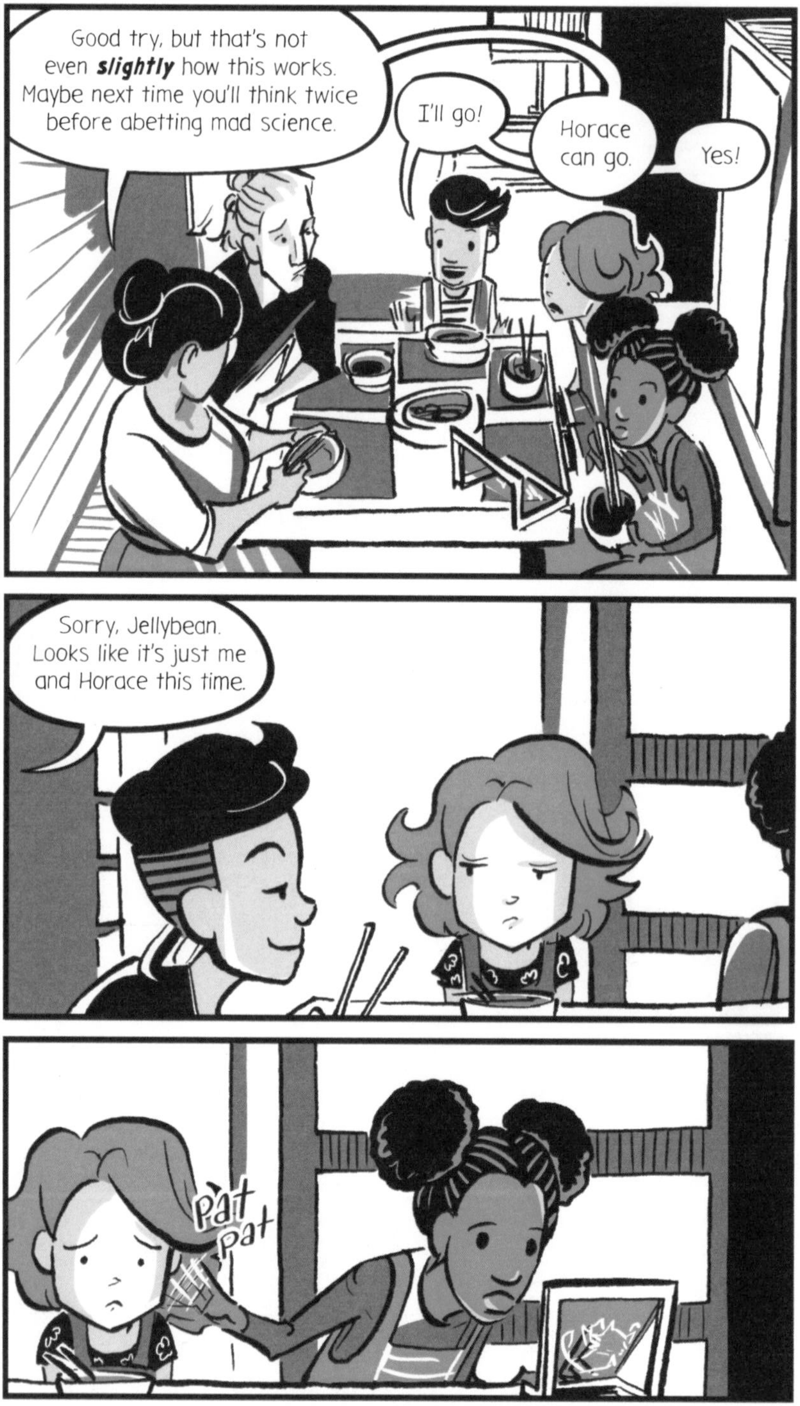
Good try, but that's not even **slightly** how this works. Maybe next time you'll think twice before abetting mad science.
I'll go!
Horace can go.
Yes!
Sorry, Jellybean. Looks like it's just me and Horace this time.
Pat pat

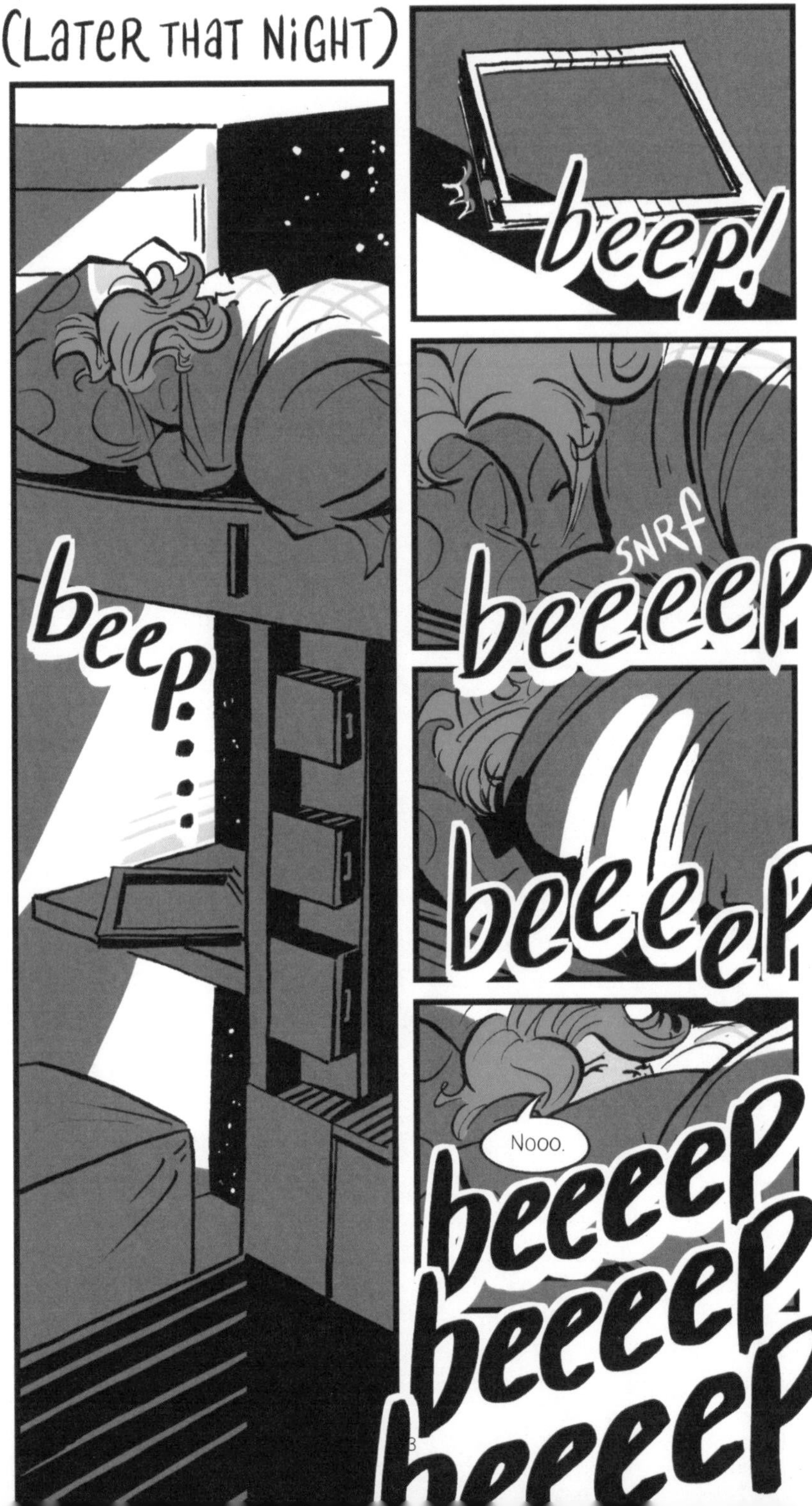
(LATER THAT NIGHT)
beep....
beep!
SNRf
beeeeep
beeeeep
Nooo.
beeeeep
beeeeep

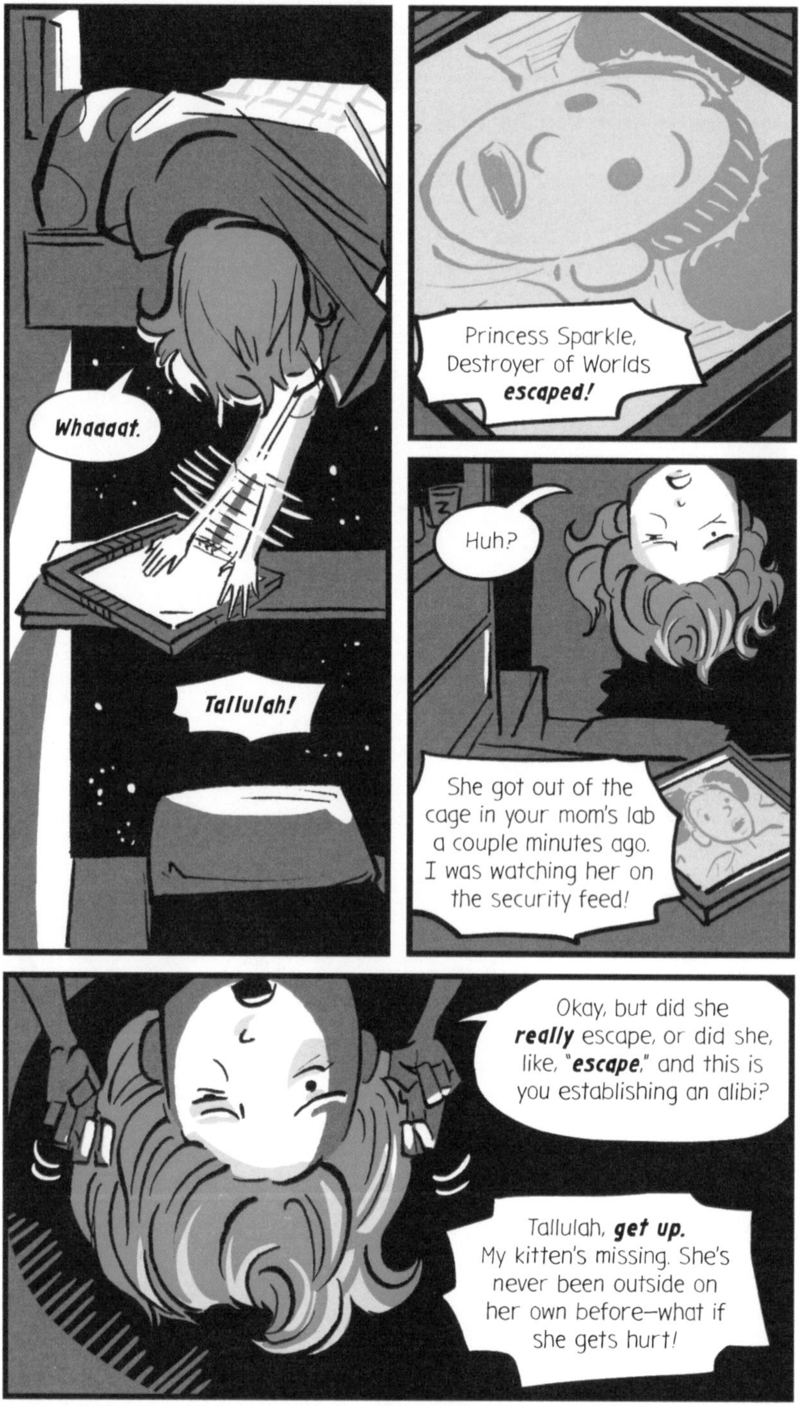
Whaaaat.
Tallulah!
Princess Sparkle, Destroyer of Worlds **escaped!**
Huh?
She got out of the cage in your mom's lab a couple minutes ago. I was watching her on the security feed!
Okay, but did she **really** escape, or did she, like, "**escape**," and this is you establishing an alibi?
Tallulah, **get up.** My kitten's missing. She's never been outside on her own before—what if she gets hurt!

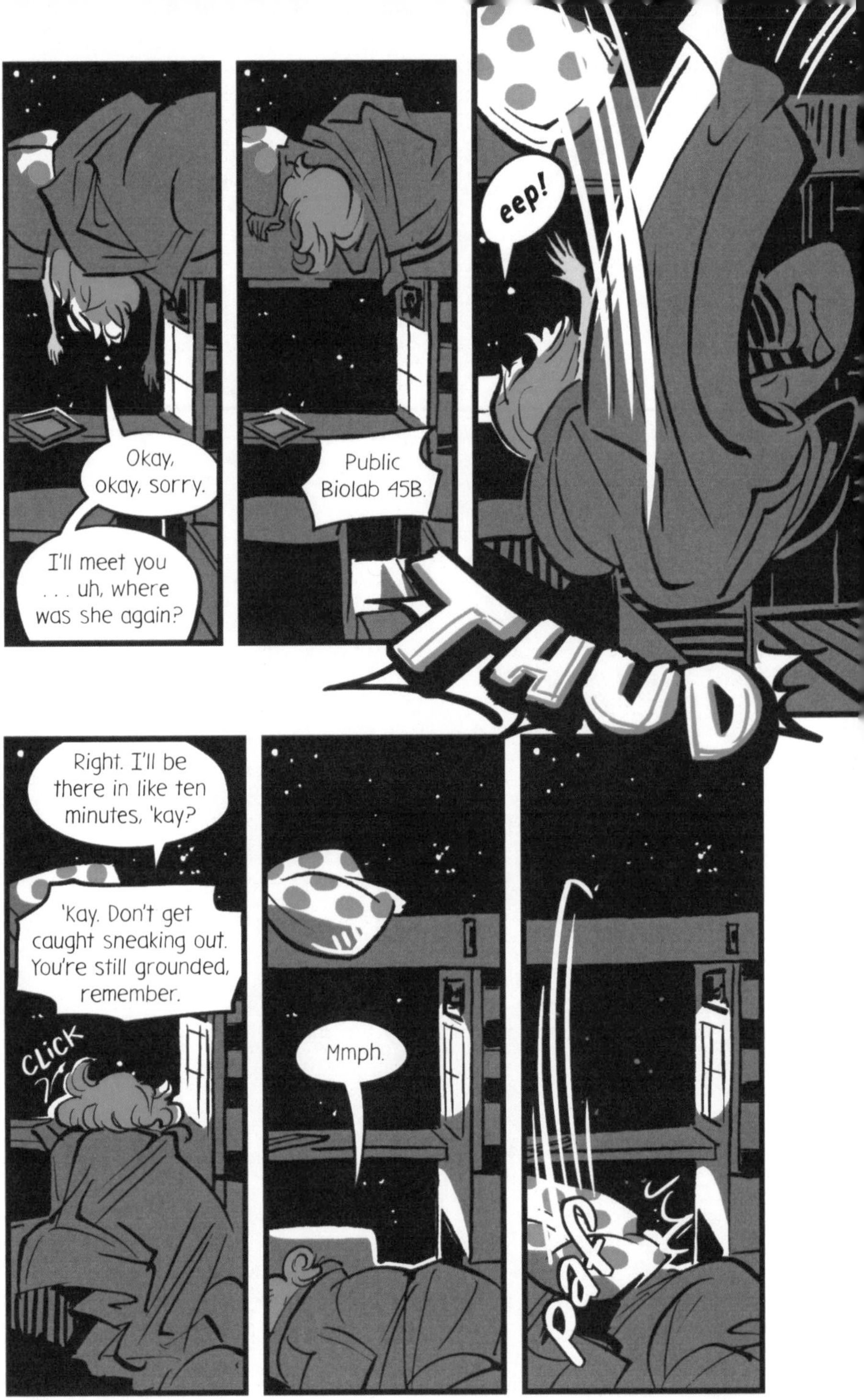
Okay, okay, sorry.
I'll meet you . . . uh, where was she again?
Public Biolab 45B.
eep!
THUD
Right. I'll be there in like ten minutes, 'kay?
'Kay. Don't get caught sneaking out. You're still grounded, remember.
CLICK
Mmph.
paf

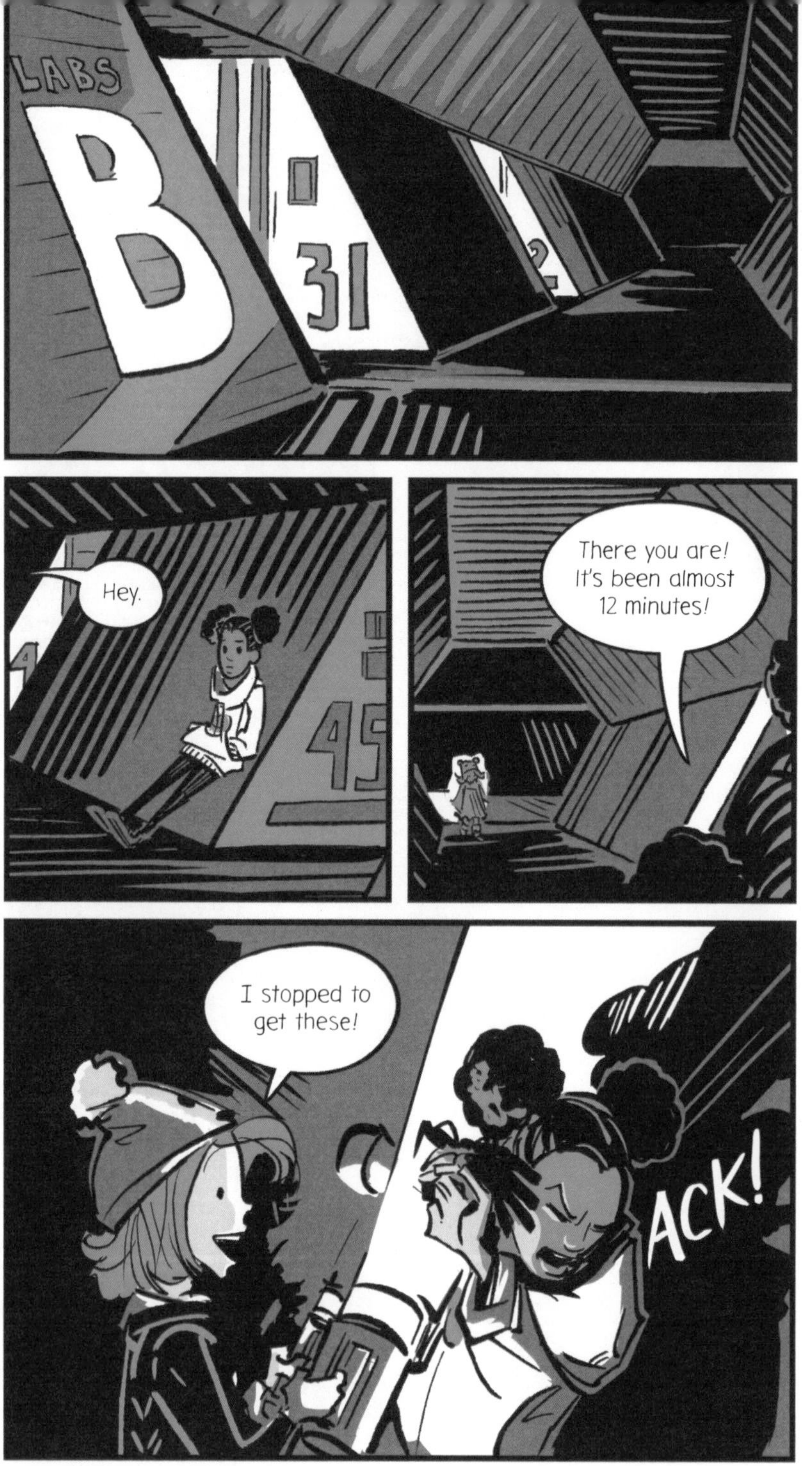
LABS
B
31
Hey.
45
There you are! It's been almost 12 minutes!
I stopped to get these!
ACK!

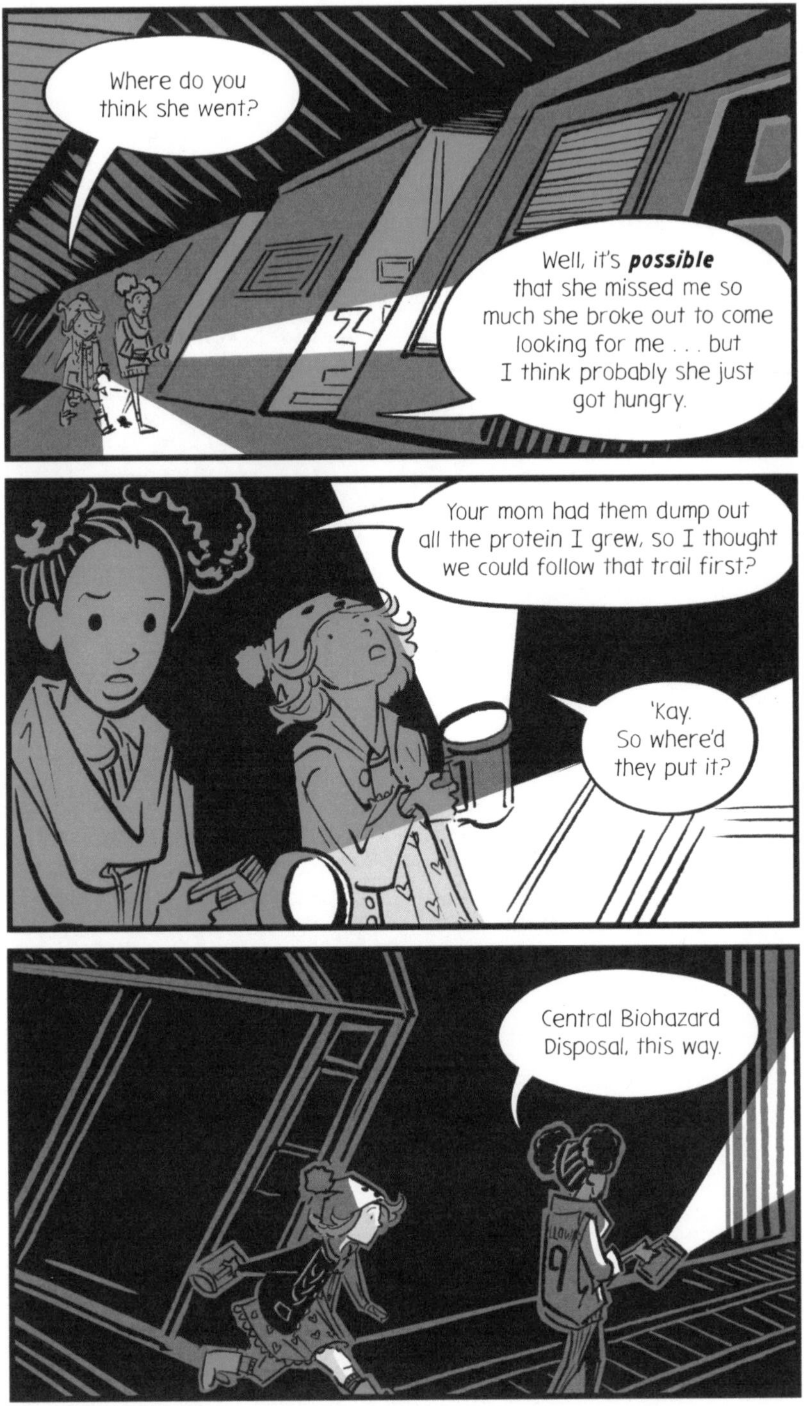
Where do you think she went?
Well, it's ***possible*** that she missed me so much she broke out to come looking for me . . . but I think probably she just got hungry.
Your mom had them dump out all the protein I grew, so I thought we could follow that trail first?
'Kay. So where'd they put it?
Central Biohazard Disposal, this way.

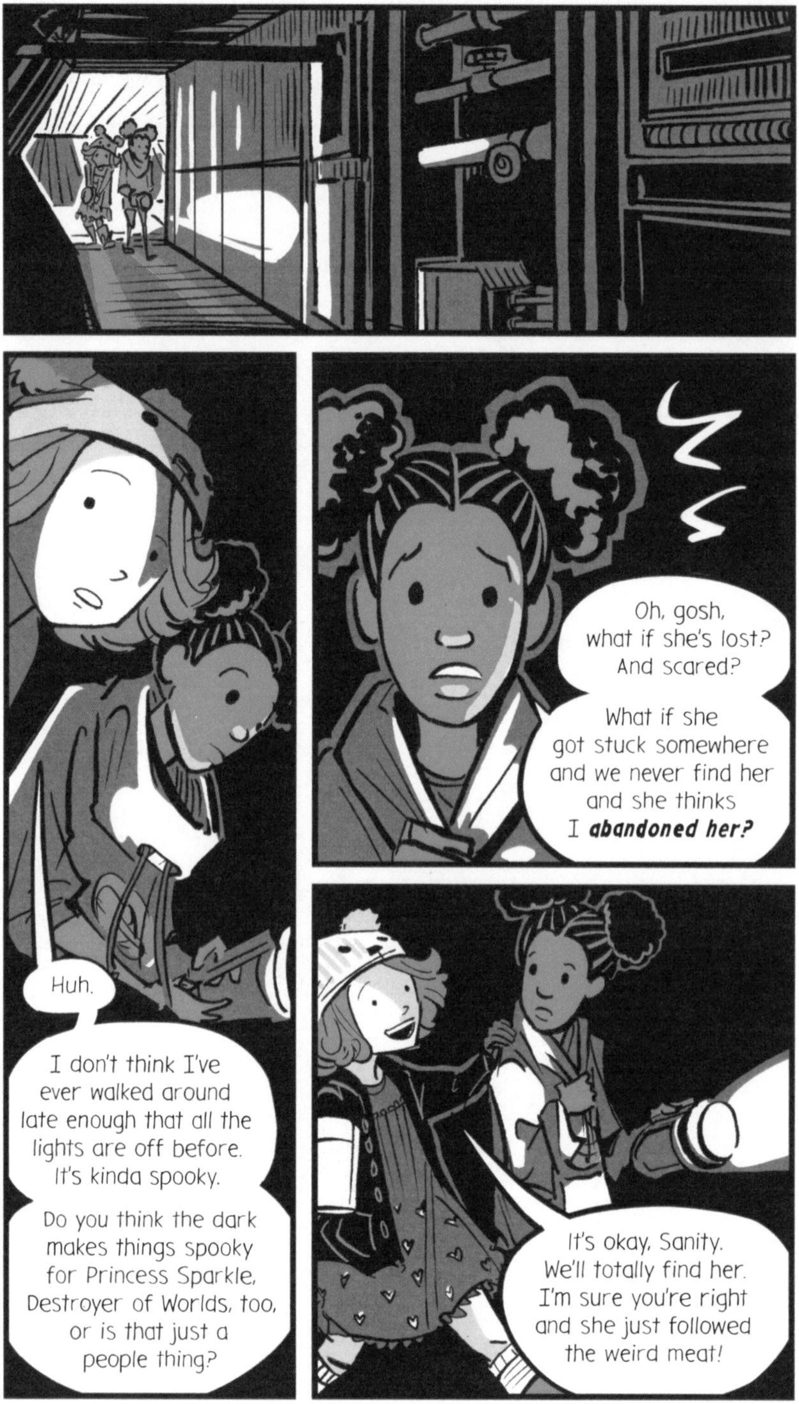
Huh.
I don't think I've ever walked around late enough that all the lights are off before. It's kinda spooky.
Do you think the dark makes things spooky for Princess Sparkle, Destroyer of Worlds, too, or is that just a people thing?
Oh, gosh, what if she's lost? And scared?
What if she got stuck somewhere and we never find her and she thinks I **abandoned her?**
It's okay, Sanity. We'll totally find her. I'm sure you're right and she just followed the weird meat!

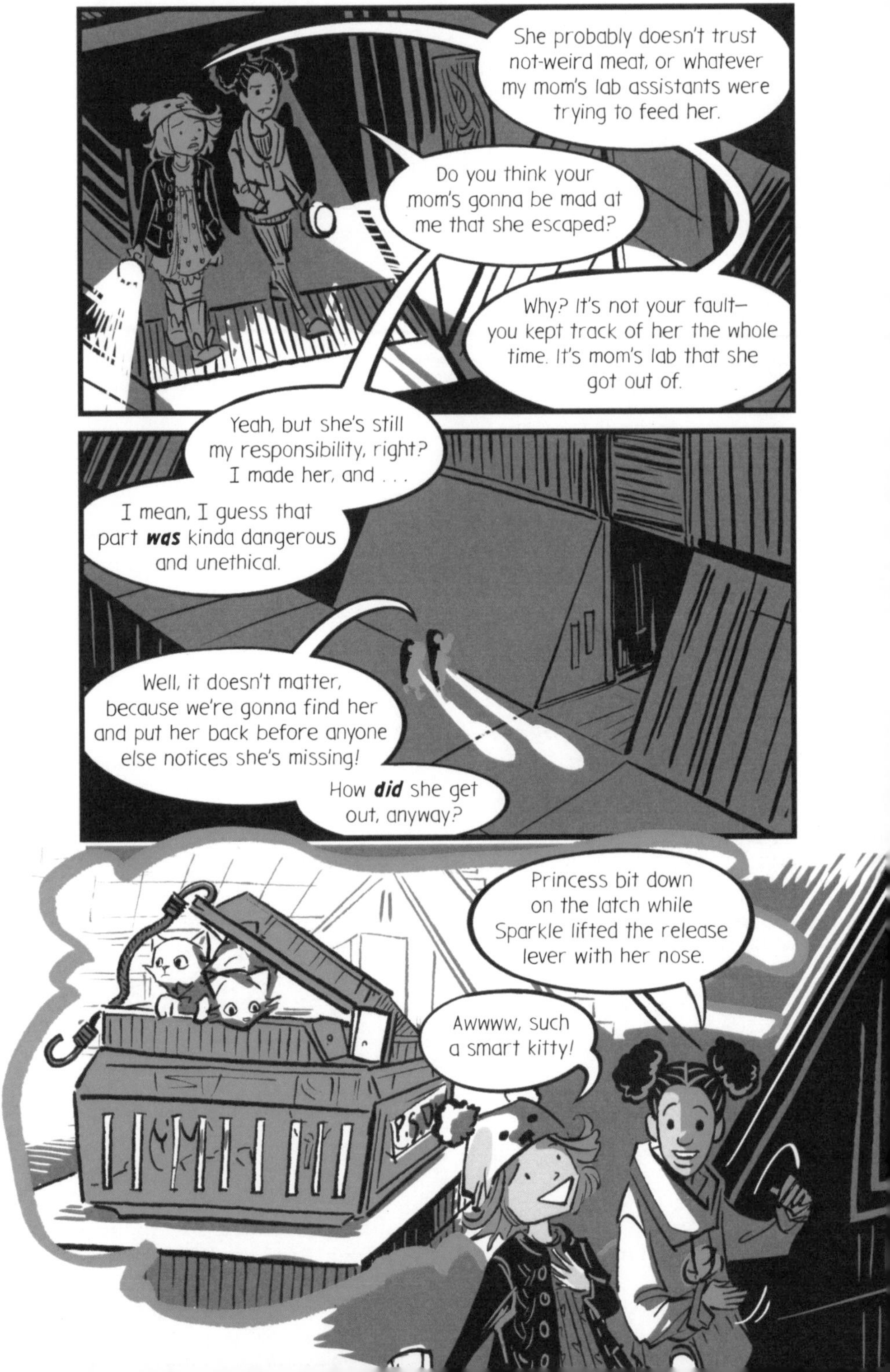
She probably doesn't trust not-weird meat, or whatever my mom's lab assistants were trying to feed her.
Do you think your mom's gonna be mad at me that she escaped?
Why? It's not your fault— you kept track of her the whole time. It's mom's lab that she got out of.
Yeah, but she's still my responsibility, right? I made her, and . . .
I mean, I guess that part ***was*** kinda dangerous and unethical.
Well, it doesn't matter, because we're gonna find her and put her back before anyone else notices she's missing!
How ***did*** she get out, anyway?
Princess bit down on the latch while Sparkle lifted the release lever with her nose.
Awwww, such a smart kitty!
P.S.D.

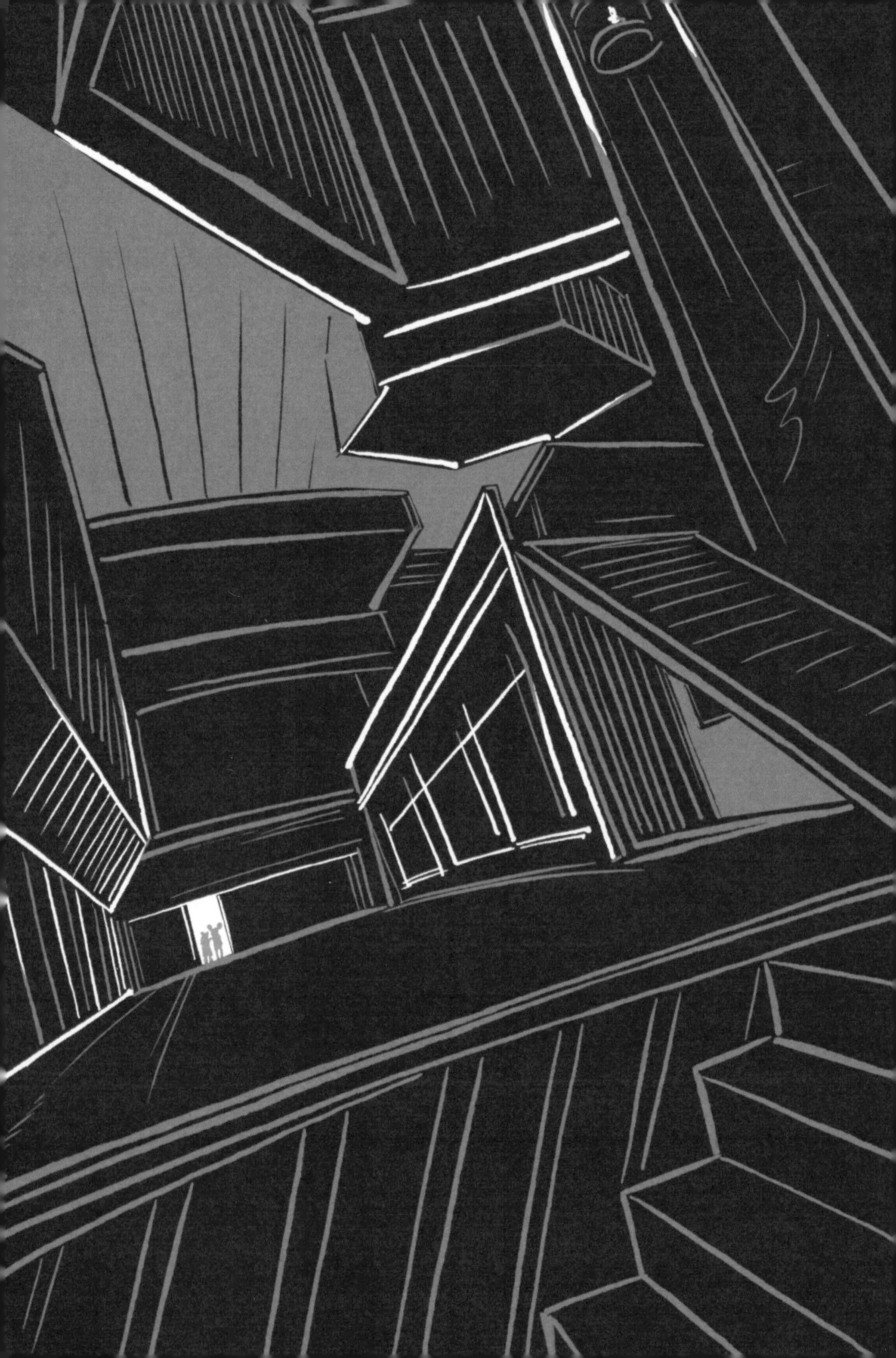

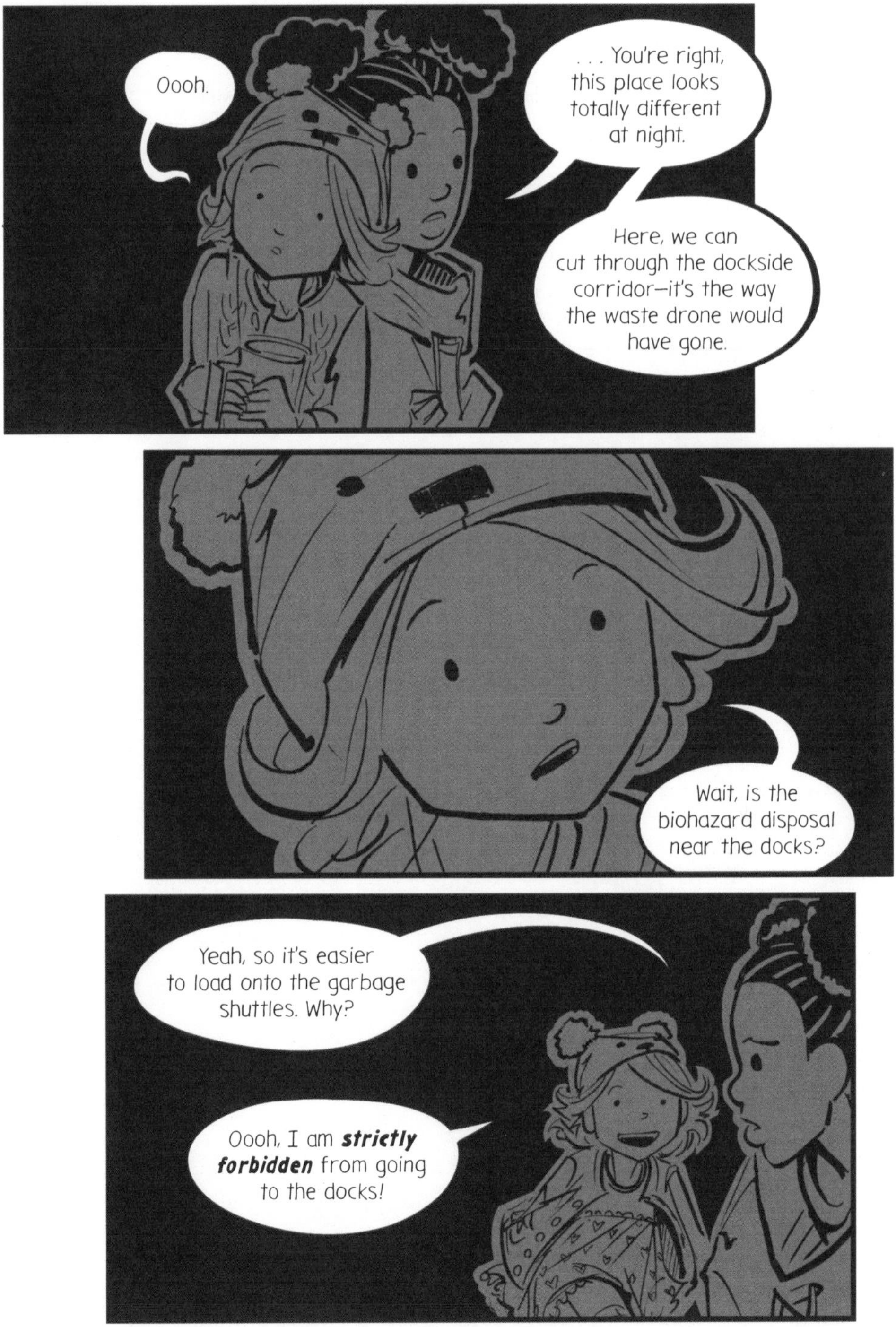
Oooh.
. . . You're right, this place looks totally different at night.
Here, we can cut through the dockside corridor—it's the way the waste drone would have gone.
Wait, is the biohazard disposal near the docks?
Yeah, so it's easier to load onto the garbage shuttles. Why?
Oooh, I am **strictly forbidden** from going to the docks!

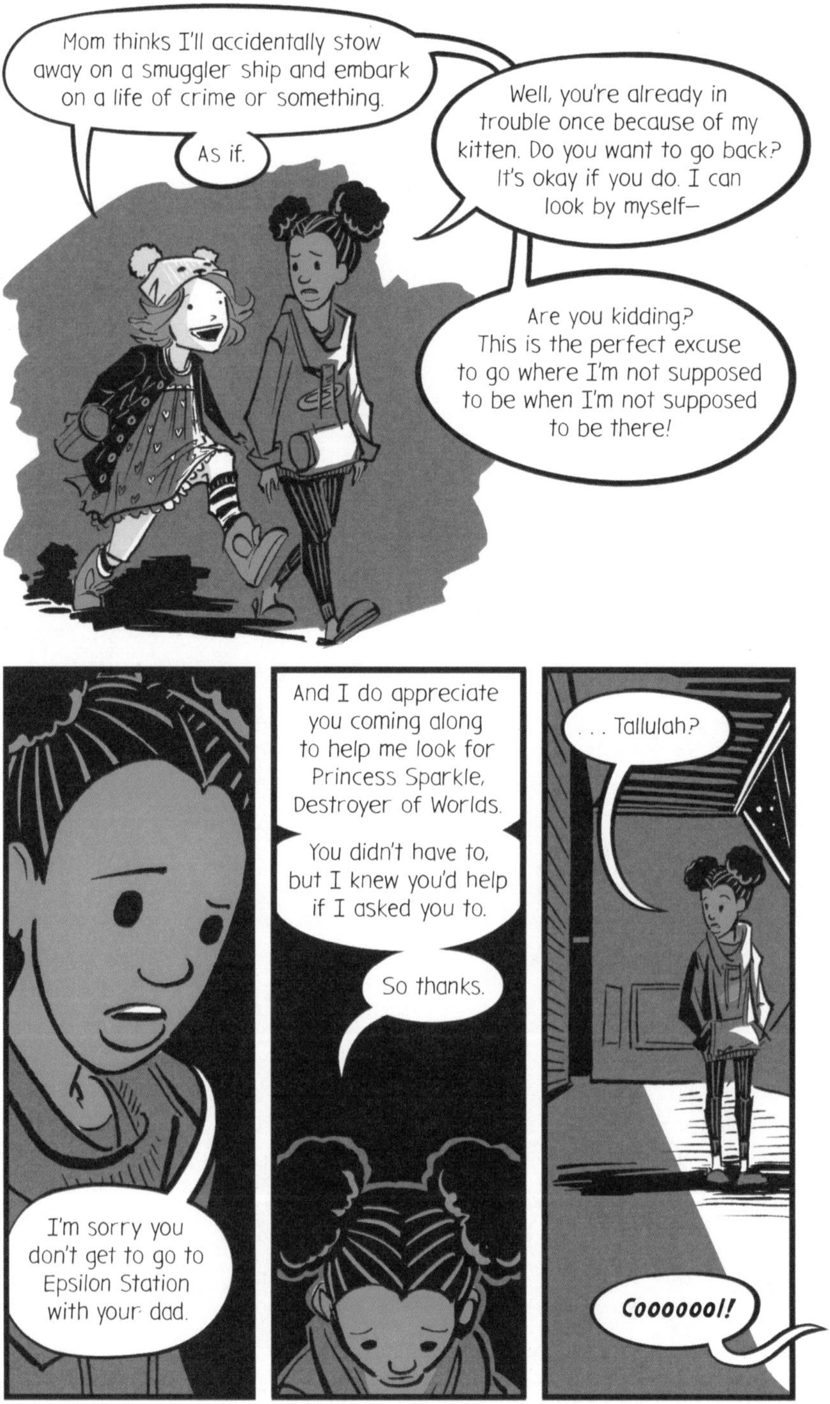
Mom thinks I'll accidentally stow away on a smuggler ship and embark on a life of crime or something.
As if.
Well, you're already in trouble once because of my kitten. Do you want to go back? It's okay if you do. I can look by myself—
Are you kidding? This is the perfect excuse to go where I'm not supposed to be when I'm not supposed to be there!
I'm sorry you don't get to go to Epsilon Station with your dad.
And I do appreciate you coming along to help me look for Princess Sparkle, Destroyer of Worlds.
You didn't have to, but I knew you'd help if I asked you to.
So thanks.
. . . Tallulah?
Coooooool!

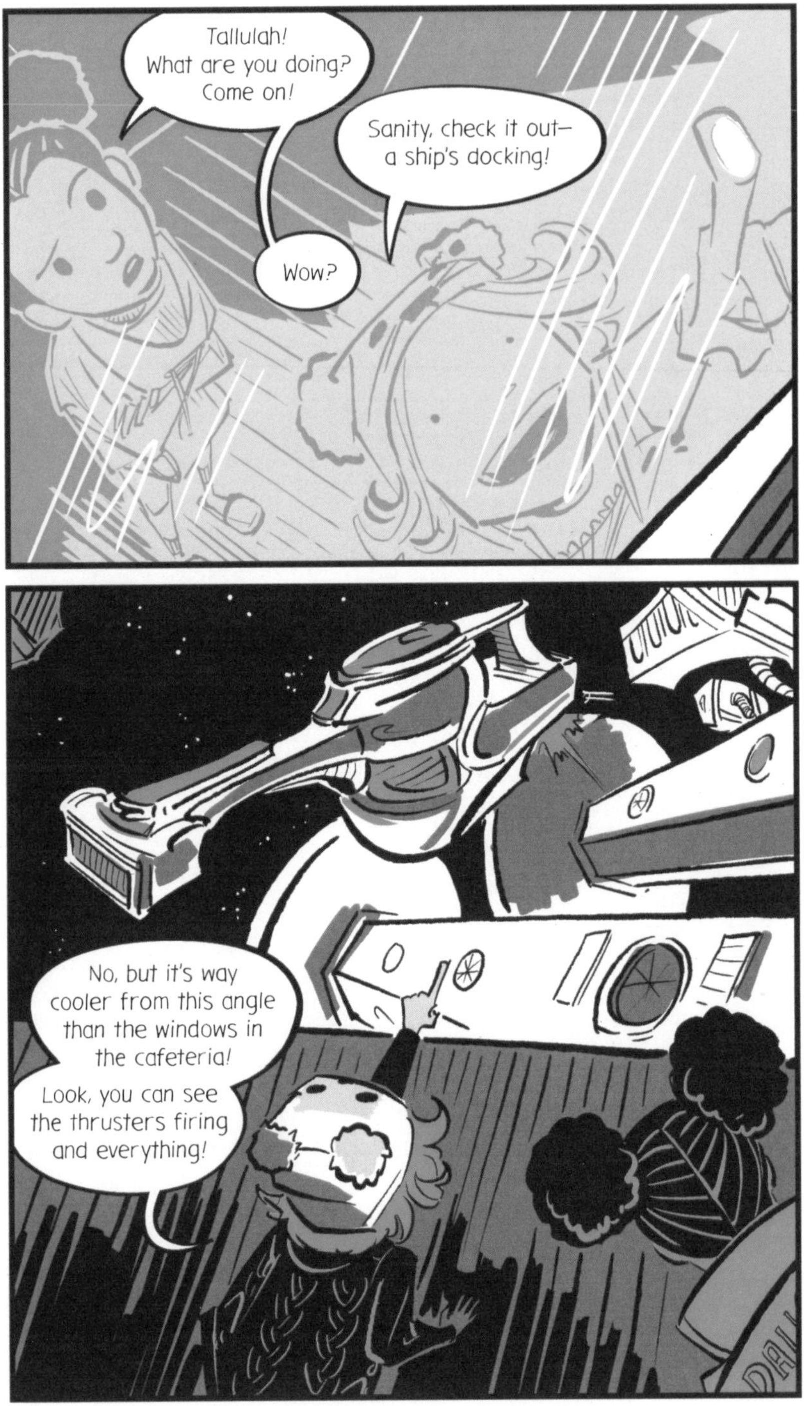
Tallulah! What are you doing? Come on!
Sanity, check it out— a ship's docking!
Wow?
No, but it's way cooler from this angle than the windows in the cafeteria!
Look, you can see the thrusters firing and everything!

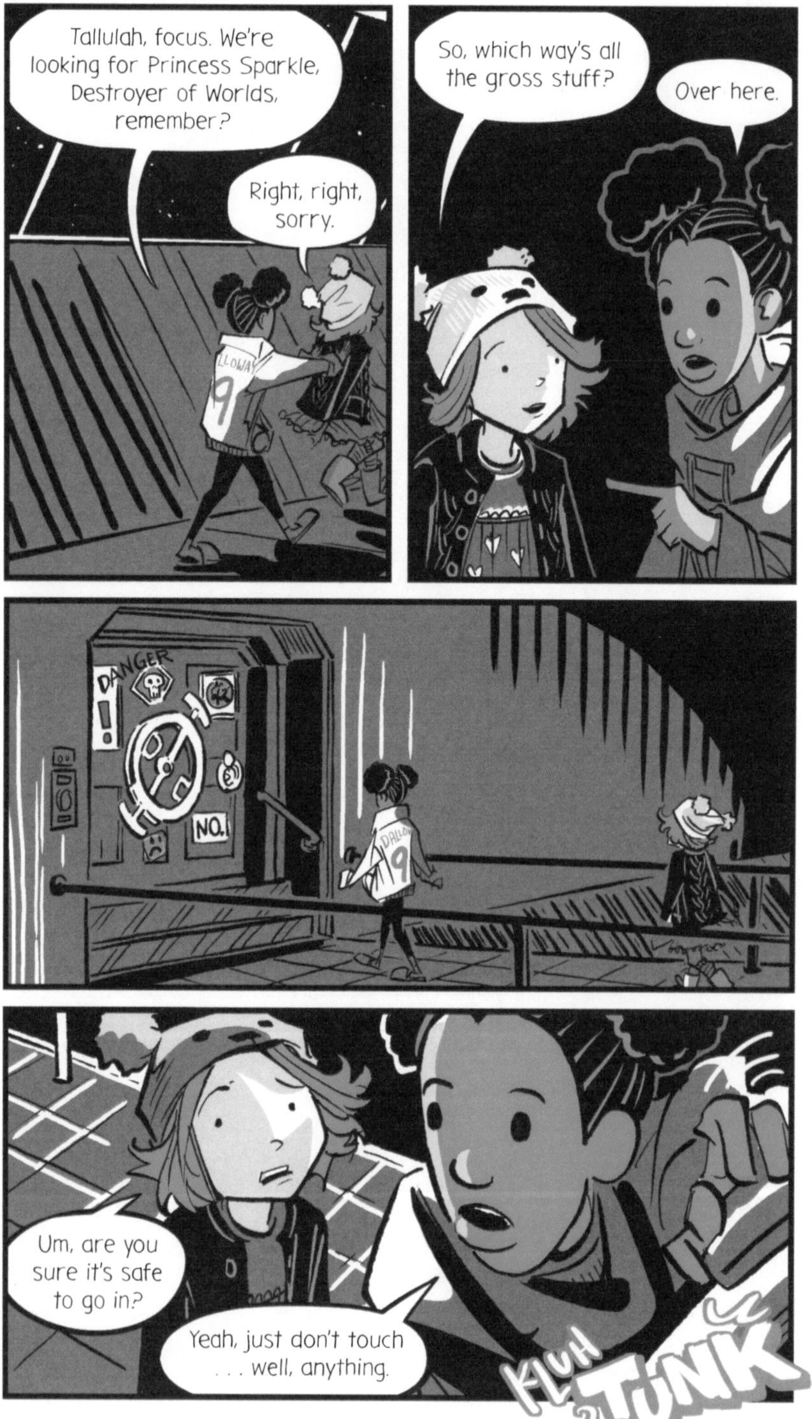
Tallulah, focus. We're looking for Princess Sparkle, Destroyer of Worlds, remember?
Right, right, sorry.
So, which way's all the gross stuff?
Over here.
DANGER
NO.
Um, are you sure it's safe to go in?
Yeah, just don't touch . . . well, anything.
KLUH TUNK

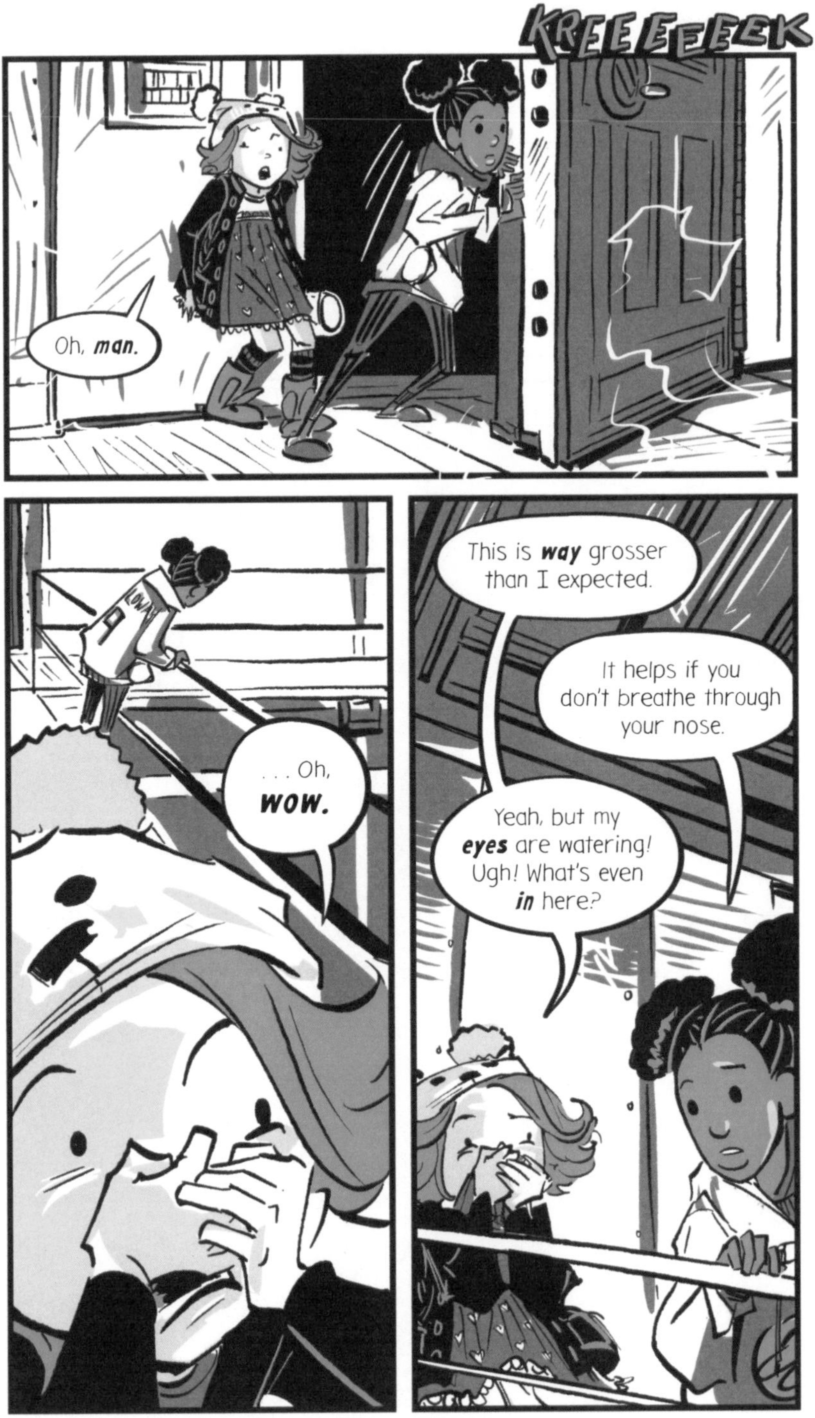
KREEEEEEEK
Oh, *man.*
. . . Oh, **WOW.**
This is **way** grosser than I expected.
It helps if you don't breathe through your nose.
Yeah, but my **eyes** are watering! Ugh! What's even **in** here?

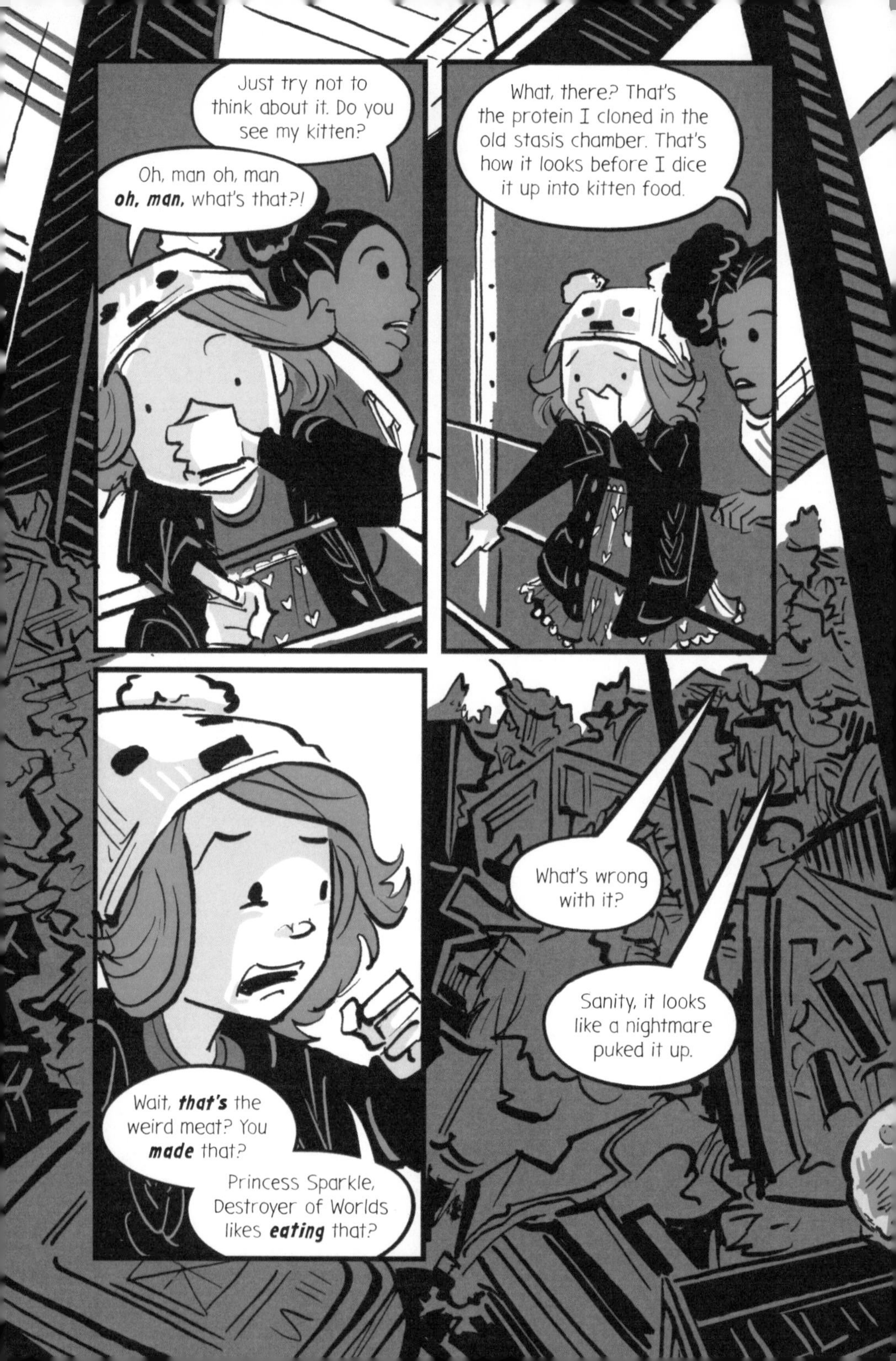
Just try not to think about it. Do you see my kitten?
Oh, man oh, man **oh, man,** what's that?!
What, there? That's the protein I cloned in the old stasis chamber. That's how it looks before I dice it up into kitten food.
What's wrong with it?
Sanity, it looks like a nightmare puked it up.
Wait, ***that's*** the weird meat? You ***made*** that?
Princess Sparkle, Destroyer of Worlds likes ***eating*** that?

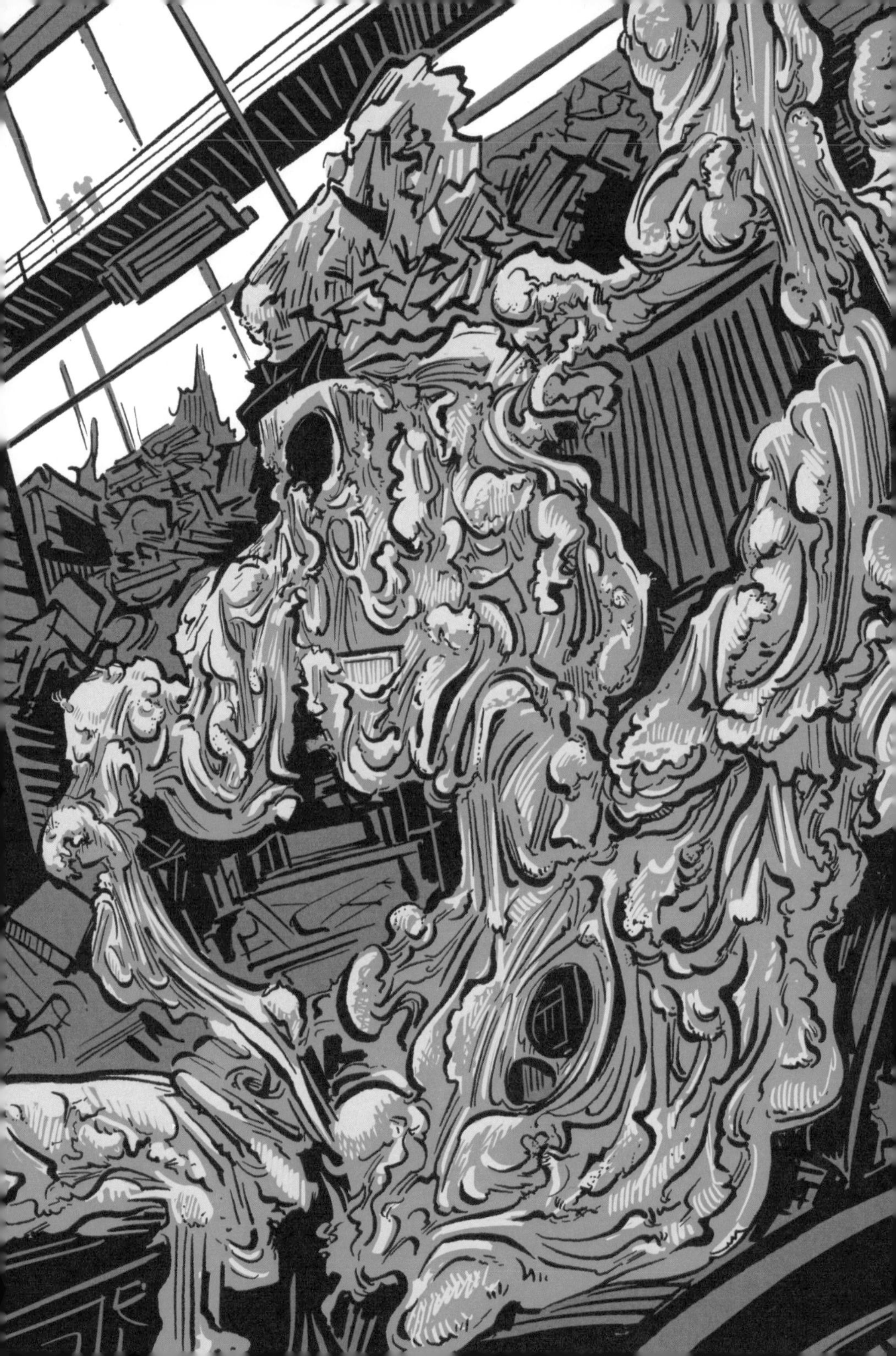

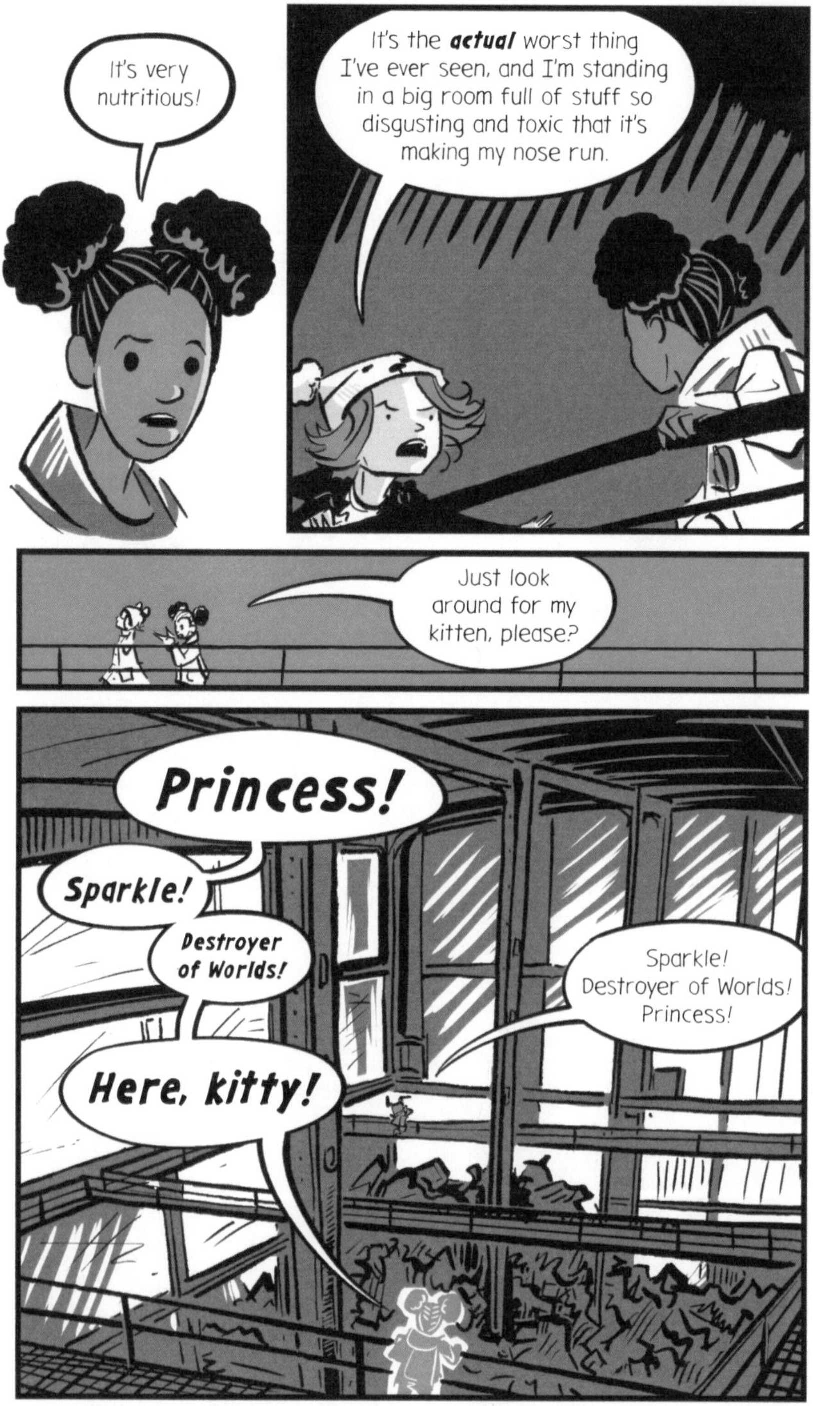
It's very nutritious!
It's the ***actual*** worst thing I've ever seen, and I'm standing in a big room full of stuff so disgusting and toxic that it's making my nose run.
Just look around for my kitten, please?
Princess!
Sparkle!
Destroyer of Worlds!
Here, kitty!
Sparkle! Destroyer of Worlds! Princess!

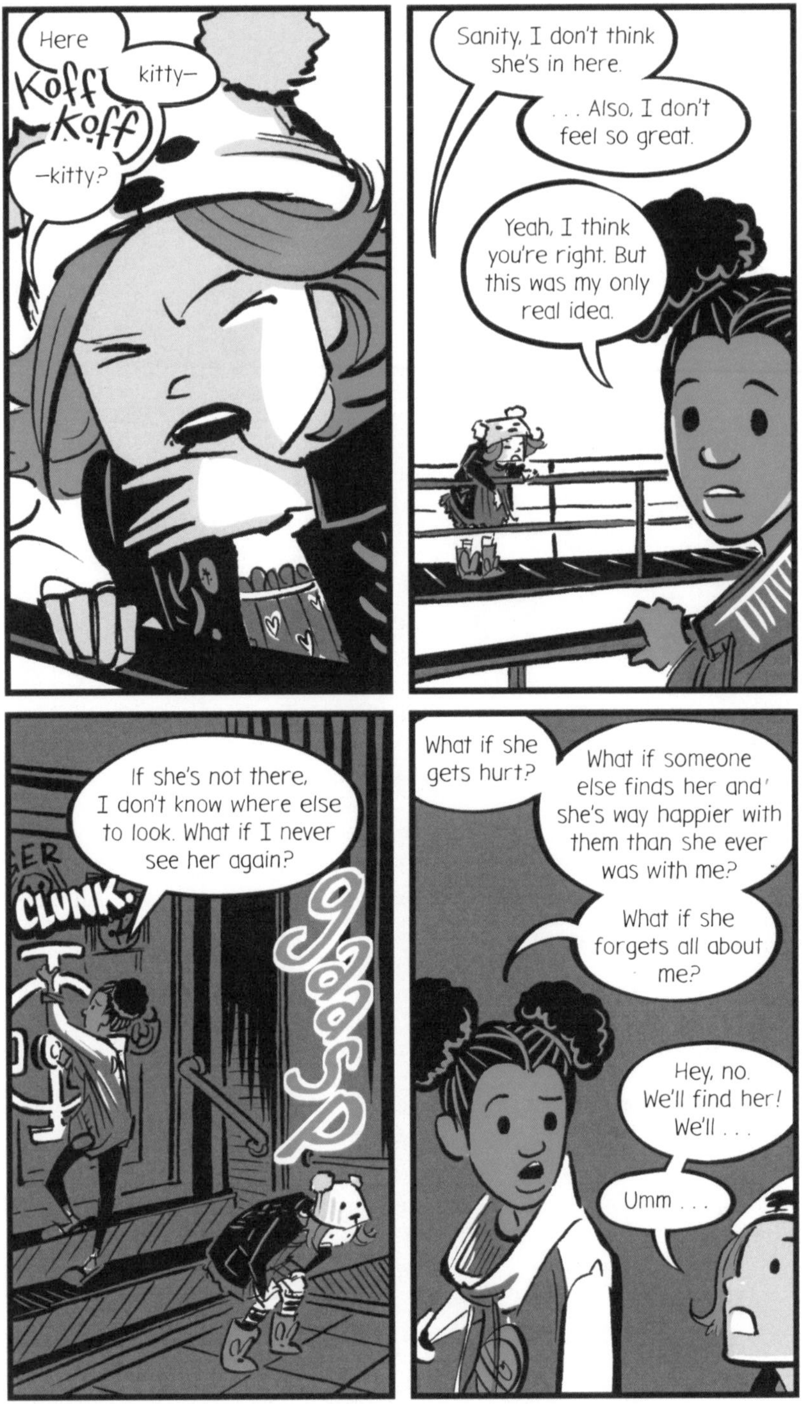
Here
kitty—
Koff
Koff
—kitty?
Sanity, I don't think she's in here.
. . . Also, I don't feel so great.
Yeah, I think you're right. But this was my only real idea.
If she's not there, I don't know where else to look. What if I never see her again?
CLUNK.
gaasp
What if she gets hurt?
What if someone else finds her and she's way happier with them than she ever was with me?
What if she forgets all about me?
Hey, no. We'll find her! We'll . . .
Umm . . .

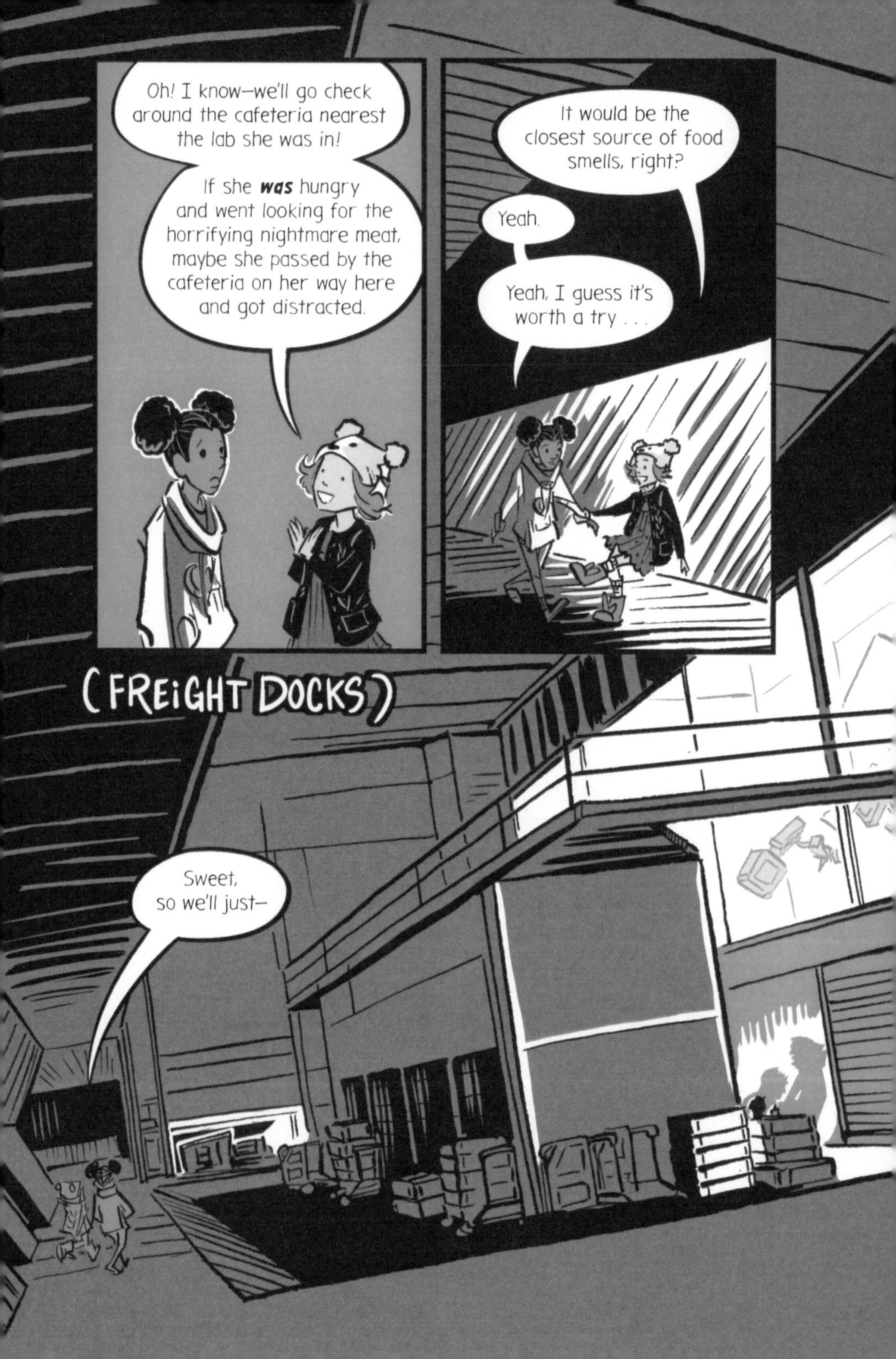

Oh! I know—we'll go check around the cafeteria nearest the lab she was in!
If she **was** hungry and went looking for the horrifying nightmare meat, maybe she passed by the cafeteria on her way here and got distracted.
It would be the closest source of food smells, right?
Yeah.
Yeah, I guess it's worth a try . . .
(FREIGHT DOCKS)
Sweet, so we'll just—

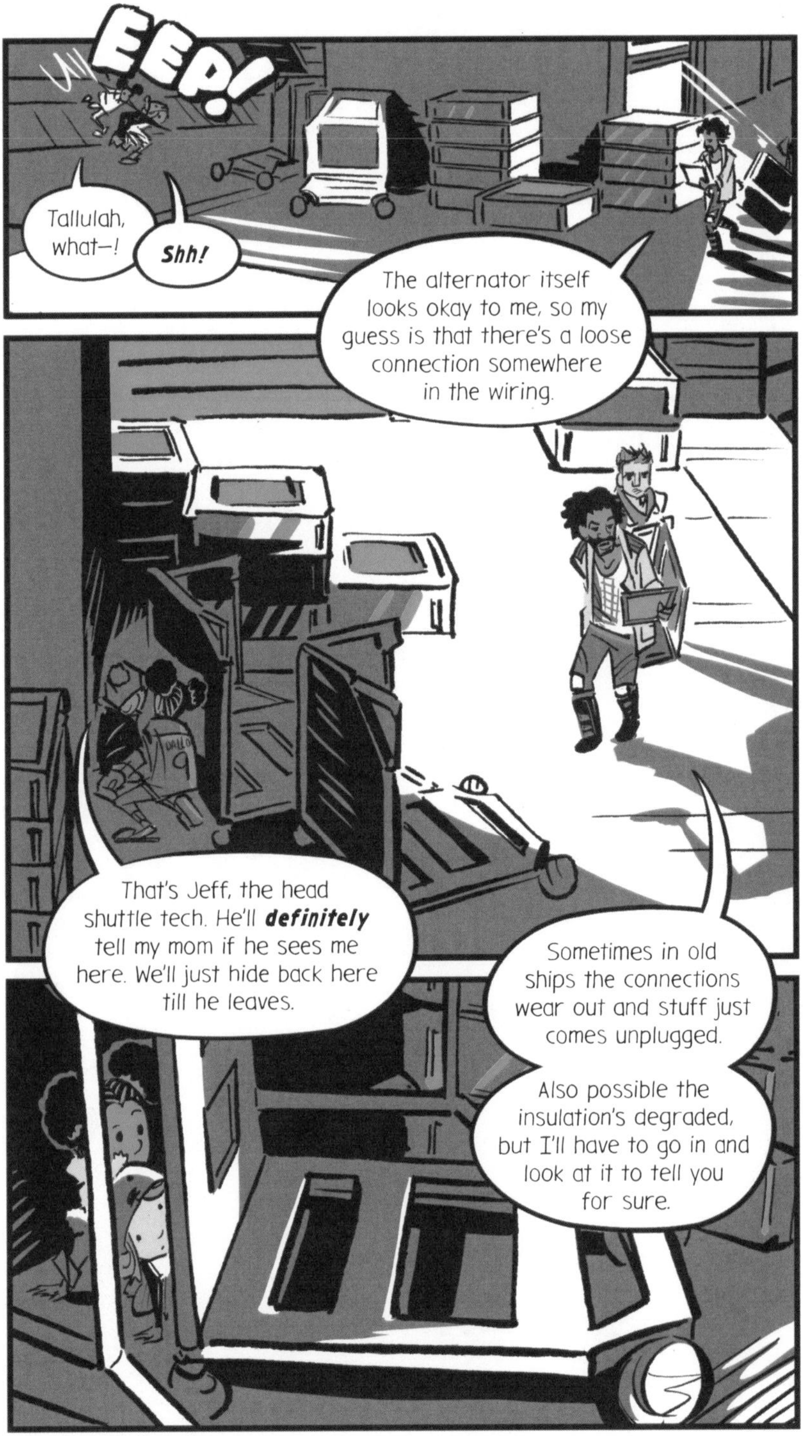
EEP!
Tallulah, what–!
Shh!
The alternator itself looks okay to me, so my guess is that there's a loose connection somewhere in the wiring.
That's Jeff, the head shuttle tech. He'll **definitely** tell my mom if he sees me here. We'll just hide back here till he leaves.
Sometimes in old ships the connections wear out and stuff just comes unplugged.
Also possible the insulation's degraded, but I'll have to go in and look at it to tell you for sure.

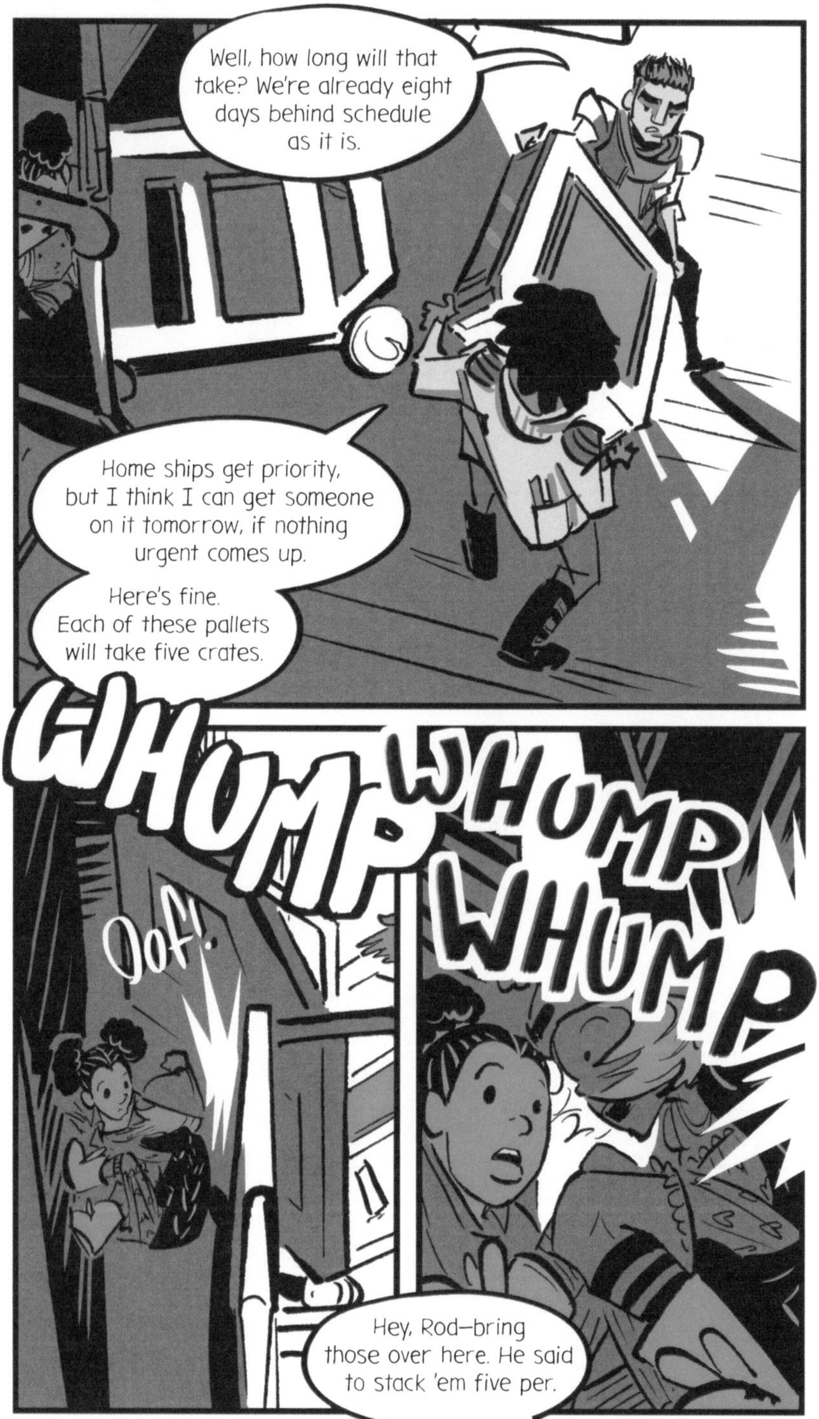
Well, how long will that take? We're already eight days behind schedule as it is.
Home ships get priority, but I think I can get someone on it tomorrow, if nothing urgent comes up.
Here's fine. Each of these pallets will take five crates.
WHUMP
WHUMP
WHUMP
Oof!
Hey, Rod—bring those over here. He said to stack 'em five per.

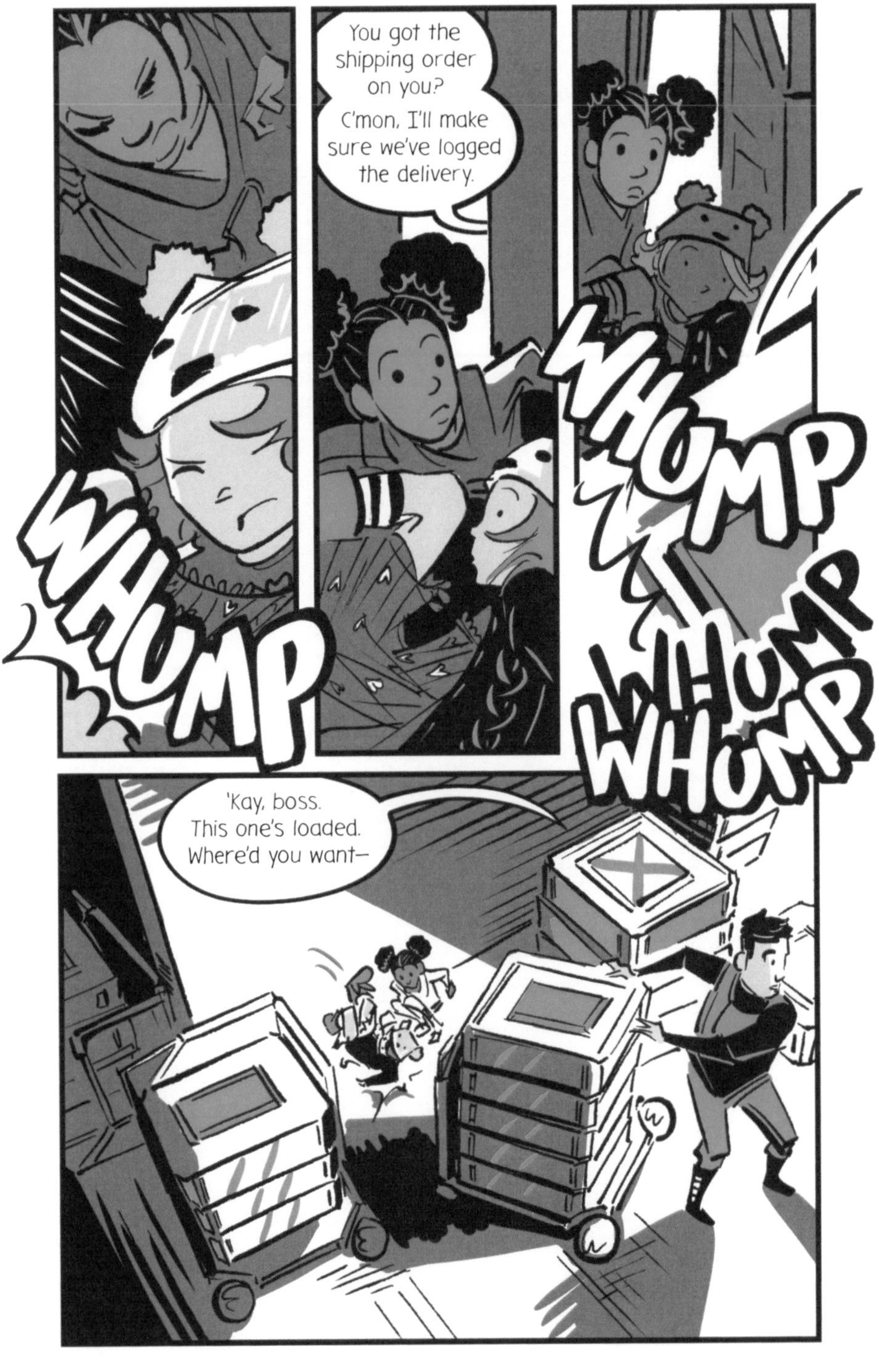
WHUMP
You got the shipping order on you?
C'mon, I'll make sure we've logged the delivery.
WHUMP
WHUMP
WHUMP
'Kay, boss. This one's loaded. Where'd you want—

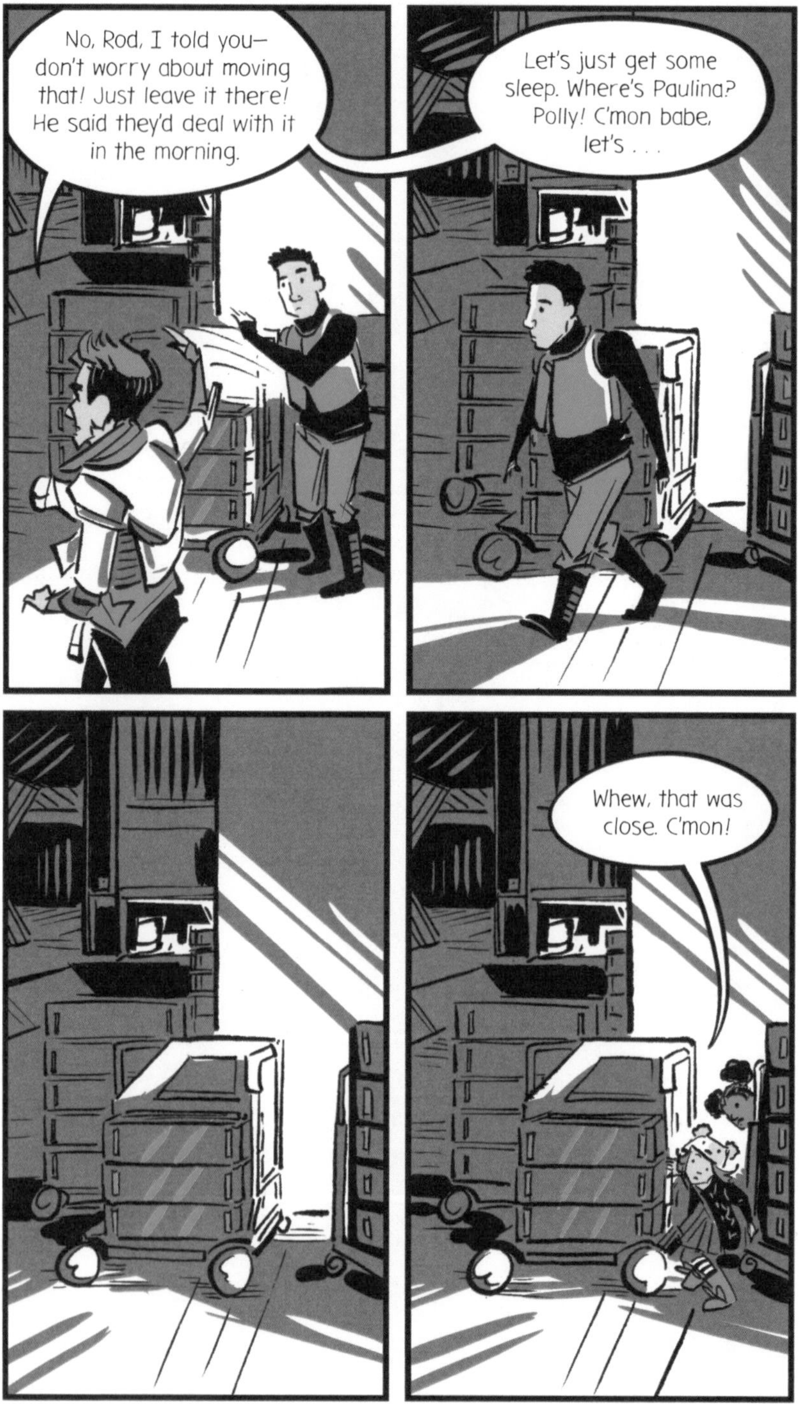
No, Rod, I told you—don't worry about moving that! Just leave it there! He said they'd deal with it in the morning.
Let's just get some sleep. Where's Paulina? Polly! C'mon babe, let's . . .
Whew, that was close. C'mon!

(RESEARCH CAFE)

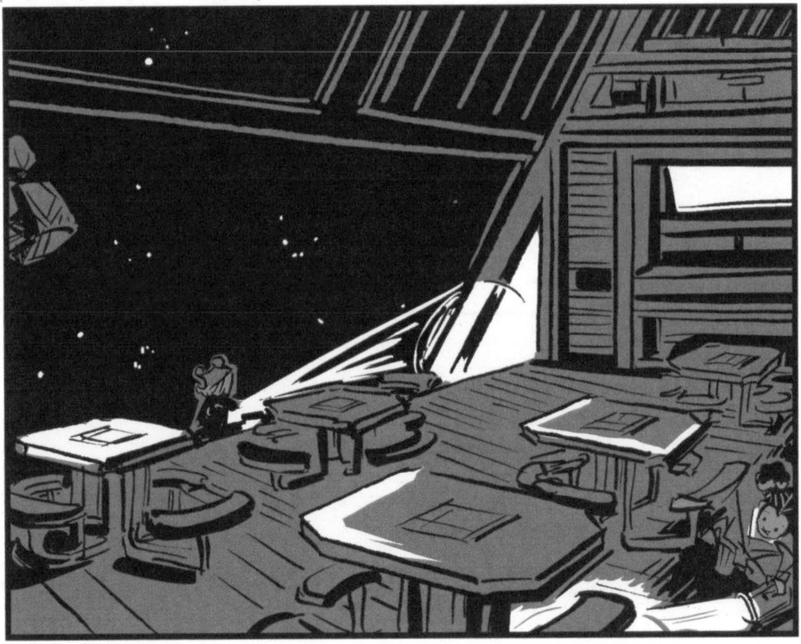

(ENGINEERING CAFE)

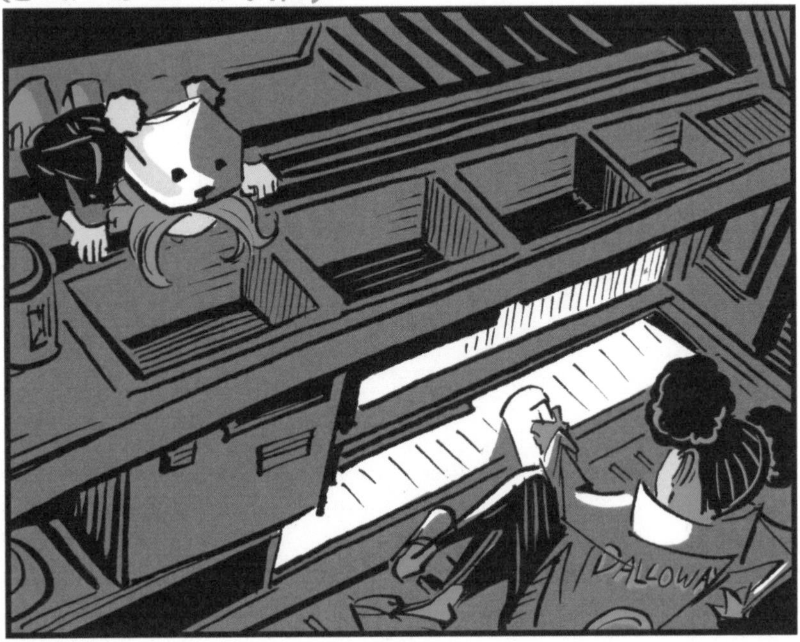
DALLOWAY

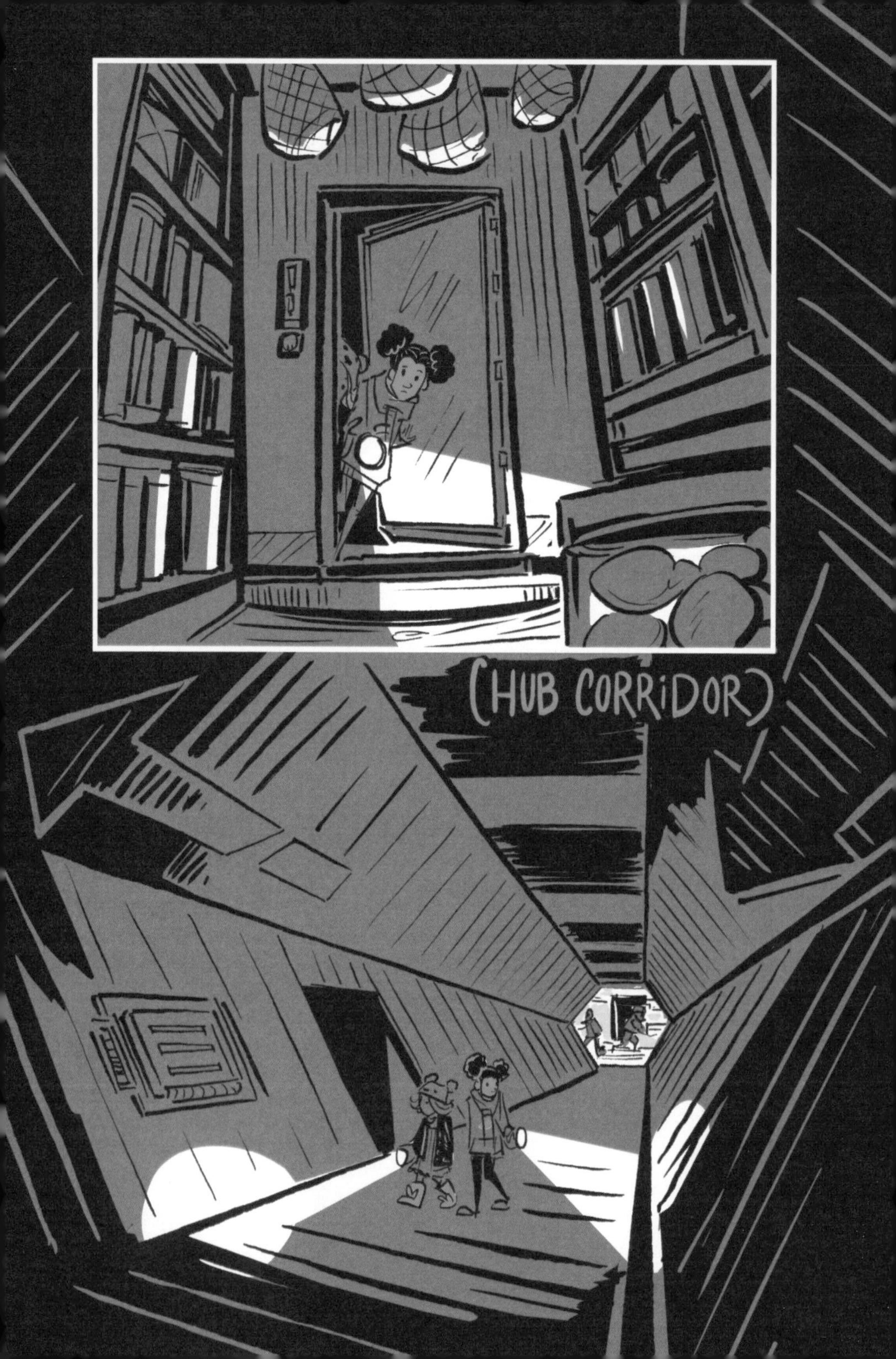
(HUB CORRIDOR)

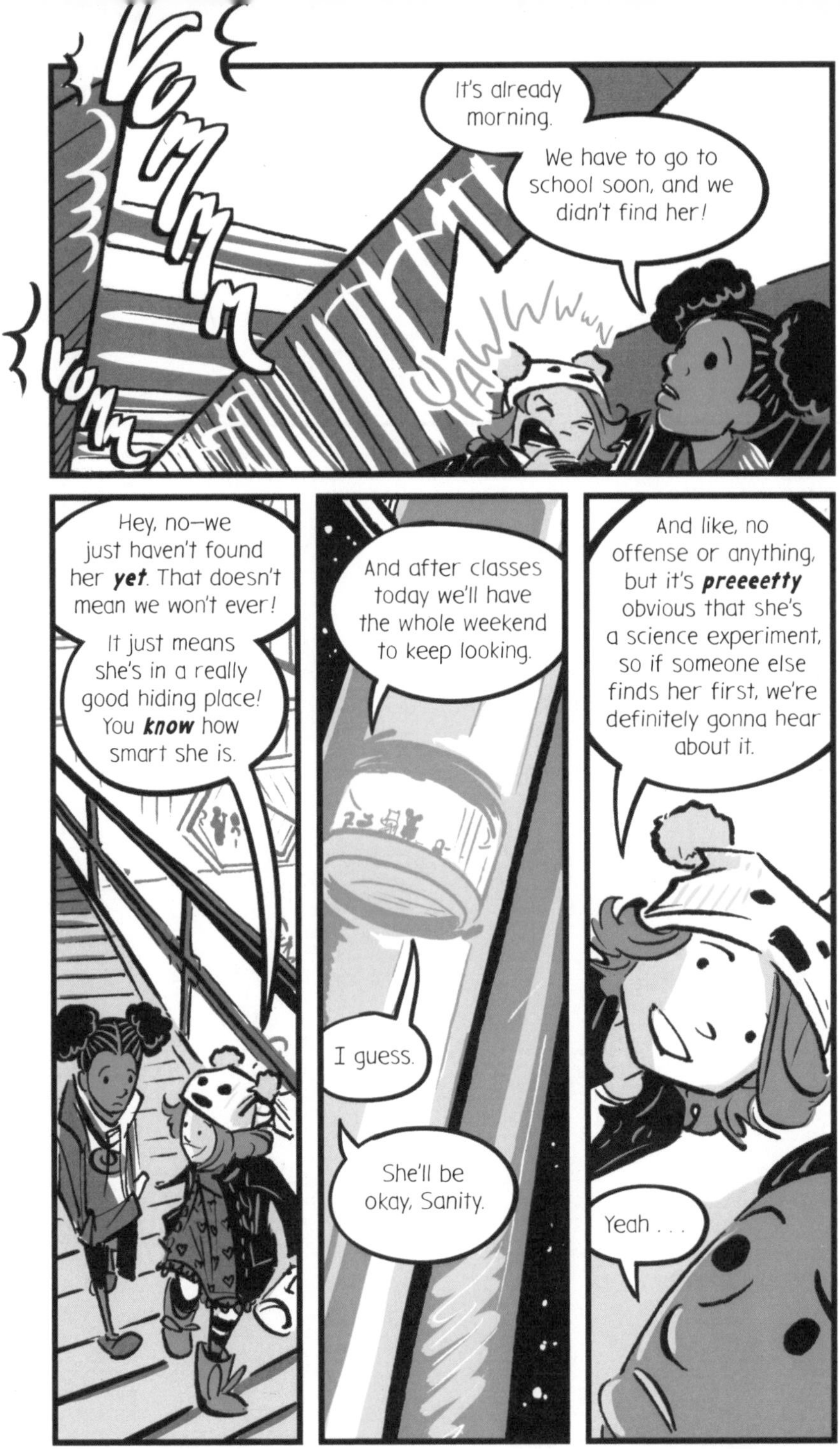
VOMMMM
VOMM
It's already morning.
We have to go to school soon, and we didn't find her!
Hey, no—we just haven't found her ***yet***. That doesn't mean we won't ever!
It just means she's in a really good hiding place! You ***know*** how smart she is.
And after classes today we'll have the whole weekend to keep looking.
I guess.
She'll be okay, Sanity.
And like, no offense or anything, but it's ***preeeetty*** obvious that she's a science experiment, so if someone else finds her first, we're definitely gonna hear about it.
Yeah . . .

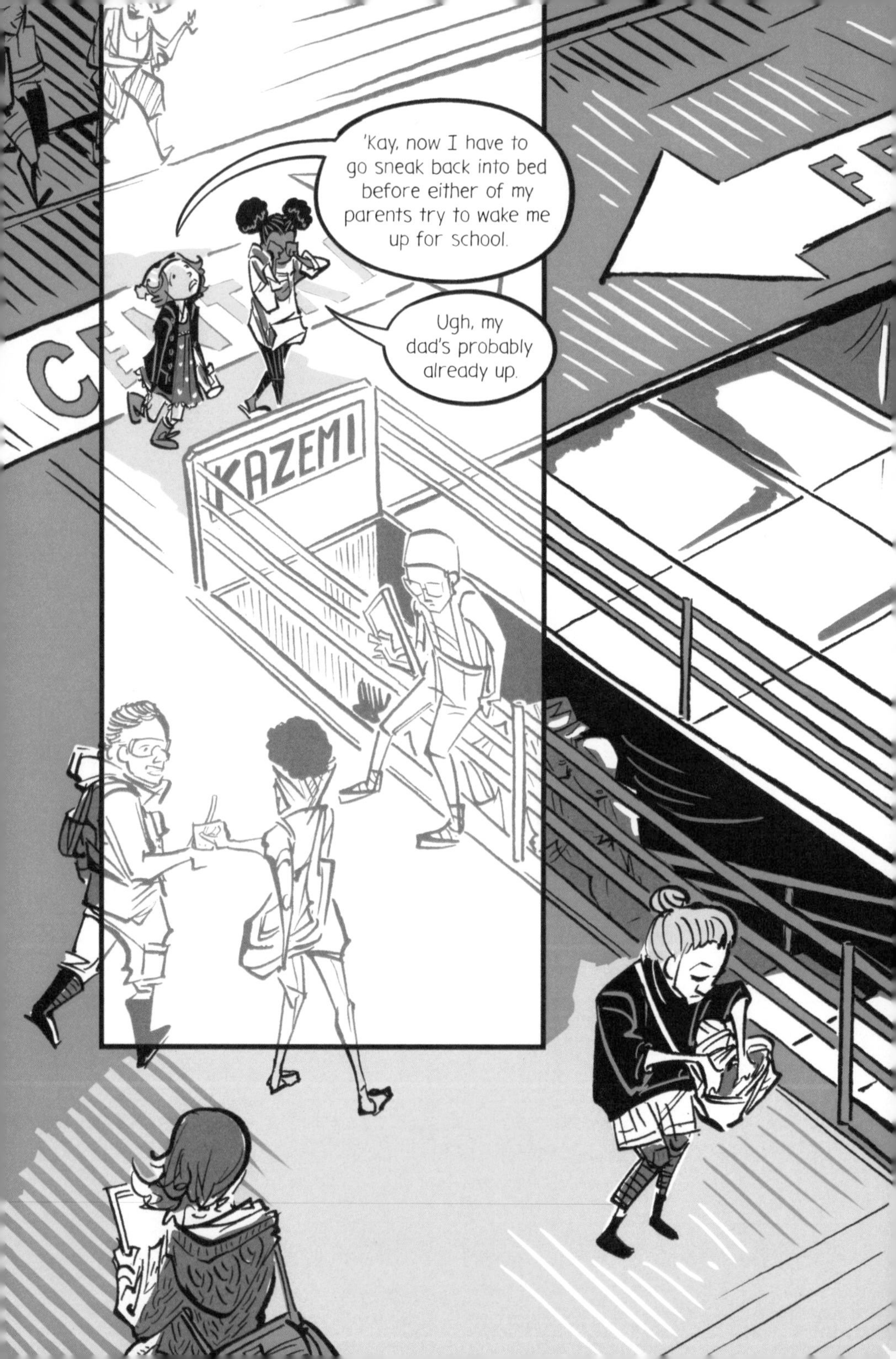
'Kay, now I have to go sneak back into bed before either of my parents try to wake me up for school.
Ugh, my dad's probably already up.
KAZEMI

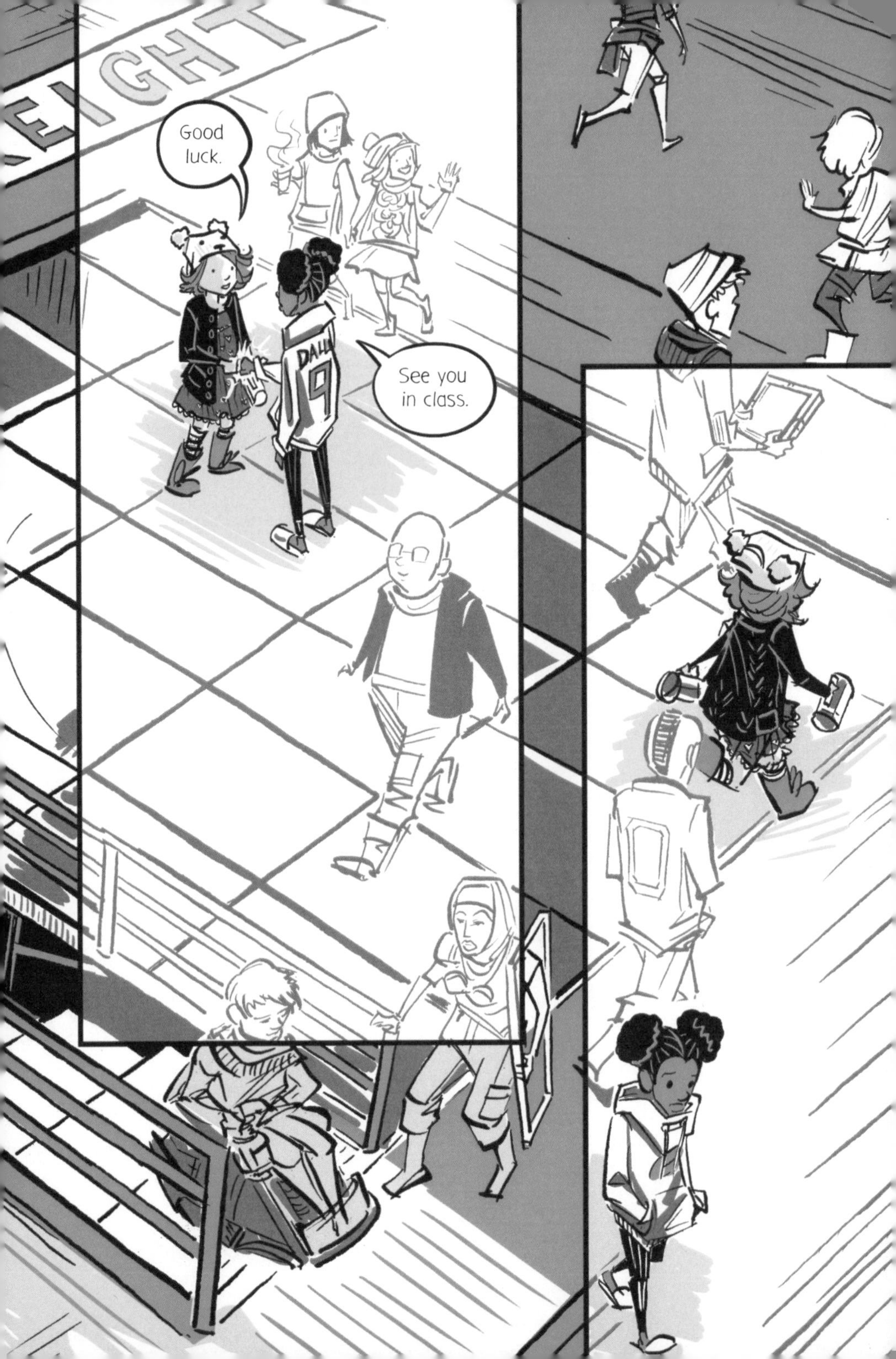
EIGHT
Good luck.
DALL 19
See you in class.

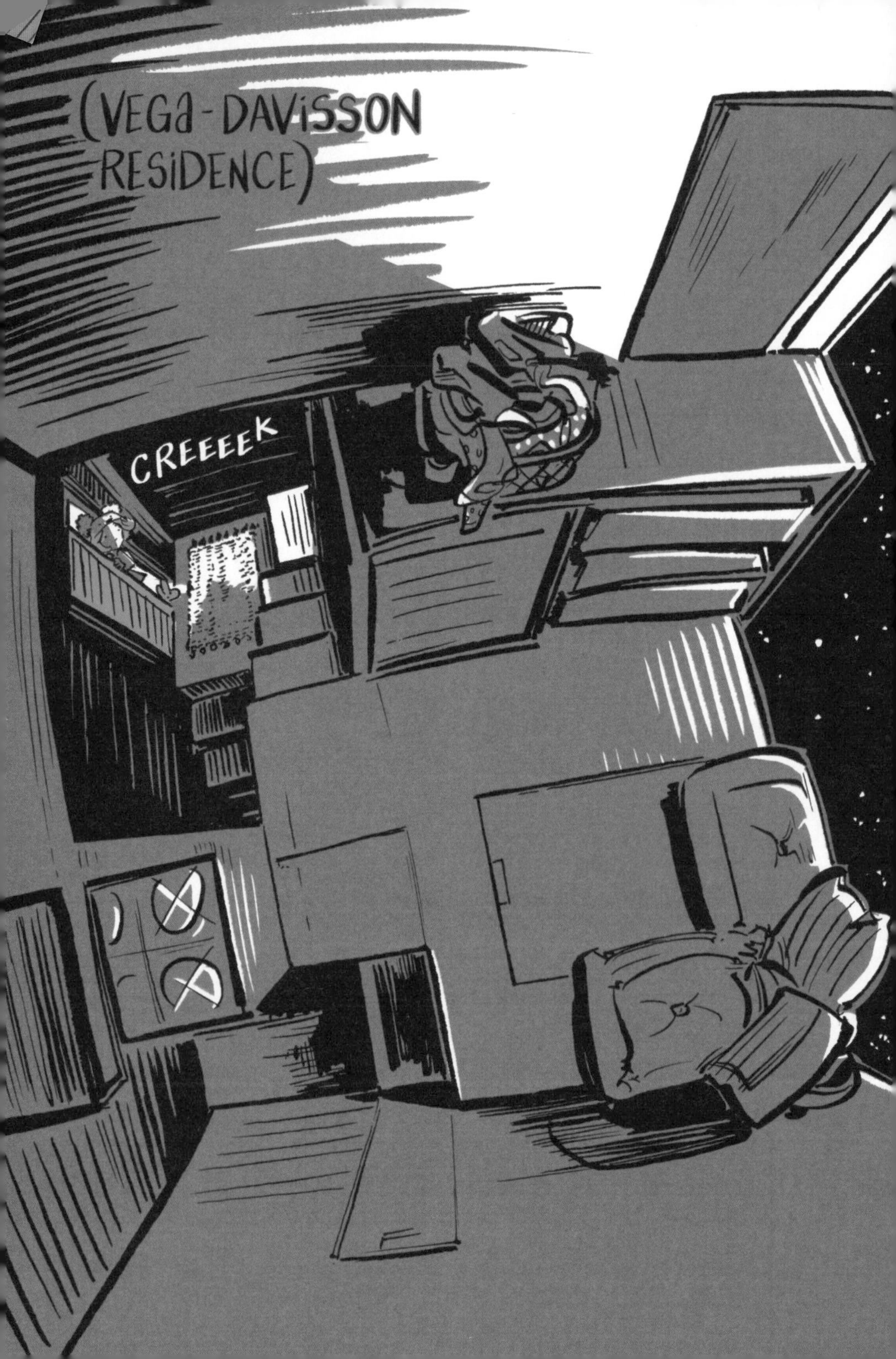
(VEGA-DAVISSON RESIDENCE)
CREEEEK

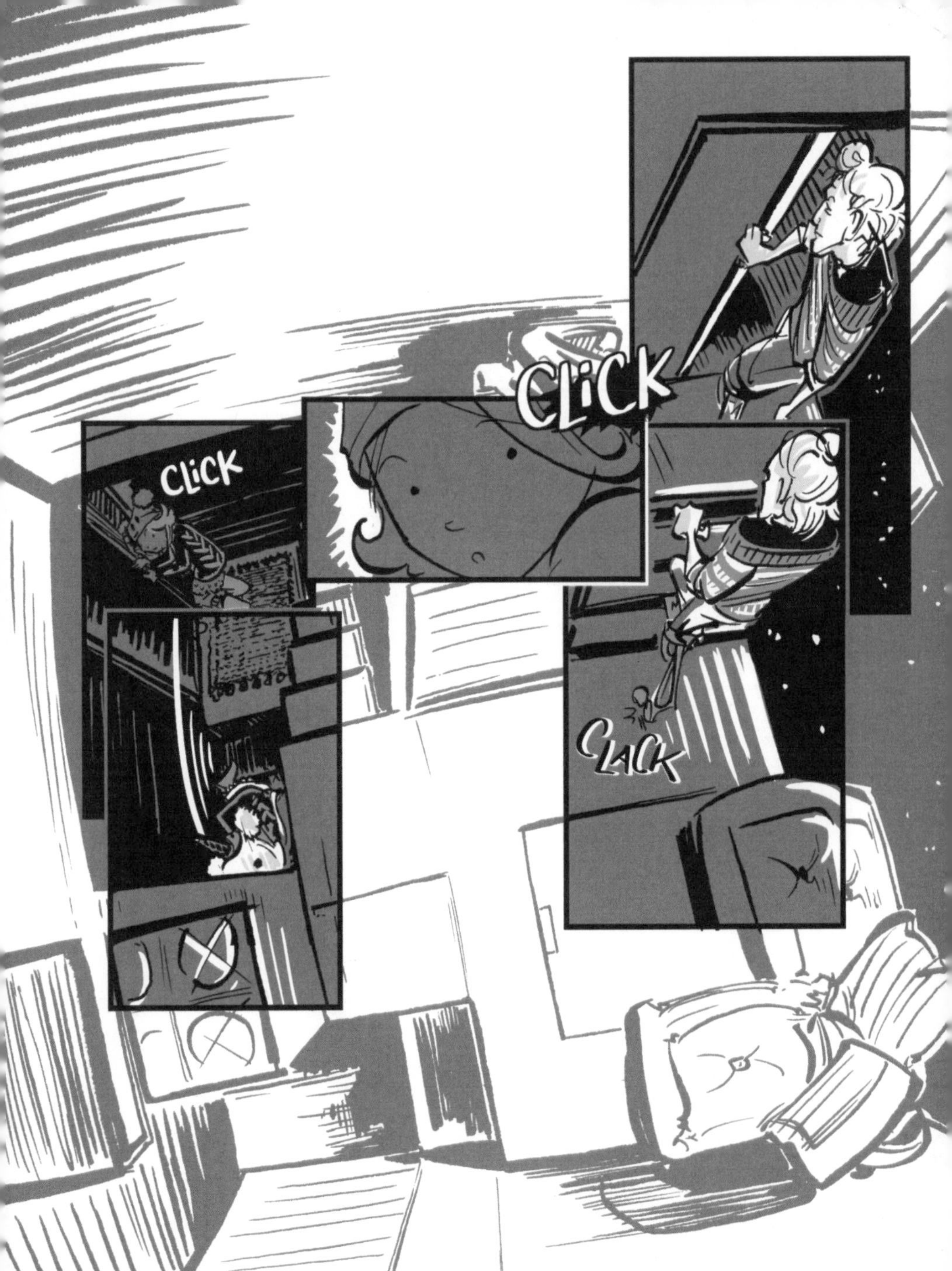
CLICK
CLICK
CLACK

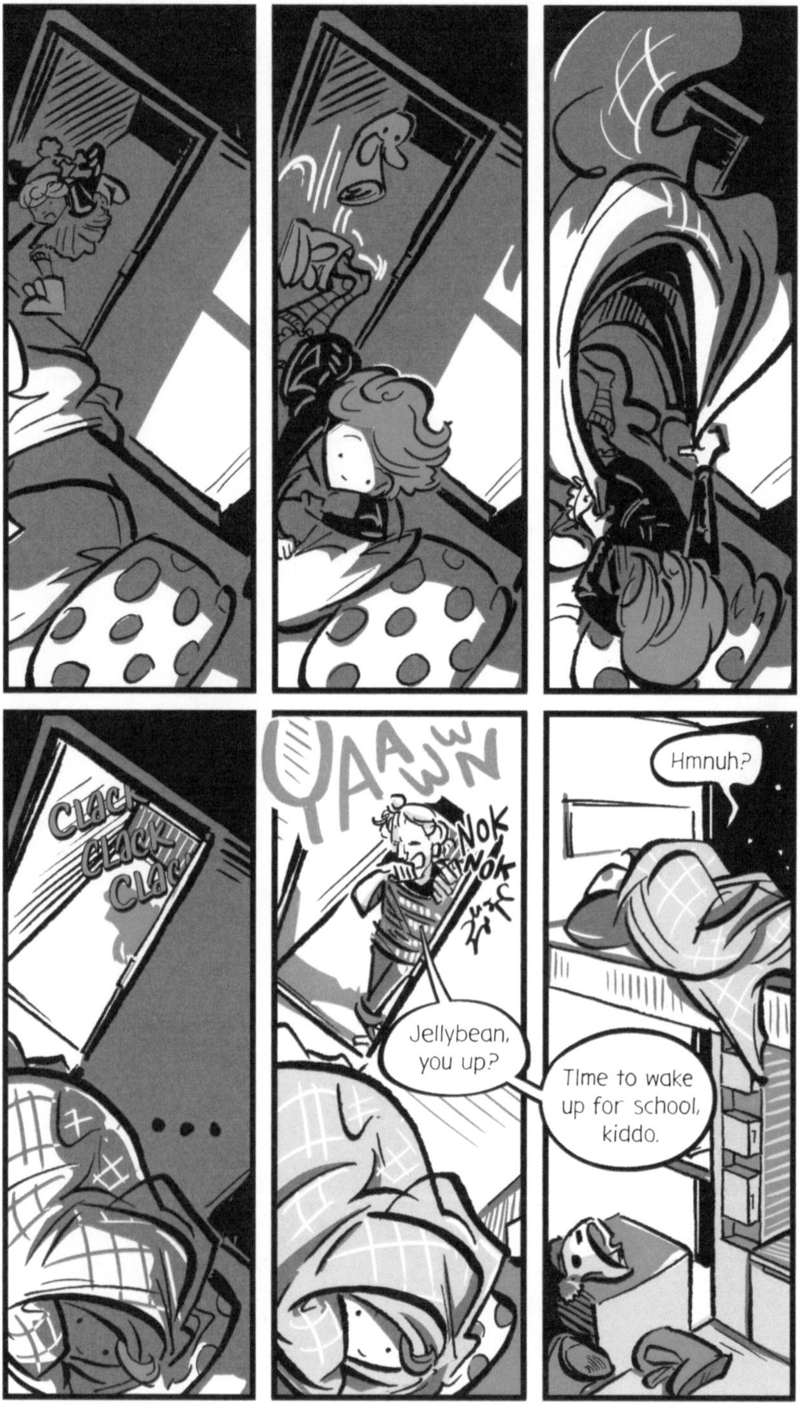
CLACK
CLACK
CLAC
. . .
YAAWWN
NOK
NOK
Jellybean, you up?
Time to wake up for school, kiddo.
Hmnuh?

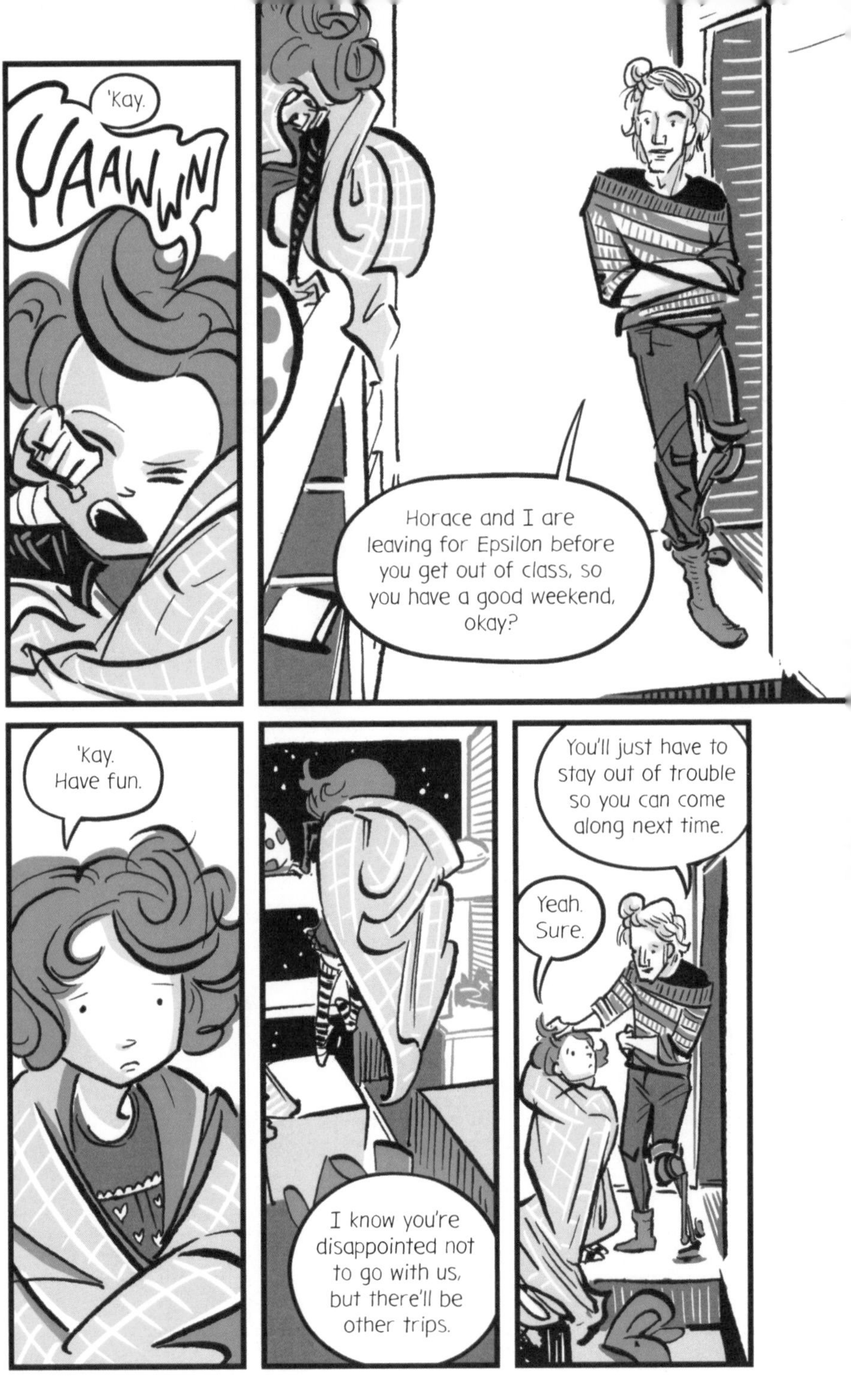

'Kay.
YAAWWN
Horace and I are leaving for Epsilon before you get out of class, so you have a good weekend, okay?
'Kay. Have fun.
I know you're disappointed not to go with us, but there'll be other trips.
You'll just have to stay out of trouble so you can come along next time.
Yeah. Sure.

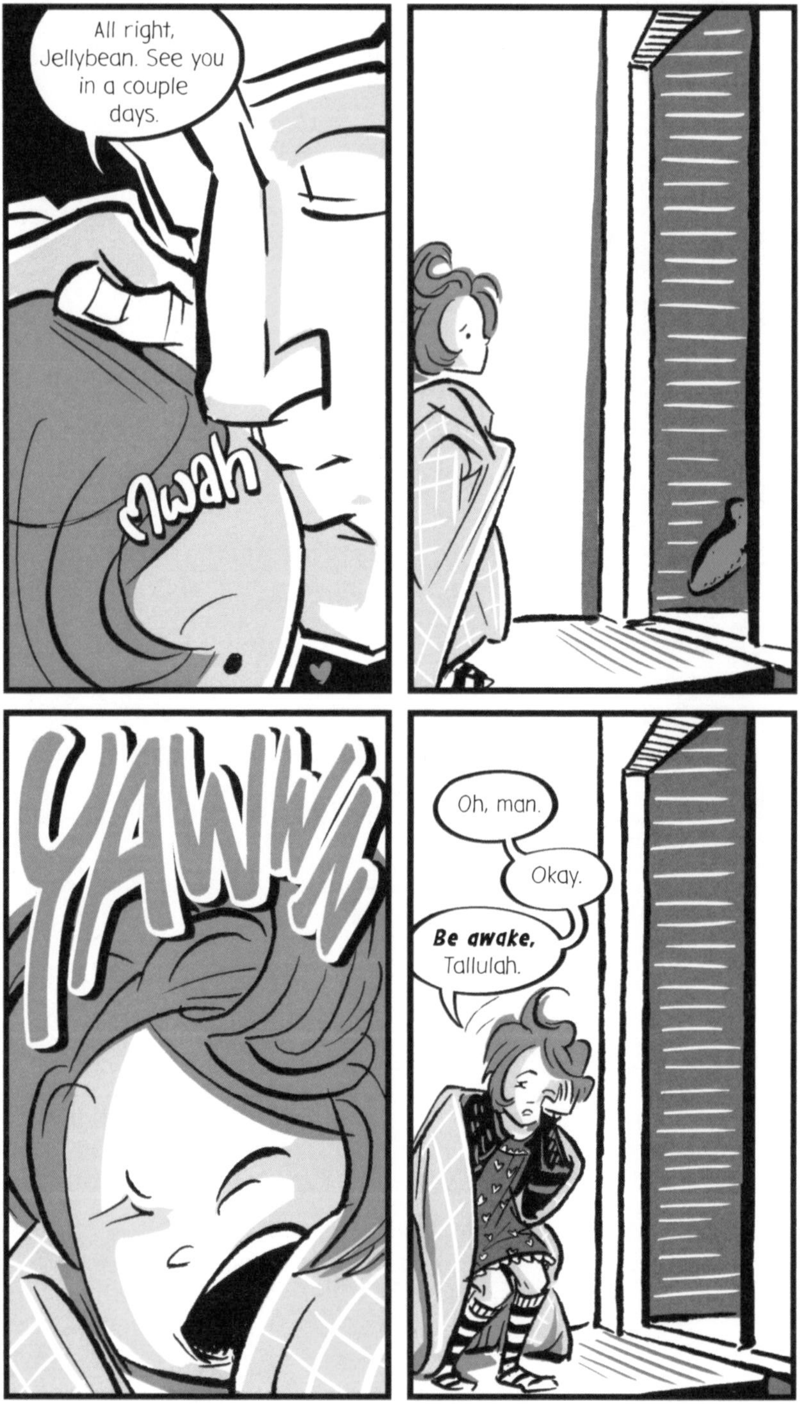
All right, Jellybean. See you in a couple days.
Mwah
YAWWN
Oh, man.
Okay.
Be awake, Tallulah.

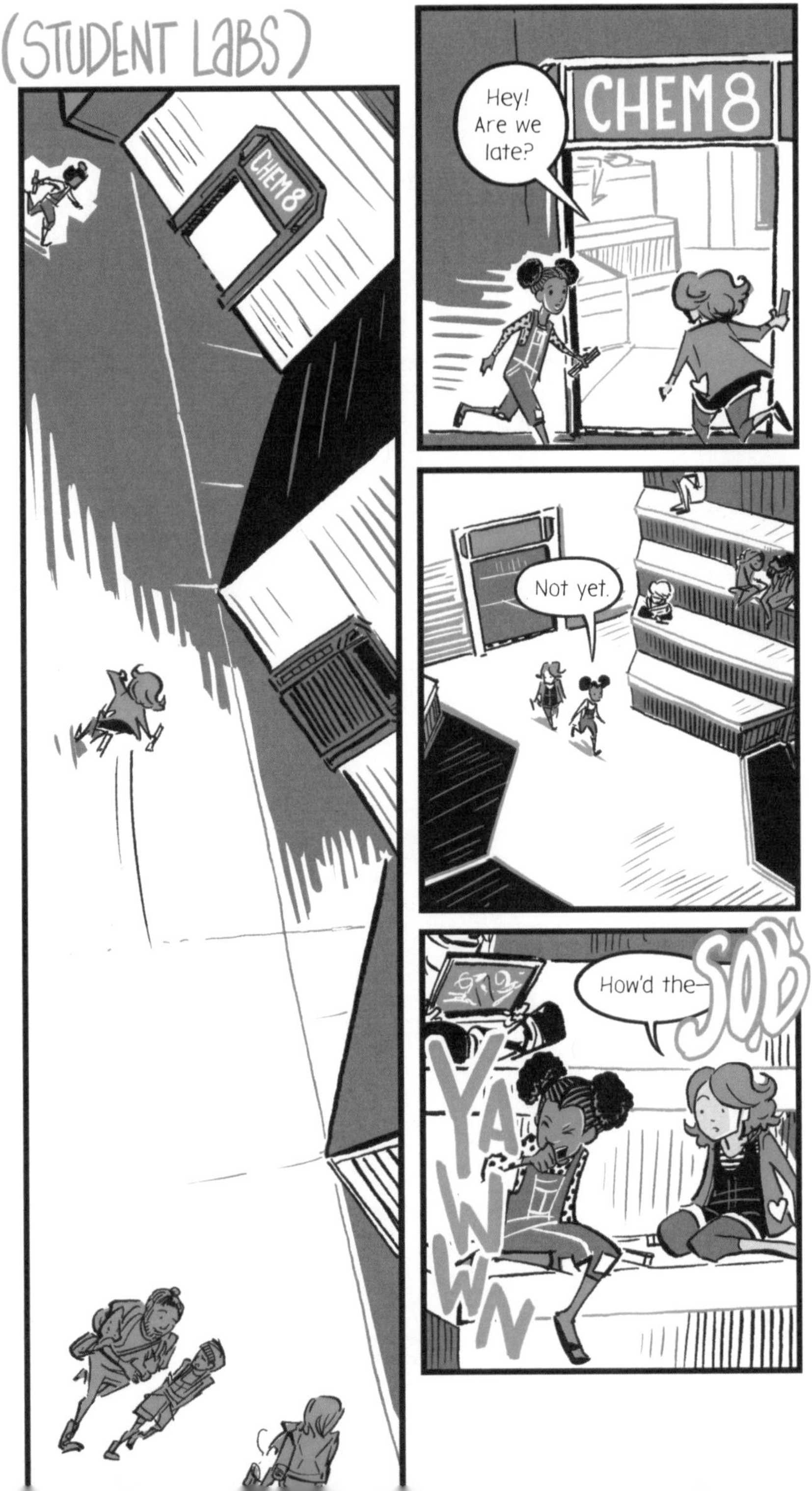
(STUDENT LABS)
CHEM 8
CHEM 8
Hey! Are we late?
Not yet.
How'd the—
SOB
YAWWN

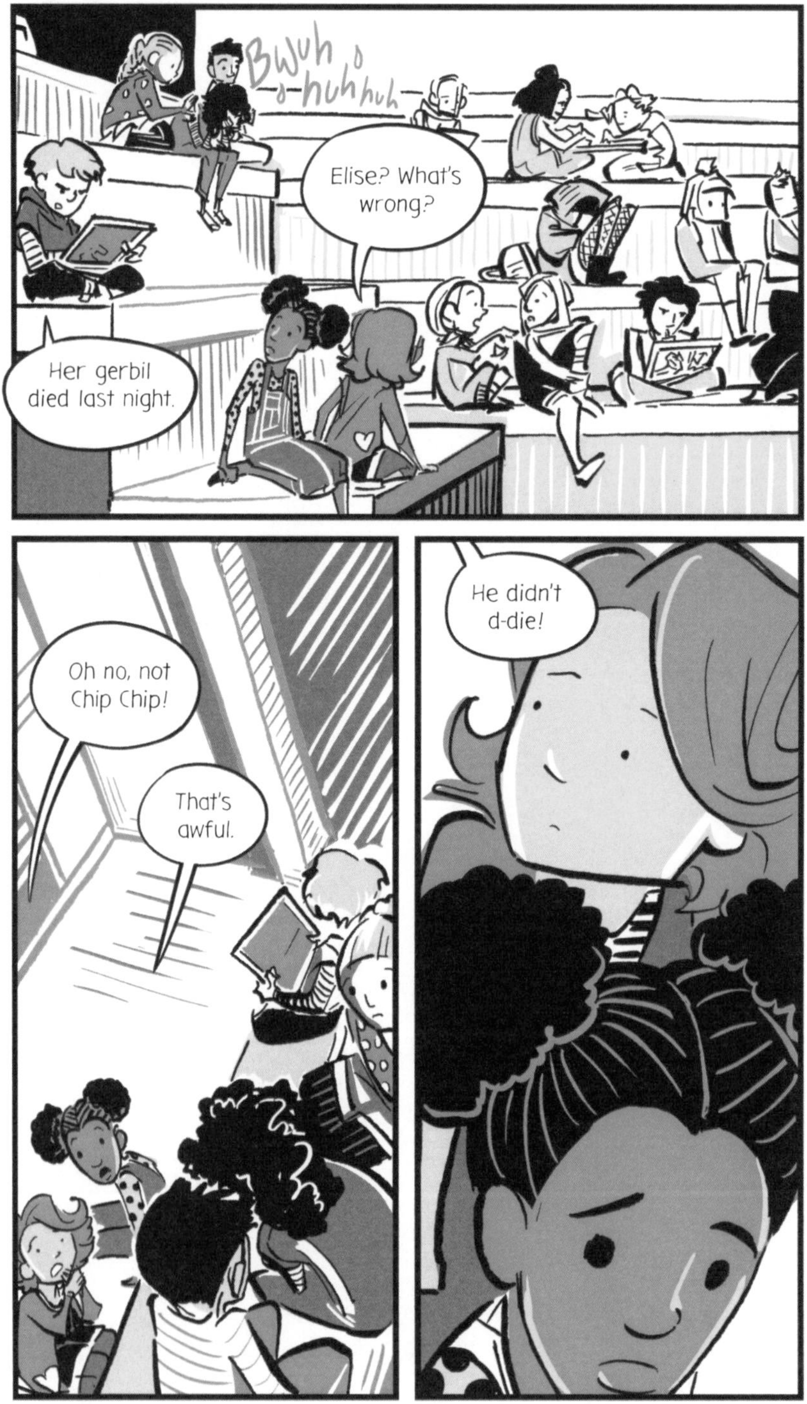
Bwuh huh huh huh
Elise? What's wrong?
Her gerbil died last night.
Oh no, not Chip Chip!
That's awful.
He didn't d-die!

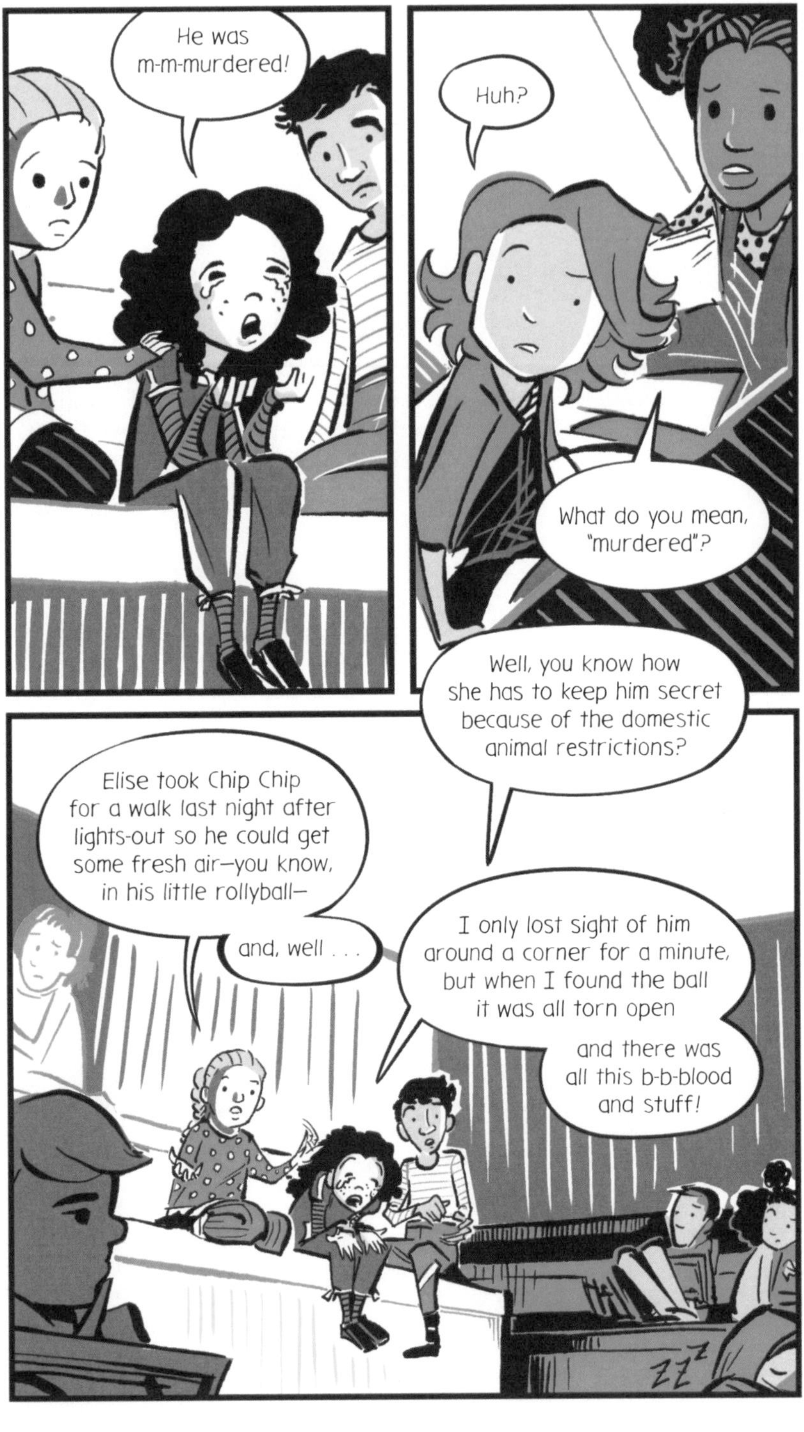
He was m-m-murdered!
Huh?
What do you mean, "murdered"?
Well, you know how she has to keep him secret because of the domestic animal restrictions?
Elise took Chip Chip for a walk last night after lights-out so he could get some fresh air—you know, in his little rollyball—
and, well . . .
I only lost sight of him around a corner for a minute, but when I found the ball it was all torn open
and there was all this b-b-blood and stuff!
ZZZ

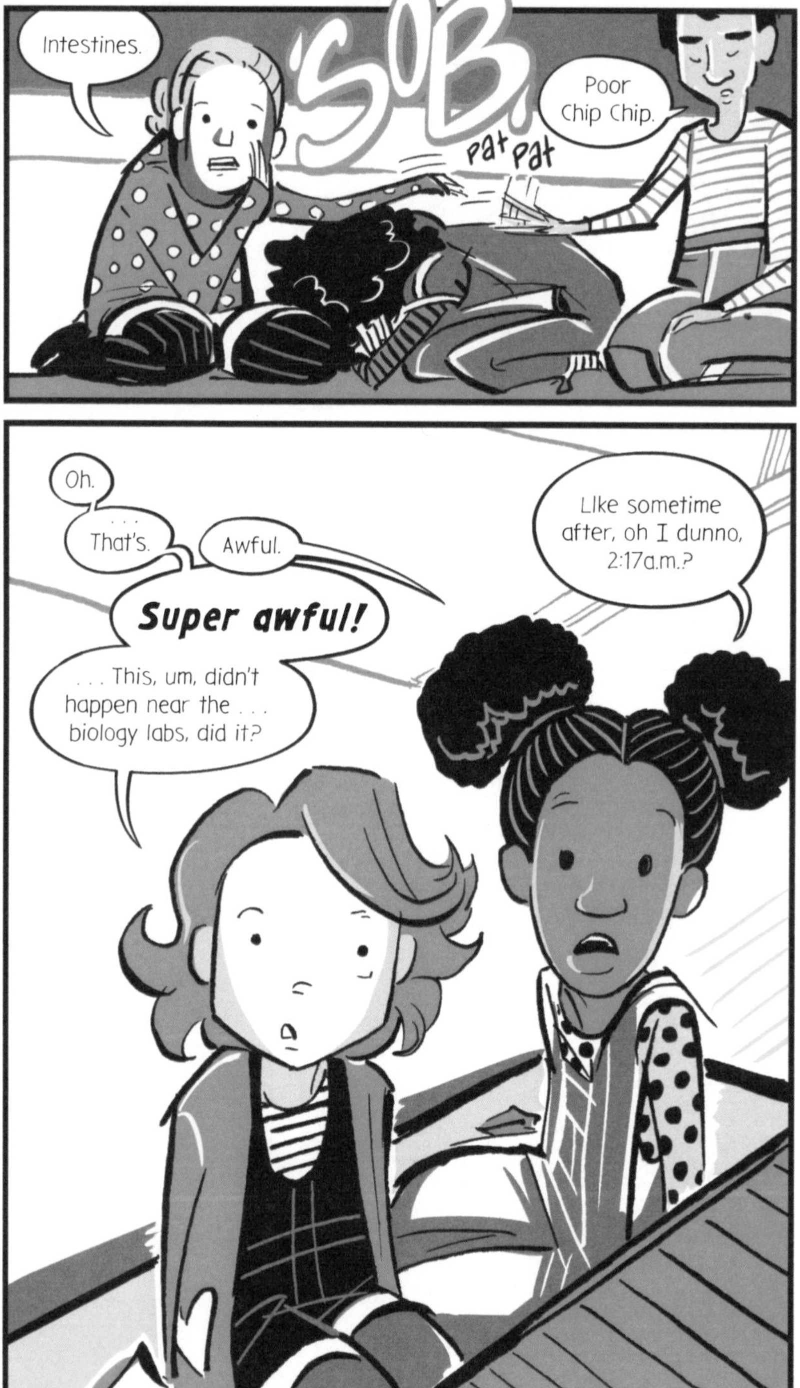
Intestines.
SOB
pat pat
Poor Chip Chip.
Oh.
. . . That's.
Awful.
Super awful!
. . . This, um, didn't happen near the . . . biology labs, did it?
Like sometime after, oh I dunno, 2:17a.m.?

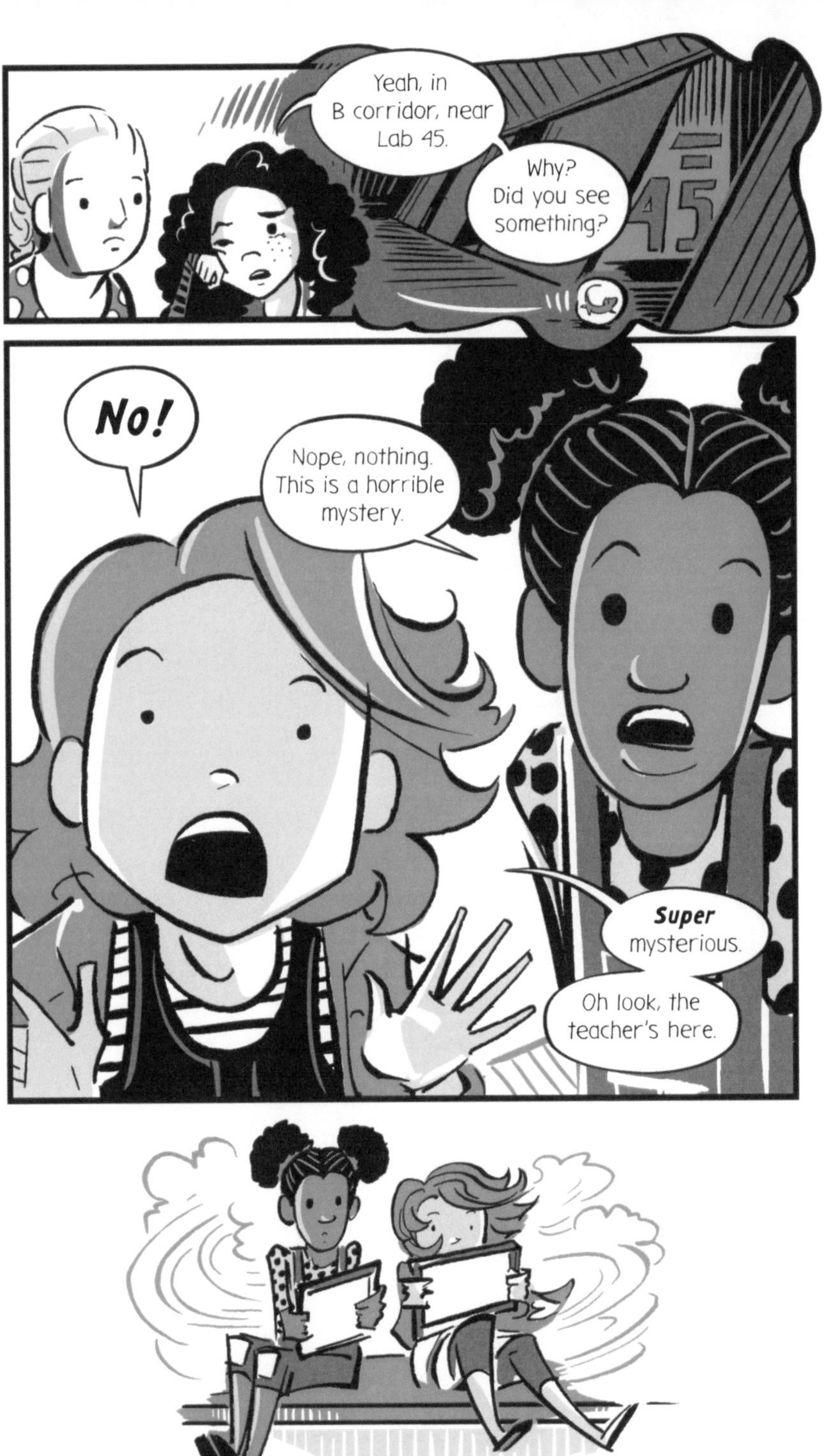
Yeah, in B corridor, near Lab 45.
Why? Did you see something?
45
No!
Nope, nothing. This is a horrible mystery.
Super mysterious.
Oh look, the teacher's here.

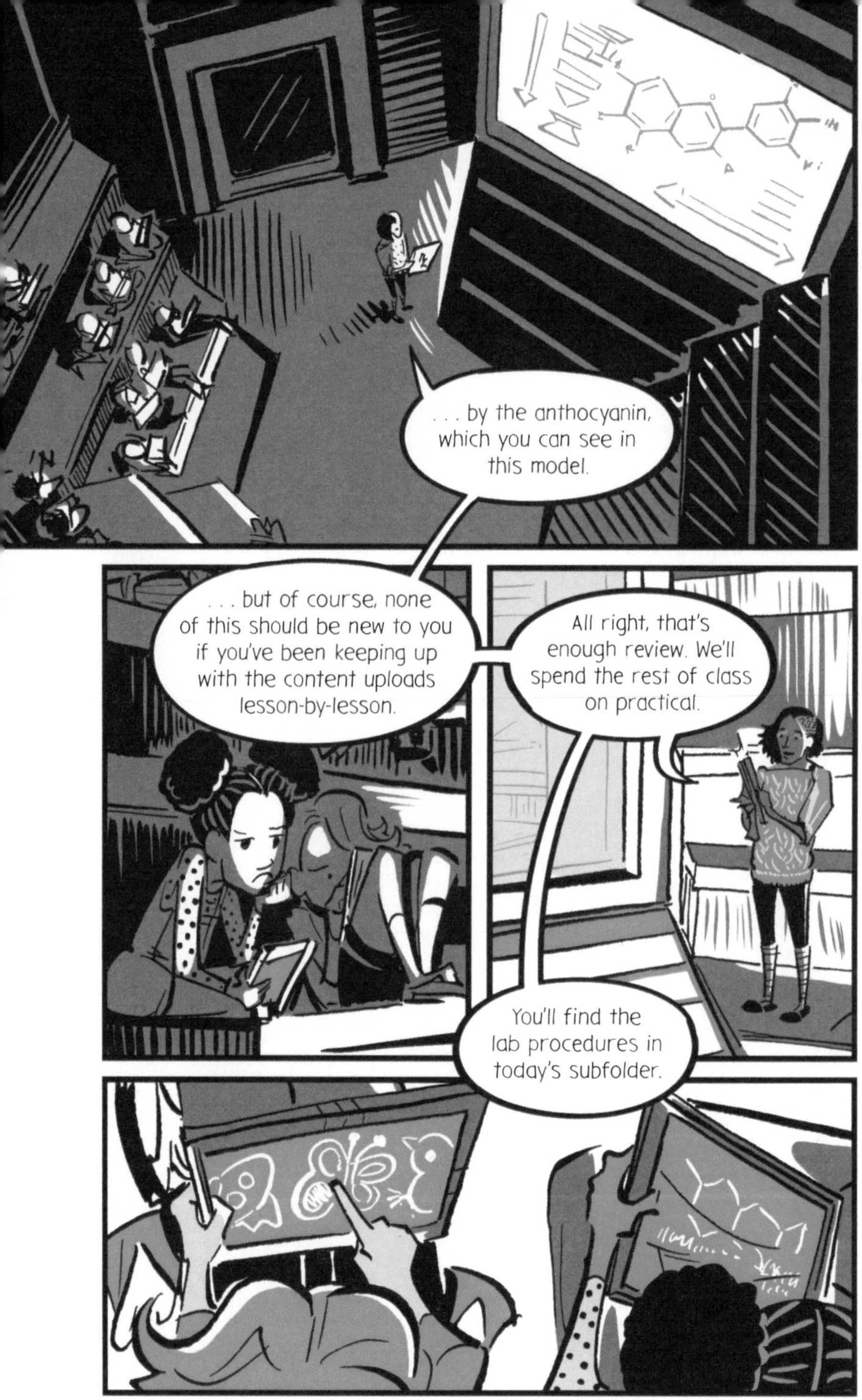
. . . by the anthocyanin, which you can see in this model.
. . . but of course, none of this should be new to you if you've been keeping up with the content uploads lesson-by-lesson.
All right, that's enough review. We'll spend the rest of class on practical.
You'll find the lab procedures in today's subfolder.

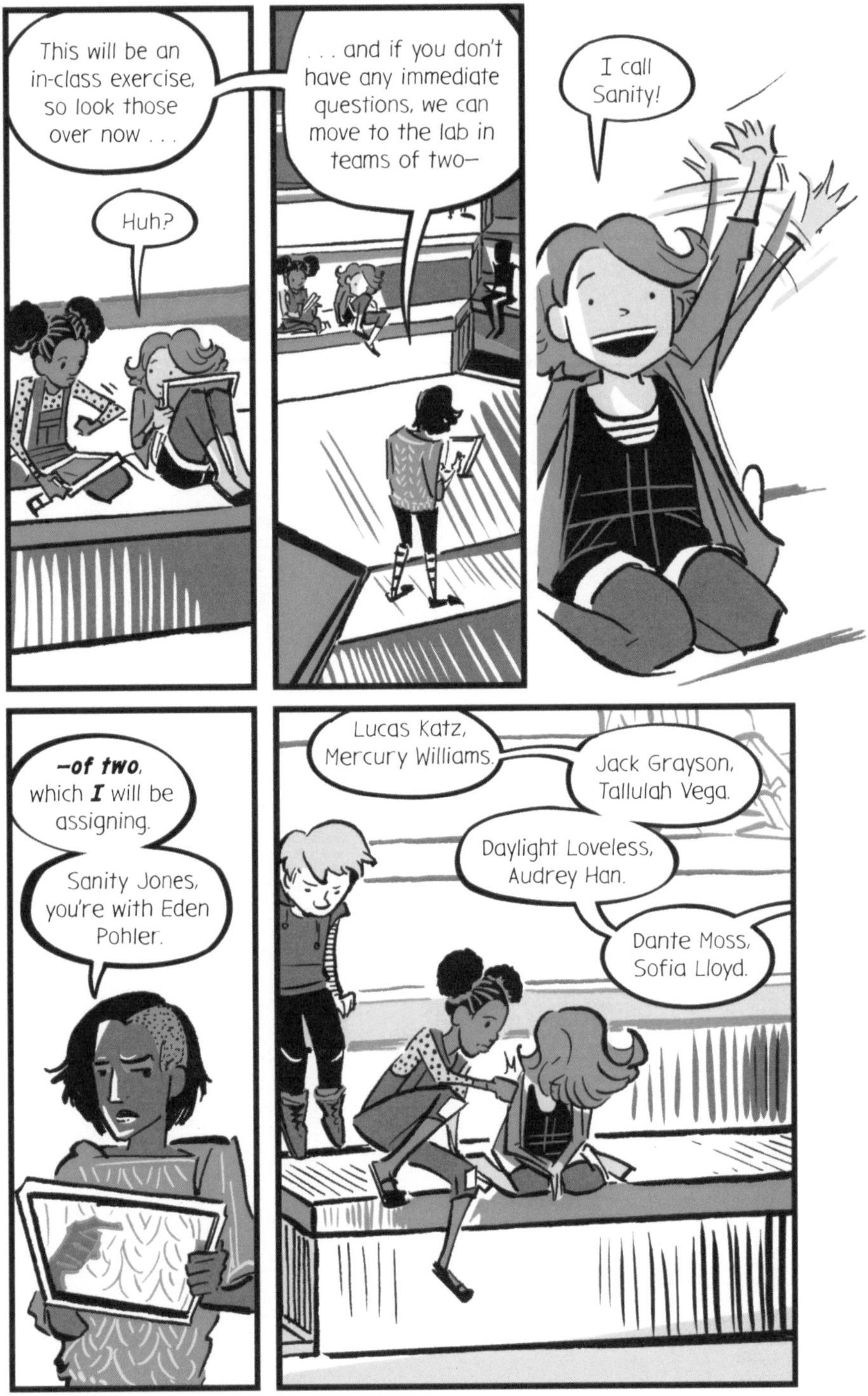
This will be an in-class exercise, so look those over now . . .
Huh?
. . . and if you don't have any immediate questions, we can move to the lab in teams of two–
I call Sanity!
–**of two**, which ***I*** will be assigning.
Sanity Jones, you're with Eden Pohler.
Lucas Katz, Mercury Williams.
Jack Grayson, Tallulah Vega.
Daylight Loveless, Audrey Han.
Dante Moss, Sofia Lloyd.

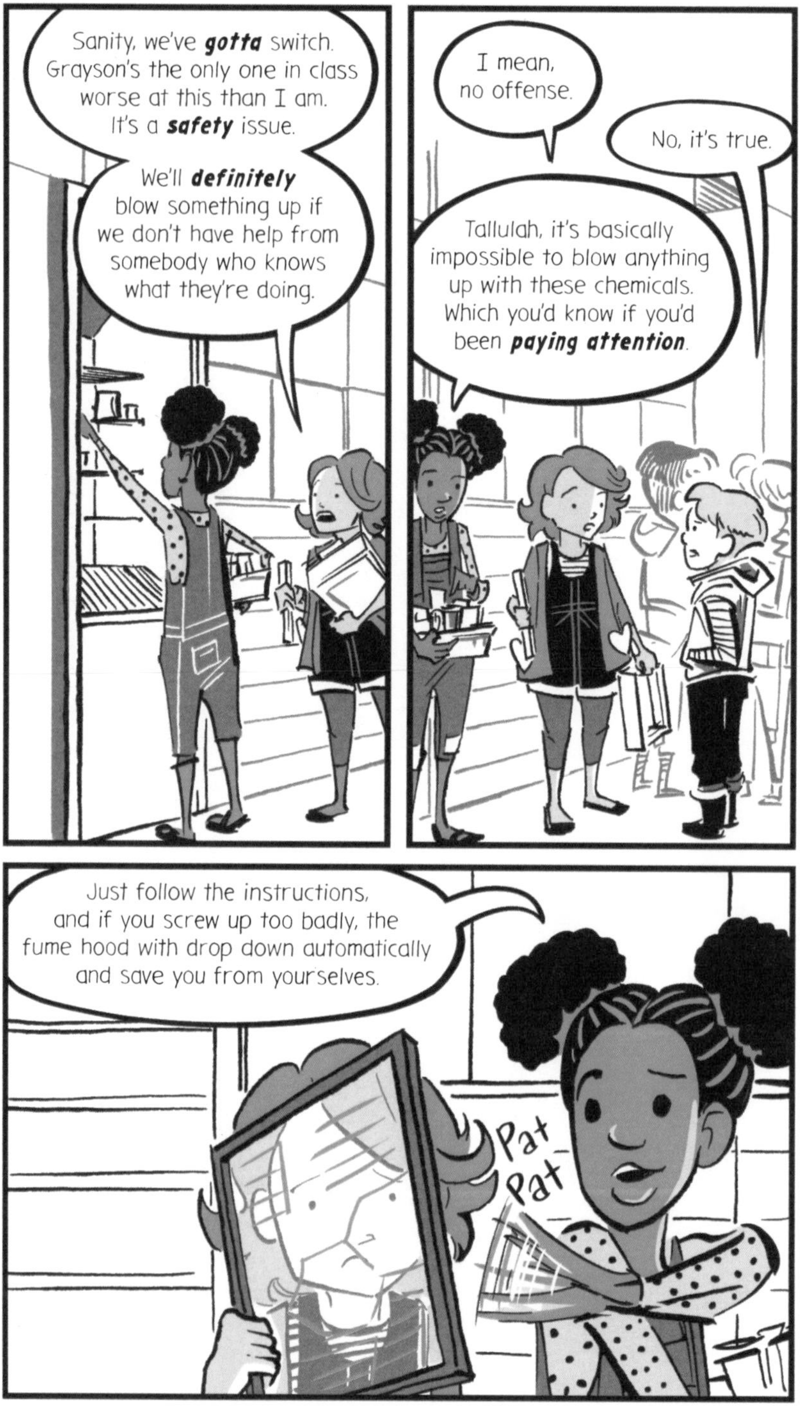
Sanity, we've **gotta** switch. Grayson's the only one in class worse at this than I am. It's a **safety** issue.
We'll **definitely** blow something up if we don't have help from somebody who knows what they're doing.
I mean, no offense.
No, it's true.
Tallulah, it's basically impossible to blow anything up with these chemicals. Which you'd know if you'd been **paying attention**.
Just follow the instructions, and if you screw up too badly, the fume hood with drop down automatically and save you from yourselves.
Pat Pat

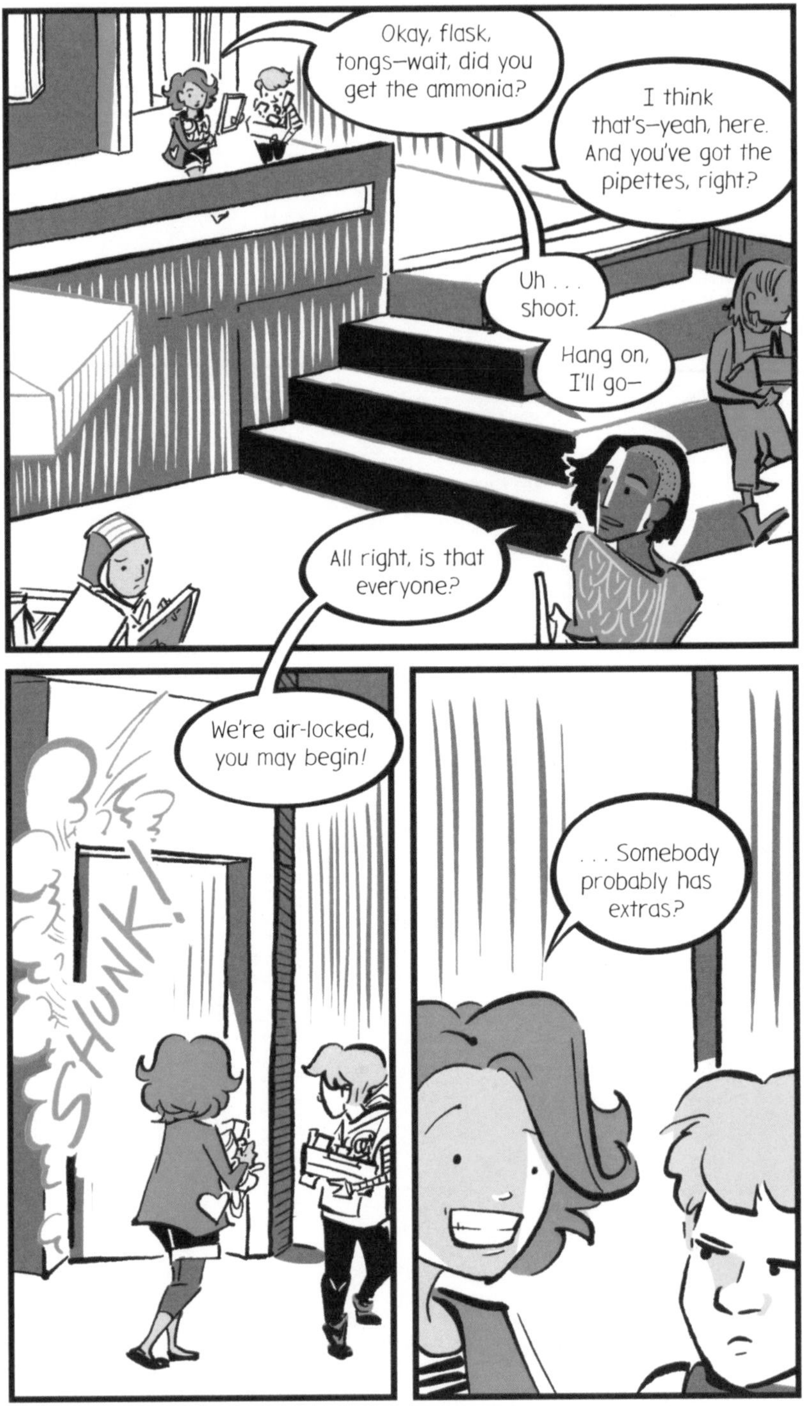
Okay, flask, tongs—wait, did you get the ammonia?
I think that's—yeah, here. And you've got the pipettes, right?
Uh . . . shoot.
Hang on, I'll go—
All right, is that everyone?
We're air-locked, you may begin!
SHUNK!
. . . Somebody probably has extras?

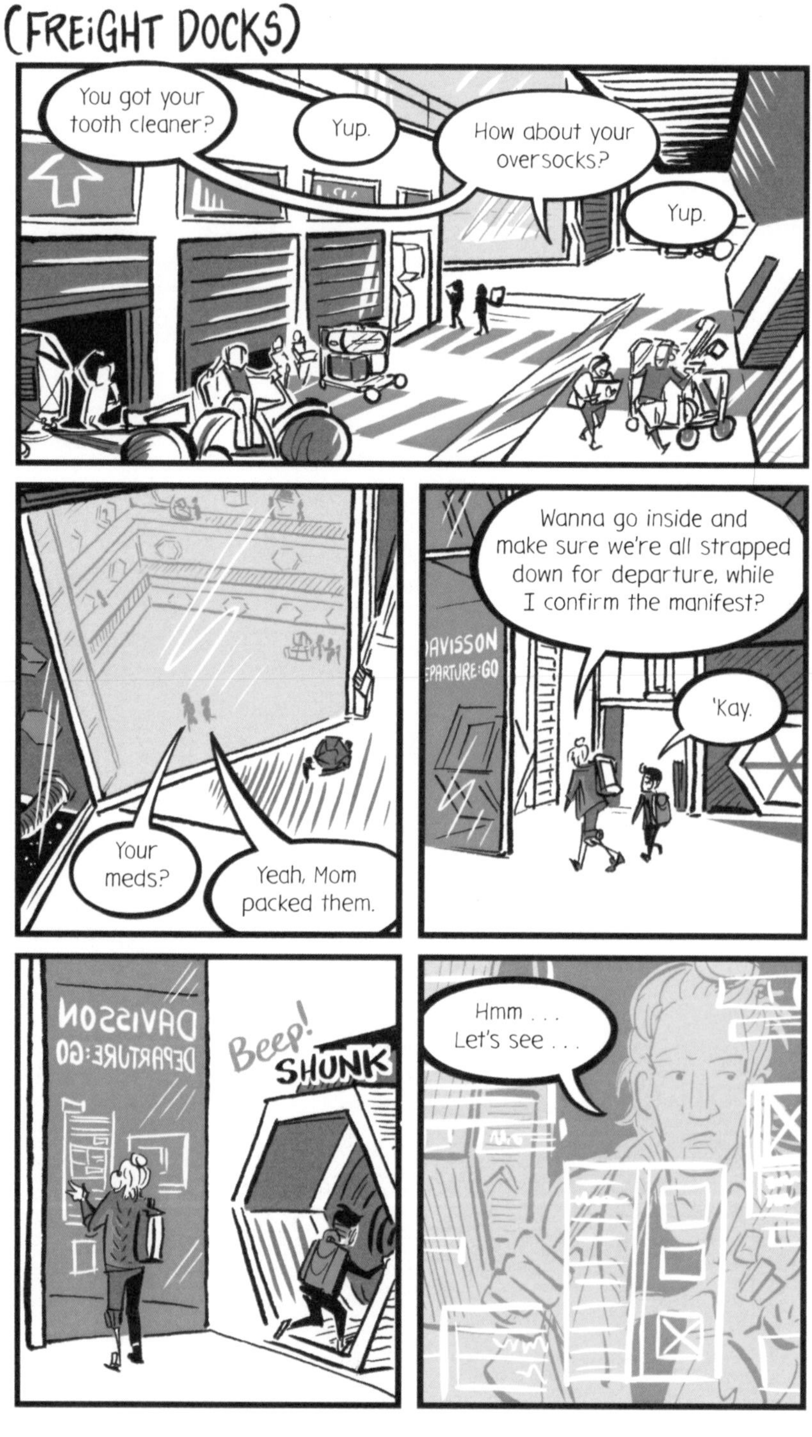
(FREIGHT DOCKS)
You got your tooth cleaner?
Yup.
How about your oversocks?
Yup.
Your meds?
Yeah, Mom packed them.
Wanna go inside and make sure we're all strapped down for departure, while I confirm the manifest?
DAVISSON
DEPARTURE:GO
'Kay.
Beep!
SHUNK
Hmm . . . Let's see . . .

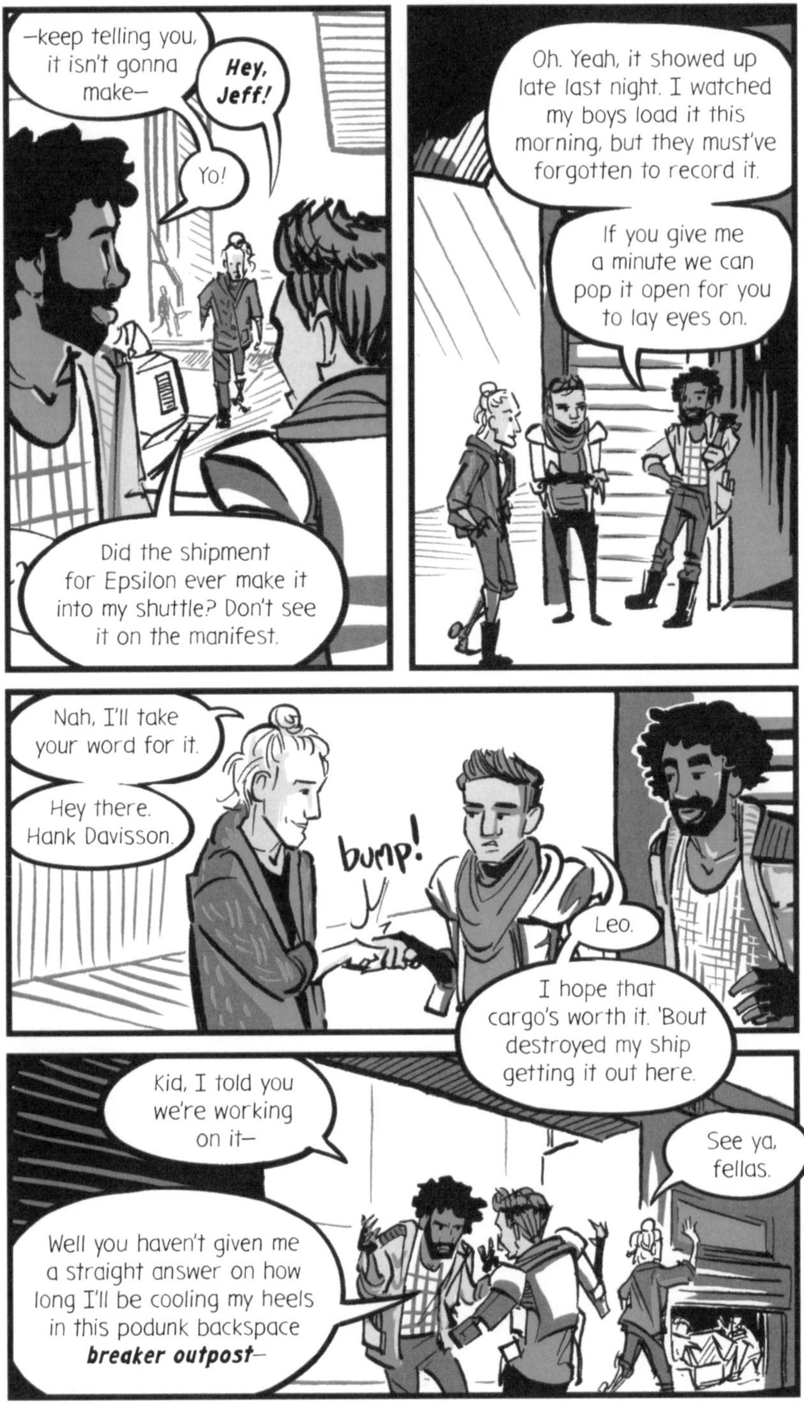

—keep telling you, it isn't gonna make—
Hey, Jeff!
Yo!
Did the shipment for Epsilon ever make it into my shuttle? Don't see it on the manifest.
Oh. Yeah, it showed up late last night. I watched my boys load it this morning, but they must've forgotten to record it.
If you give me a minute we can pop it open for you to lay eyes on.
Nah, I'll take your word for it.
Hey there. Hank Davisson.
bump!
Leo.
I hope that cargo's worth it. 'Bout destroyed my ship getting it out here.
Kid, I told you we're working on it—
See ya, fellas.
Well you haven't given me a straight answer on how long I'll be cooling my heels in this podunk backspace **breaker outpost**—

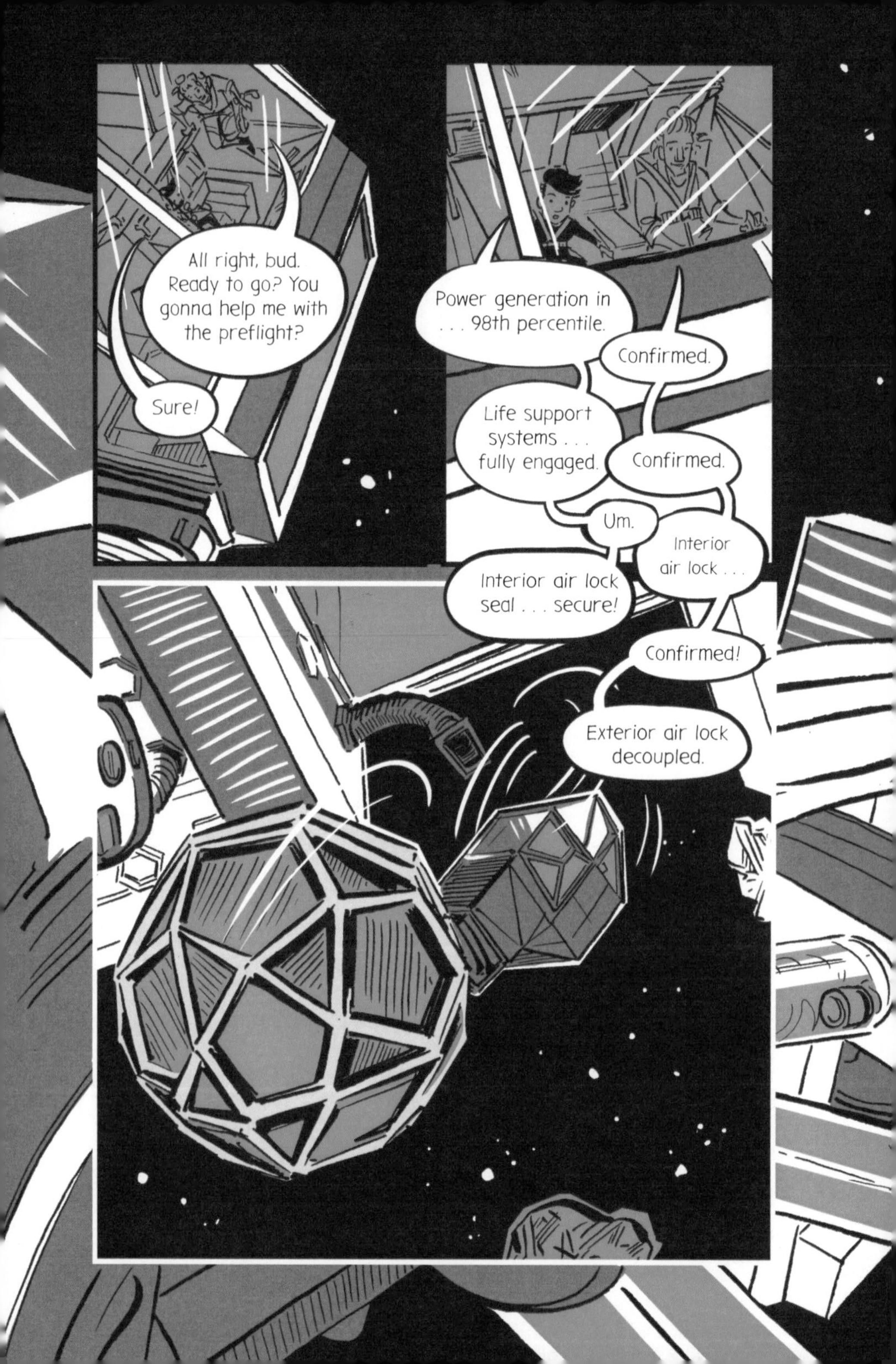
All right, bud. Ready to go? You gonna help me with the preflight?
Sure!
Power generation in . . . 98th percentile.
Confirmed.
Life support systems . . . fully engaged.
Confirmed.
Um.
Interior air lock . . .
Interior air lock seal . . . secure!
Confirmed!
Exterior air lock decoupled.

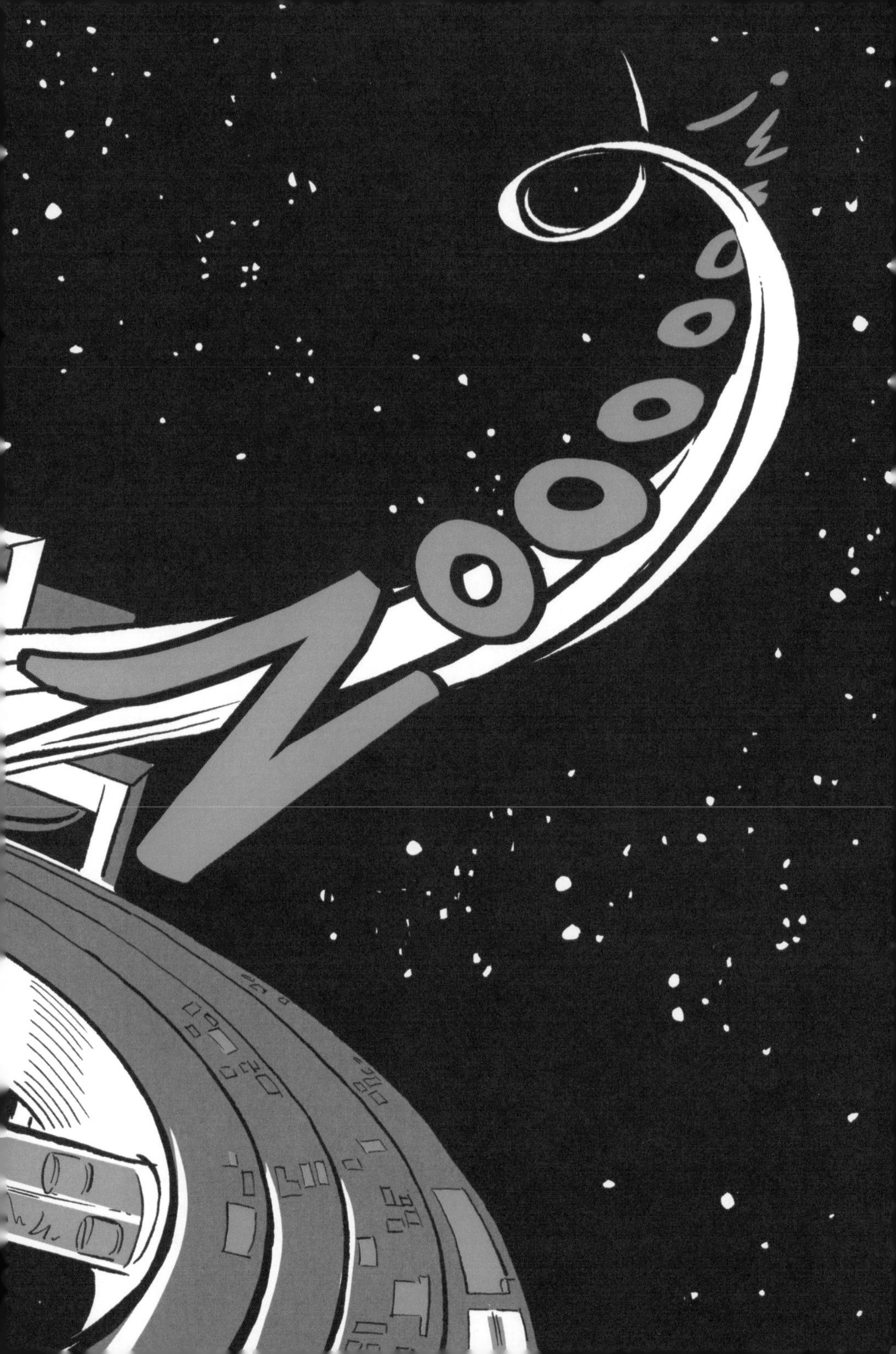
ZOOOOOM!

(ENGINEERING LAB C-12)

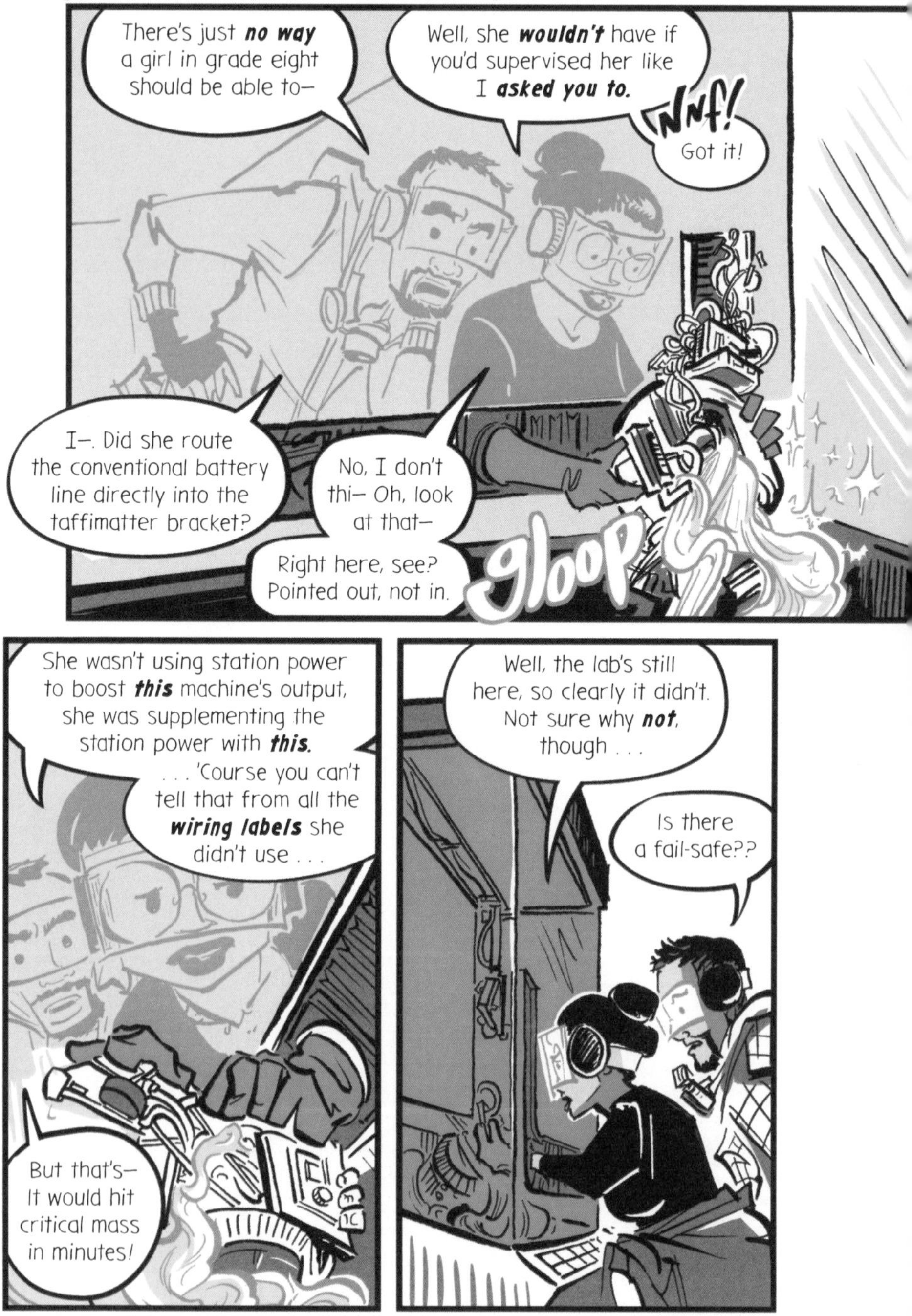
There's just **no way** a girl in grade eight should be able to—
Well, she **wouldn't** have if you'd supervised her like I **asked you to.**
Nnf!
Got it!
I—. Did she route the conventional battery line directly into the taffimatter bracket?
No, I don't thi— Oh, look at that—
Right here, see? Pointed out, not in.
gloop
She wasn't using station power to boost **this** machine's output, she was supplementing the station power with **this.**
. . . 'Course you can't tell that from all the **wiring labels** she didn't use . . .
But that's— It would hit critical mass in minutes!
Well, the lab's still here, so clearly it didn't. Not sure why **not**, though . . .
Is there a fail-safe??

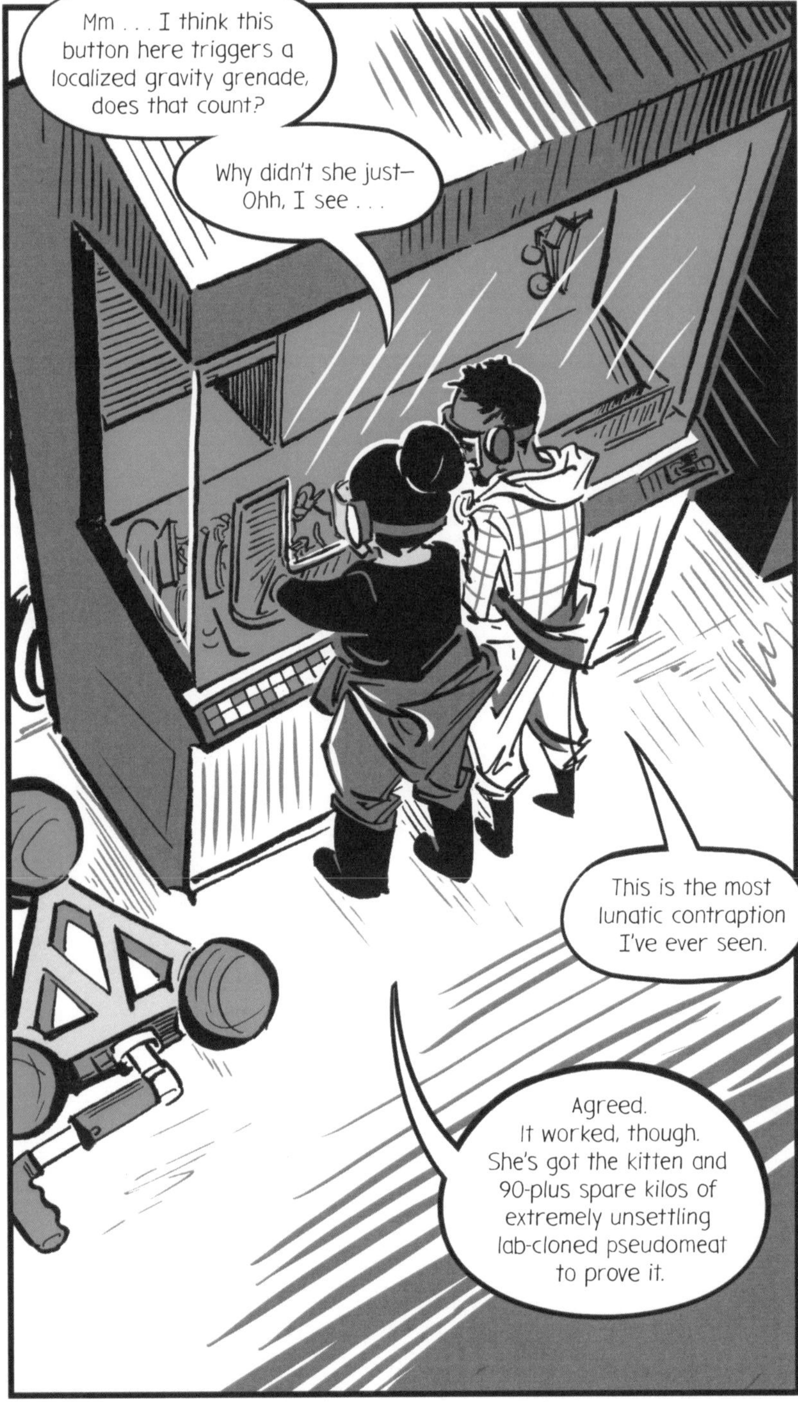
Mm . . . I think this button here triggers a localized gravity grenade, does that count?
Why didn't she just— Ohh, I see . . .
This is the most lunatic contraption I've ever seen.
Agreed. It worked, though. She's got the kitten and 90-plus spare kilos of extremely unsettling lab-cloned pseudomeat to prove it.

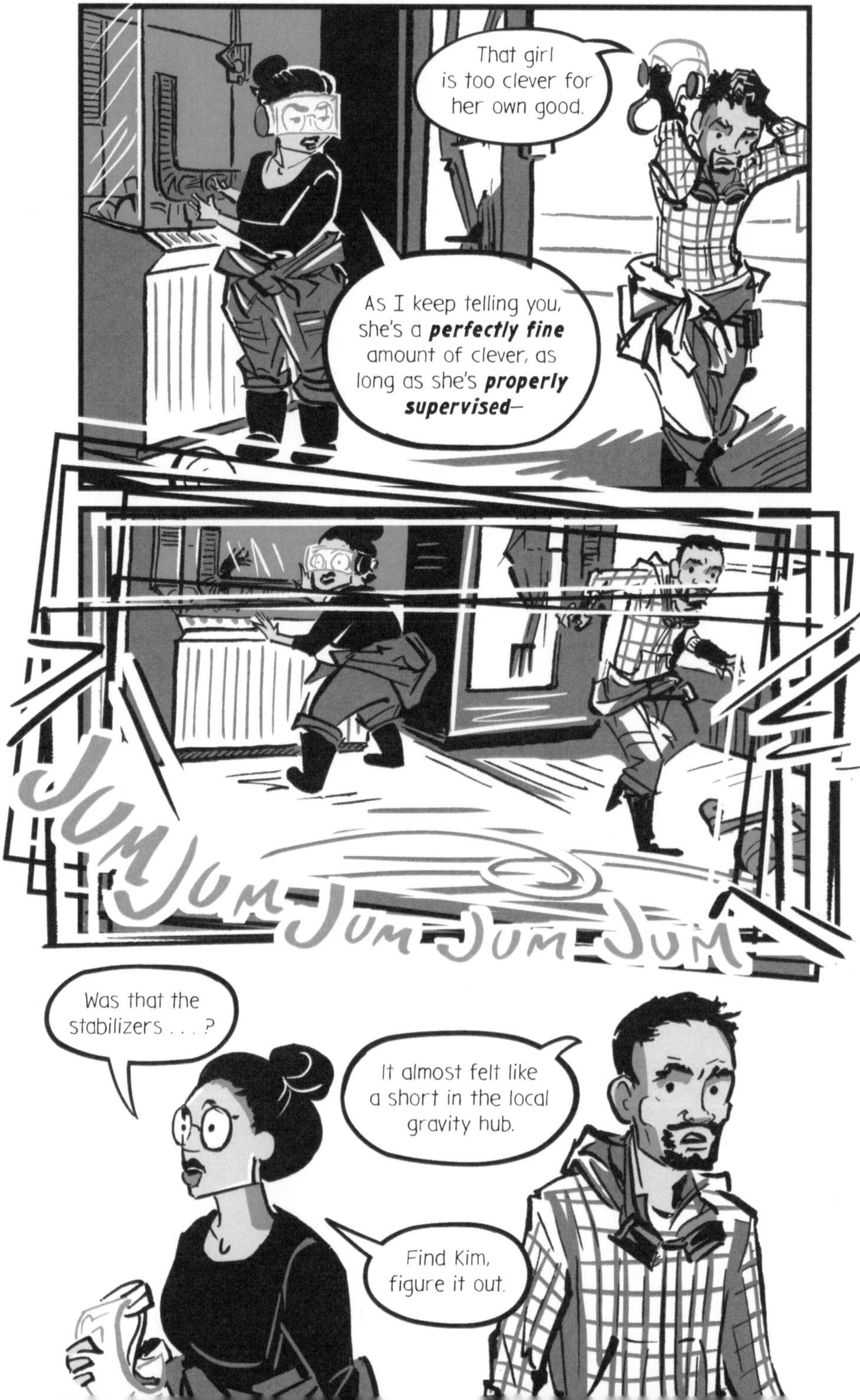
That girl is too clever for her own good.
As I keep telling you, she's a **perfectly fine** amount of clever, as long as she's **properly supervised**—
JUM JUM JUM JUM JUM
Was that the stabilizers . . . ?
It almost felt like a short in the local gravity hub.
Find Kim, figure it out.

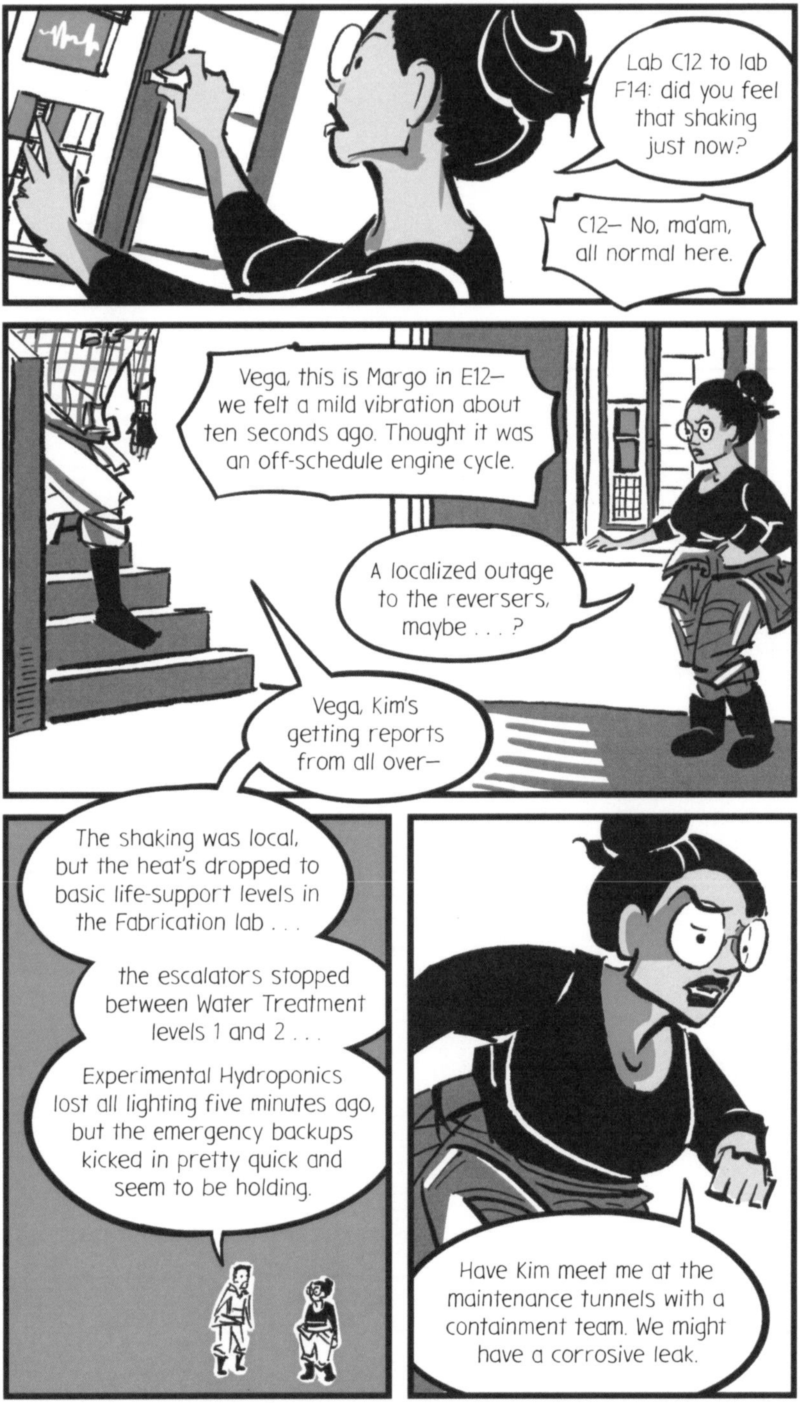
Lab C12 to lab F14: did you feel that shaking just now?
C12— No, ma'am, all normal here.
Vega, this is Margo in E12— we felt a mild vibration about ten seconds ago. Thought it was an off-schedule engine cycle.
A localized outage to the reversers, maybe . . . ?
Vega, Kim's getting reports from all over—
The shaking was local, but the heat's dropped to basic life-support levels in the Fabrication lab . . .
the escalators stopped between Water Treatment levels 1 and 2 . . .
Experimental Hydroponics lost all lighting five minutes ago, but the emergency backups kicked in pretty quick and seem to be holding.
Have Kim meet me at the maintenance tunnels with a containment team. We might have a corrosive leak.

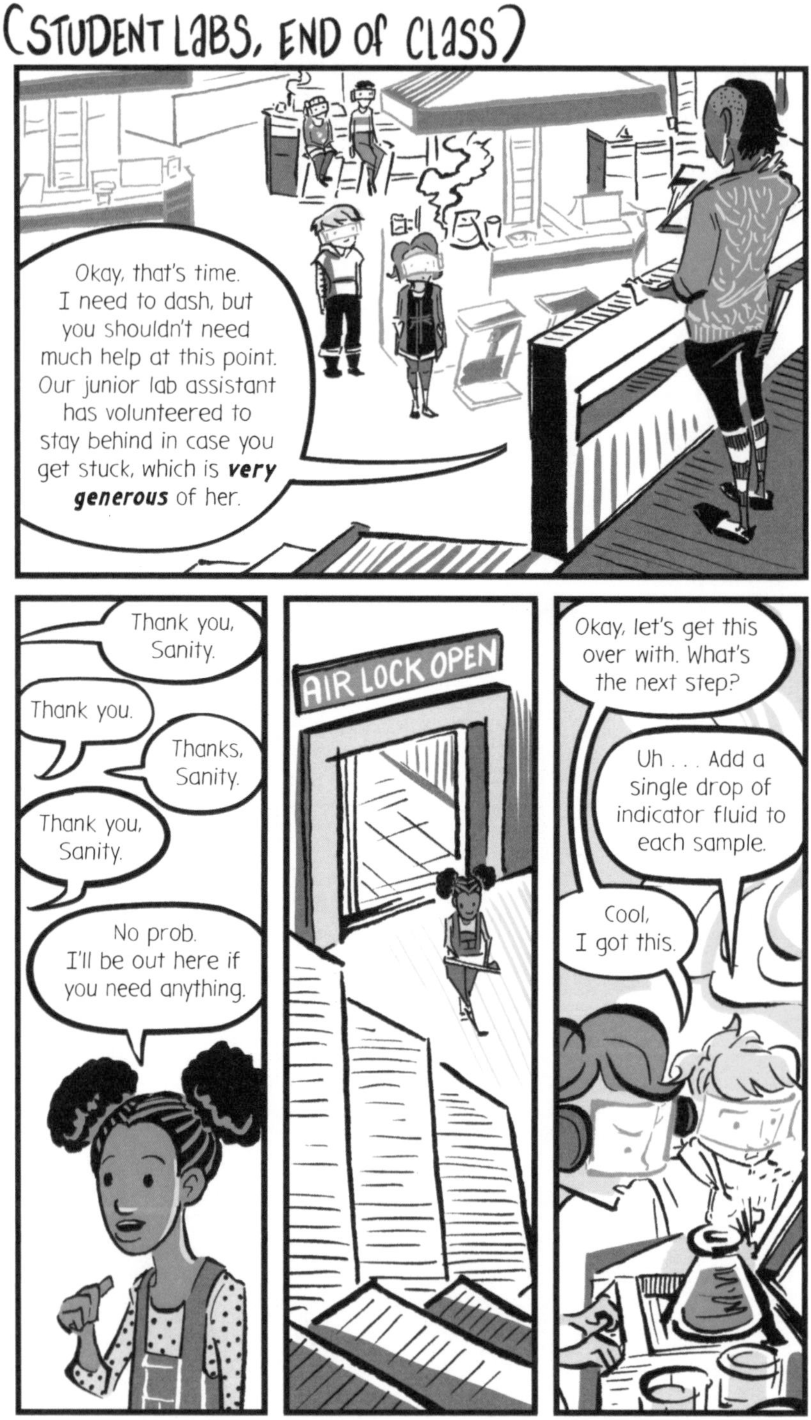
(STUDENT LABS, END OF CLASS)
Okay, that's time. I need to dash, but you shouldn't need much help at this point. Our junior lab assistant has volunteered to stay behind in case you get stuck, which is **very generous** of her.
Thank you, Sanity.
Thank you.
Thanks, Sanity.
Thank you, Sanity.
No prob. I'll be out here if you need anything.
AIR LOCK OPEN
Okay, let's get this over with. What's the next step?
Uh . . . Add a single drop of indicator fluid to each sample.
Cool, I got this.

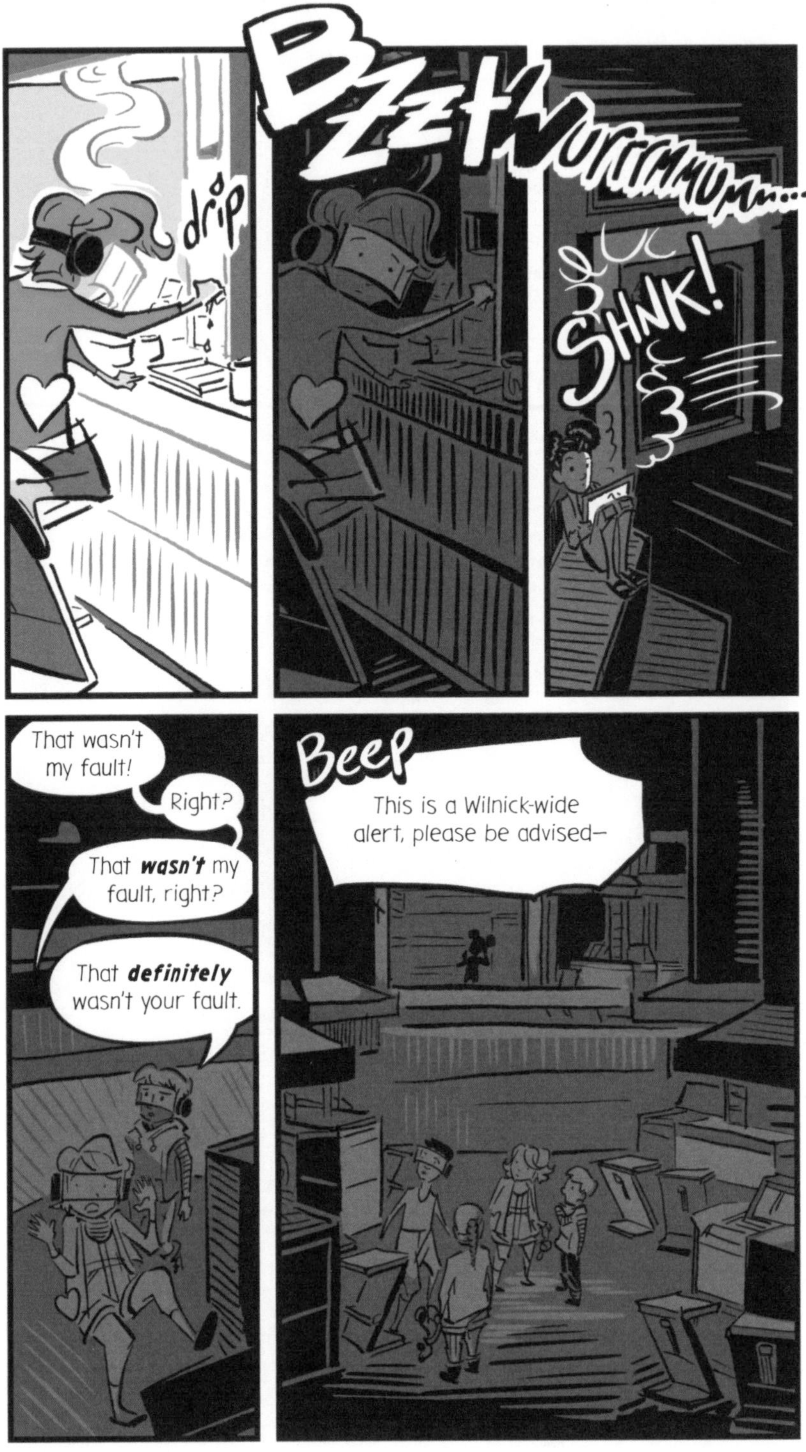
drip
BZZT'
SHNK!
That wasn't my fault!
Right?
That **wasn't** my fault, right?
That **definitely** wasn't your fault.
Beep
This is a Wilnick-wide alert, please be advised—

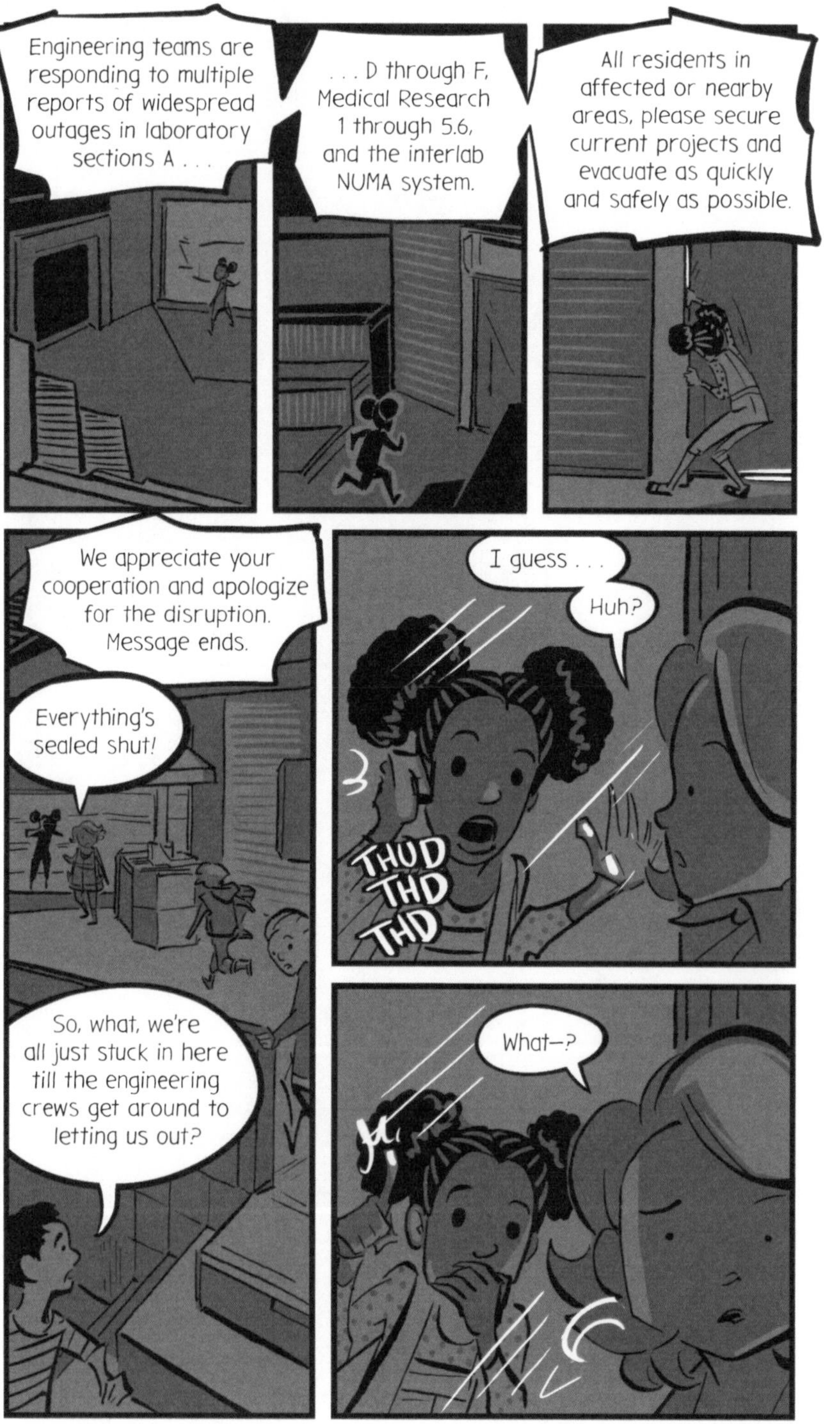
Engineering teams are responding to multiple reports of widespread outages in laboratory sections A . . .
. . . D through F, Medical Research 1 through 5.6, and the interlab NUMA system.
All residents in affected or nearby areas, please secure current projects and evacuate as quickly and safely as possible.
We appreciate your cooperation and apologize for the disruption. Message ends.
Everything's sealed shut!
So, what, we're all just stuck in here till the engineering crews get around to letting us out?
I guess . . .
Huh?
THUD
THD
THD
What–?

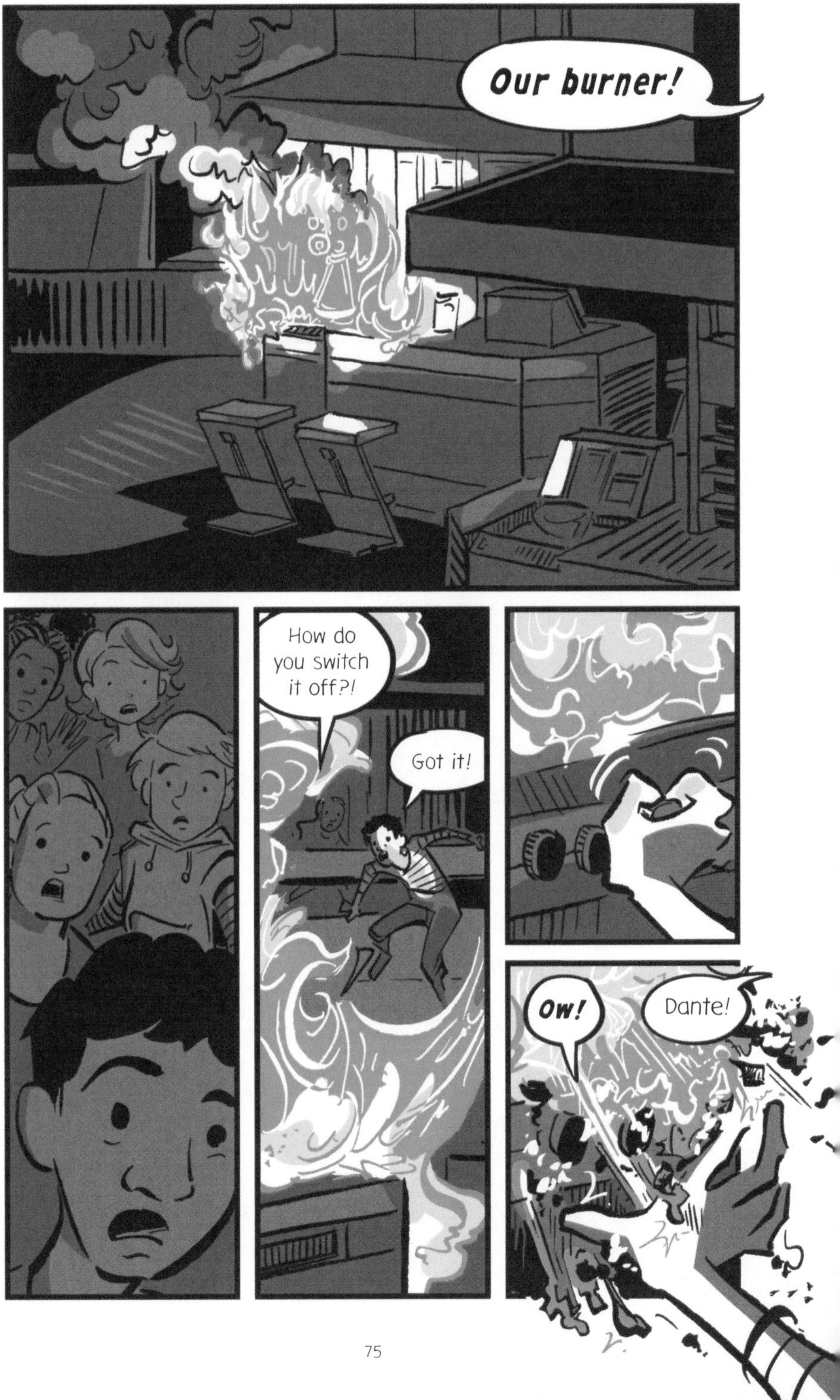
Our burner!
How do you switch it off?!
Got it!
Ow!
Dante!

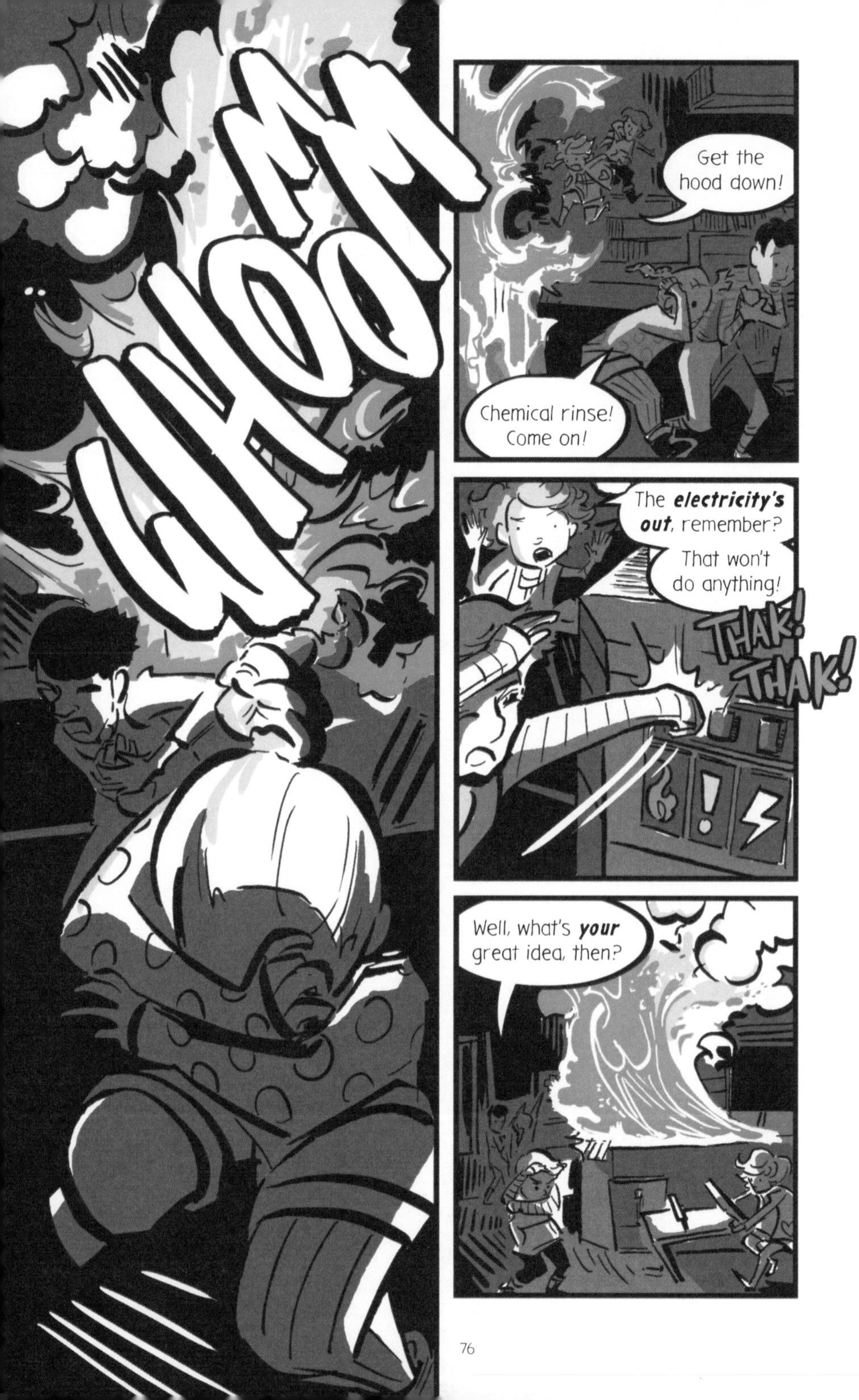
WHOOM
Get the hood down!
Chemical rinse! Come on!
The **electricity's out**, remember?
That won't do anything!
THAK! THAK!
Well, what's ***your*** great idea, then?

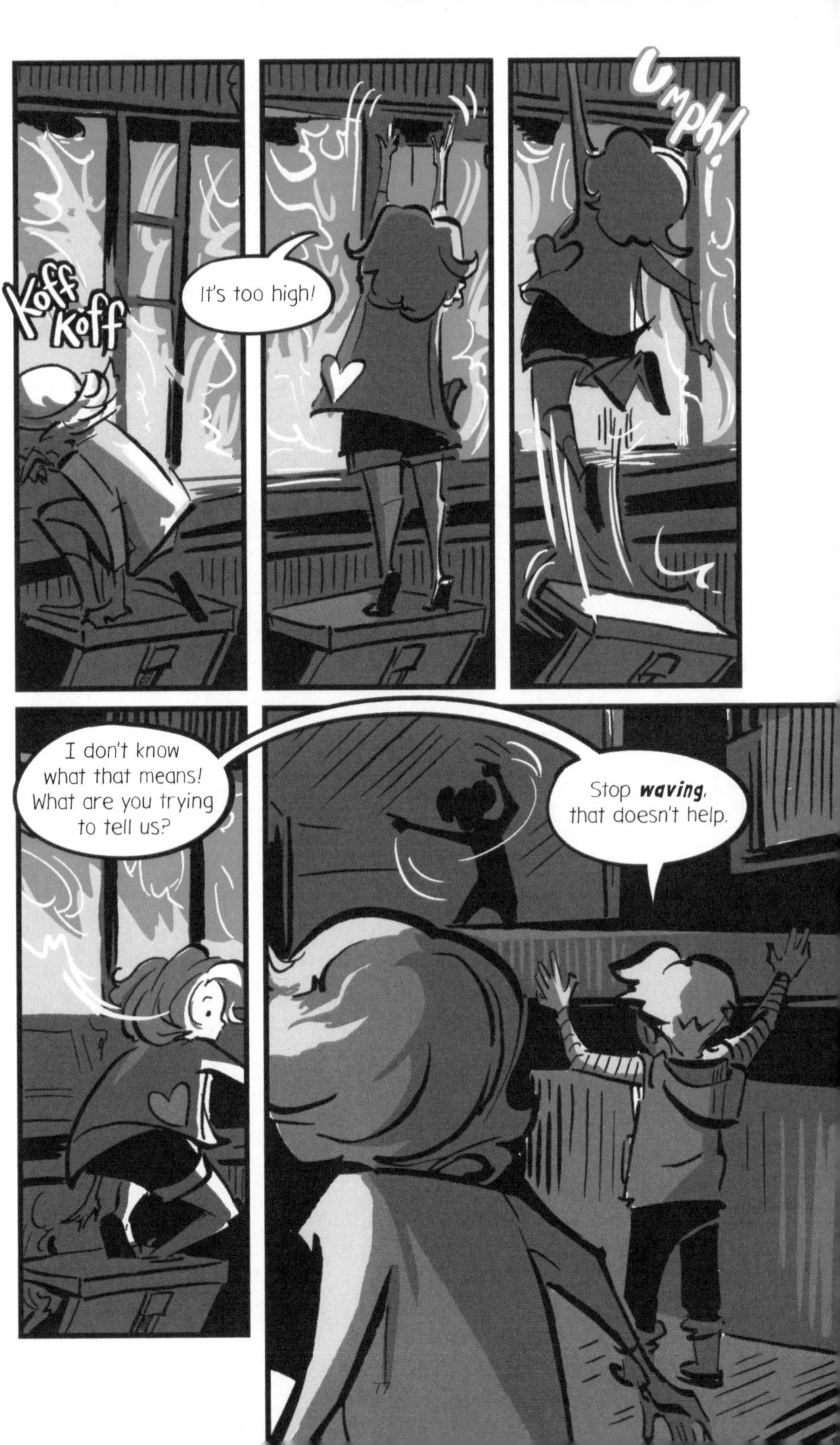
Koff
Koff
It's too high!
Umph!
I don't know what that means! What are you trying to tell us?
Stop **waving**, that doesn't help.

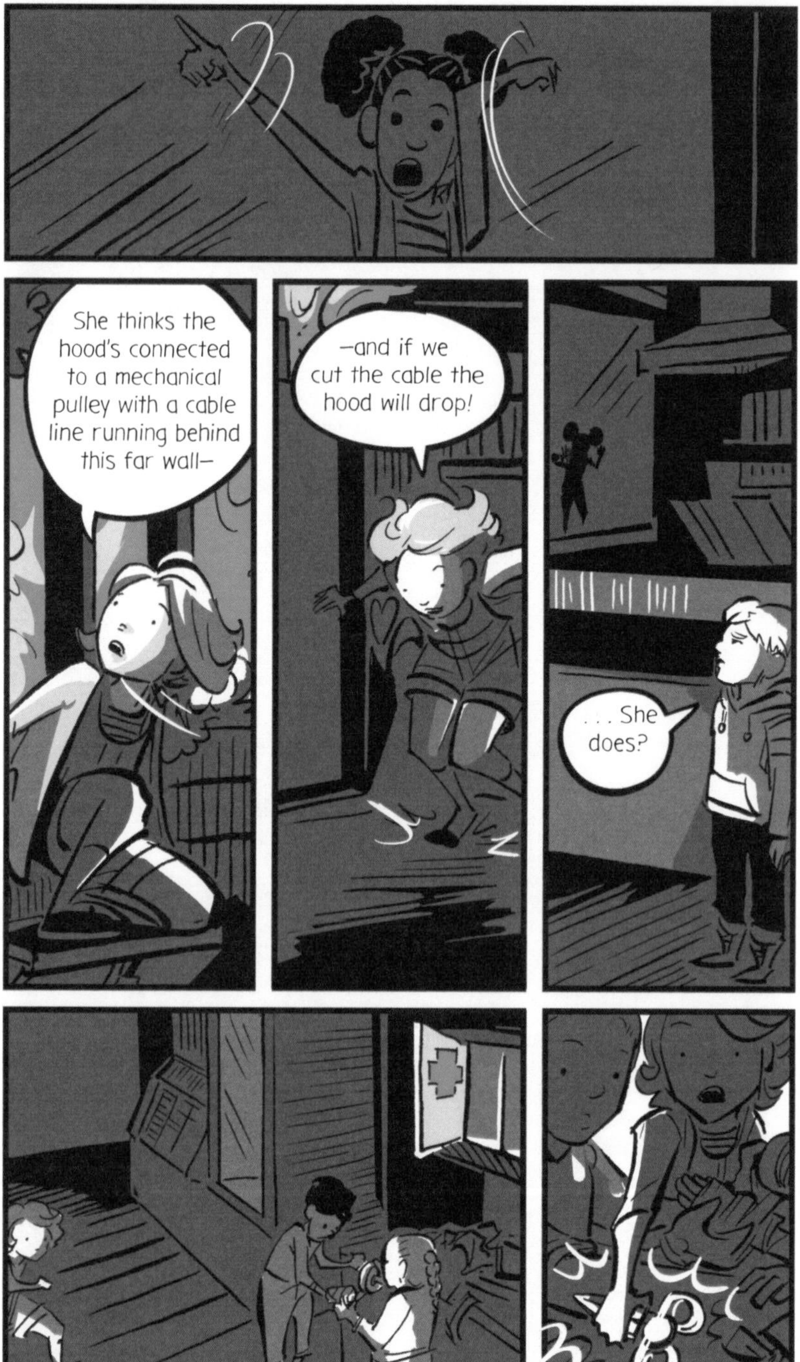
She thinks the hood's connected to a mechanical pulley with a cable line running behind this far wall—
—and if we cut the cable the hood will drop!
. . . She does?

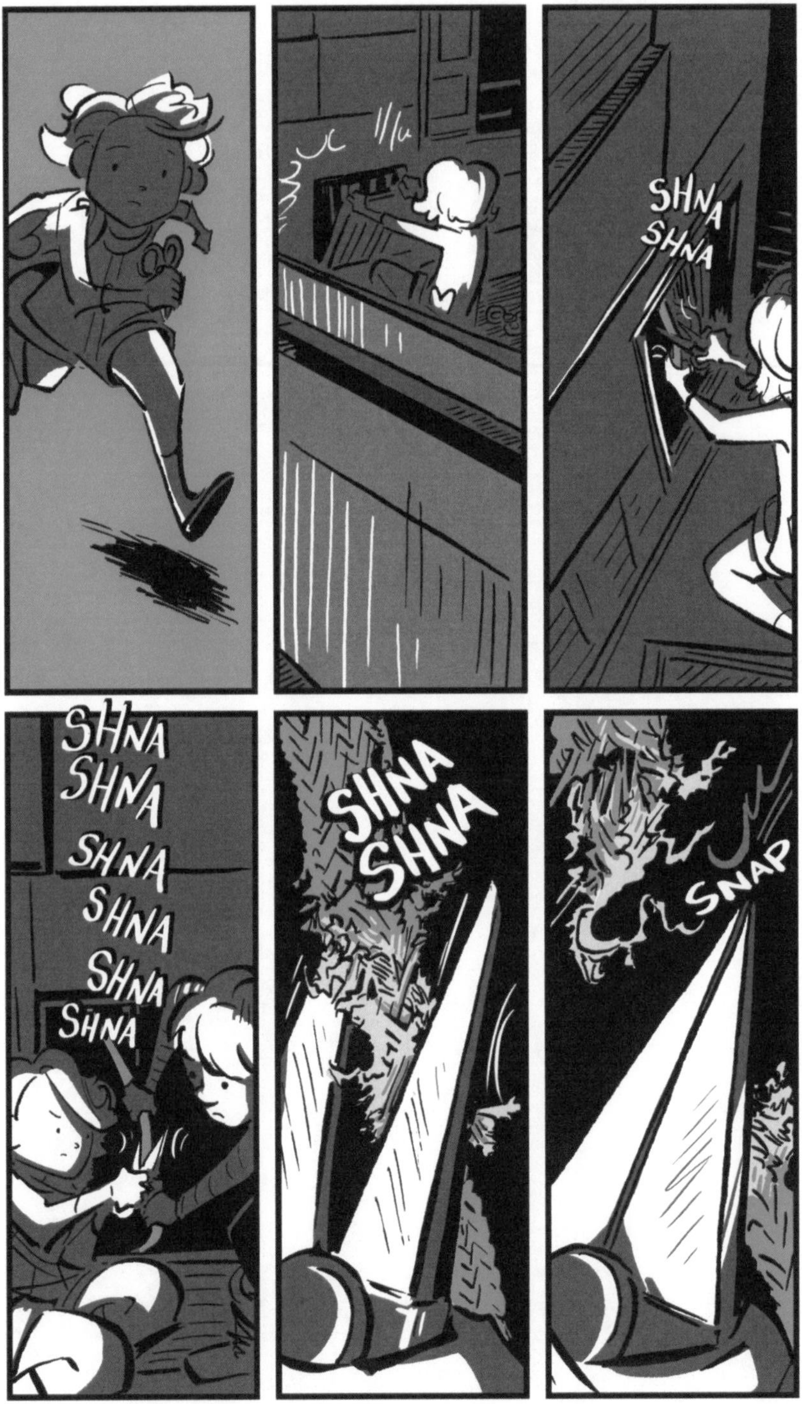
SHNA
SHNA
SHNA
SHNA
SHNA
SHNA
SHNA
SHNA
SHNA
SHNA
SNAP

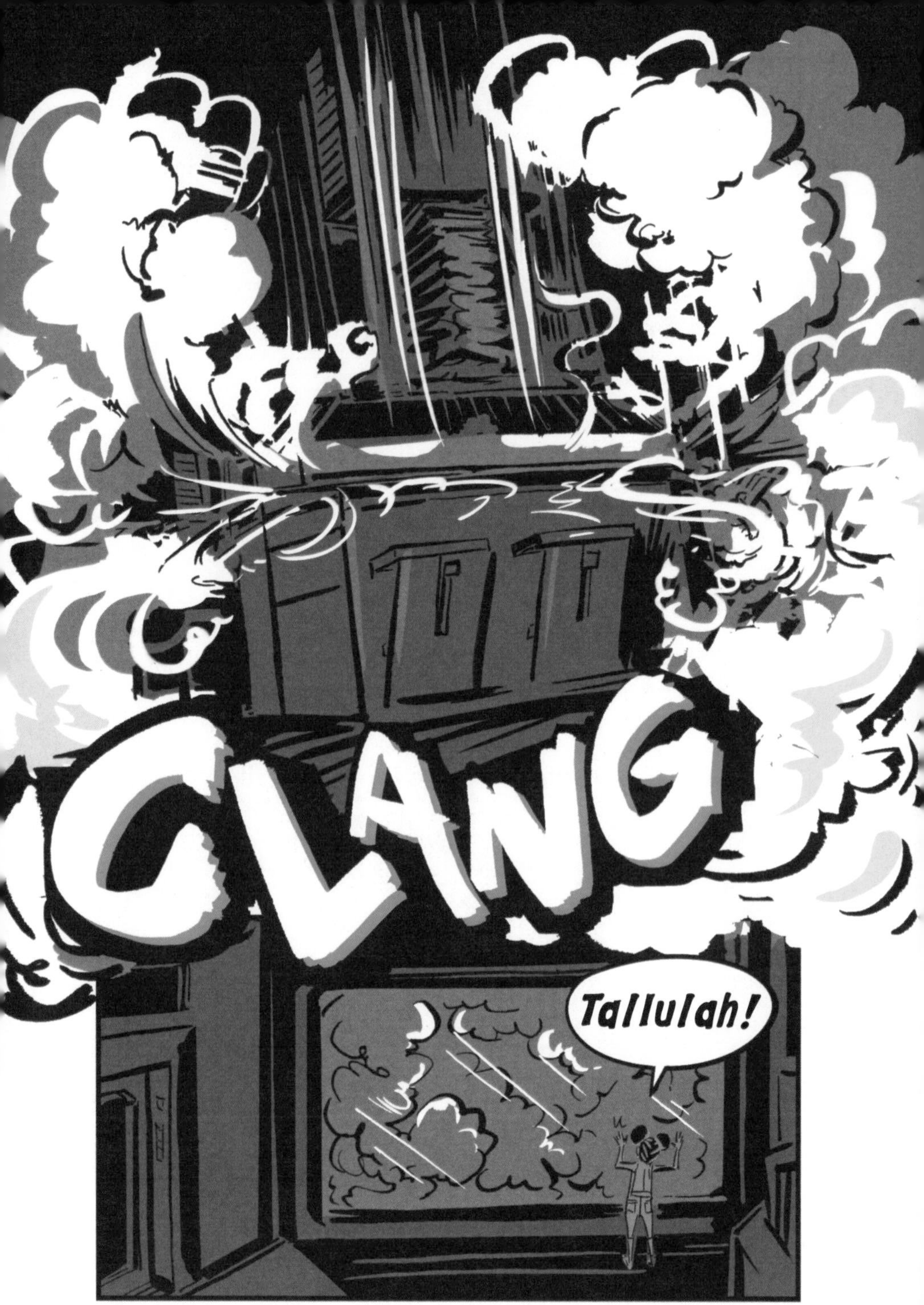
CLANG
Tallulah!

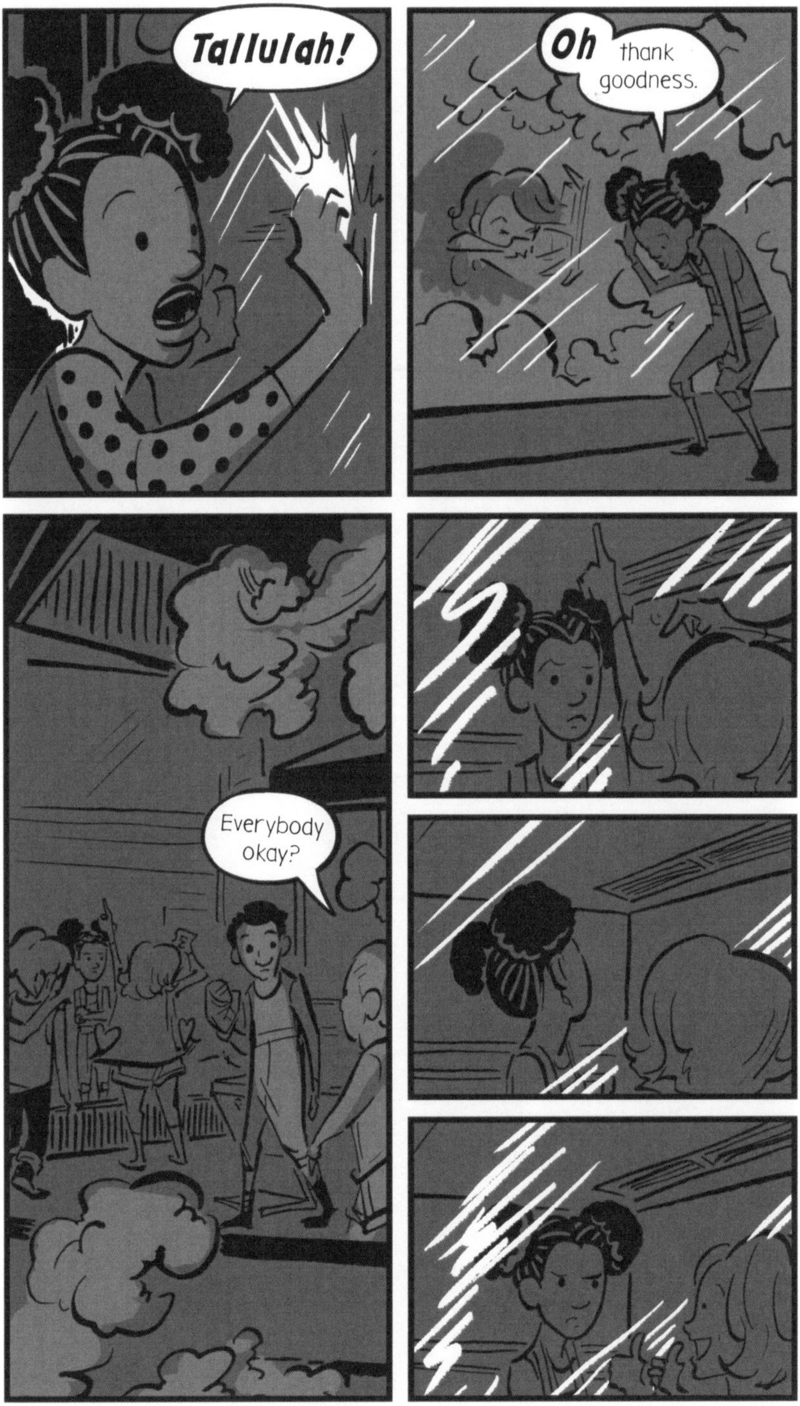
Tallulah!
Oh thank goodness.
Everybody okay?

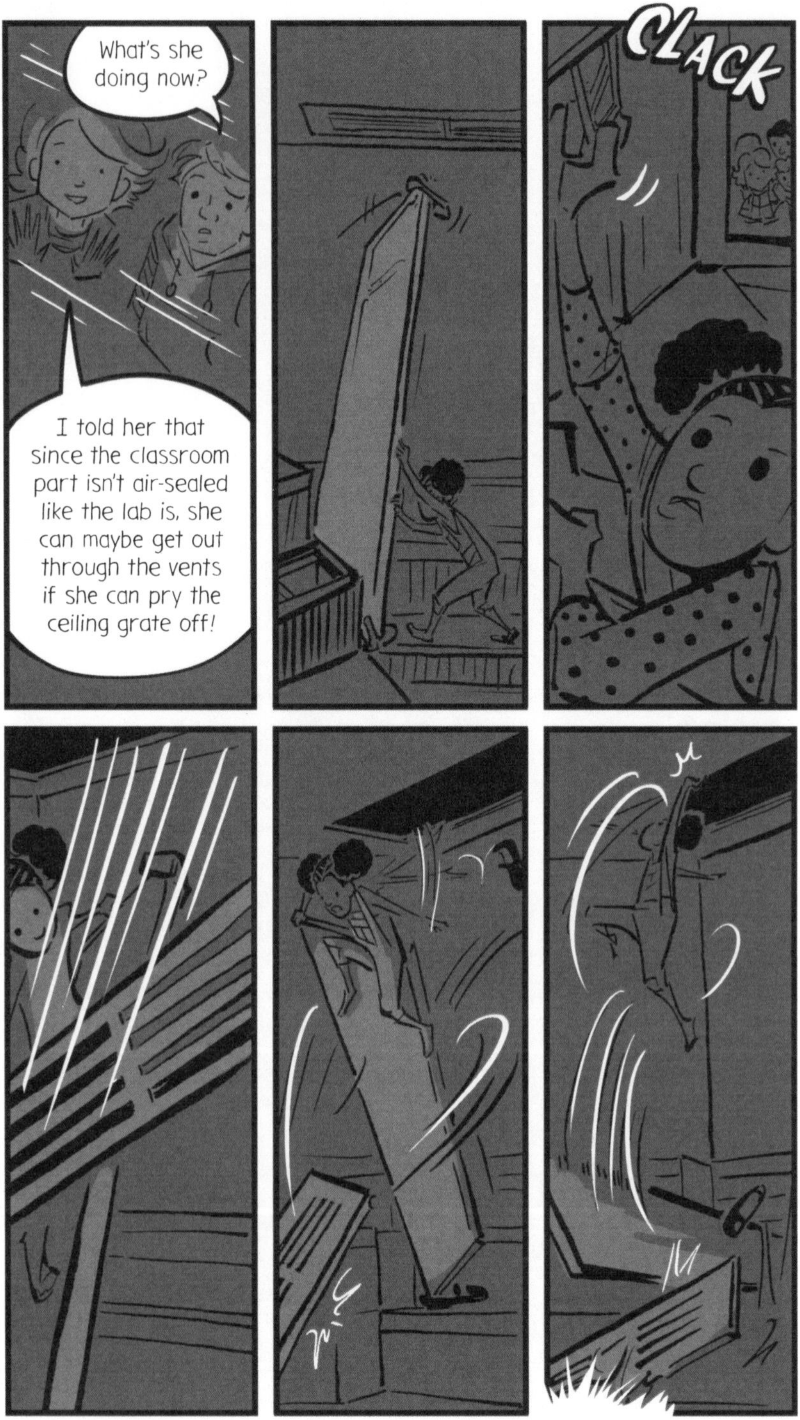
What's she doing now?
I told her that since the classroom part isn't air-sealed like the lab is, she can maybe get out through the vents if she can pry the ceiling grate off!
CLACK

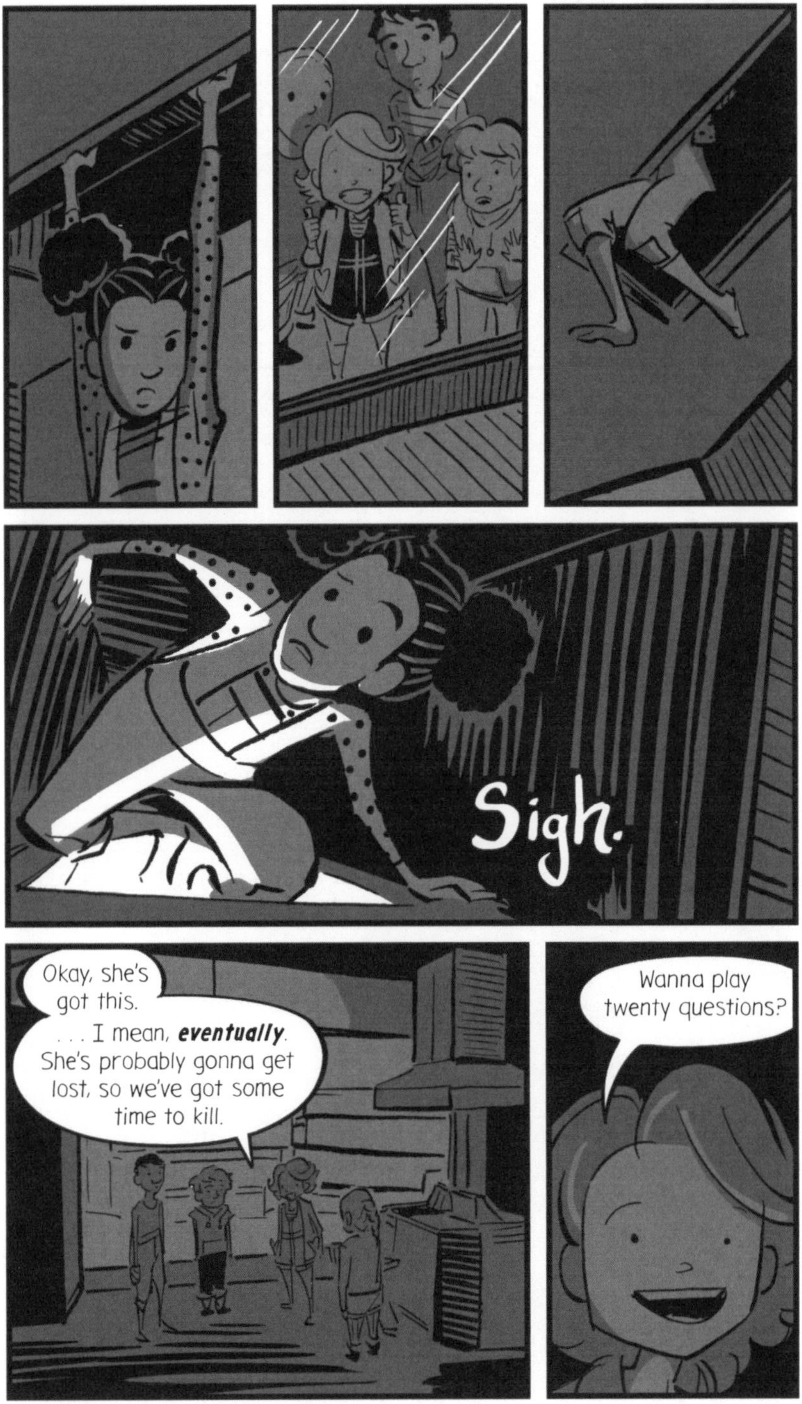
Sigh.
Okay, she's got this.
. . . I mean, **eventually**. She's probably gonna get lost, so we've got some time to kill.
Wanna play twenty questions?

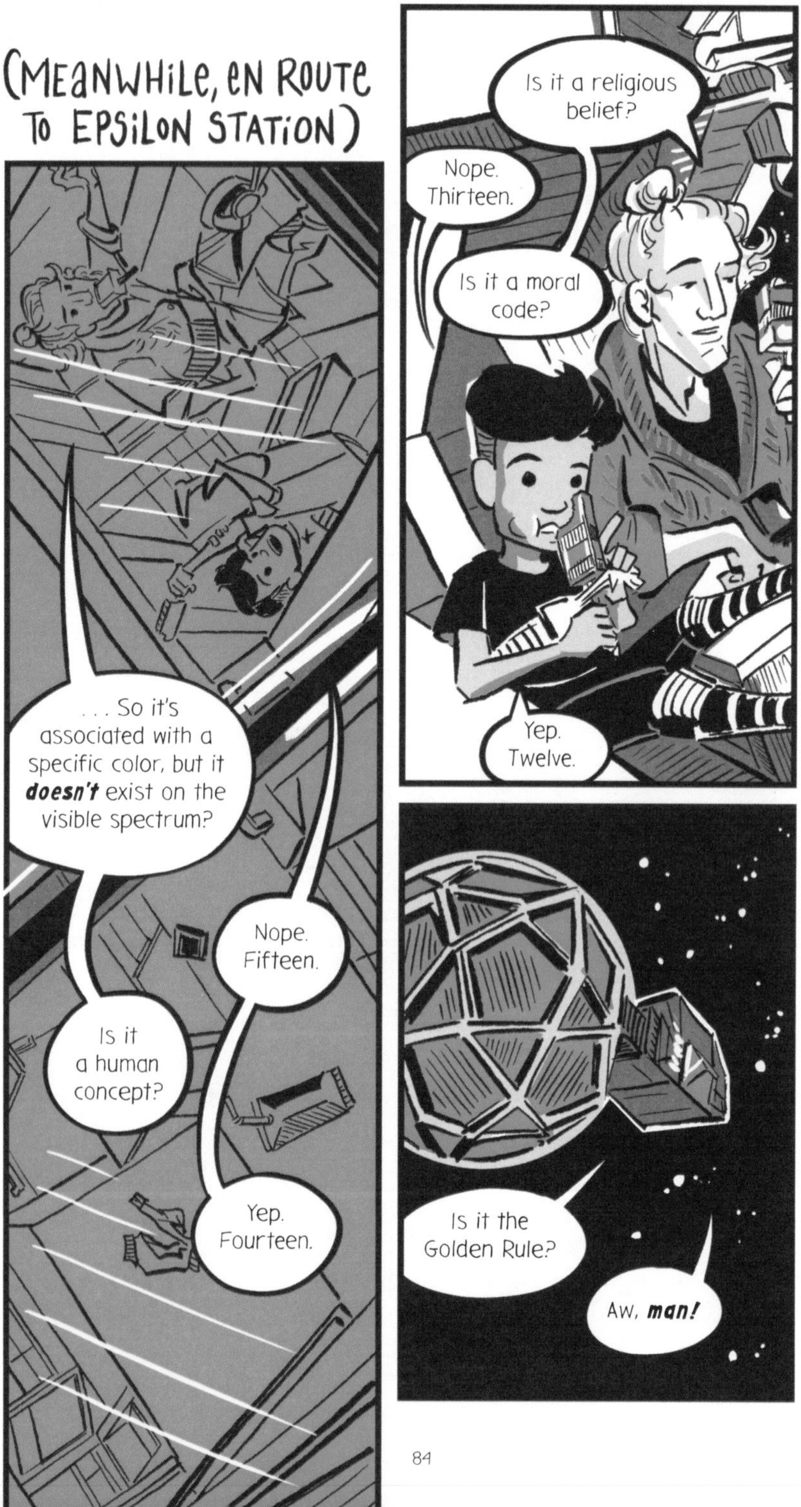
(MEANWHILE, EN ROUTE TO EPSILON STATION)
. . . So it's associated with a specific color, but it **doesn't** exist on the visible spectrum?
Nope. Fifteen.
Is it a human concept?
Yep. Fourteen.
Is it a religious belief?
Nope. Thirteen.
Is it a moral code?
Yep. Twelve.
Is it the Golden Rule?
Aw, **man!**

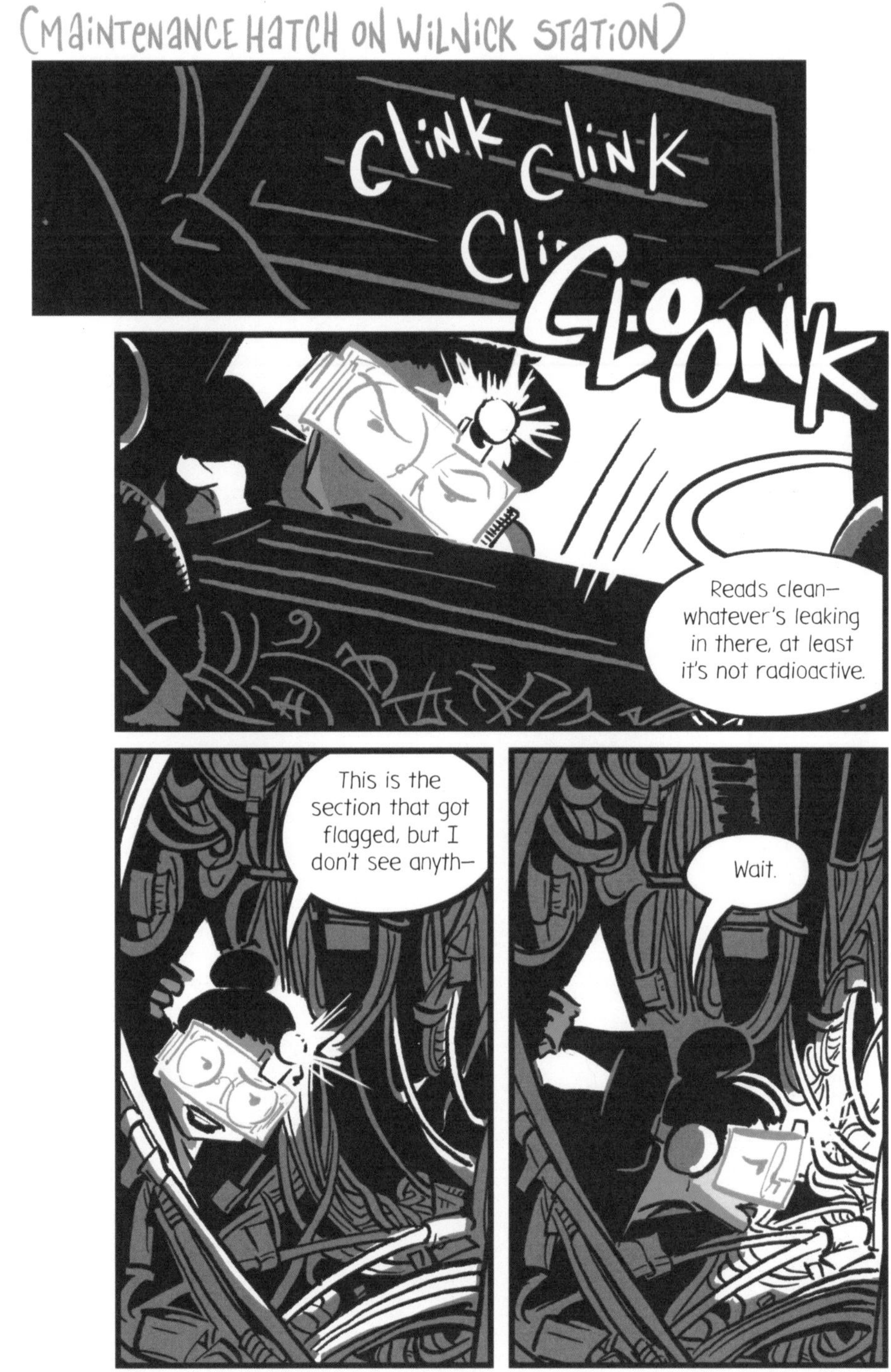
(MAINTENANCE HATCH ON WILNICK STATION)
Clink clink
Clink
Cli
CLOONK
Reads clean—whatever's leaking in there, at least it's not radioactive.
This is the section that got flagged, but I don't see anyth—
Wait.

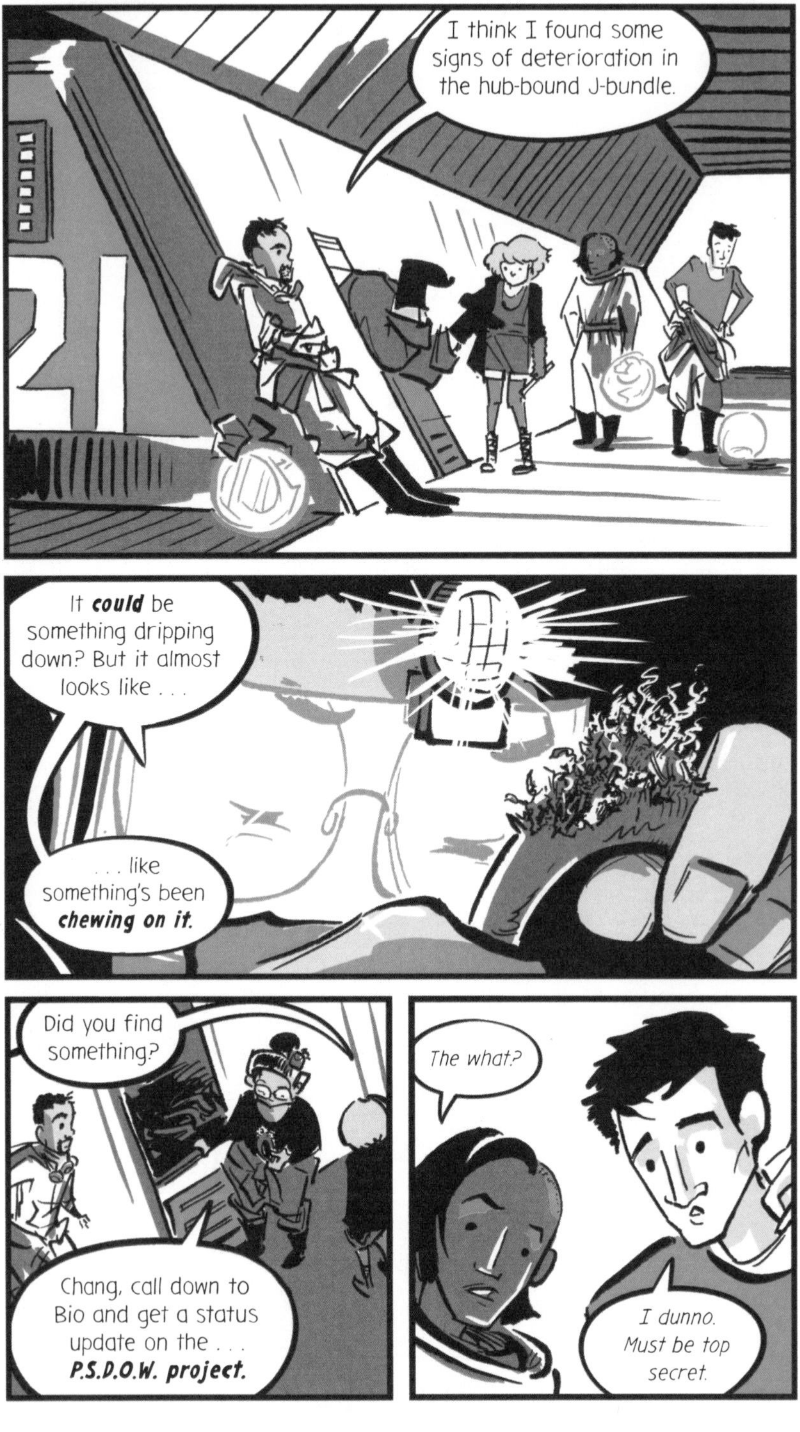
I think I found some signs of deterioration in the hub-bound J-bundle.
It **could** be something dripping down? But it almost looks like . . .
. . . like something's been **chewing on it.**
Did you find something?
Chang, call down to Bio and get a status update on the . . . **P.S.D.O.W. project.**
The what?
I dunno. Must be top secret.

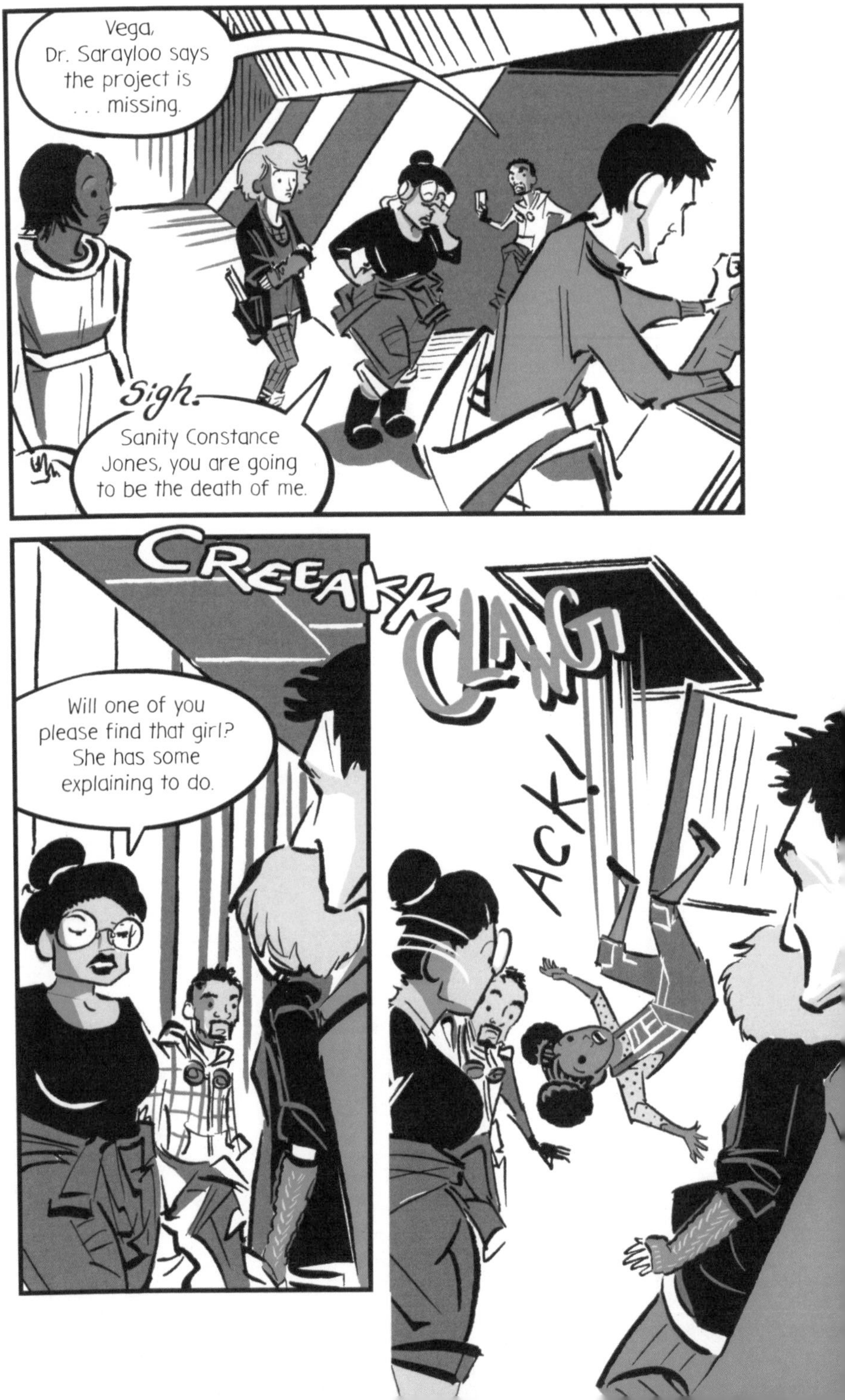

Vega, Dr. Sarayloo says the project is . . . missing.
Sigh.
Sanity Constance Jones, you are going to be the death of me.
CREEAKK
Will one of you please find that girl? She has some explaining to do.
CLANG!
ACK!

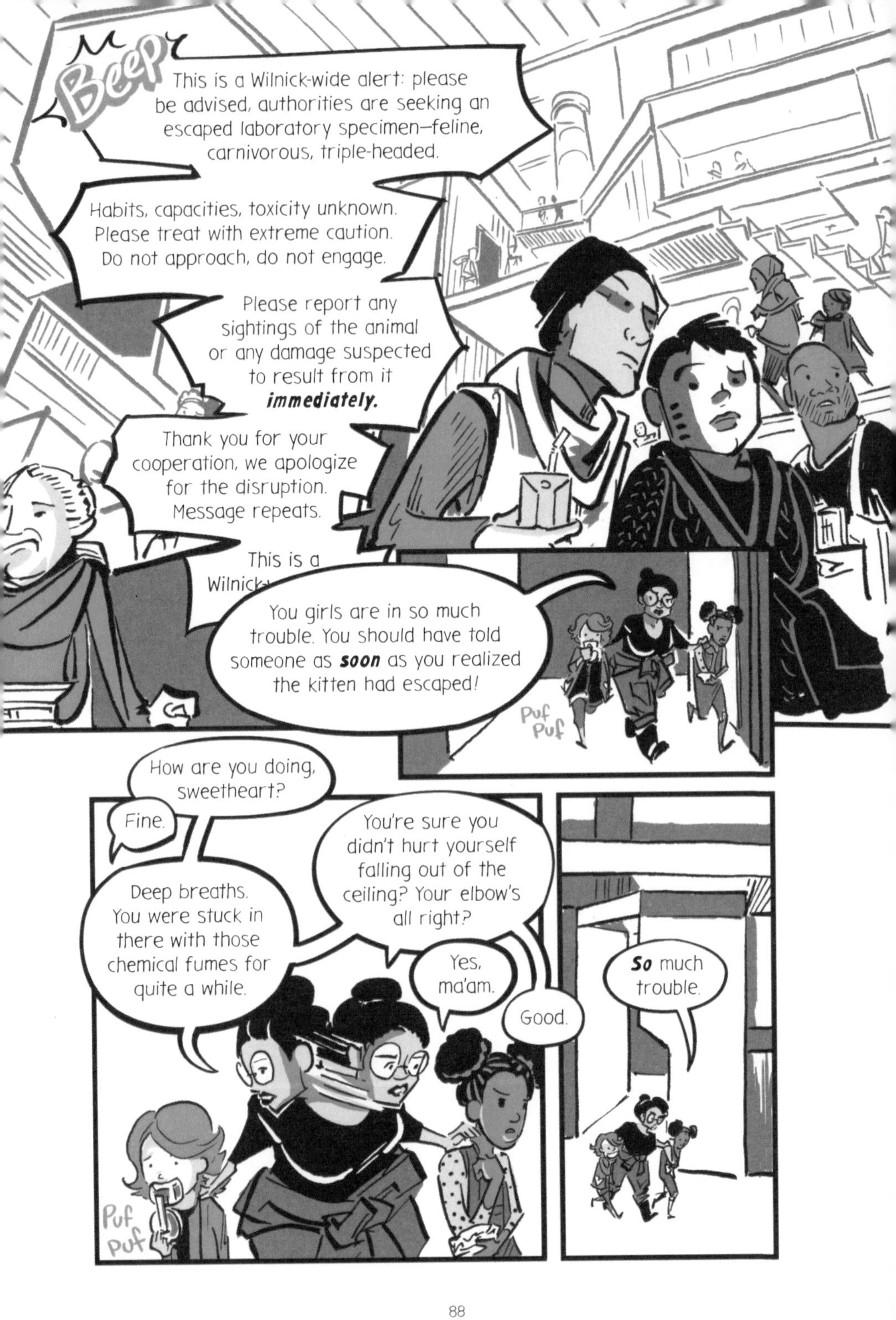
Beep
This is a Wilnick-wide alert: please be advised, authorities are seeking an escaped laboratory specimen—feline, carnivorous, triple-headed.
Habits, capacities, toxicity unknown. Please treat with extreme caution. Do not approach, do not engage.
Please report any sightings of the animal or any damage suspected to result from it ***immediately.***
Thank you for your cooperation, we apologize for the disruption. Message repeats.
This is a Wilnick-
You girls are in so much trouble. You should have told someone as ***soon*** as you realized the kitten had escaped!
Puf Puf
How are you doing, sweetheart?
Fine.
Deep breaths. You were stuck in there with those chemical fumes for quite a while.
You're sure you didn't hurt yourself falling out of the ceiling? Your elbow's all right?
Yes, ma'am.
Good.
Puf Puf
So much trouble.

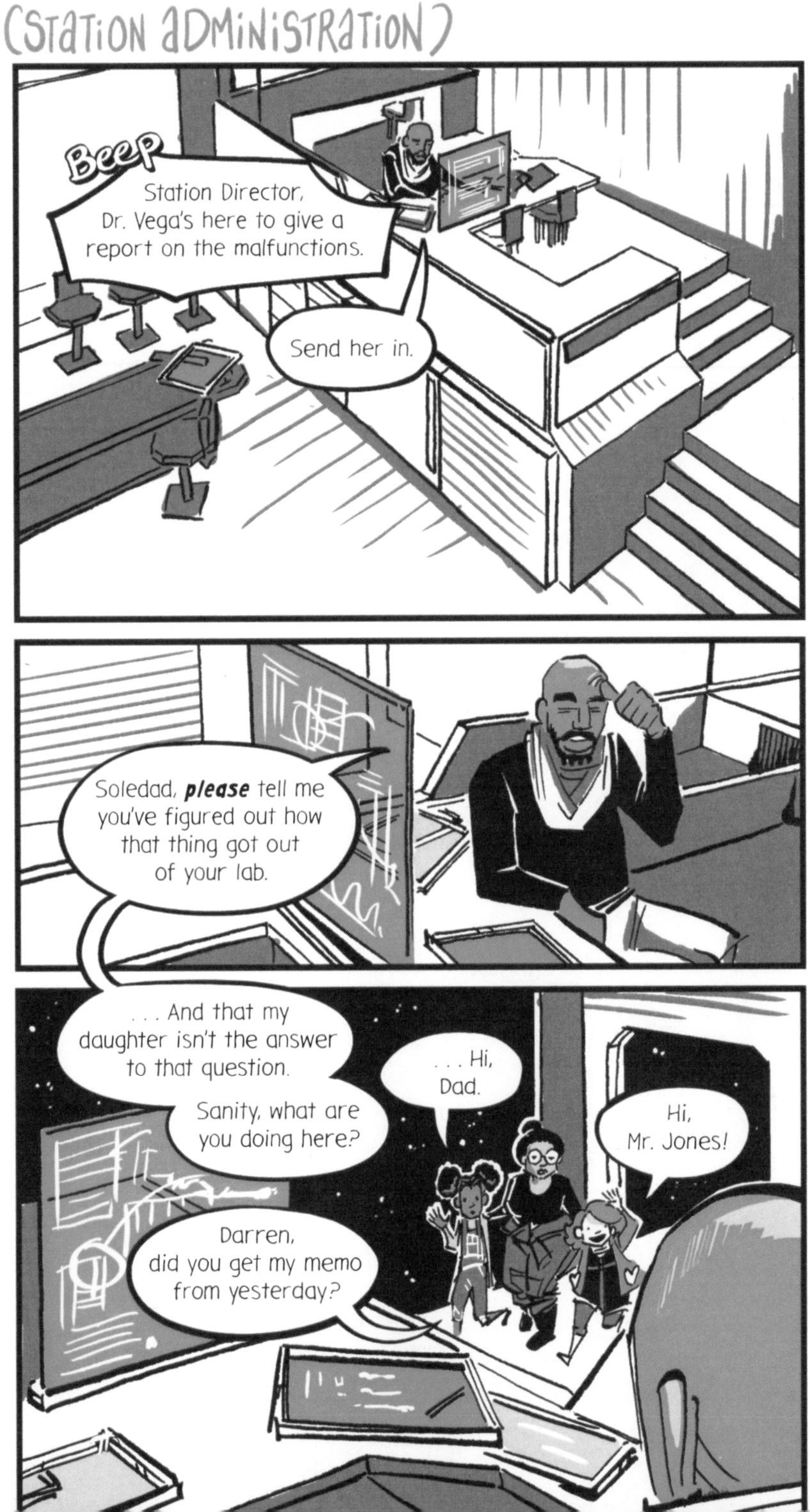
(STATION ADMINISTRATION)
Beep
Station Director, Dr. Vega's here to give a report on the malfunctions.
Send her in.
Soledad, ***please*** tell me you've figured out how that thing got out of your lab.
. . . And that my daughter isn't the answer to that question.
Sanity, what are you doing here?
. . . Hi, Dad.
Hi, Mr. Jones!
Darren, did you get my memo from yesterday?

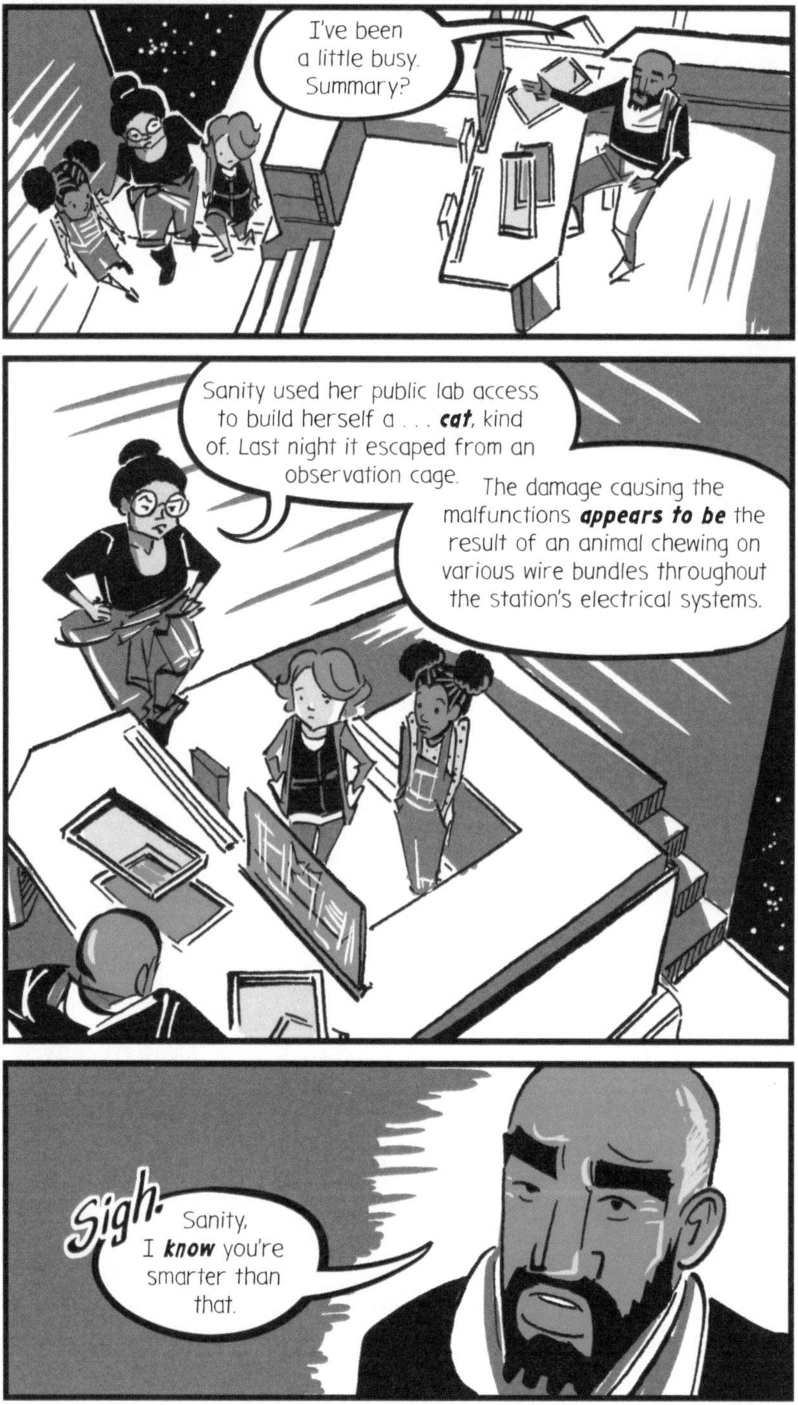

I've been a little busy. Summary?
Sanity used her public lab access to build herself a . . . **cat**, kind of. Last night it escaped from an observation cage.
The damage causing the malfunctions **appears to be** the result of an animal chewing on various wire bundles throughout the station's electrical systems.
Sigh.
Sanity, I **know** you're smarter than that.

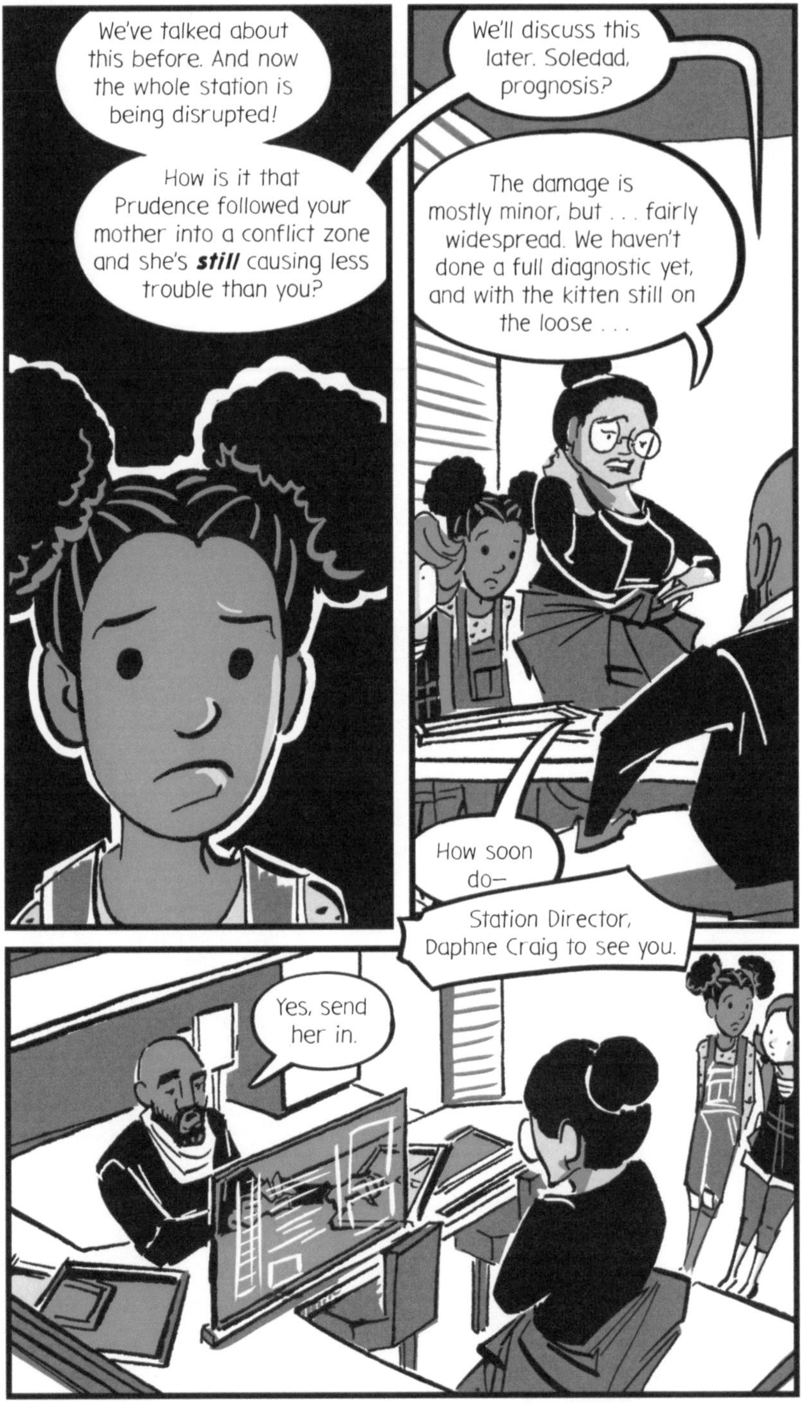
We've talked about this before. And now the whole station is being disrupted!
How is it that Prudence followed your mother into a conflict zone and she's ***still*** causing less trouble than you?
We'll discuss this later. Soledad, prognosis?
The damage is mostly minor, but . . . fairly widespread. We haven't done a full diagnostic yet, and with the kitten still on the loose . . .
How soon do—
Station Director, Daphne Craig to see you.
Yes, send her in.

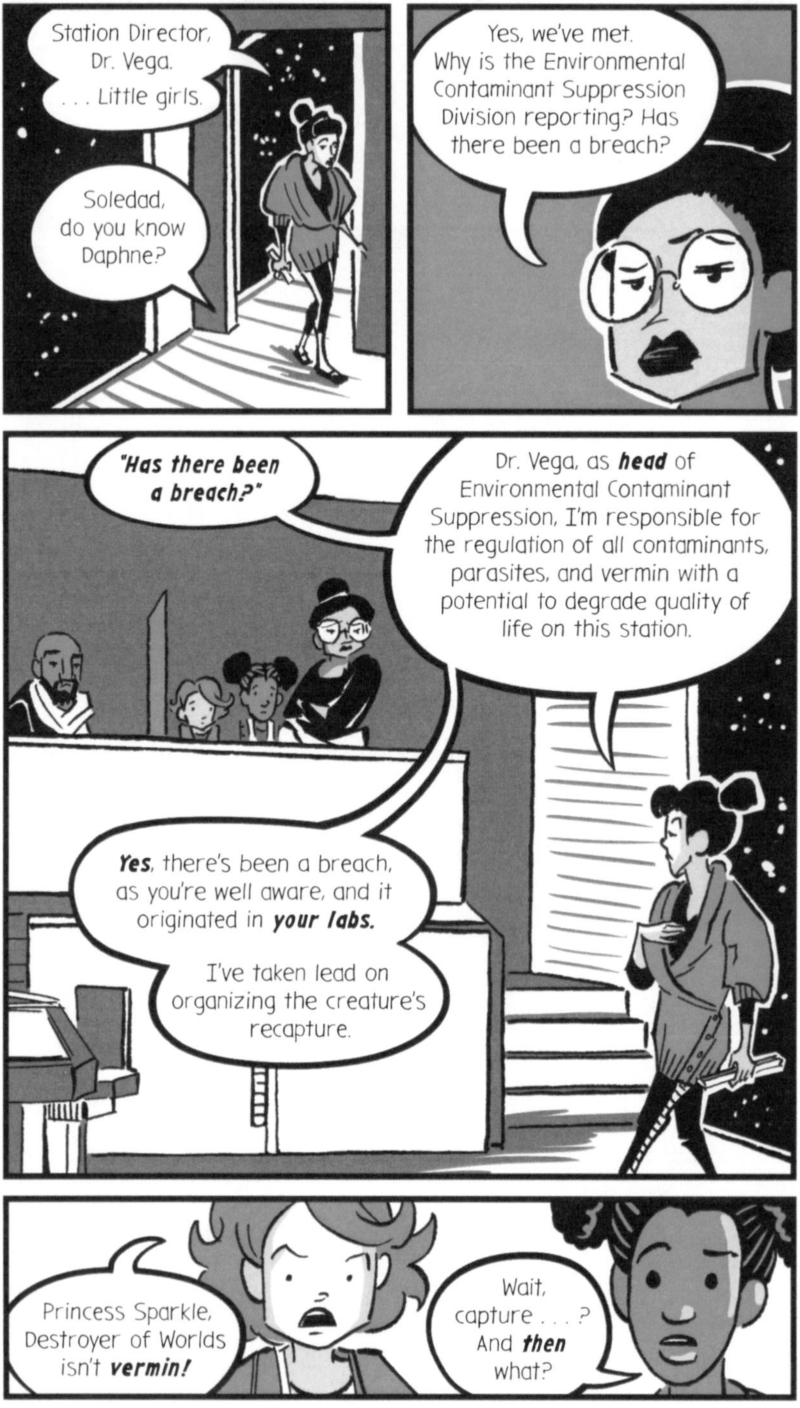
Station Director, Dr. Vega. . . . Little girls.
Soledad, do you know Daphne?
Yes, we've met. Why is the Environmental Contaminant Suppression Division reporting? Has there been a breach?
"Has there been a breach?"
Dr. Vega, as **head** of Environmental Contaminant Suppression, I'm responsible for the regulation of all contaminants, parasites, and vermin with a potential to degrade quality of life on this station.
Yes, there's been a breach, as you're well aware, and it originated in **your labs.**
I've taken lead on organizing the creature's recapture.
Princess Sparkle, Destroyer of Worlds isn't **vermin!**
Wait, capture . . . ? And **then** what?

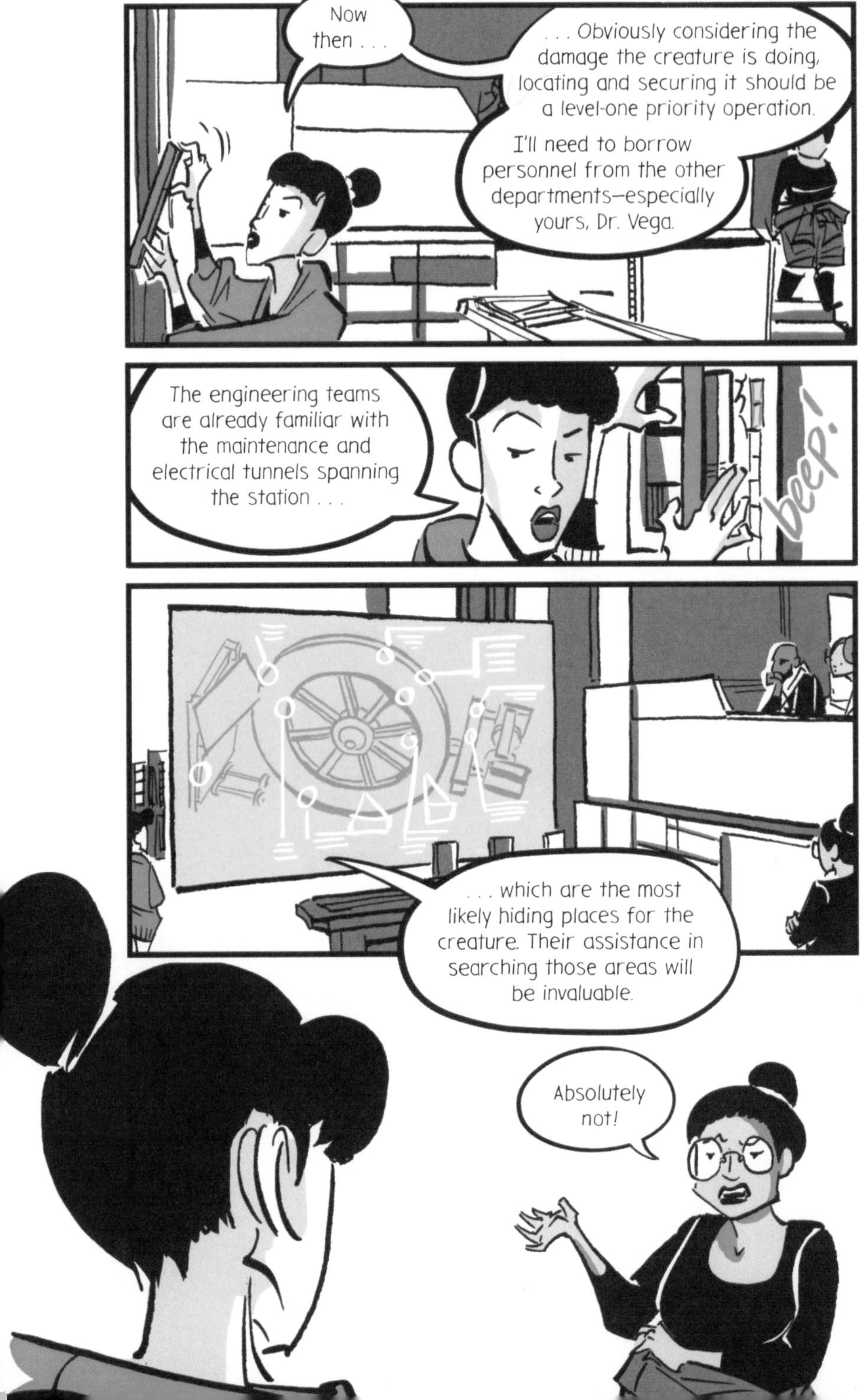
Now then . . .
. . . Obviously considering the damage the creature is doing, locating and securing it should be a level-one priority operation.
I'll need to borrow personnel from the other departments—especially yours, Dr. Vega.
The engineering teams are already familiar with the maintenance and electrical tunnels spanning the station . . .
beep!
. . . which are the most likely hiding places for the creature. Their assistance in searching those areas will be invaluable.
Absolutely not!

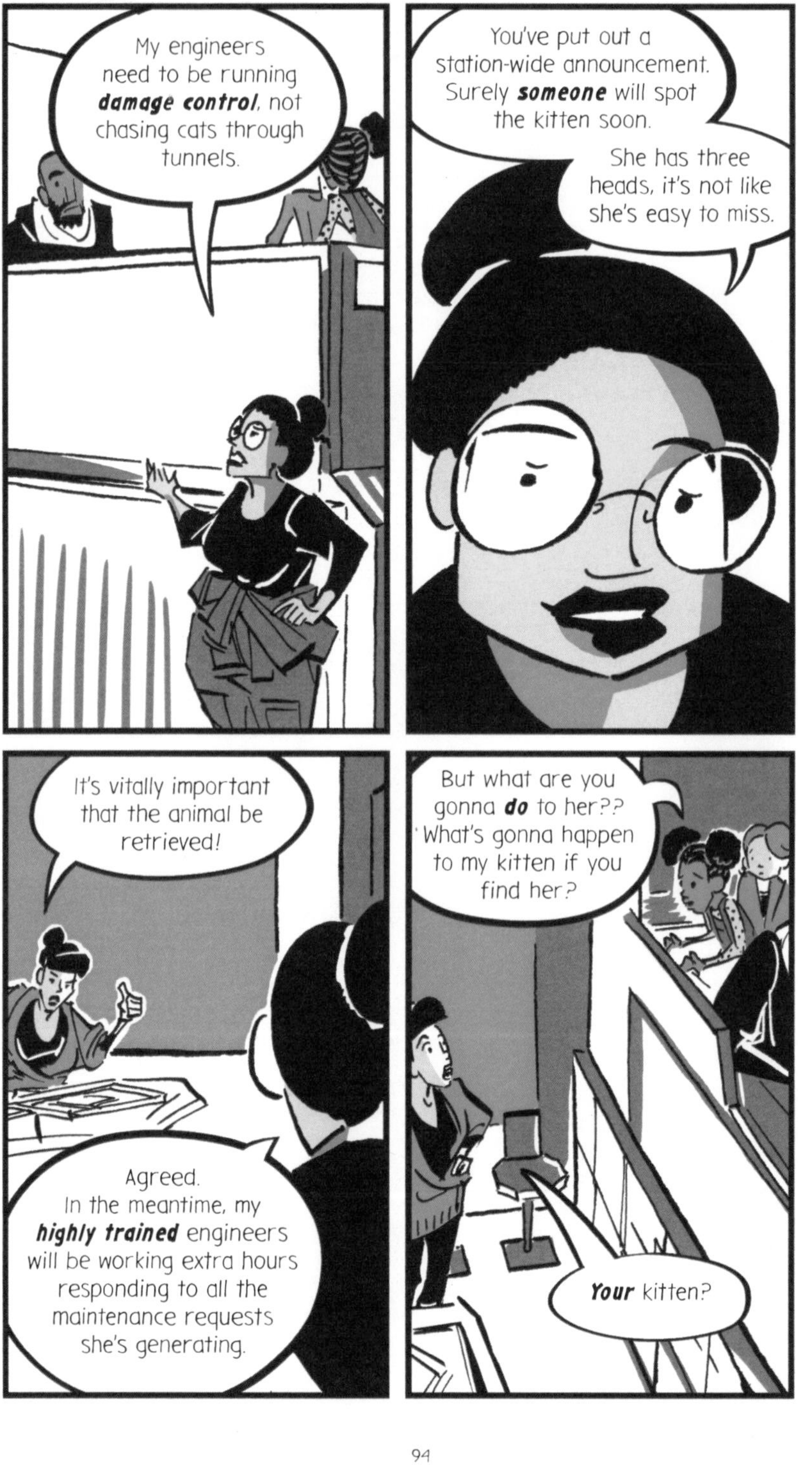
My engineers need to be running **damage control**, not chasing cats through tunnels.
You've put out a station-wide announcement. Surely **someone** will spot the kitten soon.
She has three heads, it's not like she's easy to miss.
It's vitally important that the animal be retrieved!
Agreed. In the meantime, my **highly trained** engineers will be working extra hours responding to all the maintenance requests she's generating.
But what are you gonna **do** to her?? What's gonna happen to my kitten if you find her?
Your kitten?

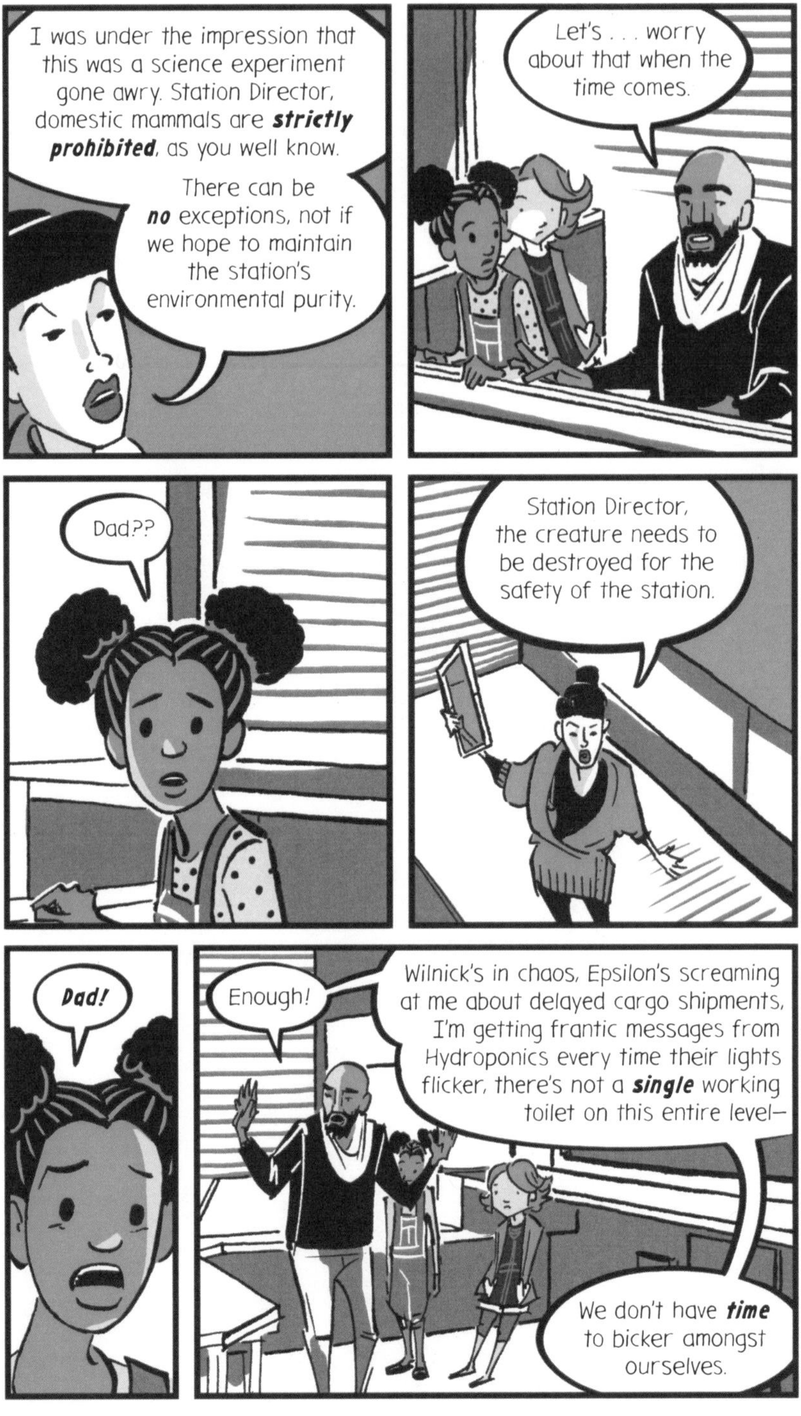
I was under the impression that this was a science experiment gone awry. Station Director, domestic mammals are **strictly prohibited**, as you well know.
There can be **no** exceptions, not if we hope to maintain the station's environmental purity.
Let's . . . worry about that when the time comes.
Dad??
Station Director, the creature needs to be destroyed for the safety of the station.
Dad!
Enough!
Wilnick's in chaos, Epsilon's screaming at me about delayed cargo shipments, I'm getting frantic messages from Hydroponics every time their lights flicker, there's not a **single** working toilet on this entire level—
We don't have **time** to bicker amongst ourselves.

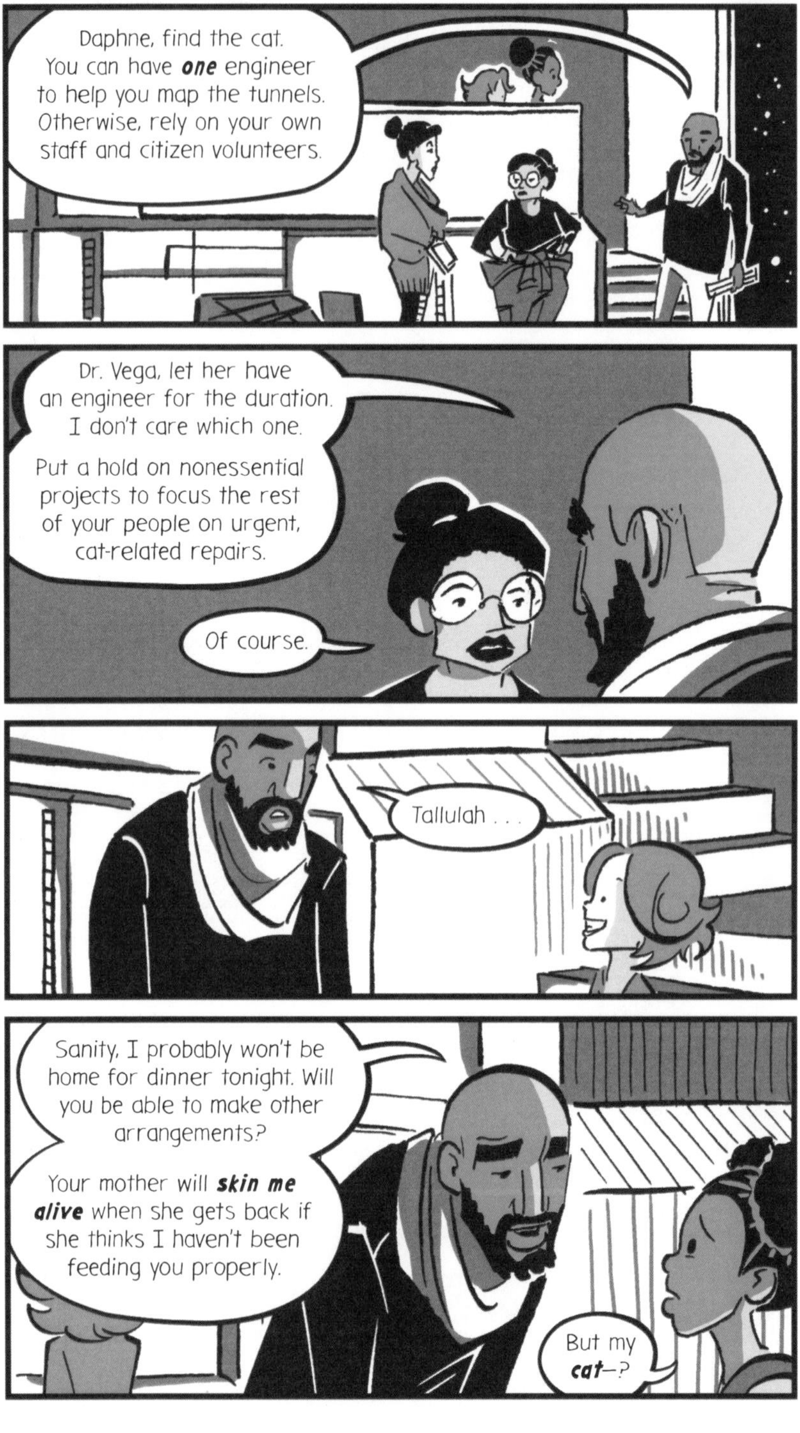
Daphne, find the cat. You can have **one** engineer to help you map the tunnels. Otherwise, rely on your own staff and citizen volunteers.
Dr. Vega, let her have an engineer for the duration. I don't care which one.
Put a hold on nonessential projects to focus the rest of your people on urgent, cat-related repairs.
Of course.
Tallulah . . .
Sanity, I probably won't be home for dinner tonight. Will you be able to make other arrangements?
Your mother will **skin me alive** when she gets back if she thinks I haven't been feeding you properly.
But my **cat**—?

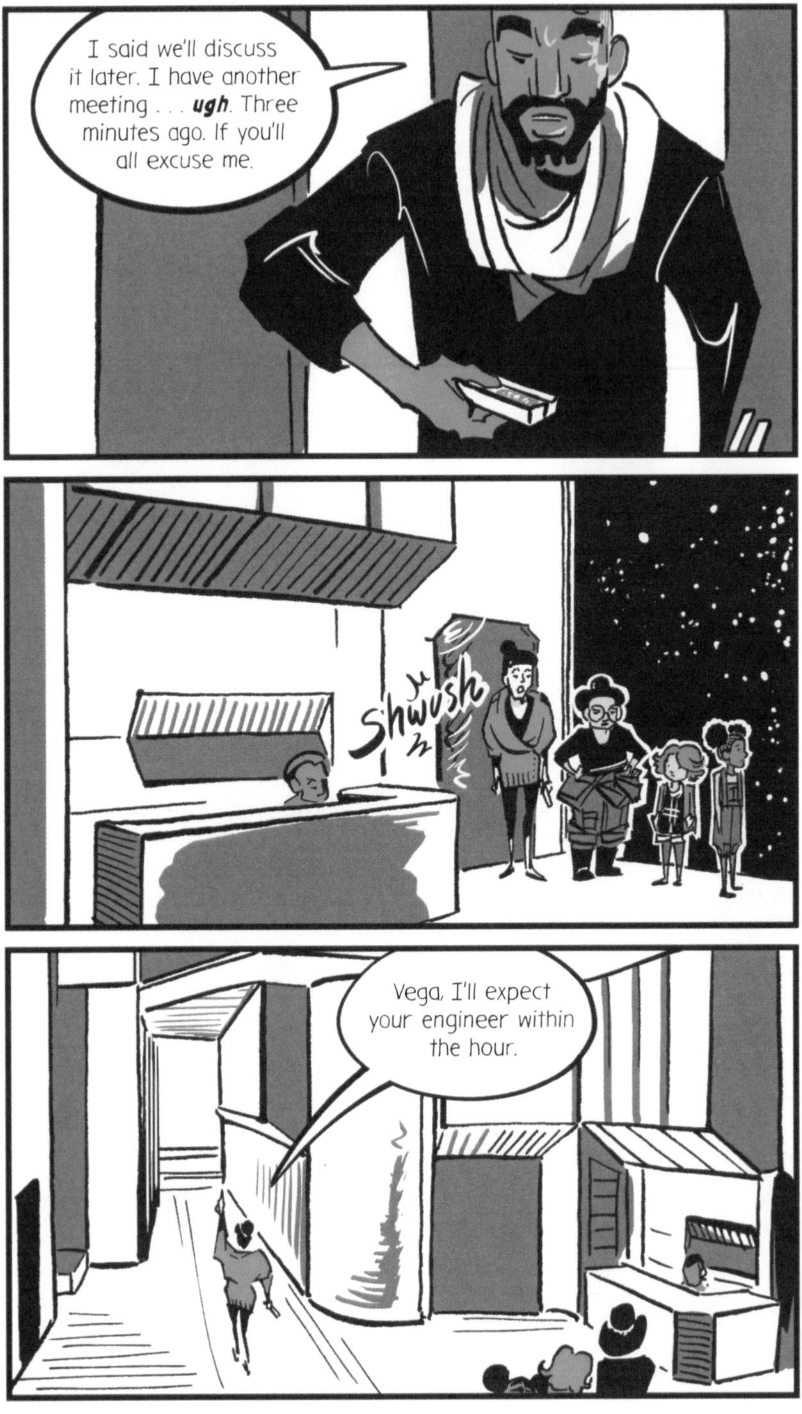
I said we'll discuss it later. I have another meeting . . . ugh. Three minutes ago. If you'll all excuse me.
Shwush
Vega, I'll expect your engineer within the hour.

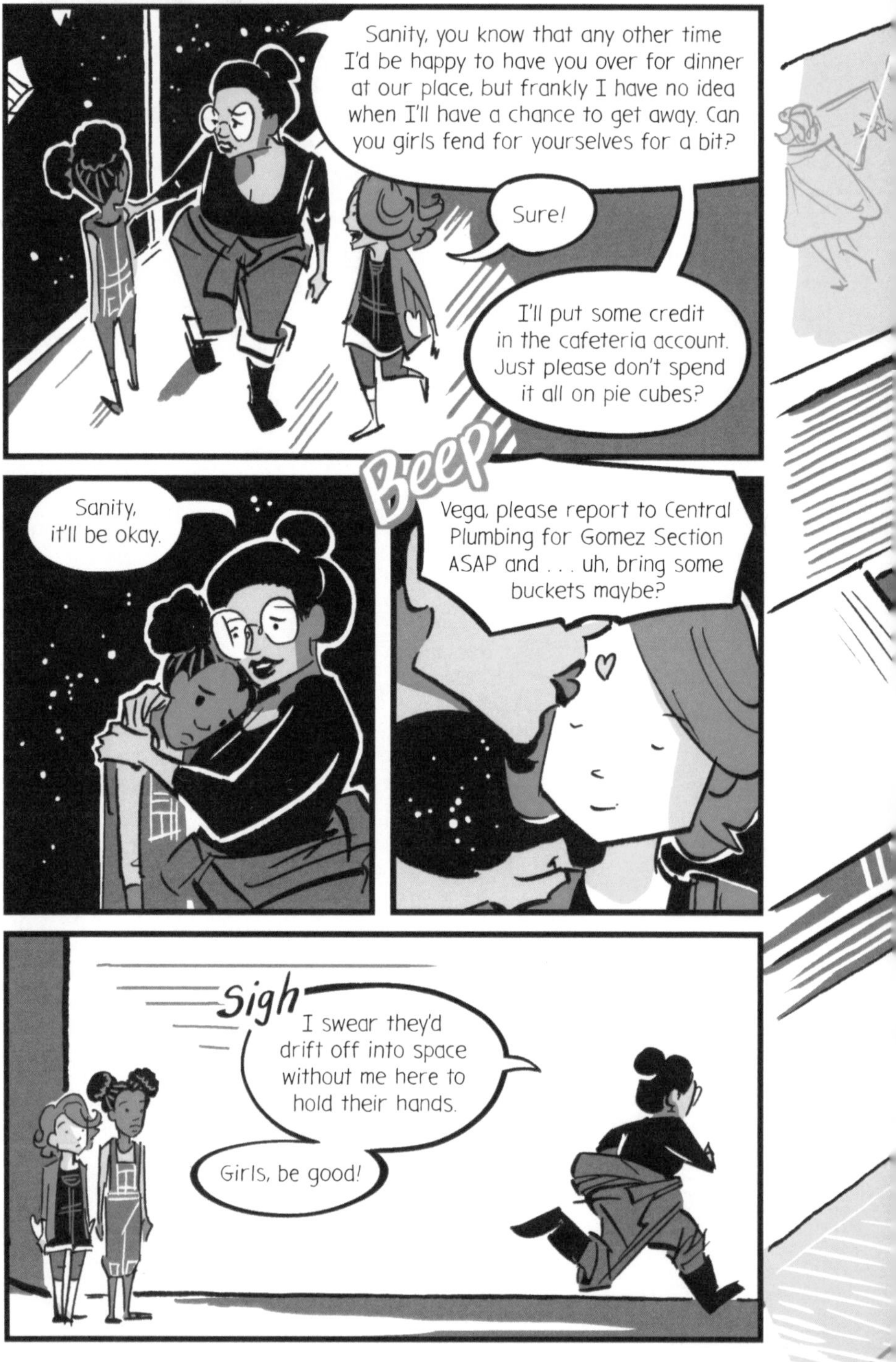
Sanity, you know that any other time I'd be happy to have you over for dinner at our place, but frankly I have no idea when I'll have a chance to get away. Can you girls fend for yourselves for a bit?
Sure!
I'll put some credit in the cafeteria account. Just please don't spend it all on pie cubes?
Beep
Sanity, it'll be okay.
Vega, please report to Central Plumbing for Gomez Section ASAP and . . . uh, bring some buckets maybe?
Sigh
I swear they'd drift off into space without me here to hold their hands.
Girls, be good!

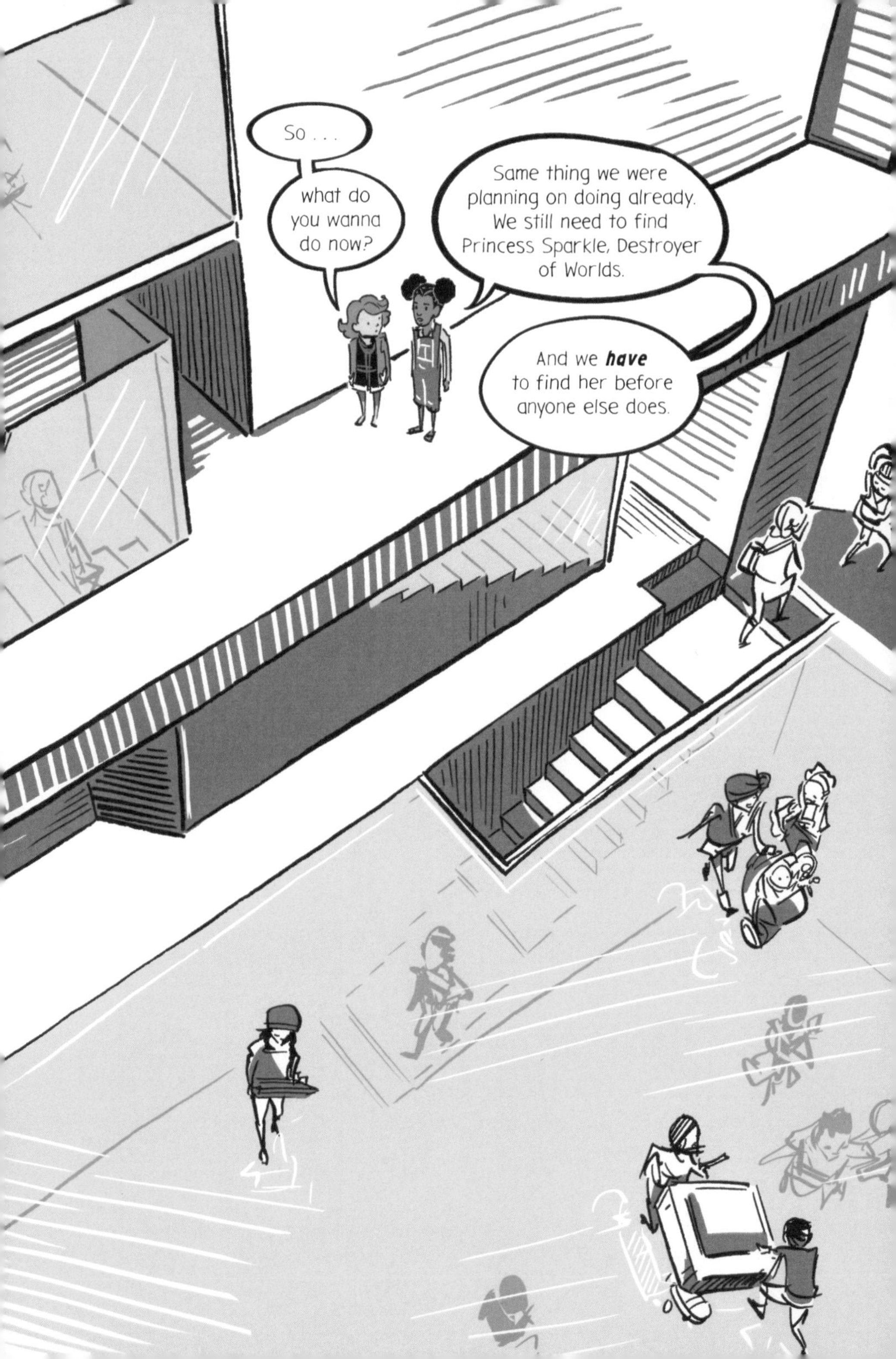
So . . .
what do you wanna do now?
Same thing we were planning on doing already. We still need to find Princess Sparkle, Destroyer of Worlds.
And we ***have*** to find her before anyone else does.

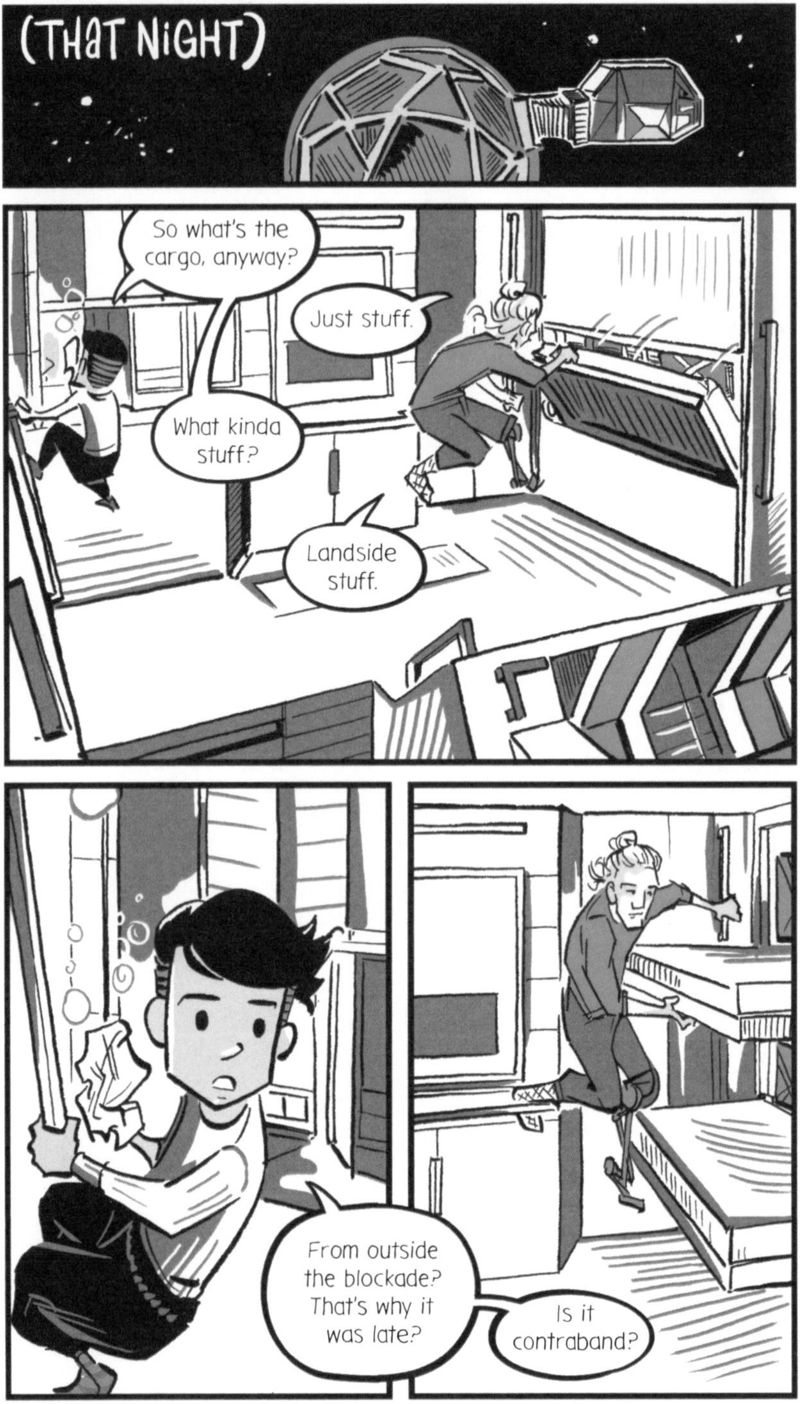
(THAT NIGHT)
So what's the cargo, anyway?
Just stuff.
What kinda stuff?
Landside stuff.
From outside the blockade? That's why it was late?
Is it contraband?

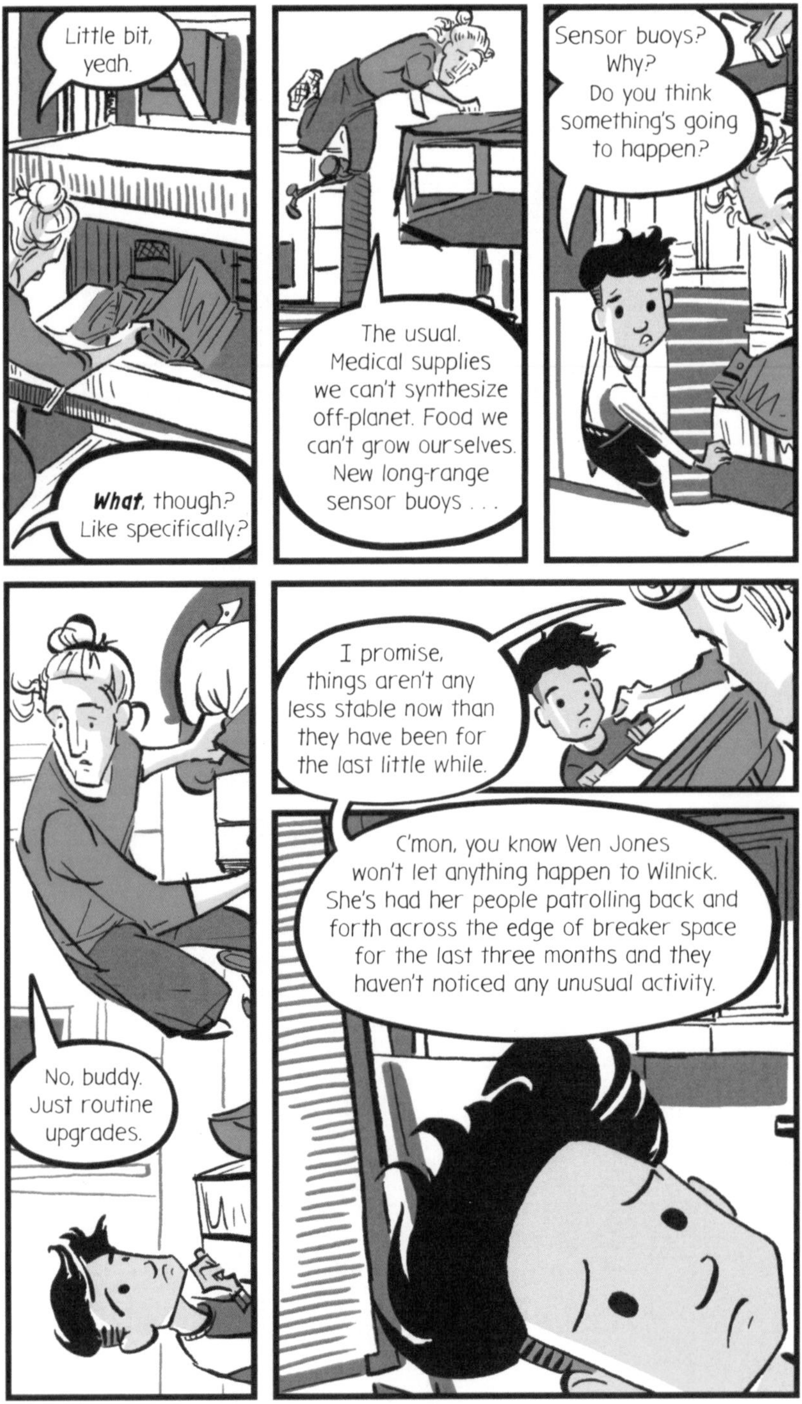

Little bit, yeah.
What, though? Like specifically?
The usual. Medical supplies we can't synthesize off-planet. Food we can't grow ourselves. New long-range sensor buoys . . .
Sensor buoys? Why? Do you think something's going to happen?
No, buddy. Just routine upgrades.
I promise, things aren't any less stable now than they have been for the last little while.
C'mon, you know Ven Jones won't let anything happen to Wilnick. She's had her people patrolling back and forth across the edge of breaker space for the last three months and they haven't noticed any unusual activity.

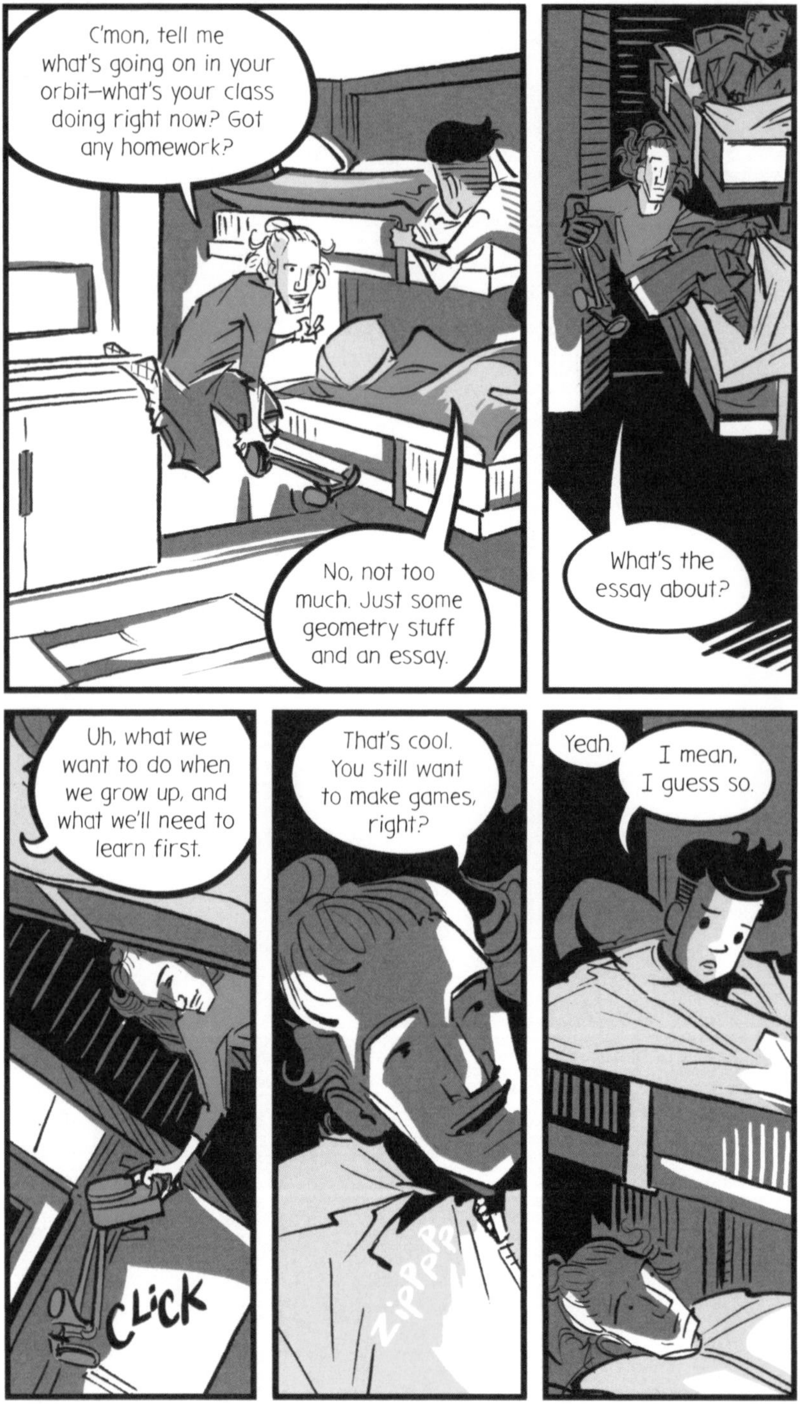
C'mon, tell me what's going on in your orbit—what's your class doing right now? Got any homework?
No, not too much. Just some geometry stuff and an essay.
What's the essay about?
Uh, what we want to do when we grow up, and what we'll need to learn first.
CLICK
That's cool. You still want to make games, right?
ZIPPPP
Yeah.
I mean, I guess so.

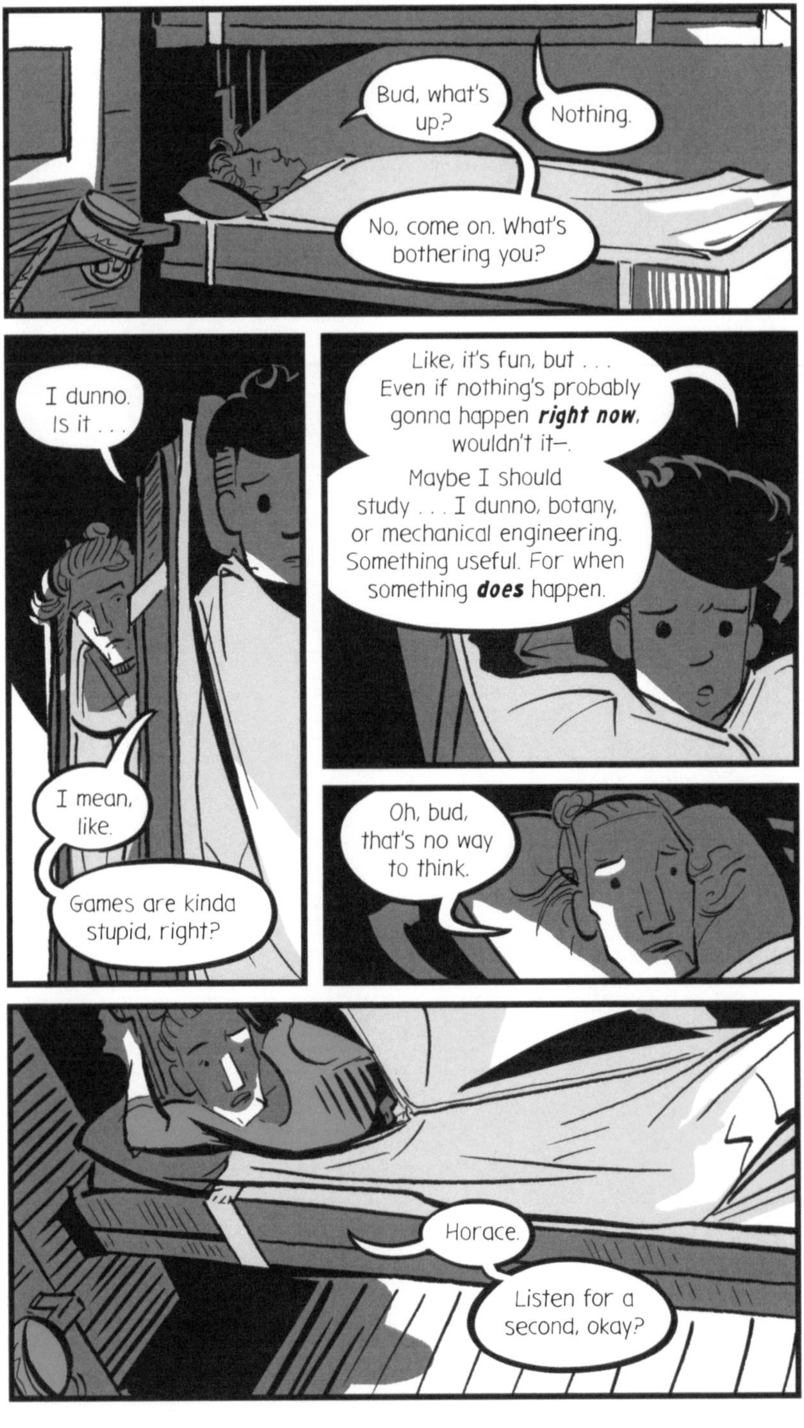
Bud, what's up?
Nothing.
No, come on. What's bothering you?
I dunno. Is it . . .
I mean, like.
Games are kinda stupid, right?
Like, it's fun, but . . . Even if nothing's probably gonna happen **right now**, wouldn't it–.
Maybe I should study . . . I dunno, botany, or mechanical engineering. Something useful. For when something **does** happen.
Oh, bud, that's no way to think.
Horace.
Listen for a second, okay?

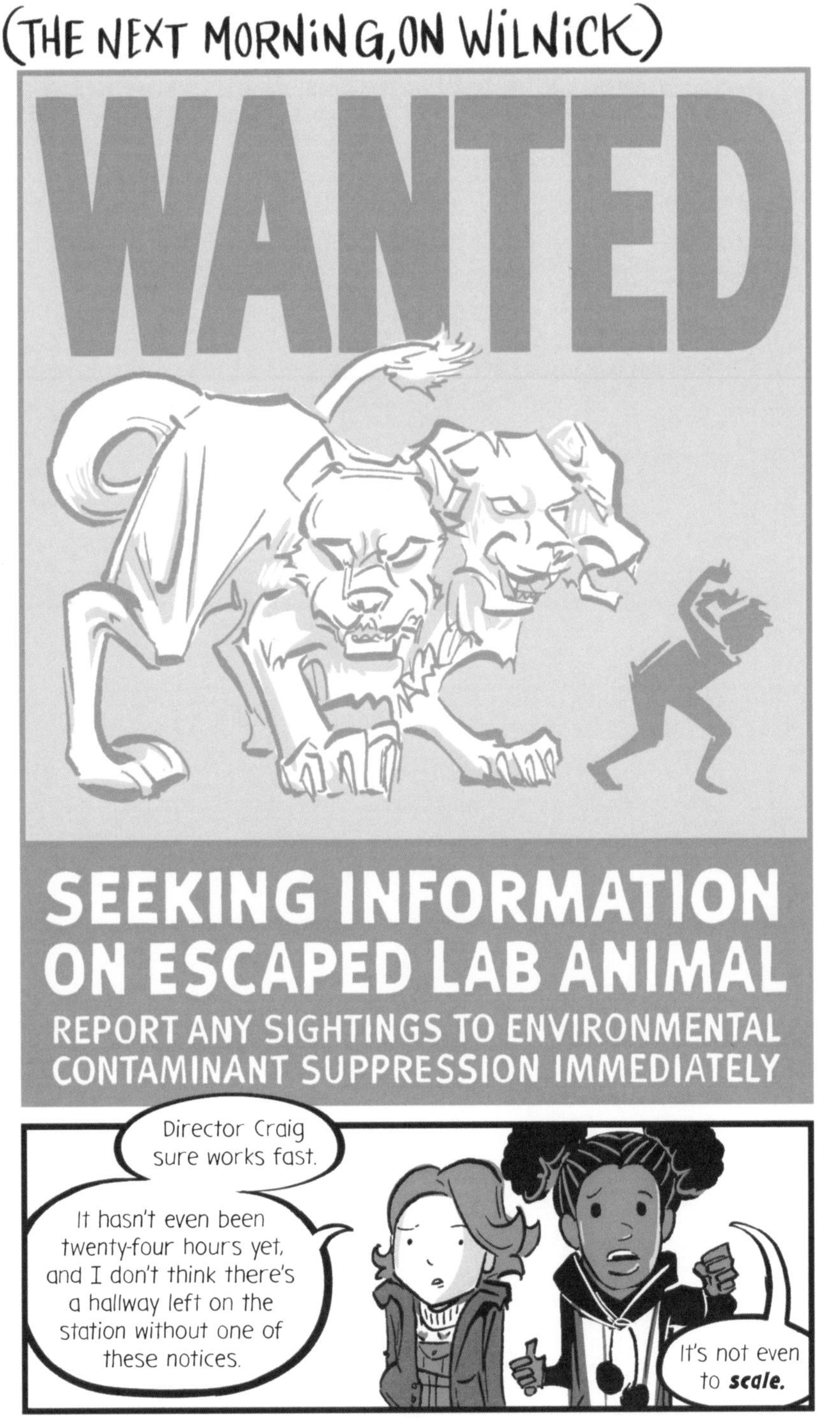
(THE NEXT MORNING, ON WILNICK)
WANTED
SEEKING INFORMATION ON ESCAPED LAB ANIMAL
REPORT ANY SIGHTINGS TO ENVIRONMENTAL CONTAMINANT SUPPRESSION IMMEDIATELY
Director Craig sure works fast.
It hasn't even been twenty-four hours yet, and I don't think there's a hallway left on the station without one of these notices.
It's not even to **scale.**

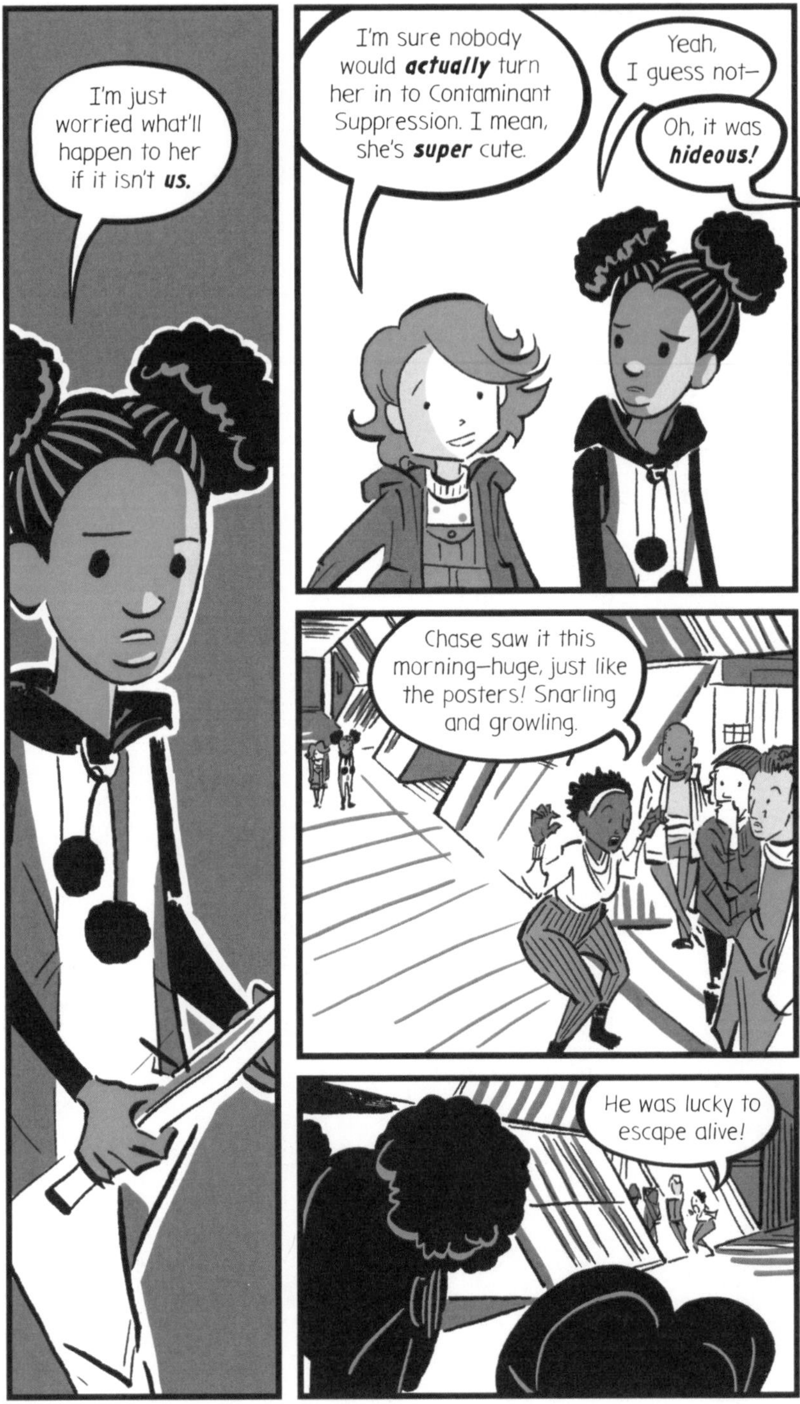
I'm just worried what'll happen to her if it isn't **us.**
I'm sure nobody would **actually** turn her in to Contaminant Suppression. I mean, she's **super** cute.
Yeah, I guess not—
Oh, it was **hideous!**
Chase saw it this morning—huge, just like the posters! Snarling and growling.
He was lucky to escape alive!

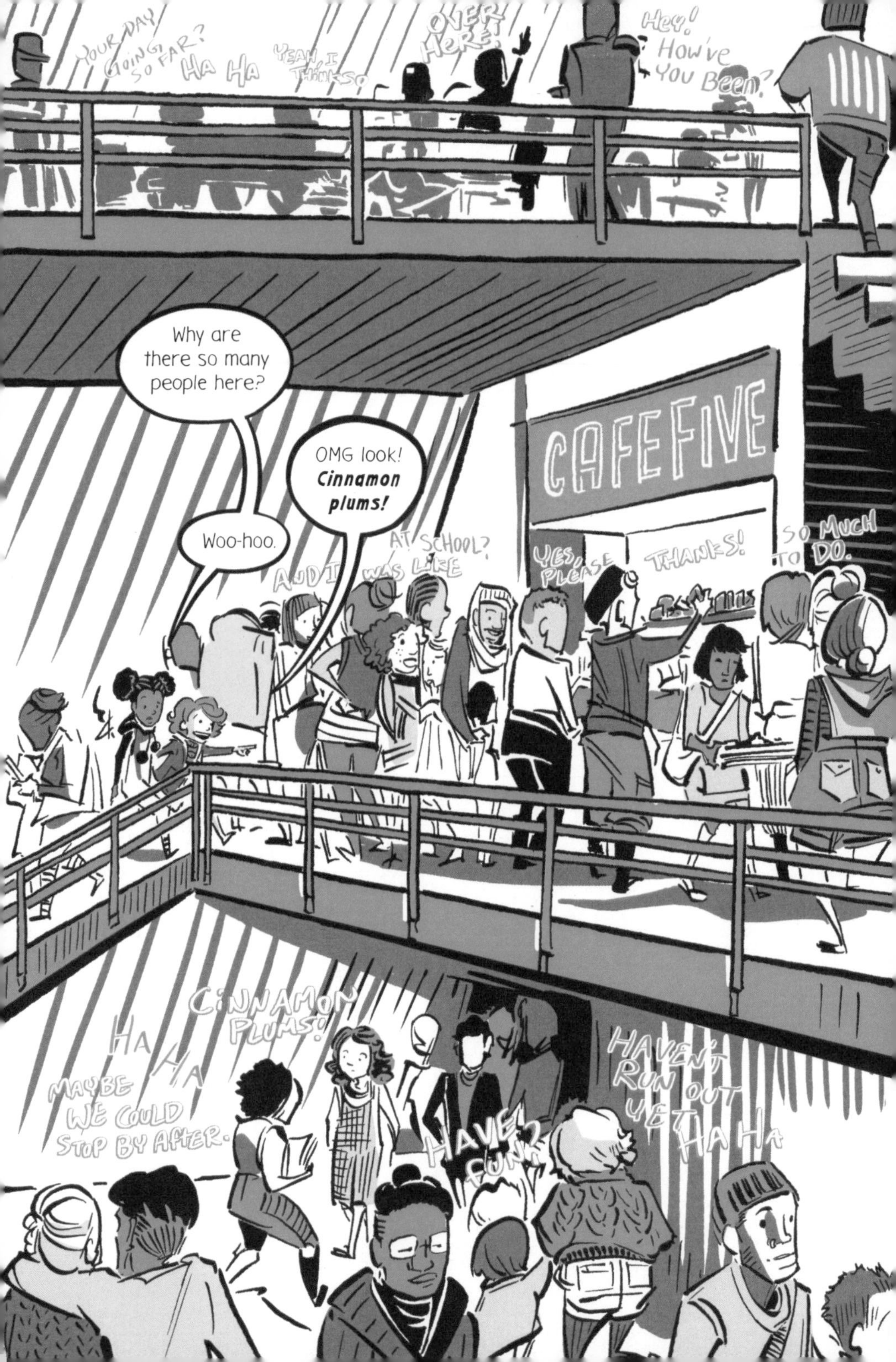
YOUR DAY GOING SO FAR?
HA HA
YEAH, I THINK SO
OVER HERE!
Hey! How've You Been?
Why are there so many people here?
OMG look! Cinnamon plums!
Woo-hoo.
AT SCHOOL?
AND I WAS LIKE
YES, PLEASE
THANKS!
SO MUCH TO DO.
CINNAMON PLUMS!
HA HA
MAYBE WE COULD STOP BY AFTER.
HAVEN'T RUN OUT YET HA HA
HAVE FUN

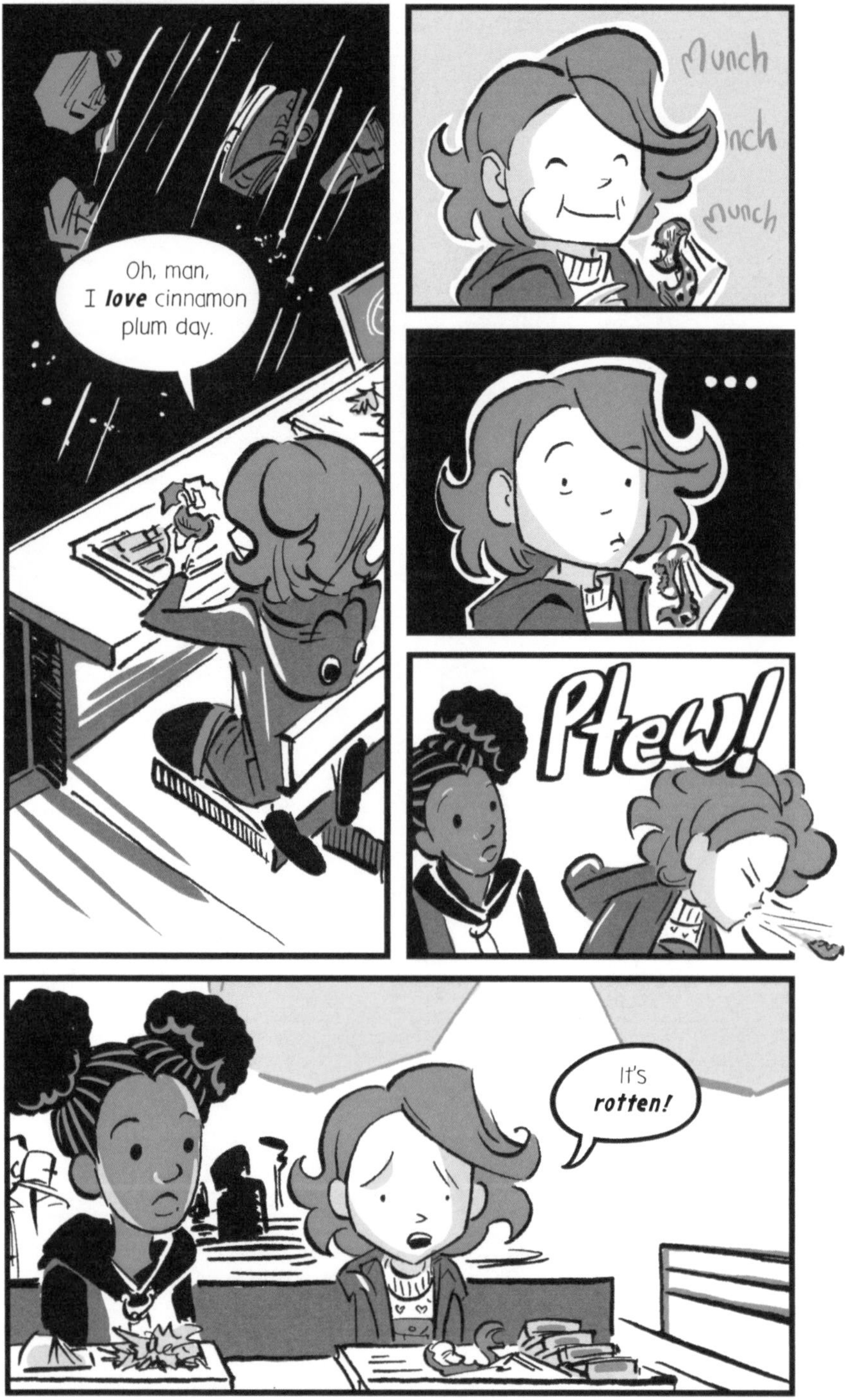
Oh, man, I **love** cinnamon plum day.
Munch
Munch
Munch
...
Ptew!
It's **rotten!**

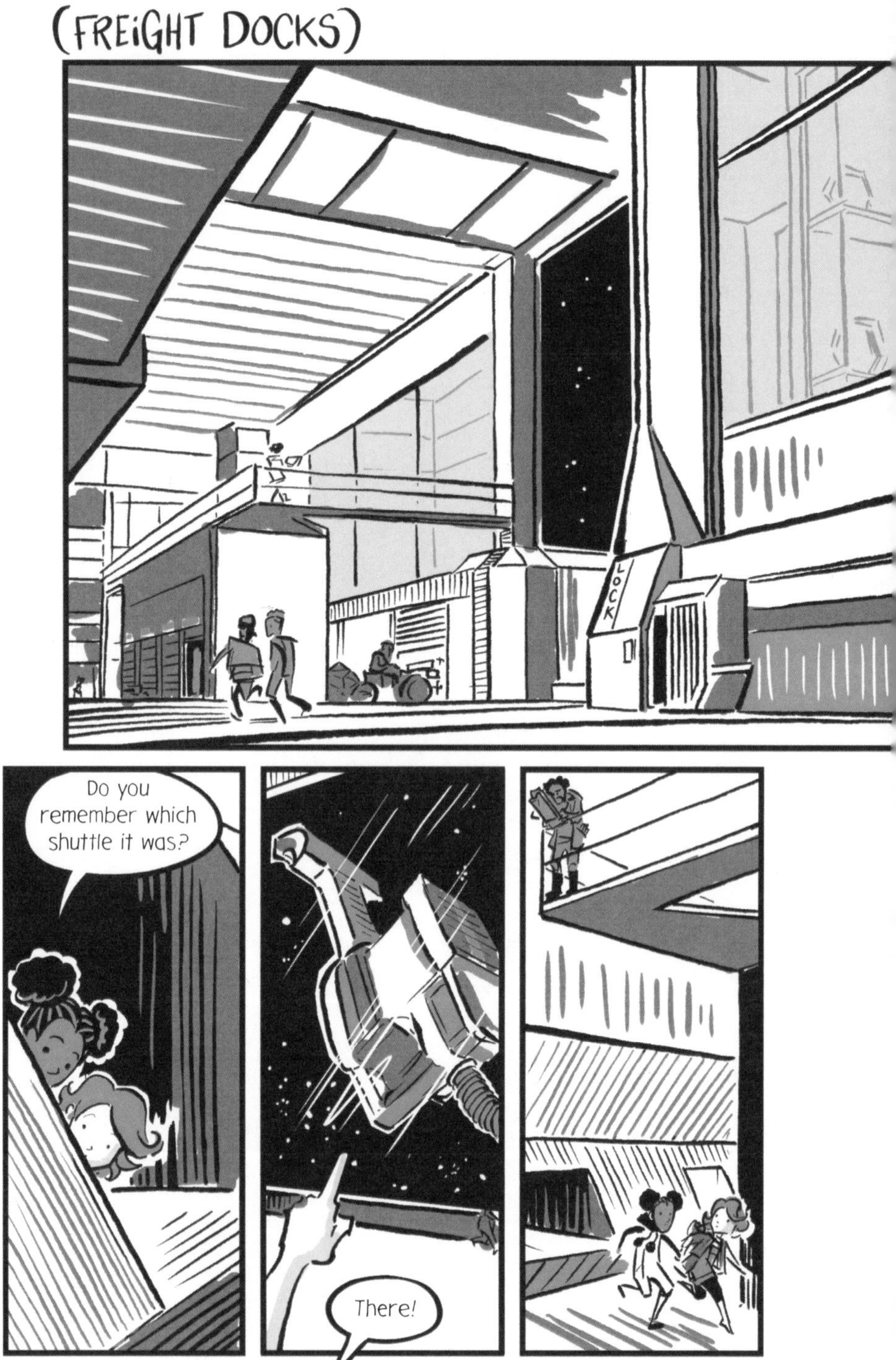
(FREIGHT DOCKS)
LOCK
Do you remember which shuttle it was?
There!

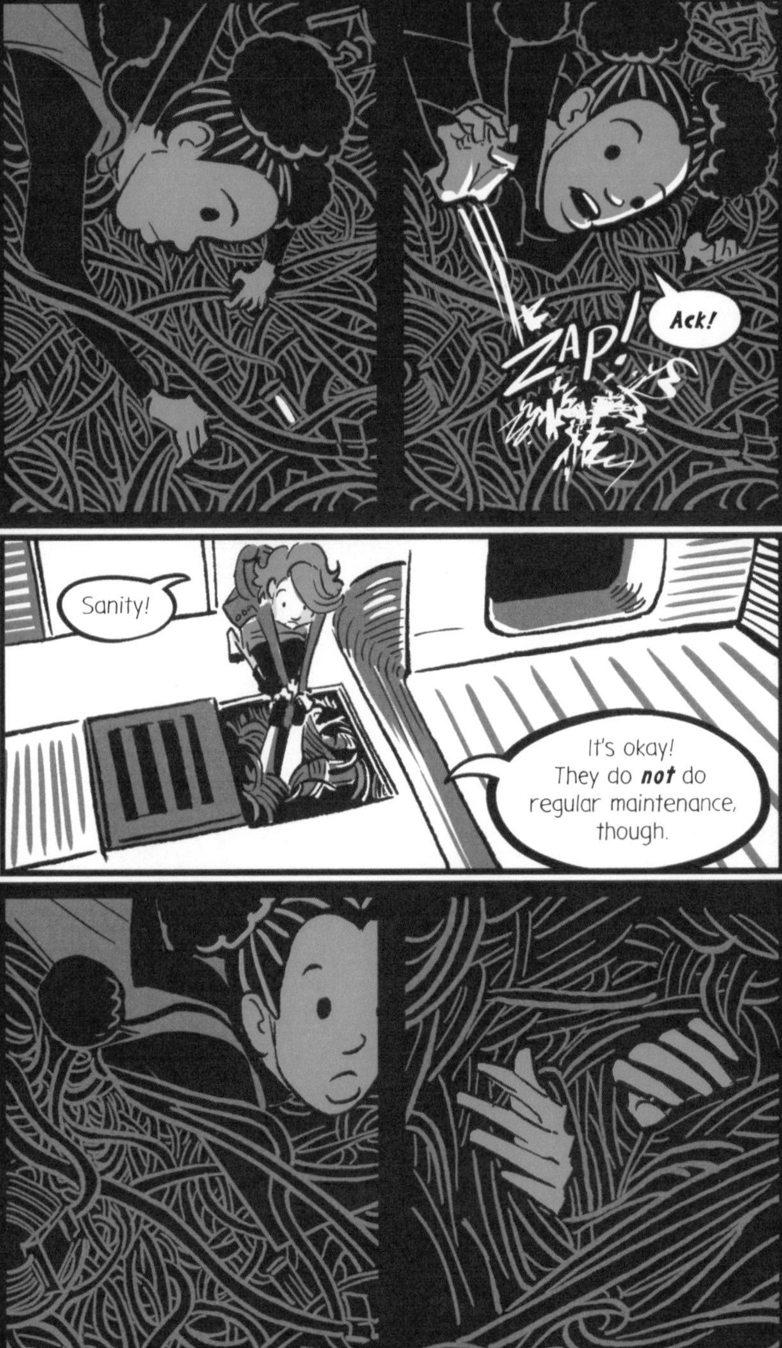
ZAP!
Ack!
Sanity!
It's okay!
They do **not** do
regular maintenance,
though.

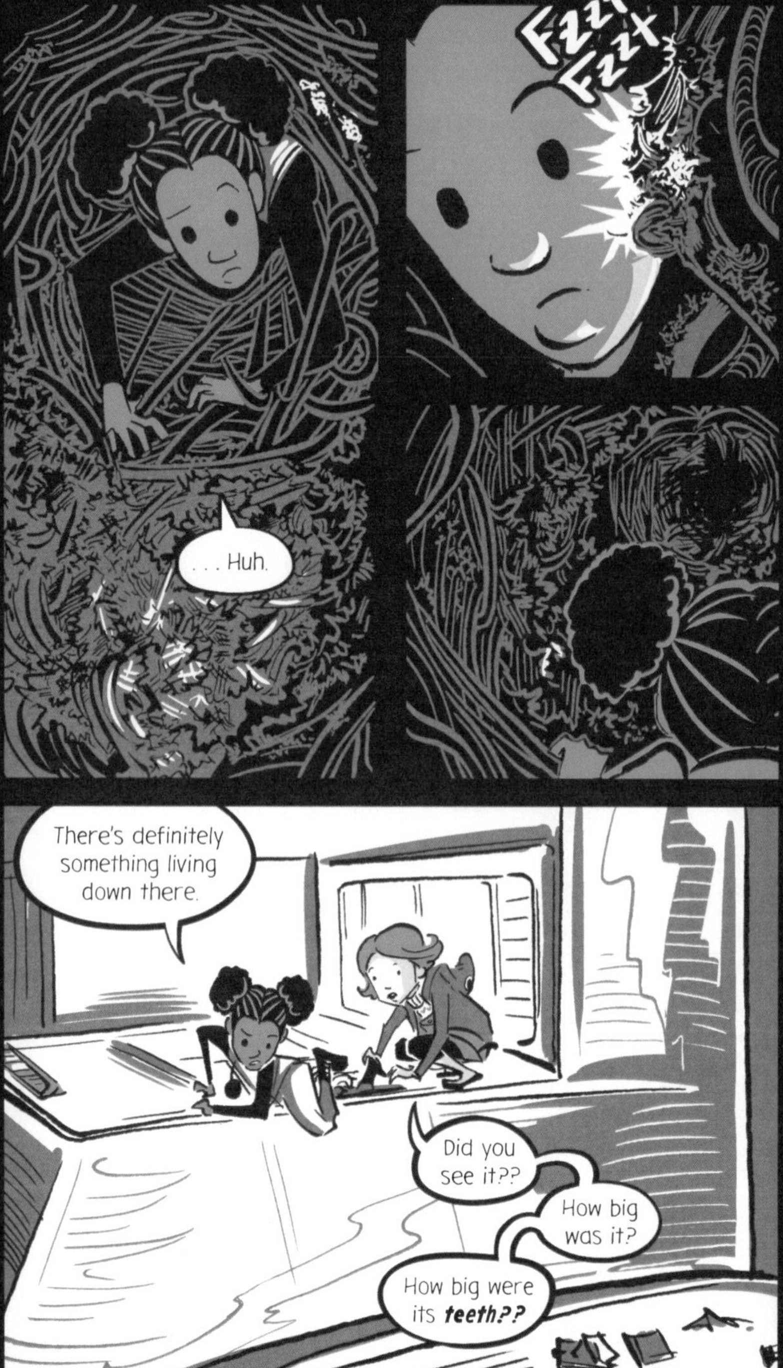

Fzzt
Fzzt
. . . Huh.
There's definitely something living down there.
Did you see it??
How big was it?
How big were its ***teeth??***

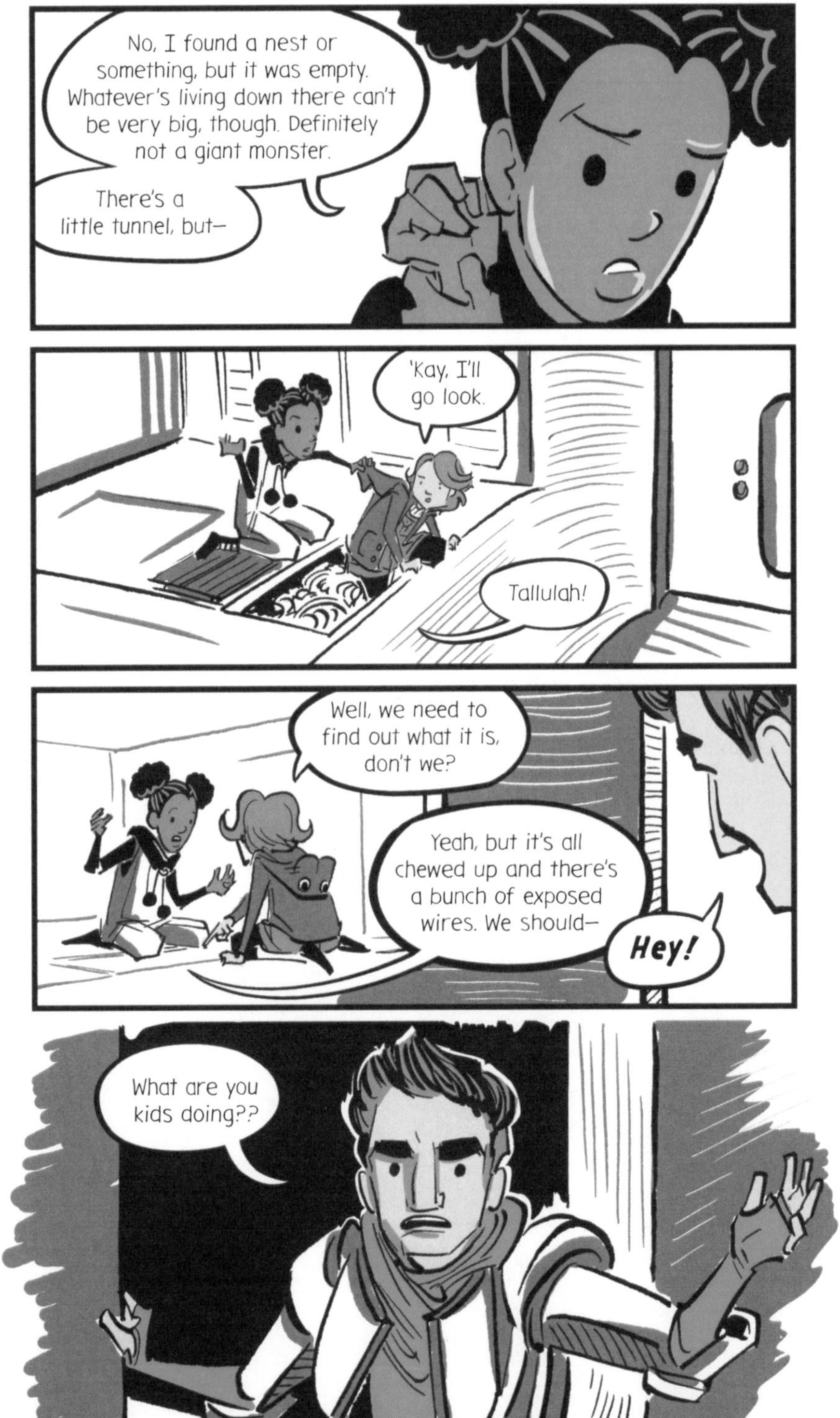
No, I found a nest or something, but it was empty. Whatever's living down there can't be very big, though. Definitely not a giant monster.
There's a little tunnel, but–
'Kay, I'll go look.
Tallulah!
Well, we need to find out what it is, don't we?
Yeah, but it's all chewed up and there's a bunch of exposed wires. We should–
Hey!
What are you kids doing??

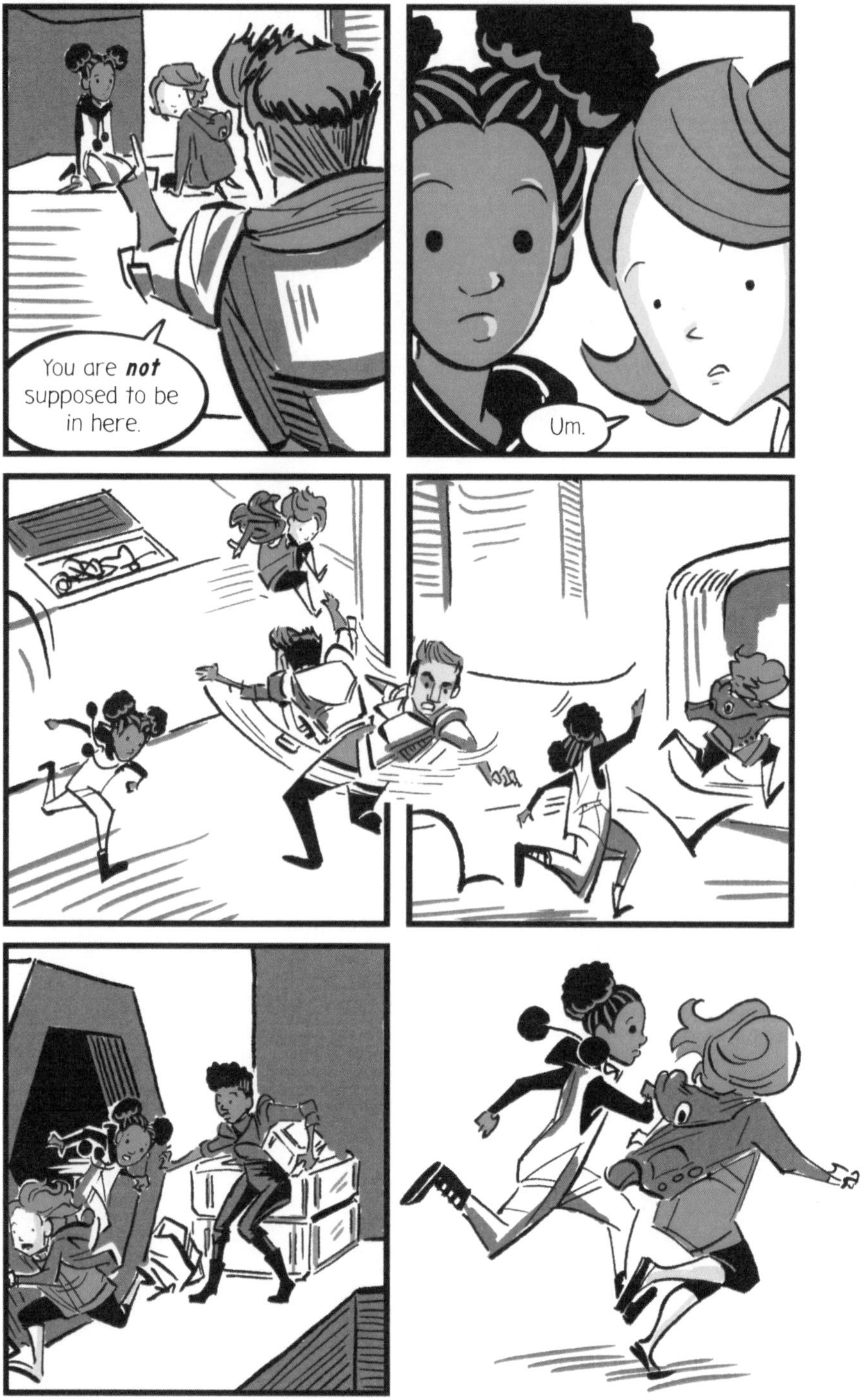
You are **not** supposed to be in here.
Um.

(Halfway to Epsilon Station)

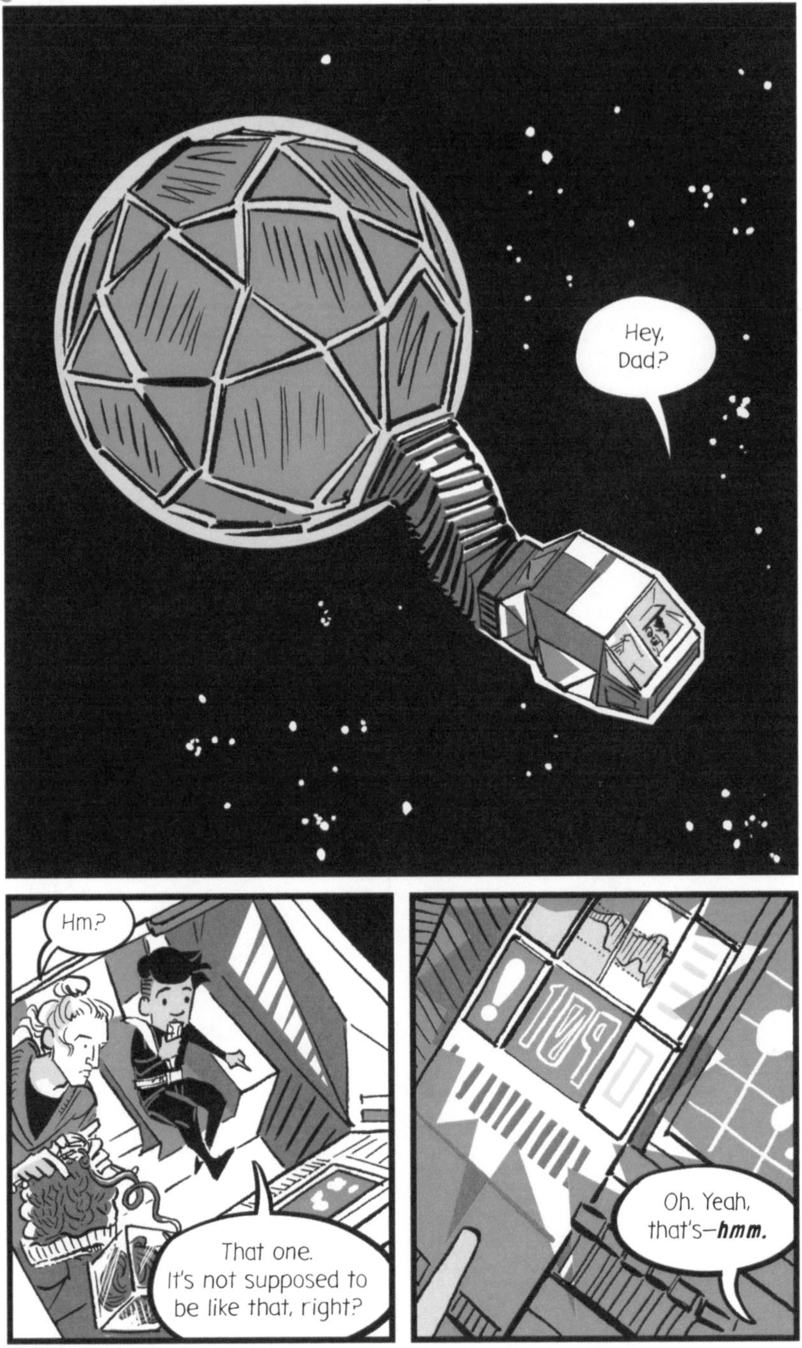
Hey, Dad?
Hm?
That one. It's not supposed to be like that, right?
Oh. Yeah, that's—***hmm.***

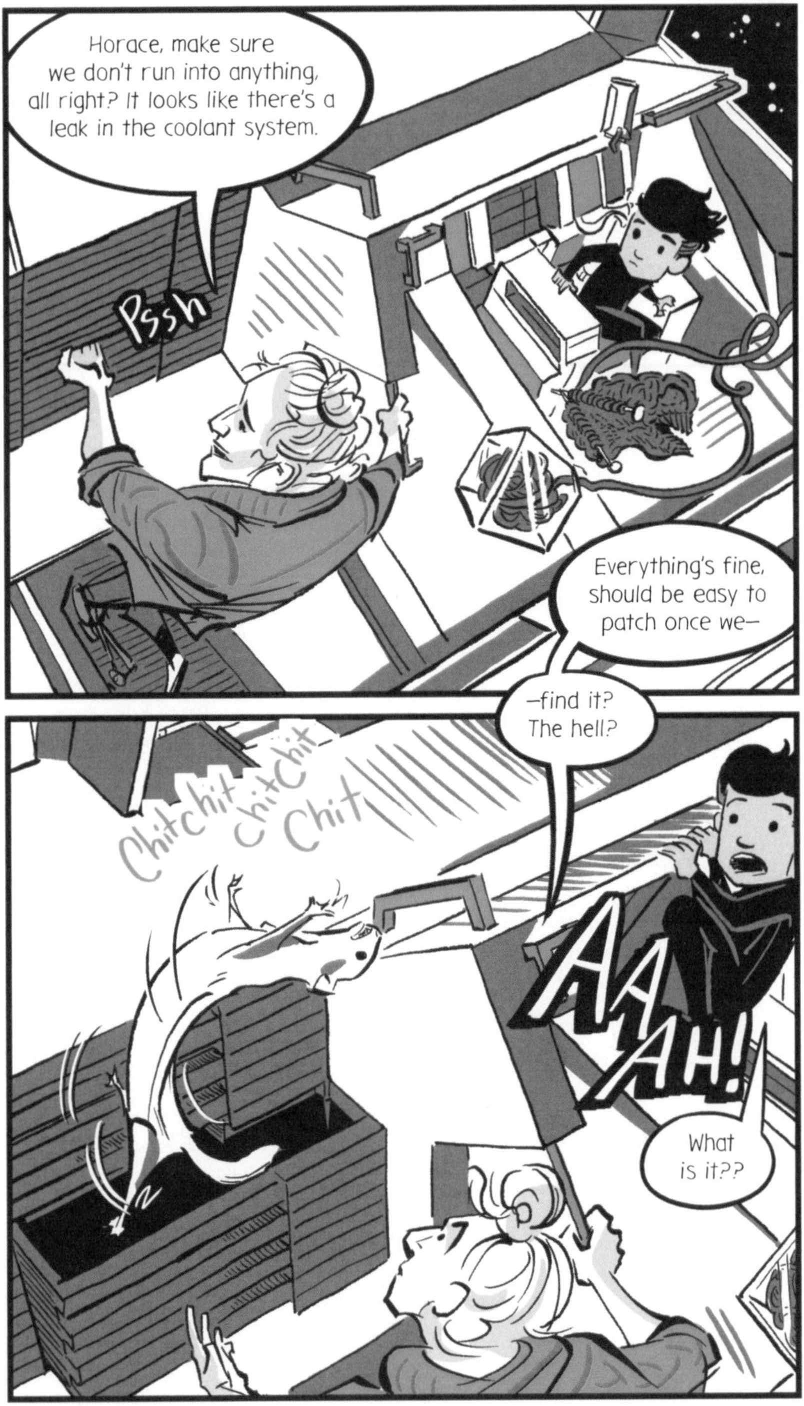

Horace, make sure we don't run into anything, all right? It looks like there's a leak in the coolant system.
Pssh
Everything's fine, should be easy to patch once we—
—find it? The hell?
Chitchit chitchit Chit
AAAAH!
What is it??

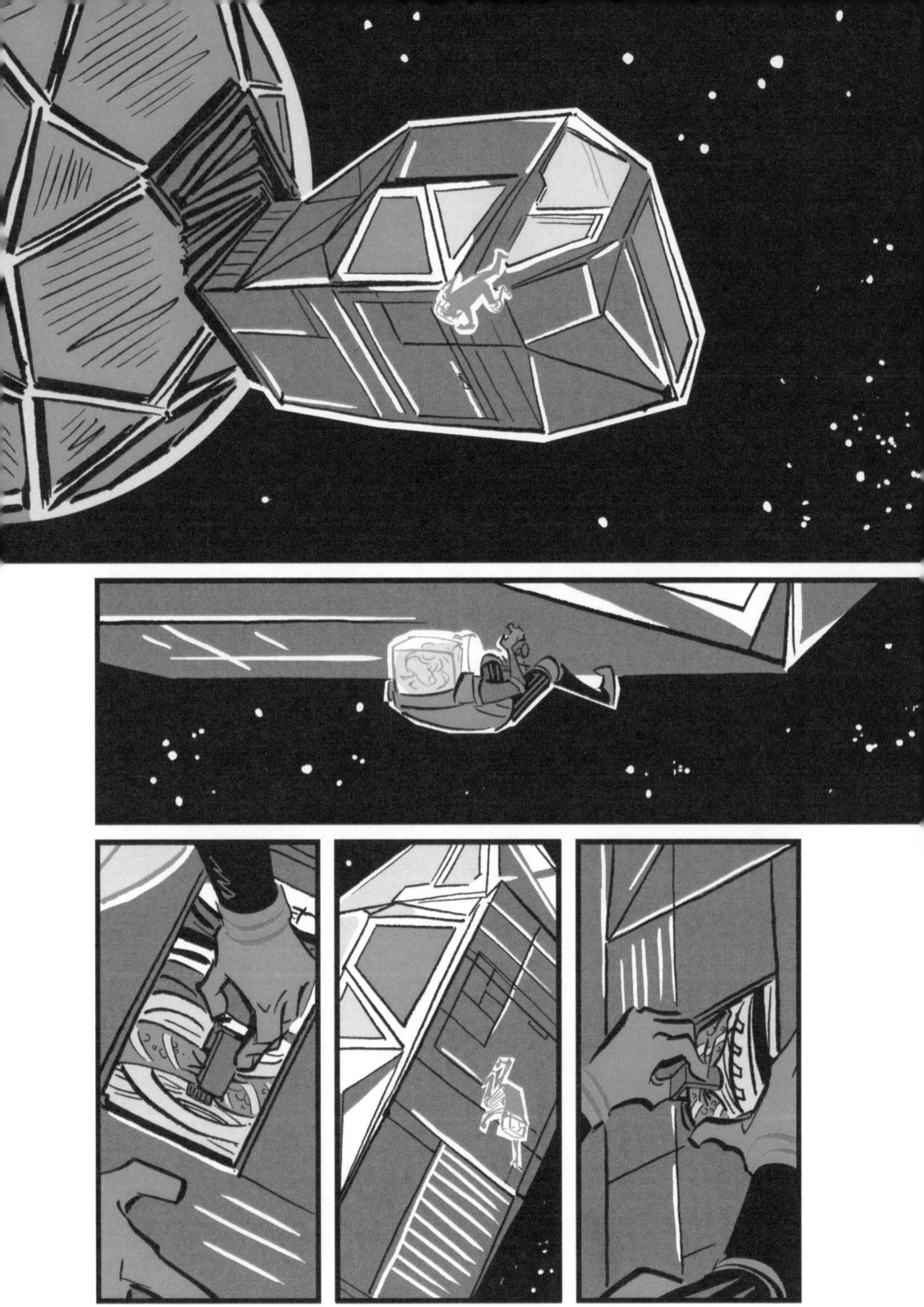

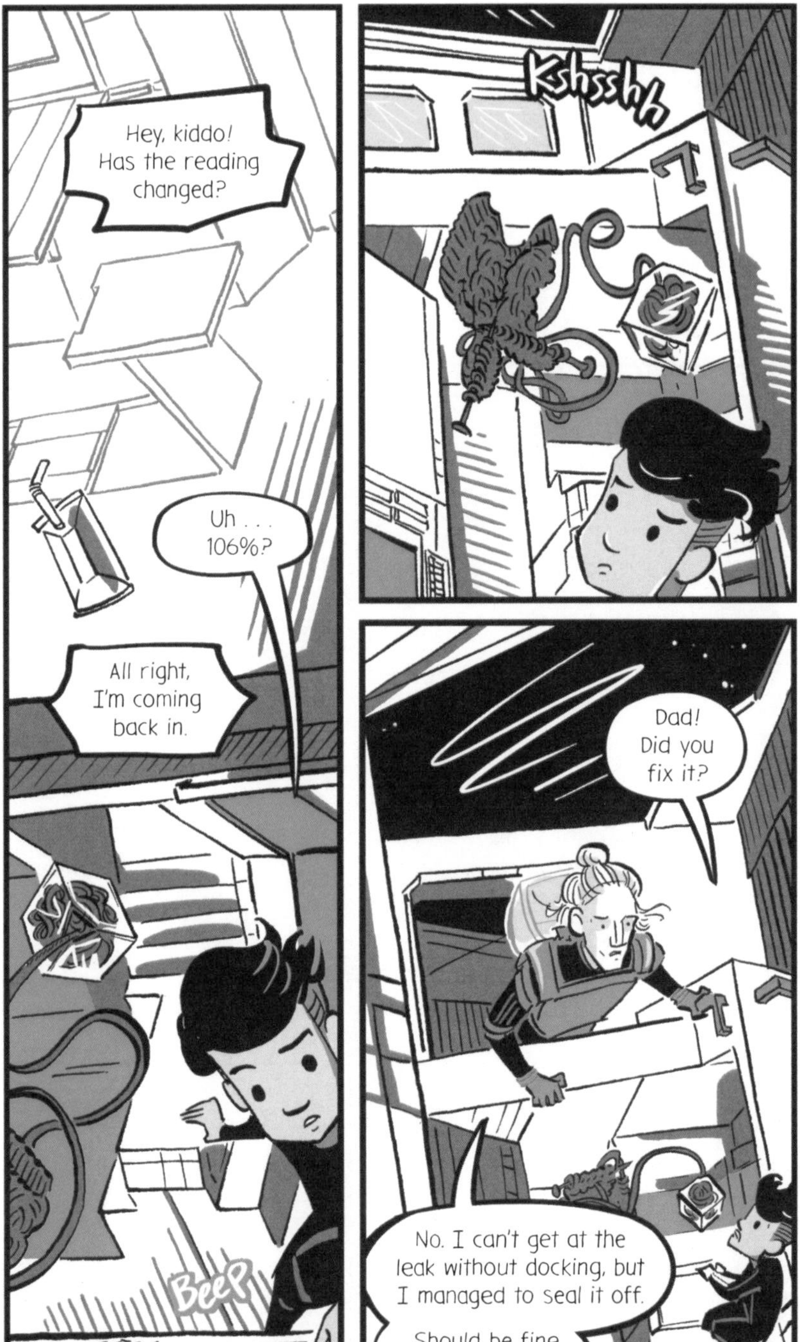
Hey, kiddo! Has the reading changed?
Uh . . . 106%?
All right, I'm coming back in.
Beep
Kshssshh
Dad! Did you fix it?
No. I can't get at the leak without docking, but I managed to seal it off.
Should be fine, short-term.

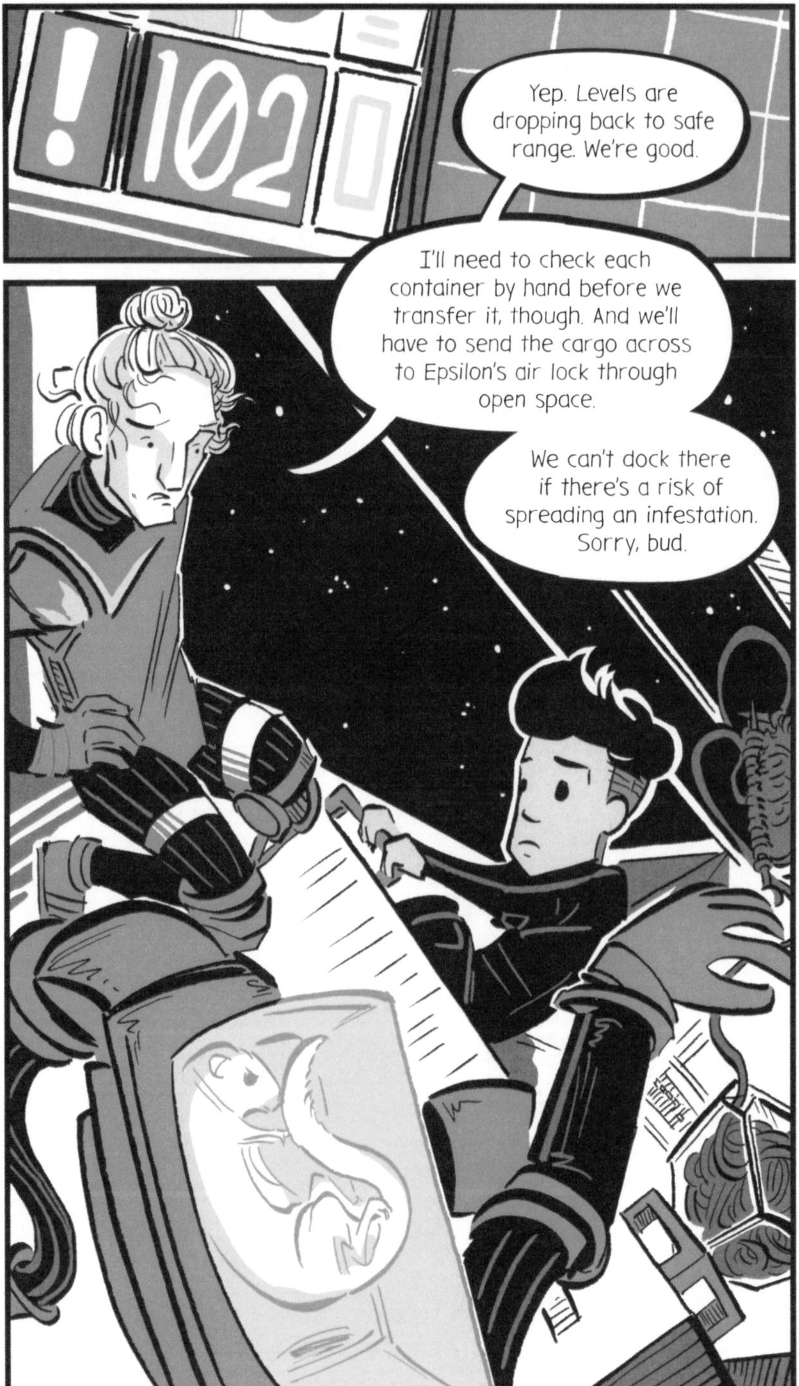
102
Yep. Levels are dropping back to safe range. We're good.
I'll need to check each container by hand before we transfer it, though. And we'll have to send the cargo across to Epsilon's air lock through open space.
We can't dock there if there's a risk of spreading an infestation. Sorry, bud.

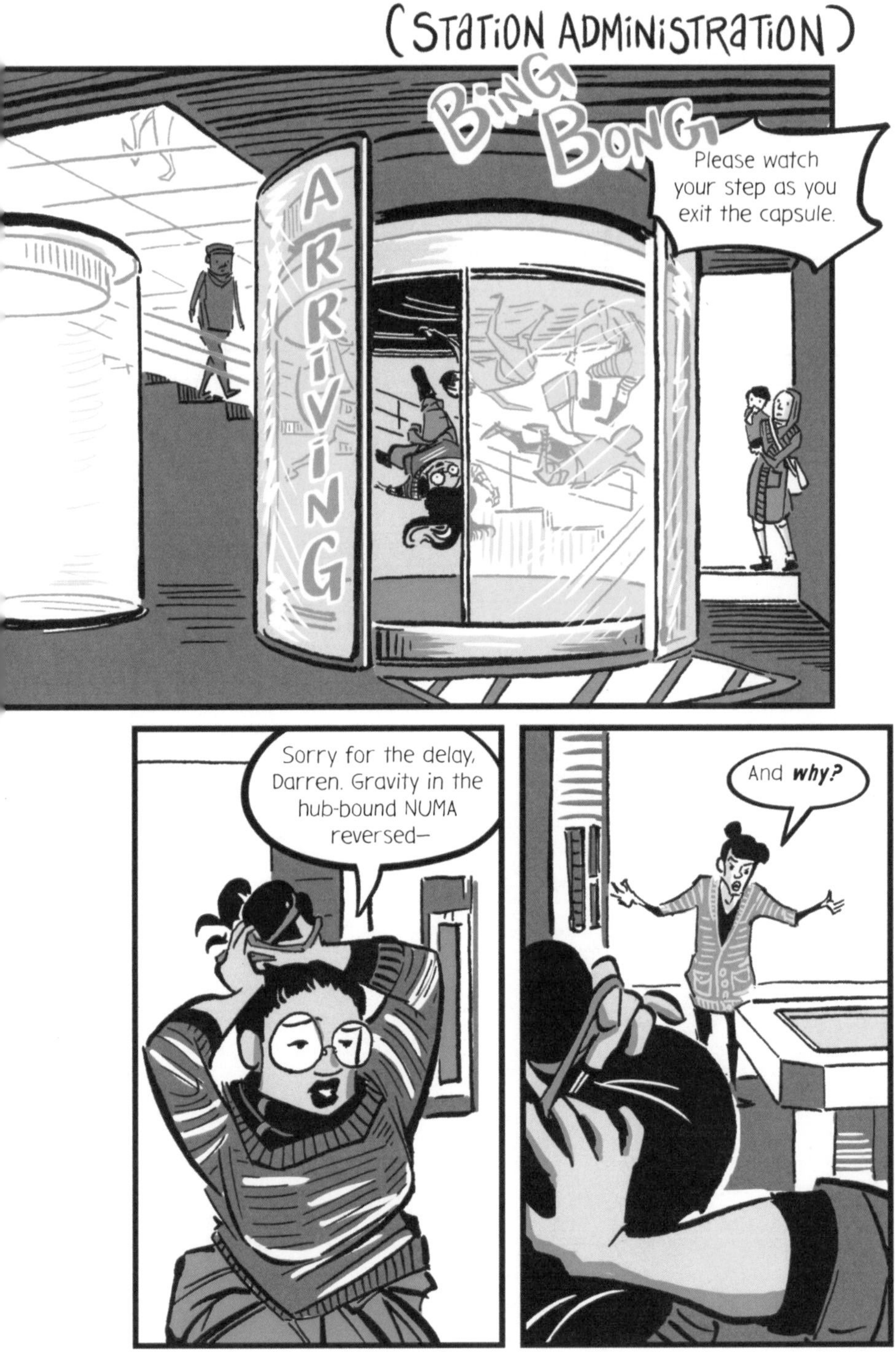
(STATION ADMINISTRATION)
BING BONG
ARRIVING
Please watch your step as you exit the capsule.
Sorry for the delay, Darren. Gravity in the hub-bound NUMA reversed—
And **why?**

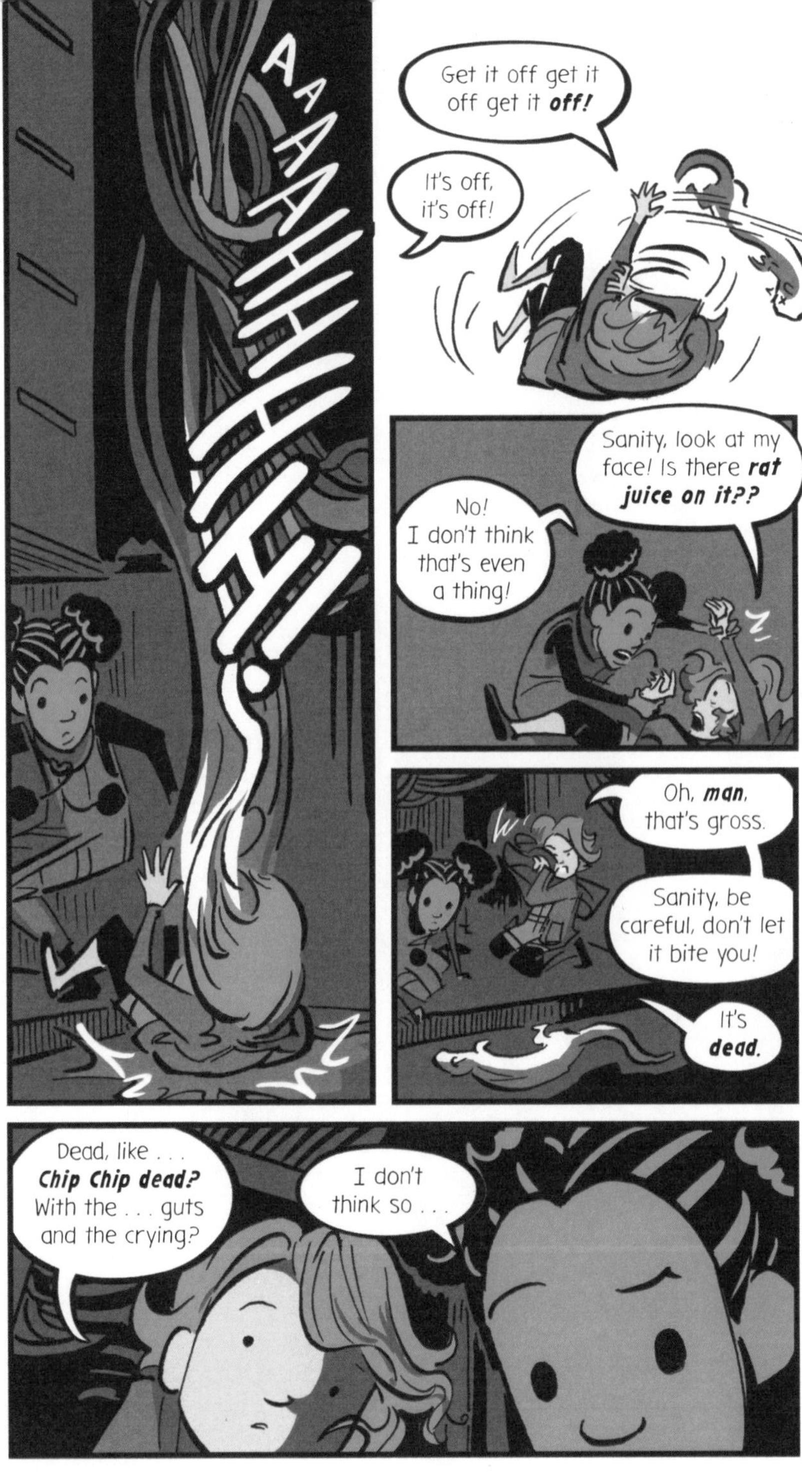

AAAAAHHHHHHHHH!
Get it off get it off get it **off!**
It's off, it's off!
Sanity, look at my face! Is there **rat juice on it??**
No! I don't think that's even a thing!
Oh, **man,** that's gross.
Sanity, be careful, don't let it bite you!
It's **dead.**
Dead, like . . . ***Chip Chip dead?*** With the . . . guts and the crying?
I don't think so . . .

(EPSILON STATION)

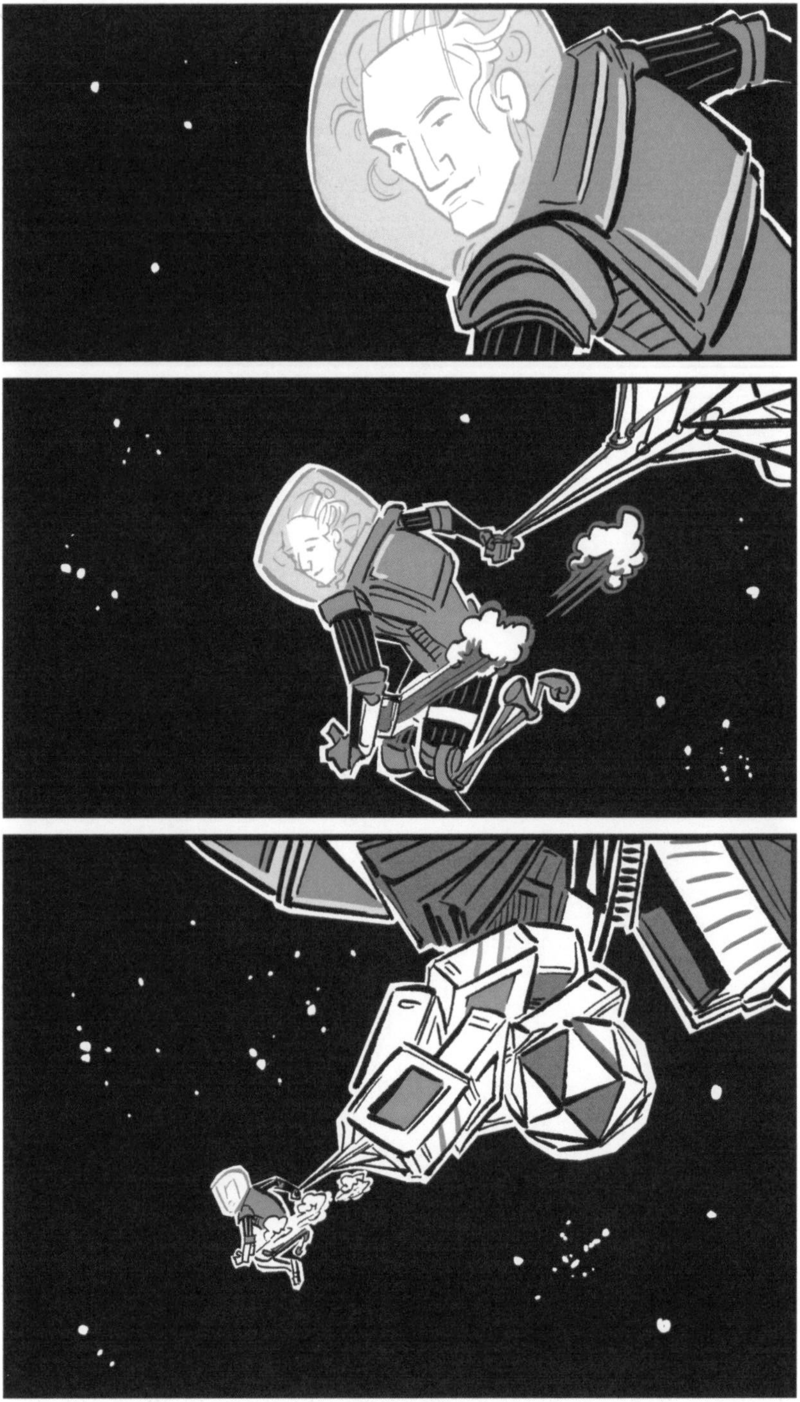

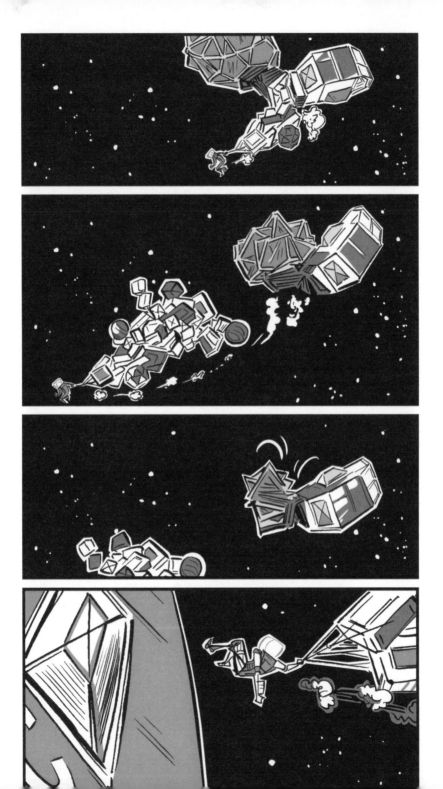

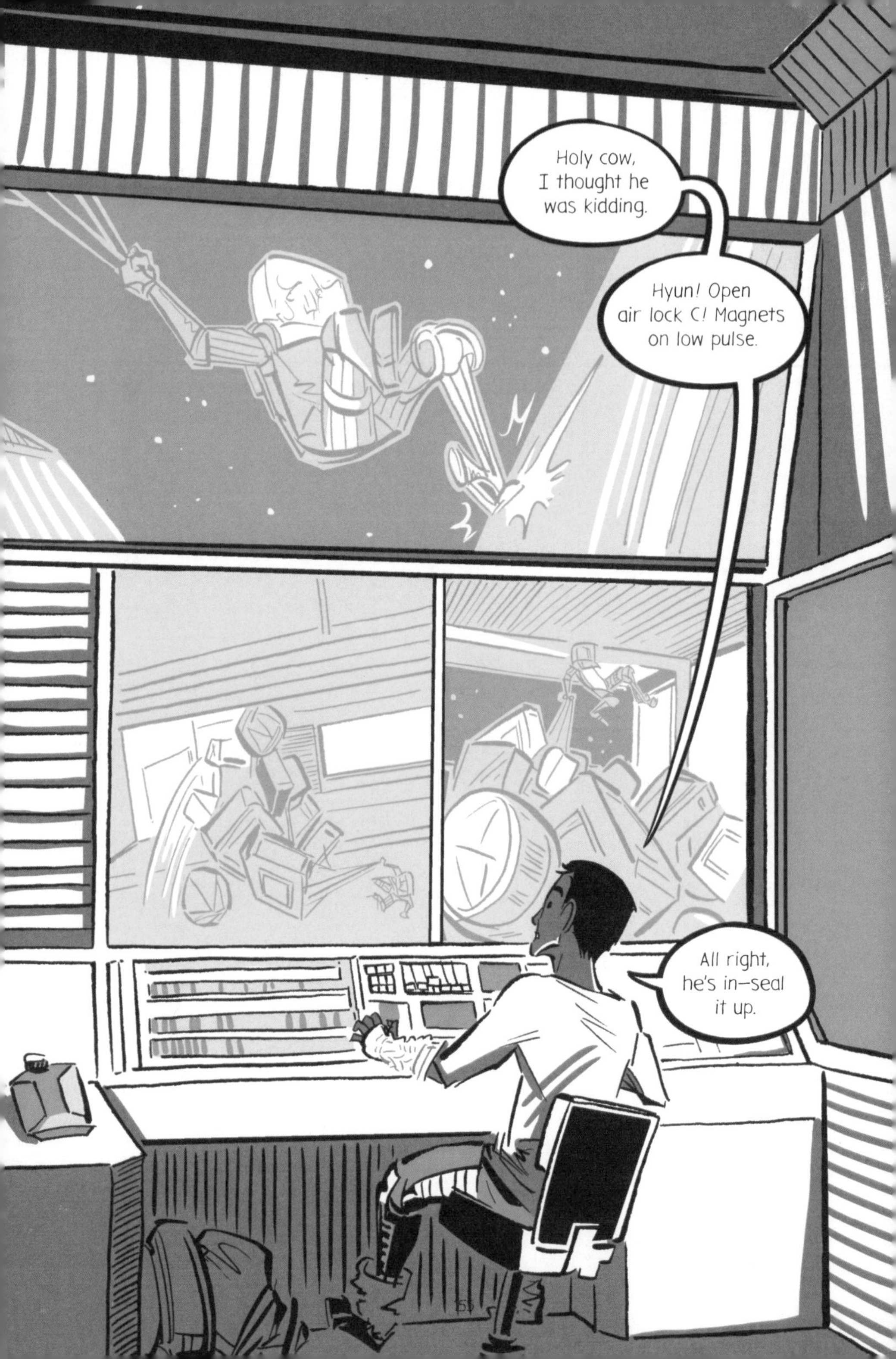
Holy cow, I thought he was kidding.
Hyun! Open air lock C! Magnets on low pulse.
All right, he's in—seal it up.

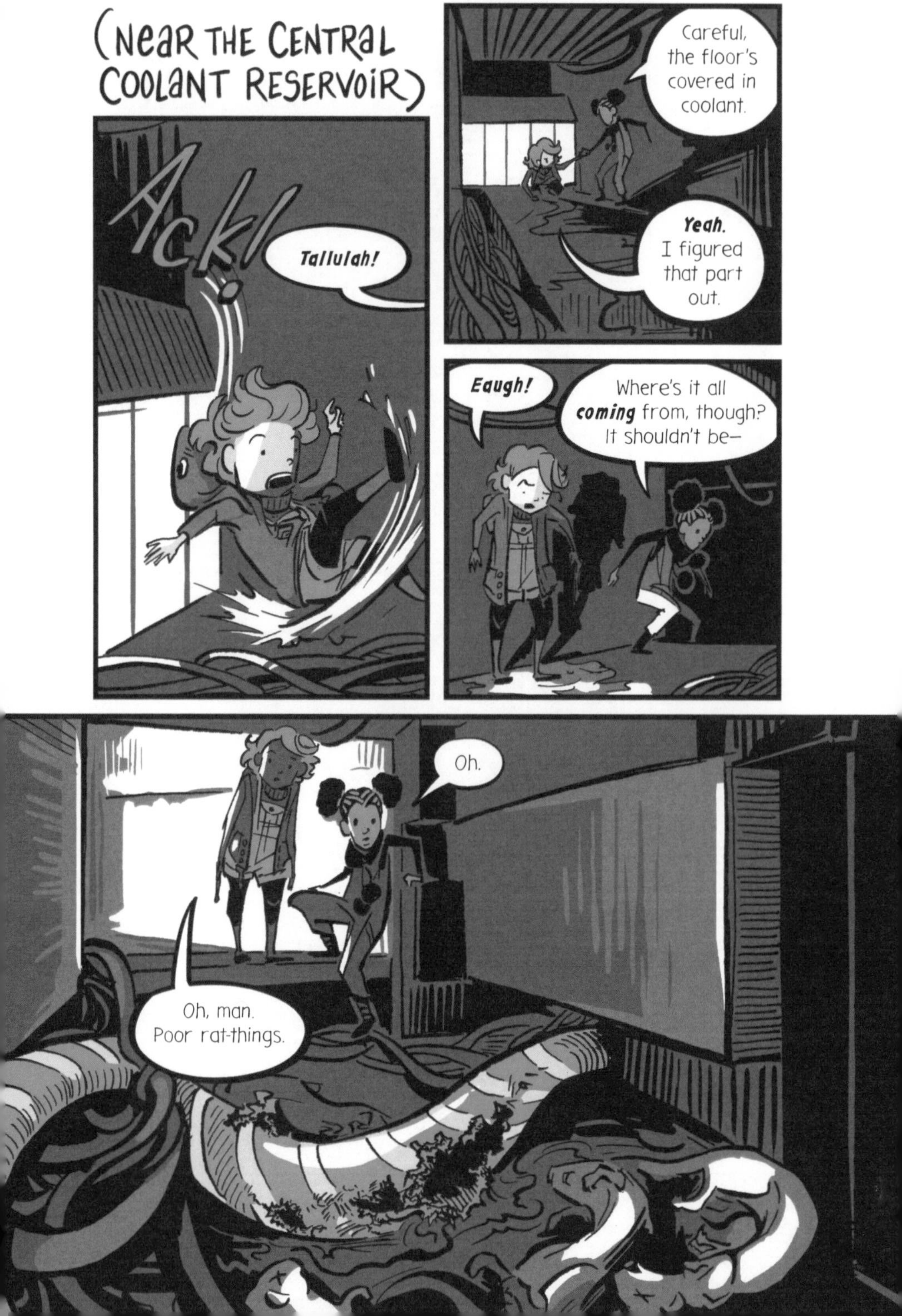
(NEAR THE CENTRAL COOLANT RESERVOIR)
ACK!
Tallulah!
Careful, the floor's covered in coolant.
Yeah. I figured that part out.
Eaugh!
Where's it all coming from, though? It shouldn't be—
Oh.
Oh, man. Poor rat-things.

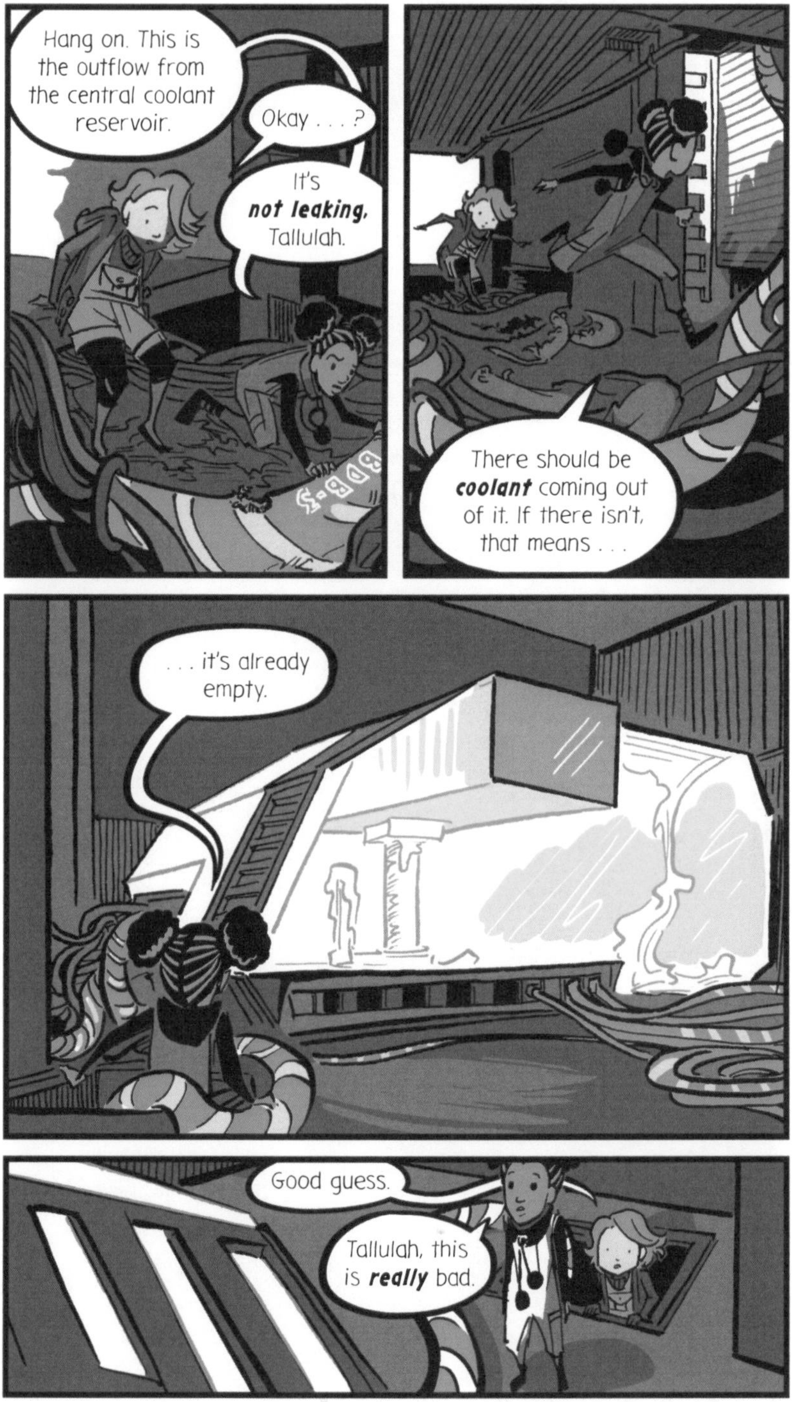
Hang on. This is the outflow from the central coolant reservoir.
Okay . . . ?
It's **not leaking,** Tallulah.
BDB-3
There should be **coolant** coming out of it. If there isn't, that means . . .
. . . it's already empty.
Good guess.
Tallulah, this is **really** bad.

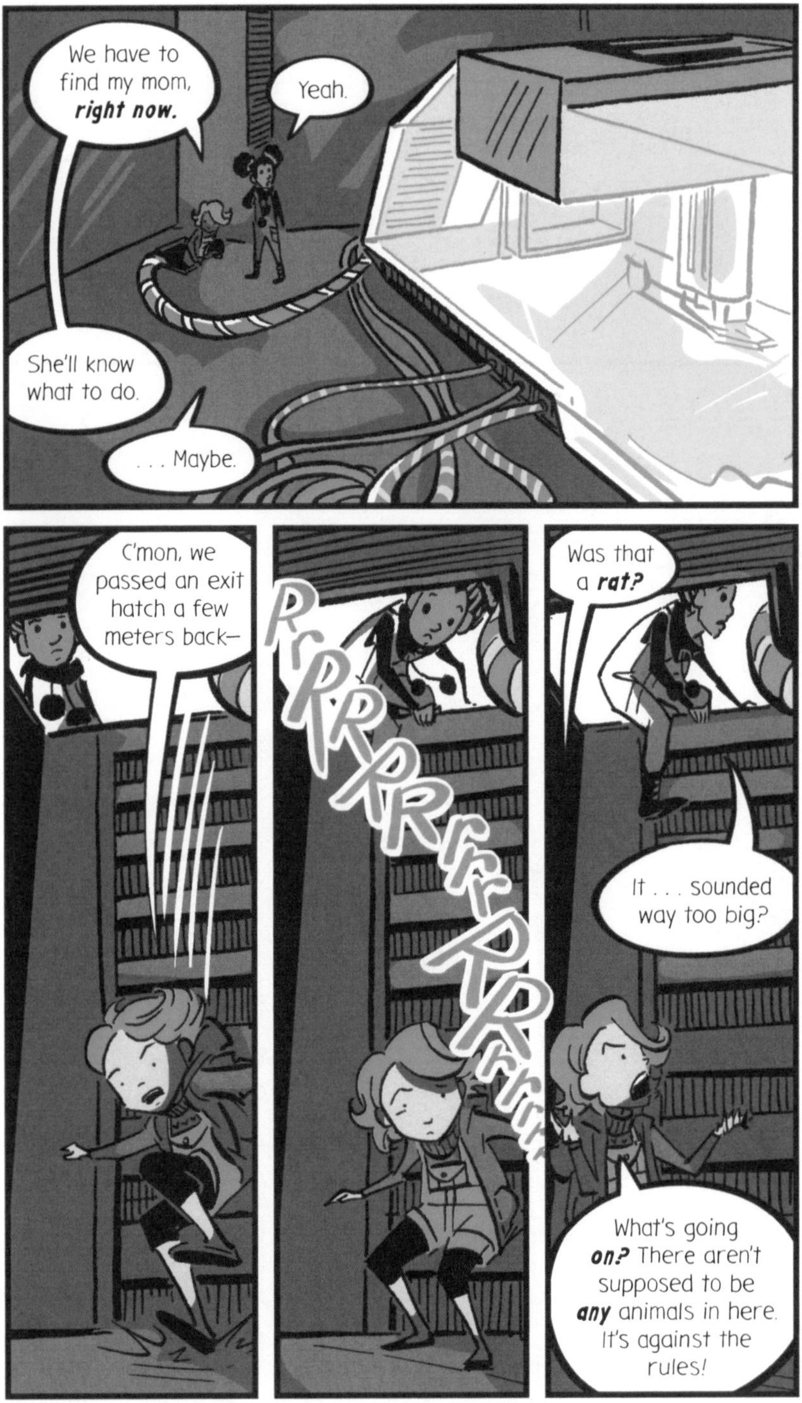
We have to find my mom, **right now.**
Yeah.
She'll know what to do.
. . . Maybe.
C'mon, we passed an exit hatch a few meters back—
RrRRRRrrrRRRrrrr
Was that a **rat?**
It . . . sounded way too big?
What's going **on?** There aren't supposed to be **any** animals in here. It's against the rules!

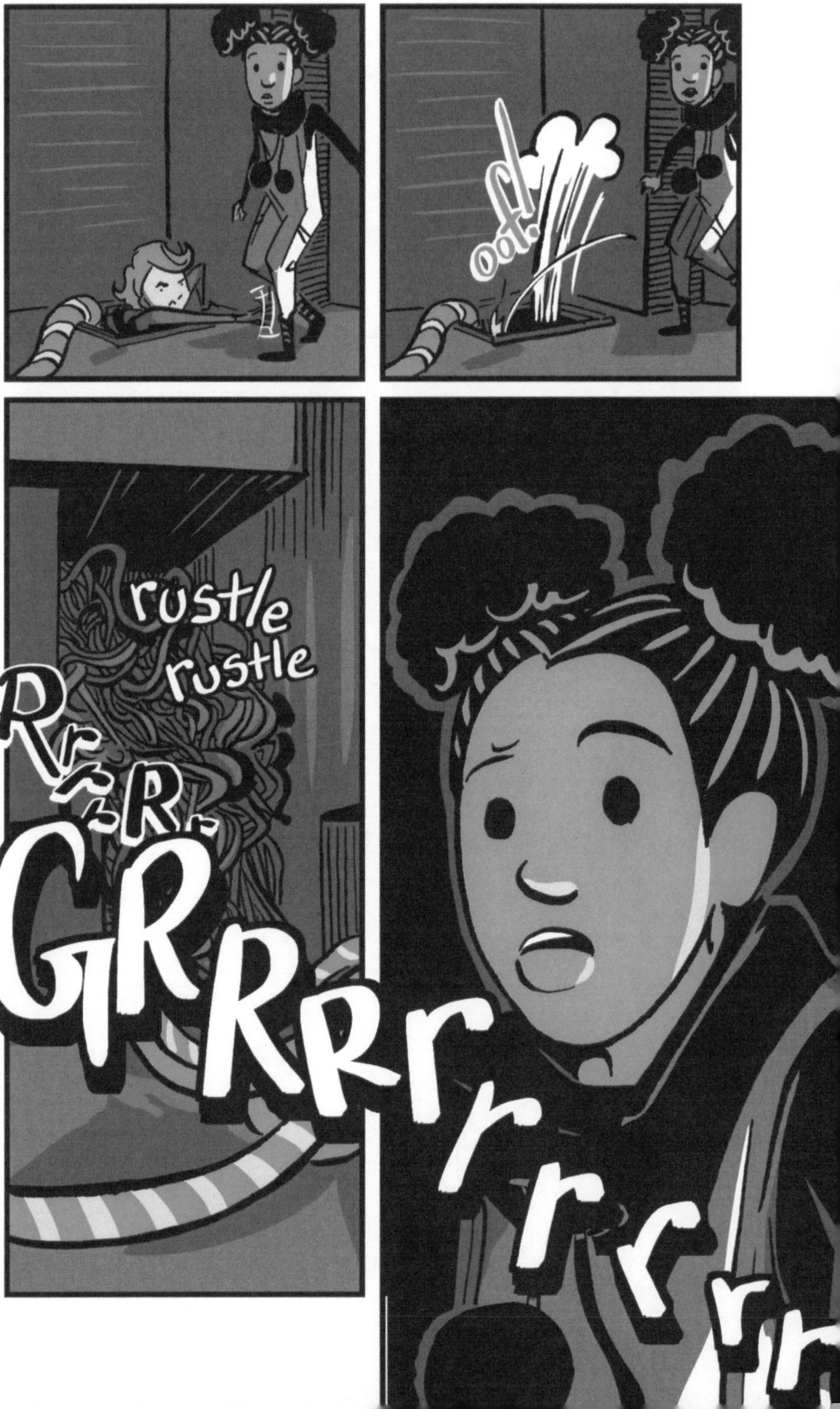
oof!
rustle
rustle
GRRRrrrrr

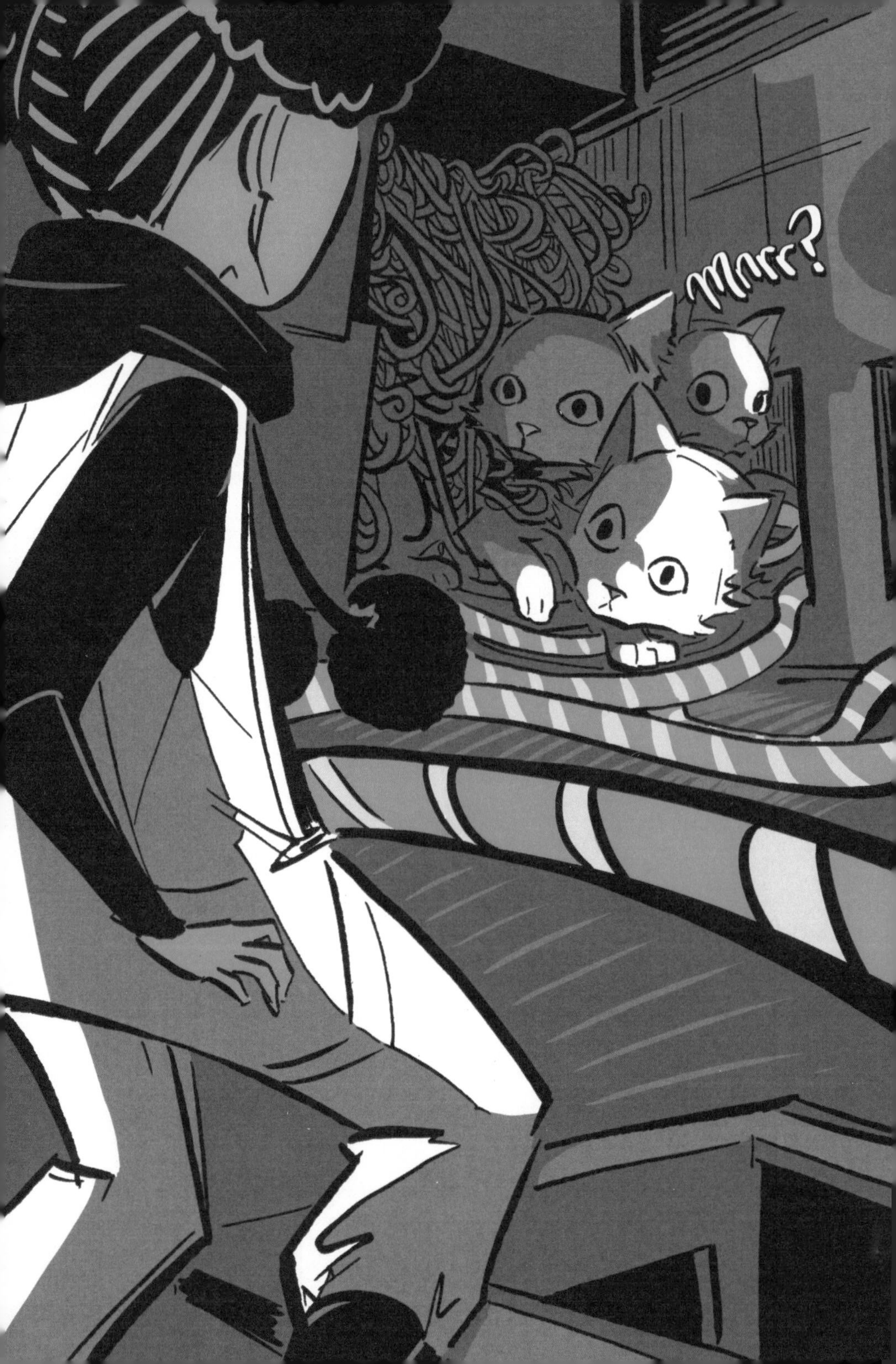
Mrrr?

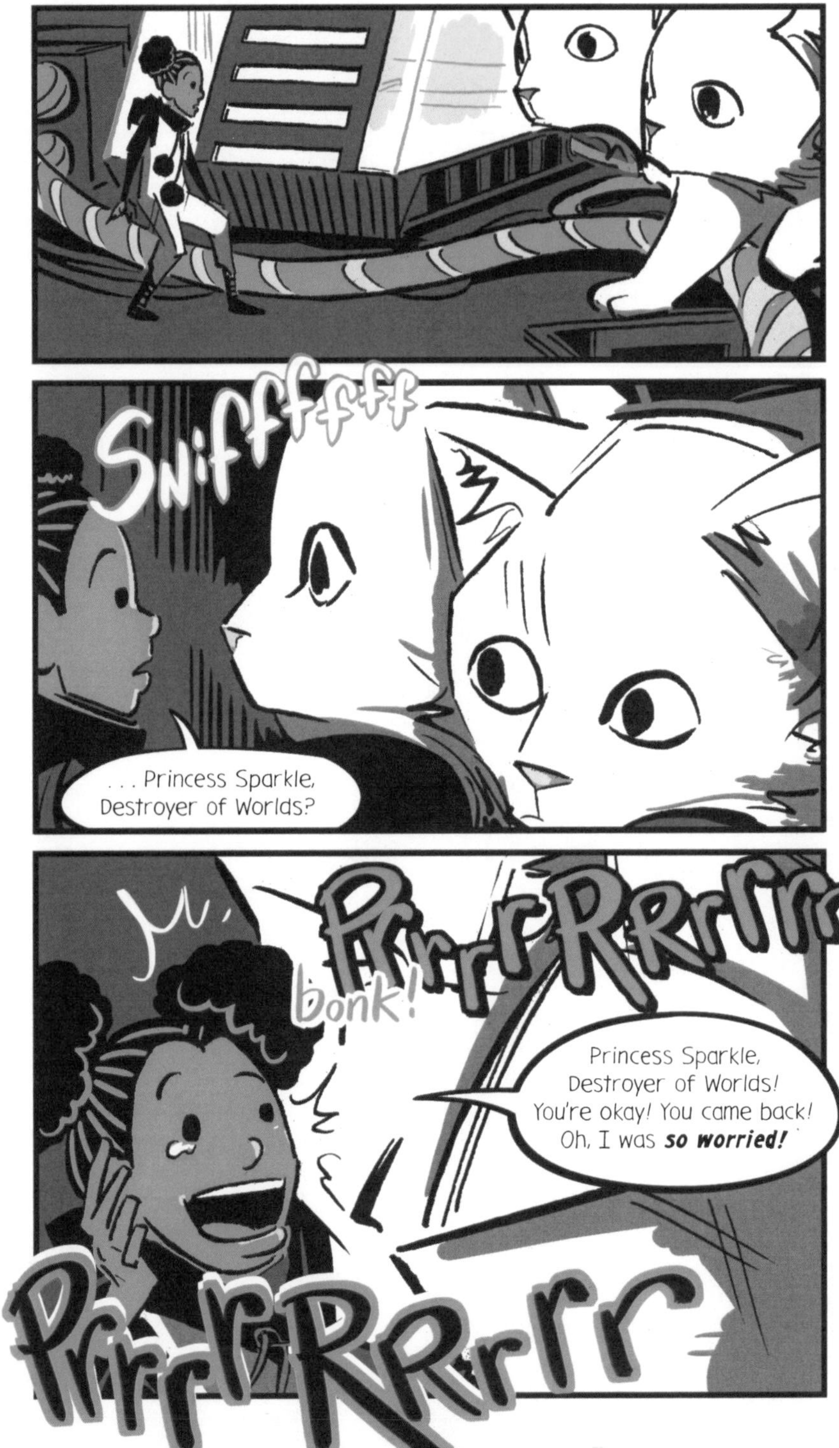
Sniffffff
. . . Princess Sparkle, Destroyer of Worlds?
PrrrrRRrrrr
bonk!
Princess Sparkle, Destroyer of Worlds! You're okay! You came back! Oh, I was **so worried!**
PrrrrRRrrrr

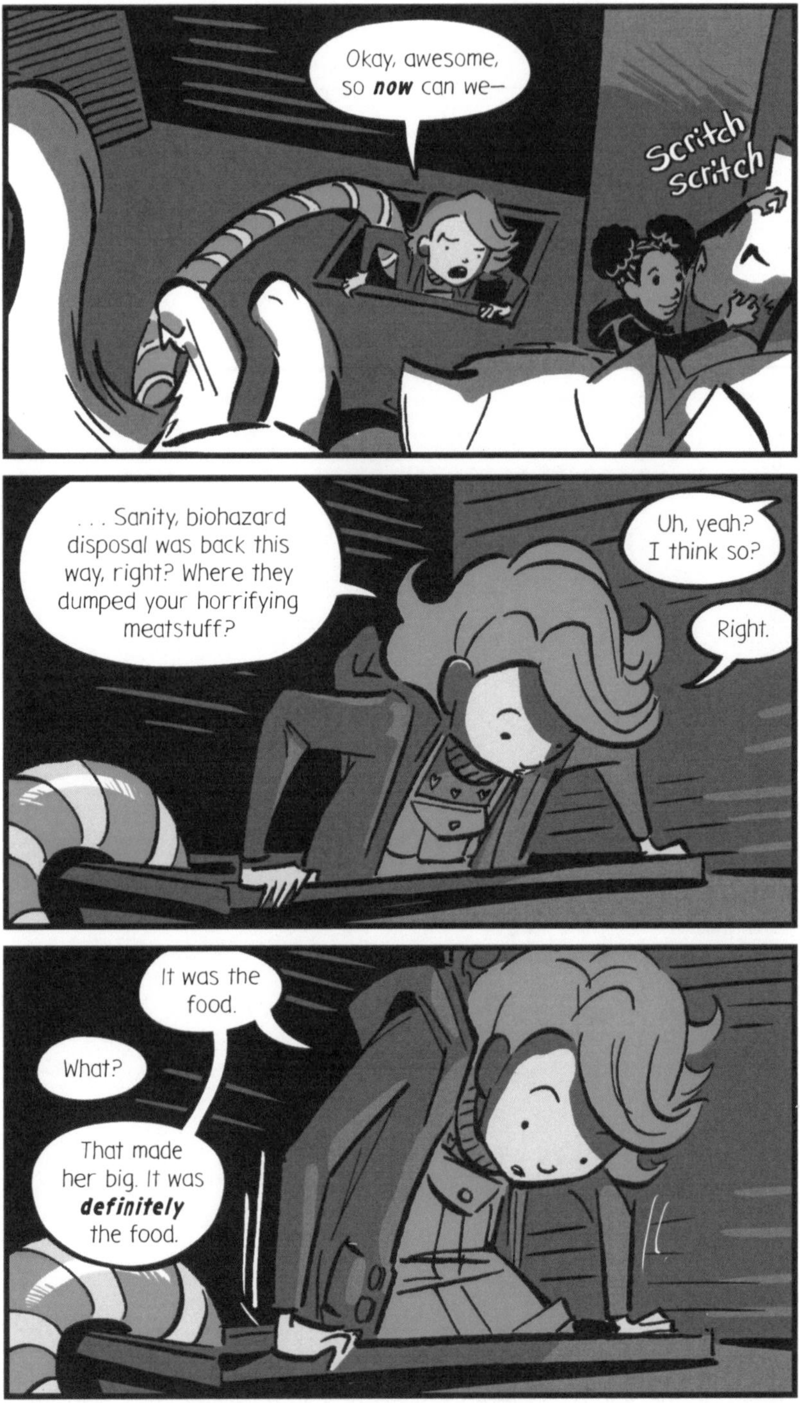
Okay, awesome, so **now** can we–
Scritch scritch
. . . Sanity, biohazard disposal was back this way, right? Where they dumped your horrifying meatstuff?
Uh, yeah? I think so?
Right.
It was the food.
What?
That made her big. It was **definitely** the food.

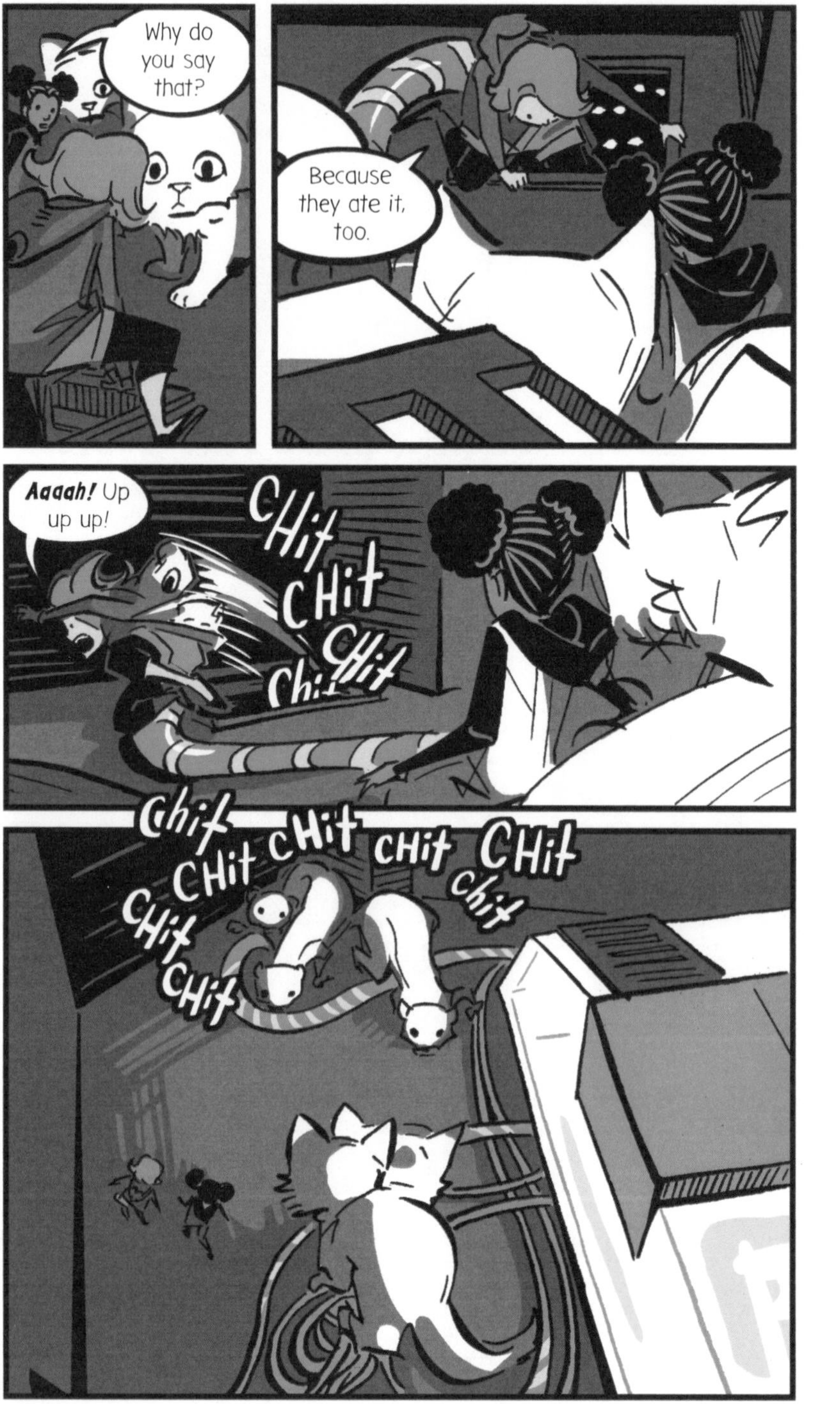
Why do you say that?
Because they ate it, too.
Aaaah! Up up up!
CHit CHit CHit Chit
Chit CHit cHit cHit CHit chit
CHit CHit

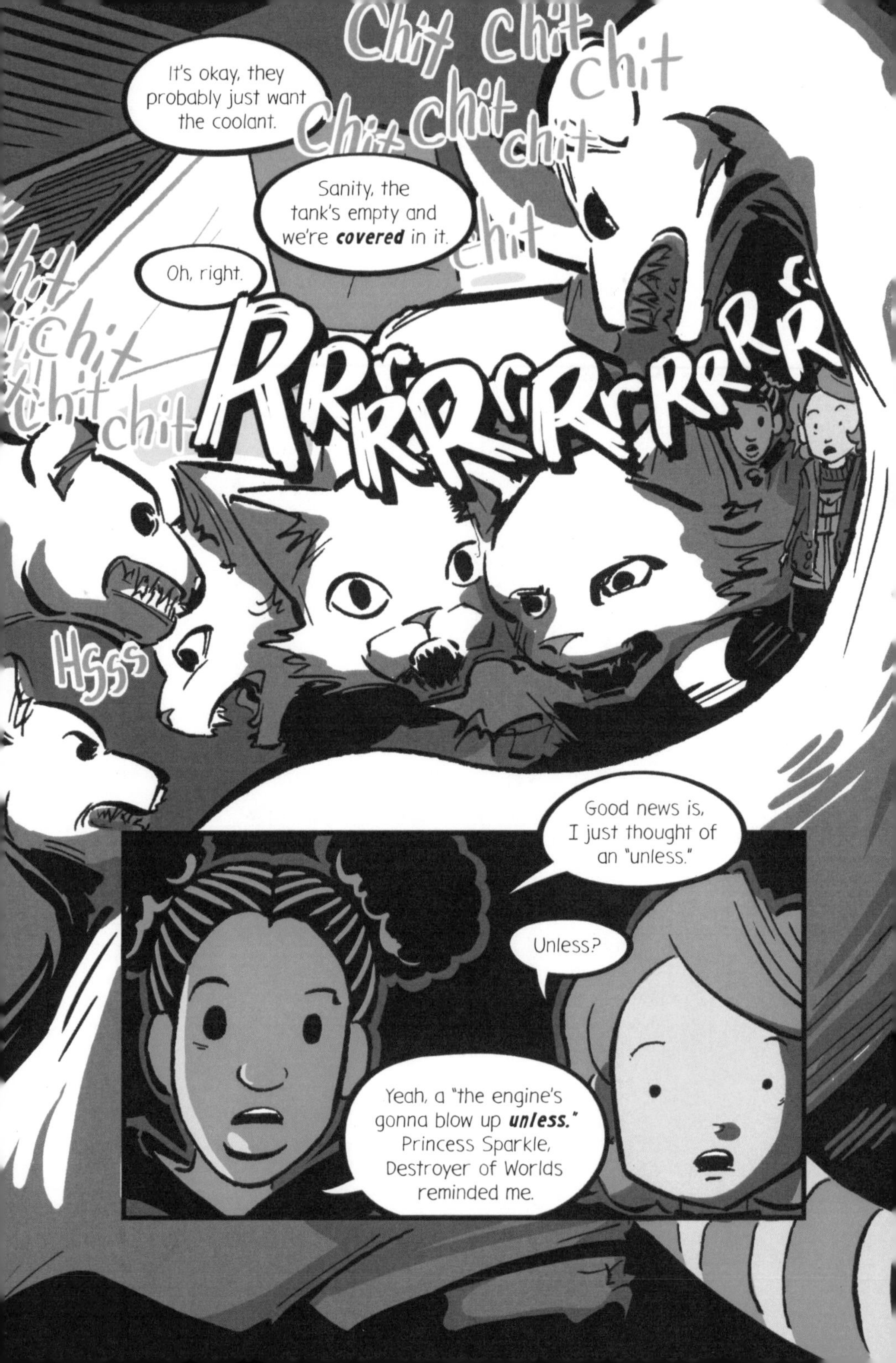
Chit chit chit
It's okay, they probably just want the coolant.
Chit chit chit
Sanity, the tank's empty and we're **covered** in it.
chit
Oh, right.
chit chit chit chit
RRRRRRRRRRRR
Hsss
Good news is, I just thought of an "unless."
Unless?
Yeah, a "the engine's gonna blow up **unless.**" Princess Sparkle, Destroyer of Worlds reminded me.

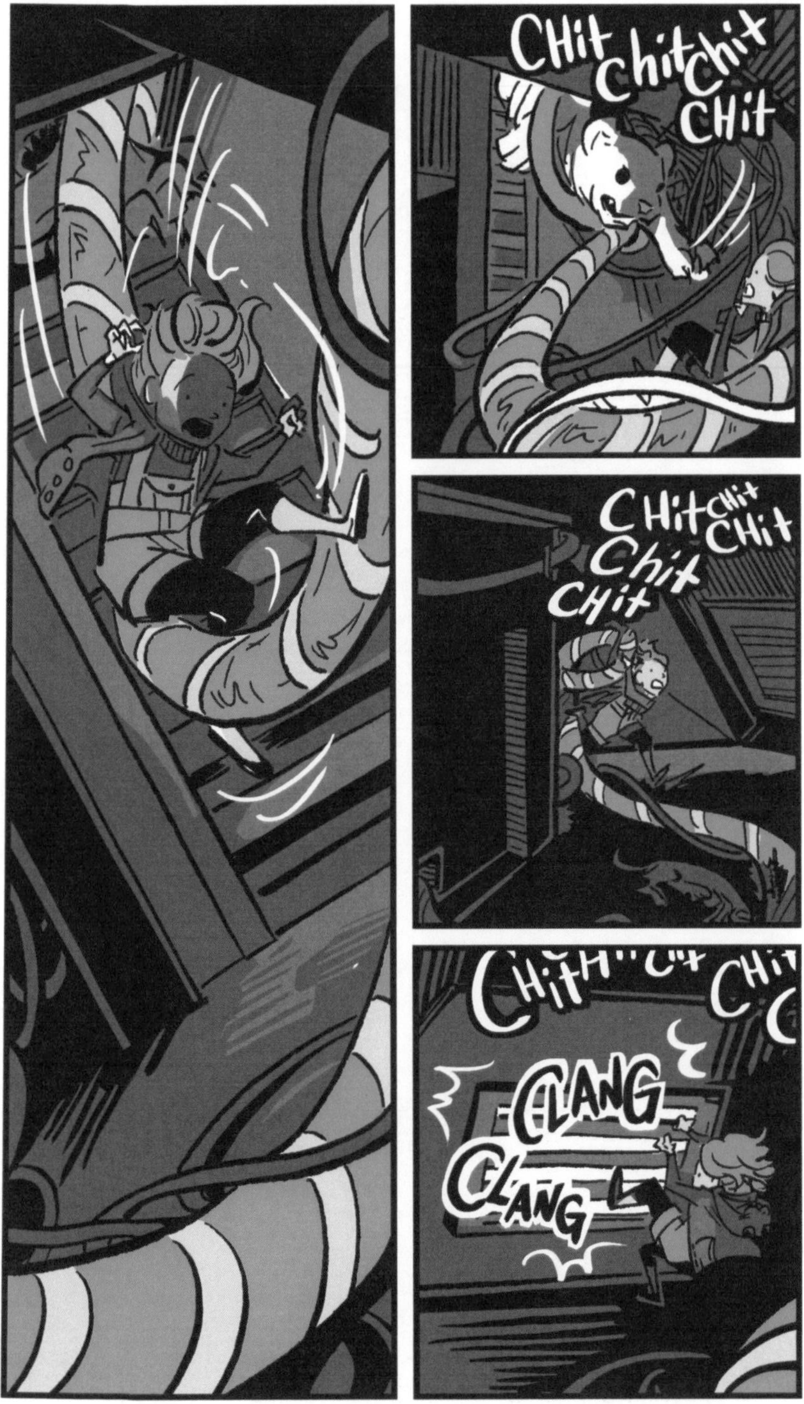
CHIT chitchit CHIT
CHITCHIT CHIT CHIT CHIT
CLANG
CLANG

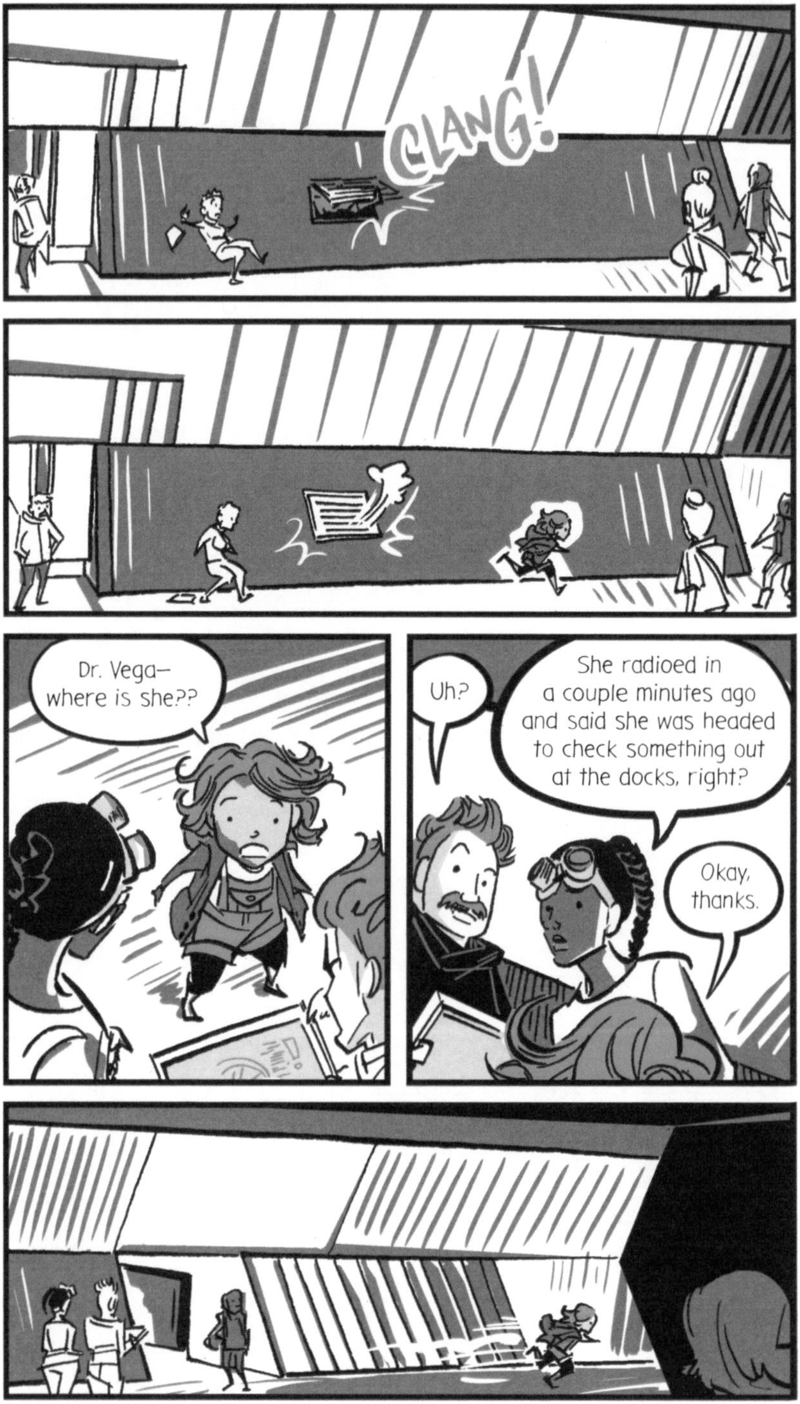
CLANG!
Dr. Vega—where is she??
Uh?
She radioed in a couple minutes ago and said she was headed to check something out at the docks, right?
Okay, thanks.

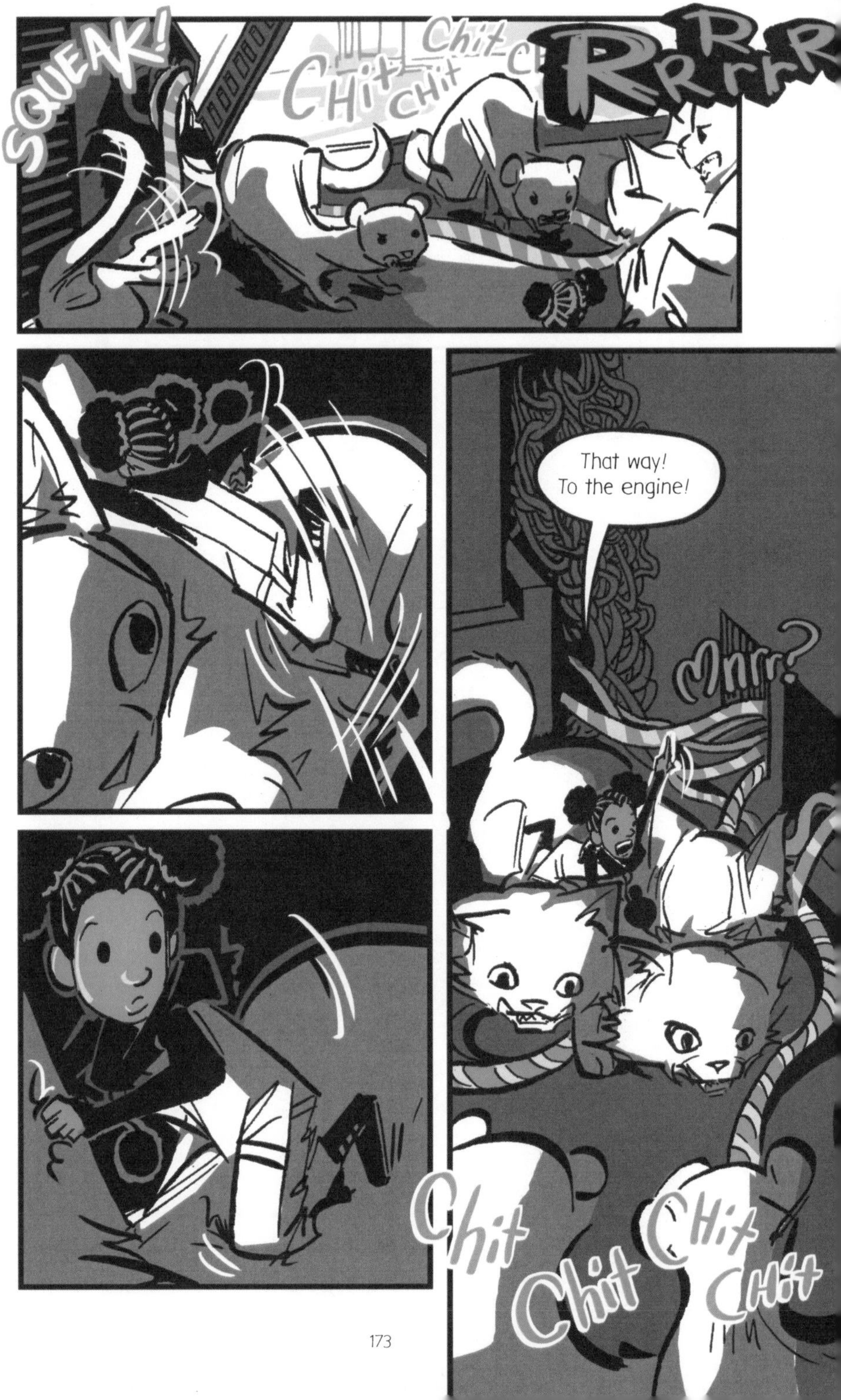
SQUEAK!
Chit Chit
Chit Chit
RRRRrrr
That way!
To the engine!
Mnrr?
Chit
Chit Chit
Chit

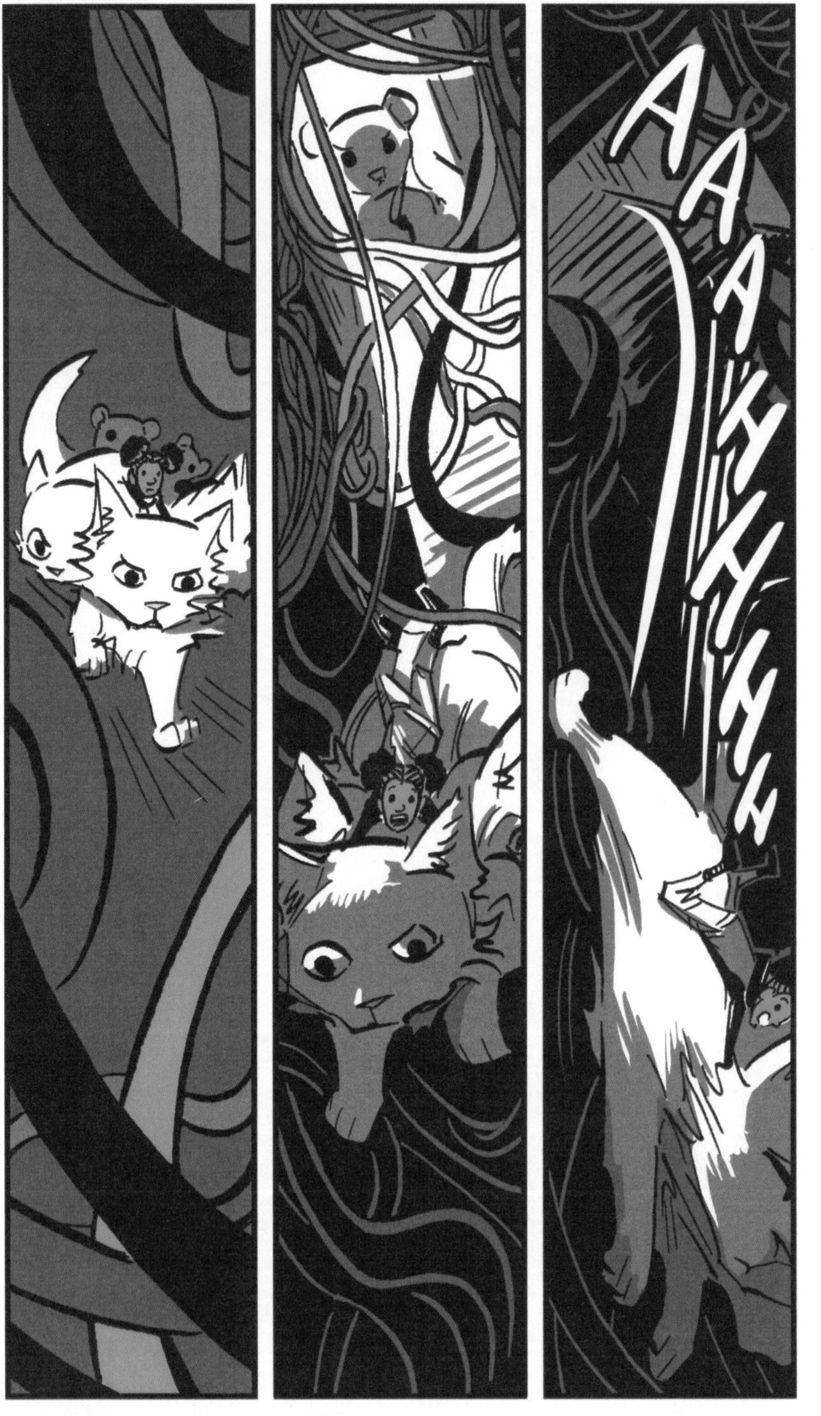
AAAHHHHHH

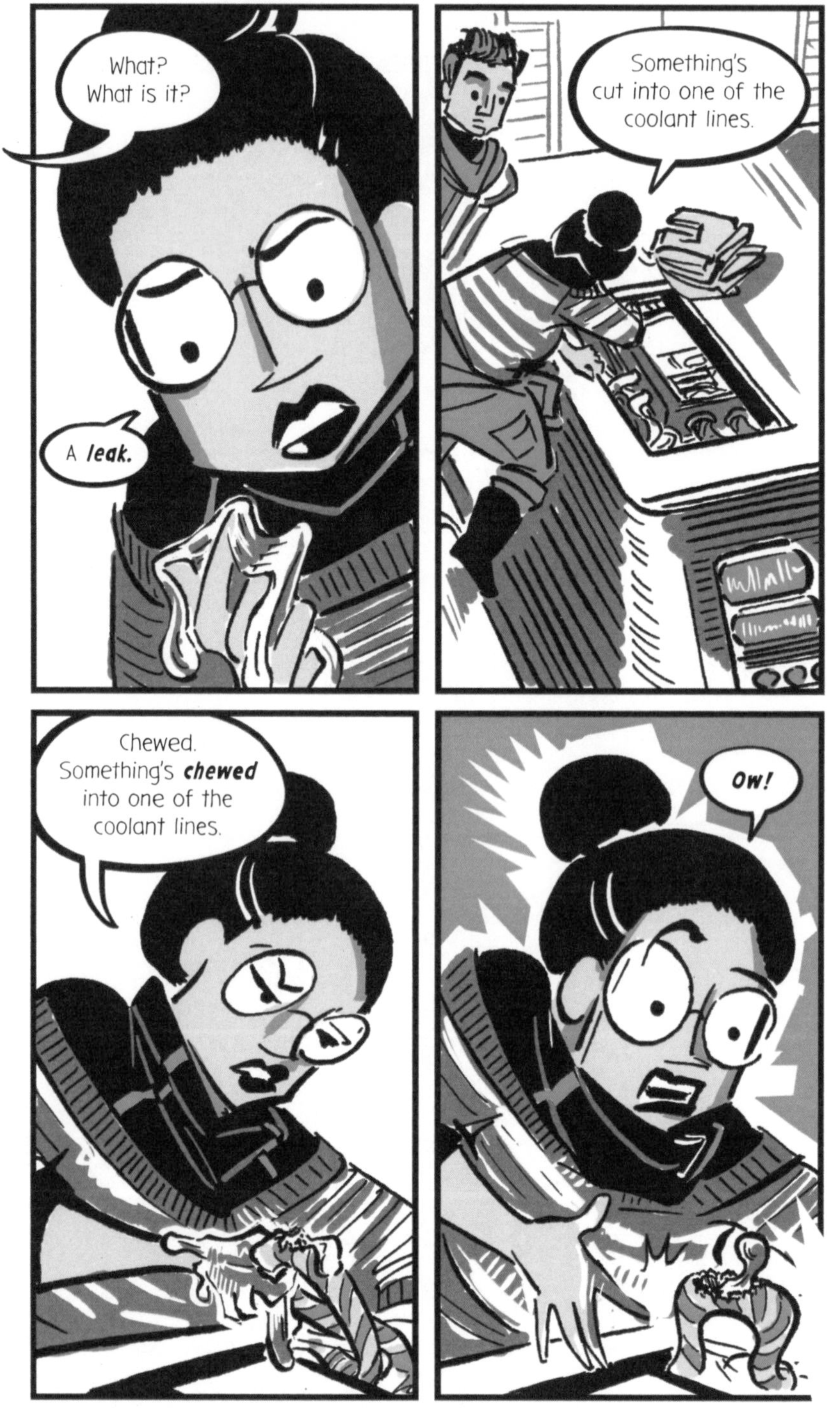
What? What is it?
A leak.
Something's cut into one of the coolant lines.
Chewed. Something's chewed into one of the coolant lines.
Ow!

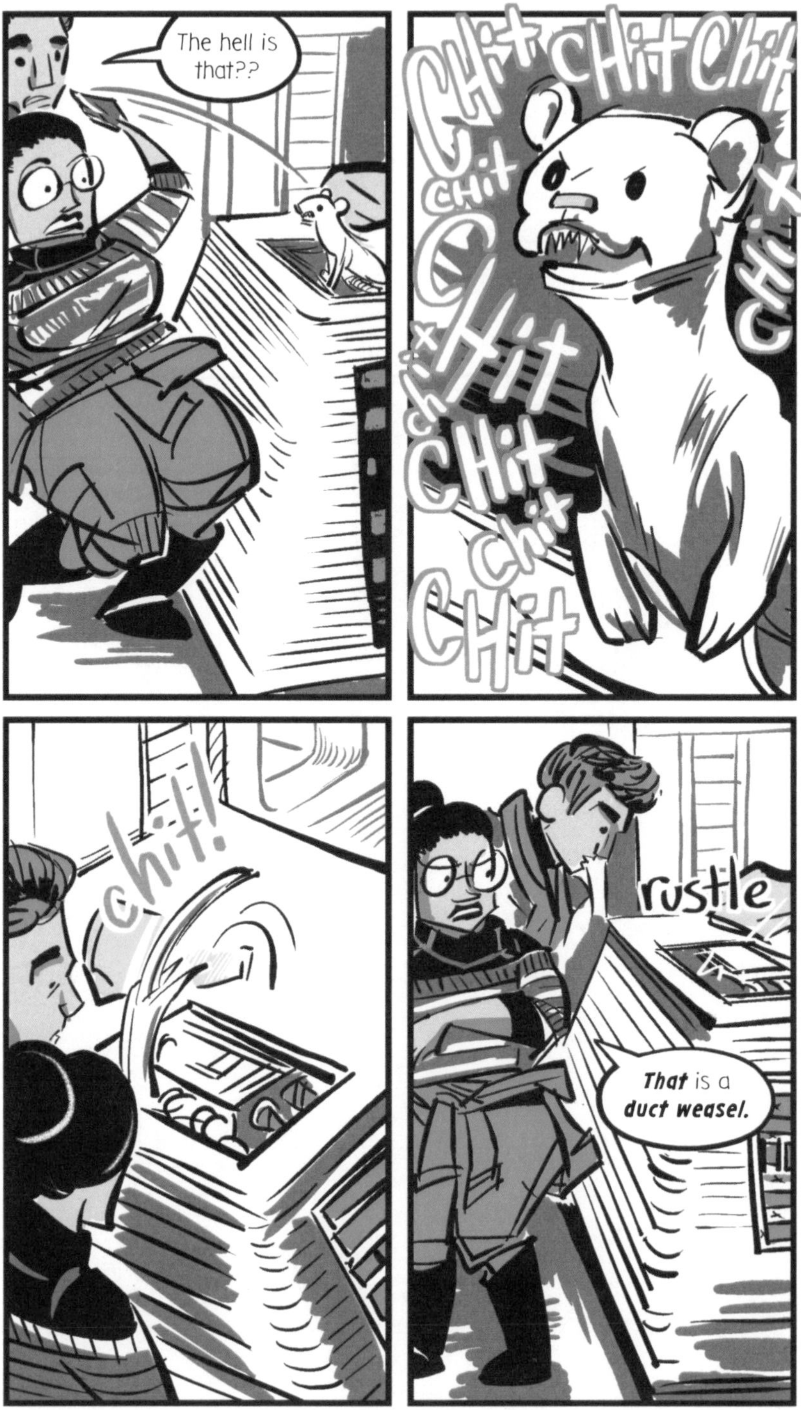
The hell is that??
CHit CHit CHit
Chit
CHit
CHit
Chit
CHit
chit!
rustle
That is a duct weasel.

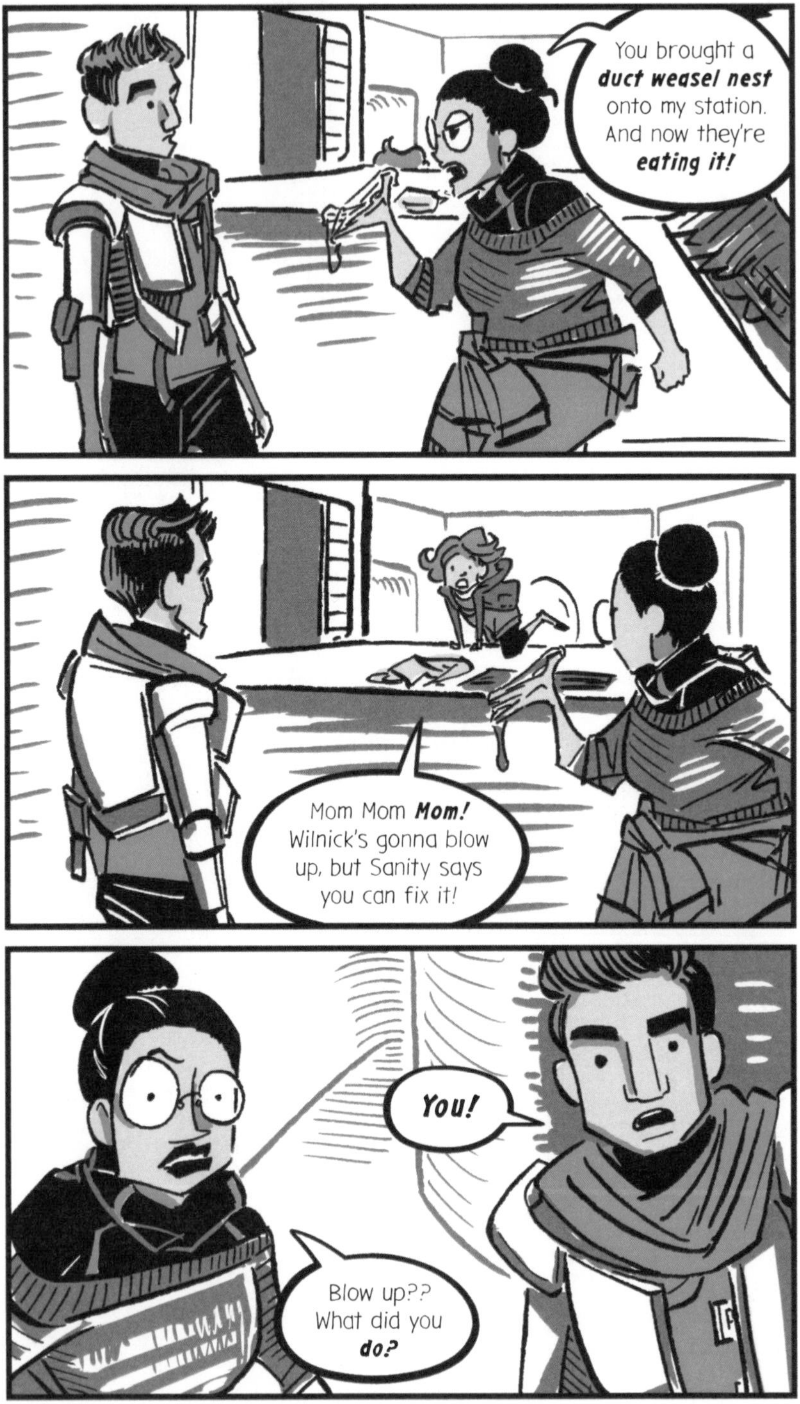
You brought a **duct weasel nest** onto my station. And now they're **eating it!**
Mom Mom **Mom!** Wilnick's gonna blow up, but Sanity says you can fix it!
You!
Blow up?? What did you **do?**

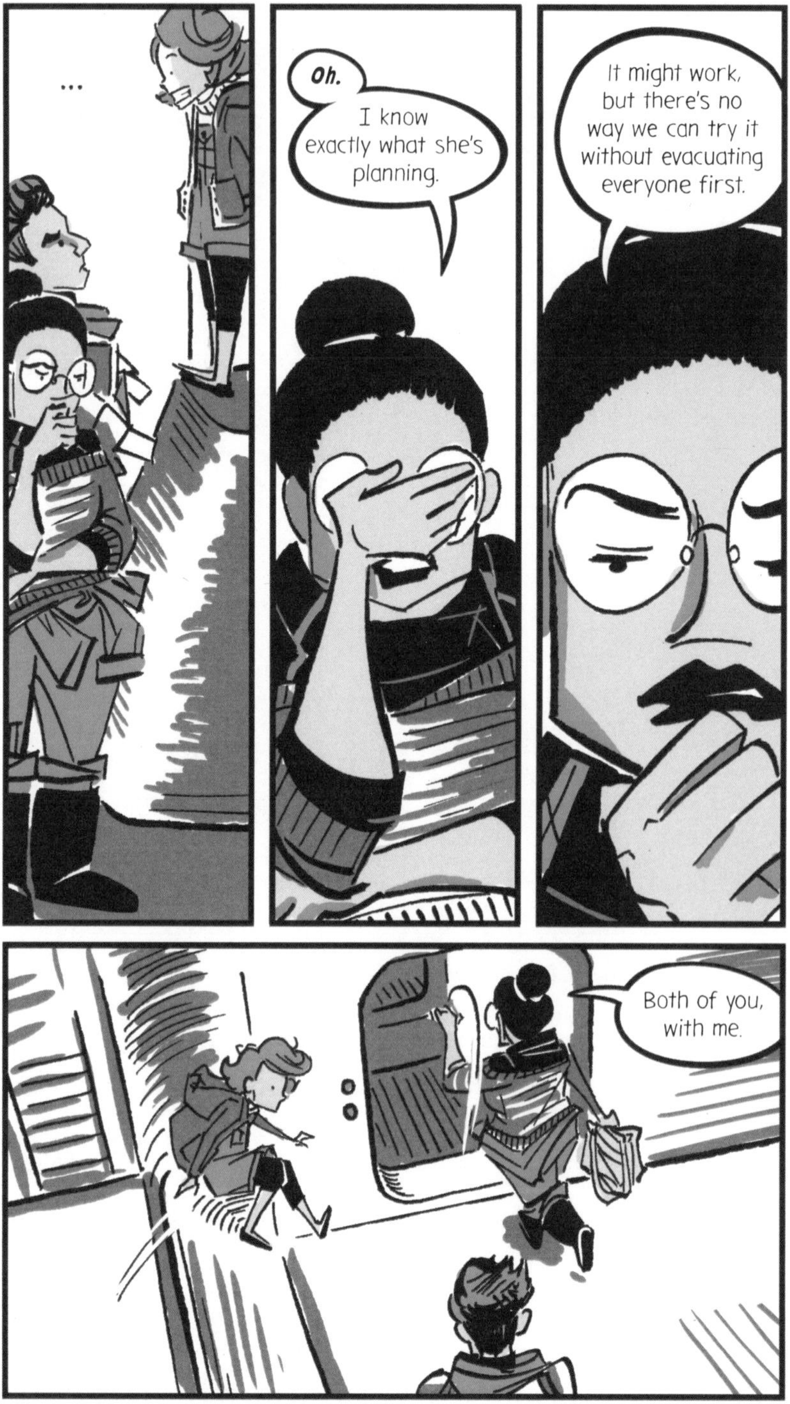
...
Oh.
I know exactly what she's planning.
It might work, but there's no way we can try it without evacuating everyone first.
Both of you, with me.

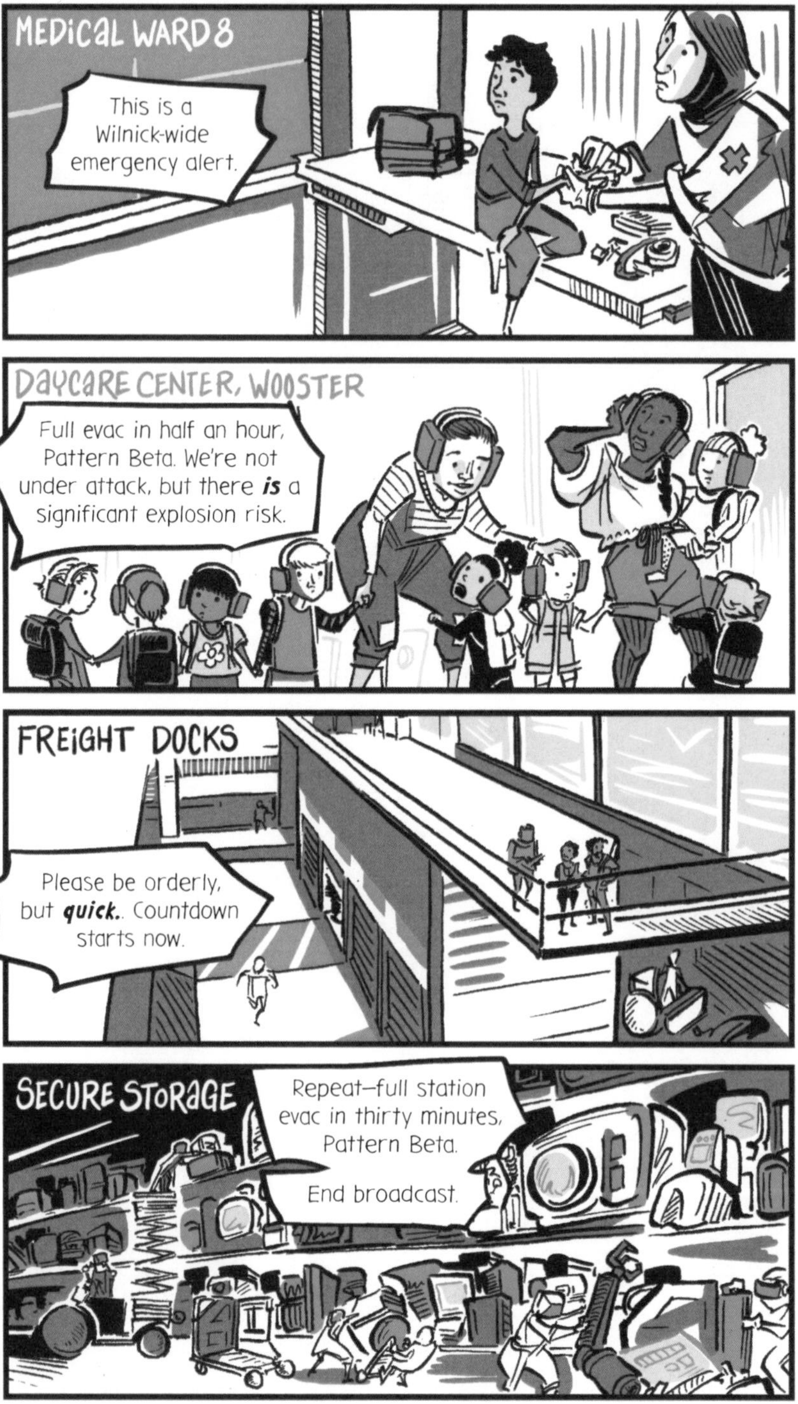
MEDICAL WARD 8
This is a Wilnick-wide emergency alert.
DAYCARE CENTER, WOOSTER
Full evac in half an hour, Pattern Beta. We're not under attack, but there **is** a significant explosion risk.
FREIGHT DOCKS
Please be orderly, but **quick.**. Countdown starts now.
SECURE STORAGE
Repeat—full station evac in thirty minutes, Pattern Beta.
End broadcast.

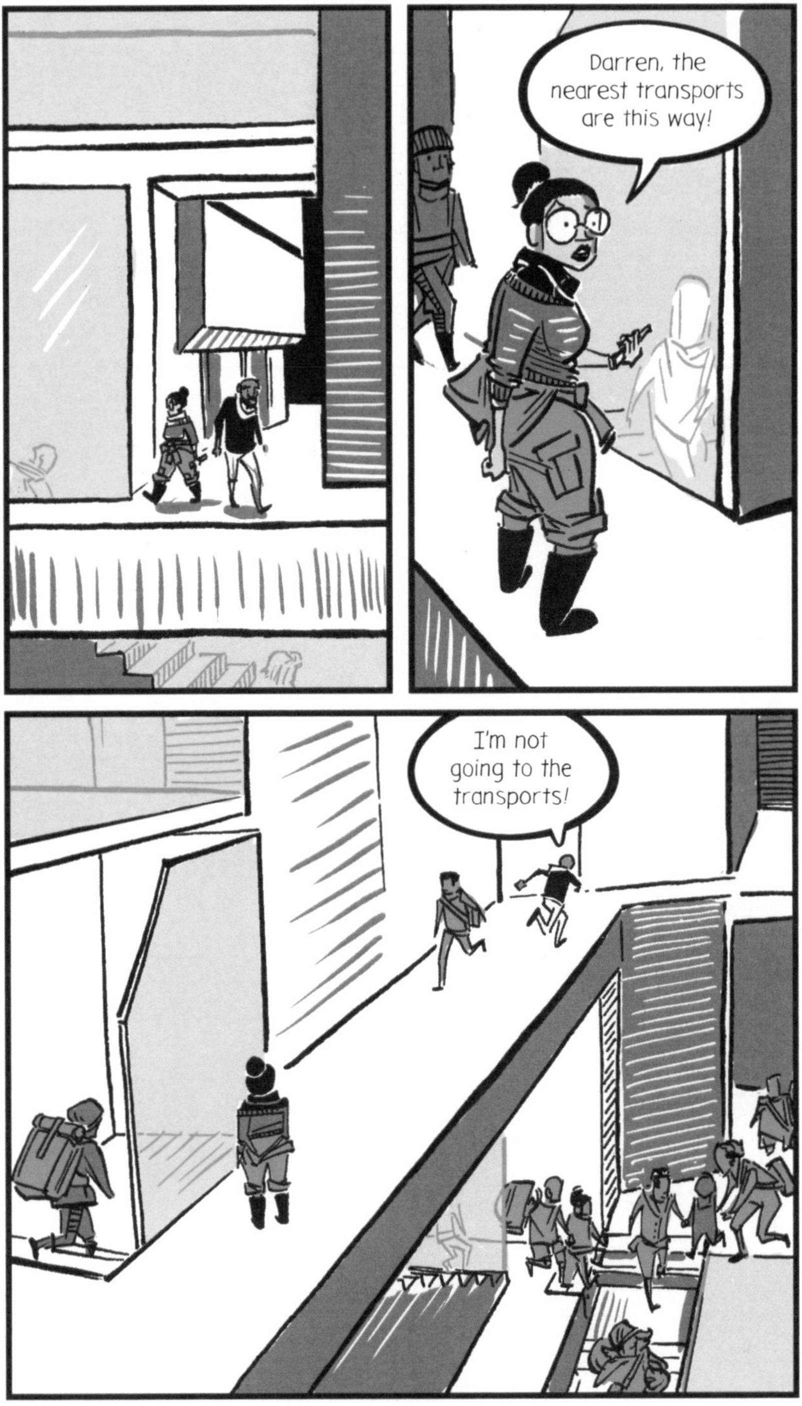
Darren, the nearest transports are this way!
I'm not going to the transports!

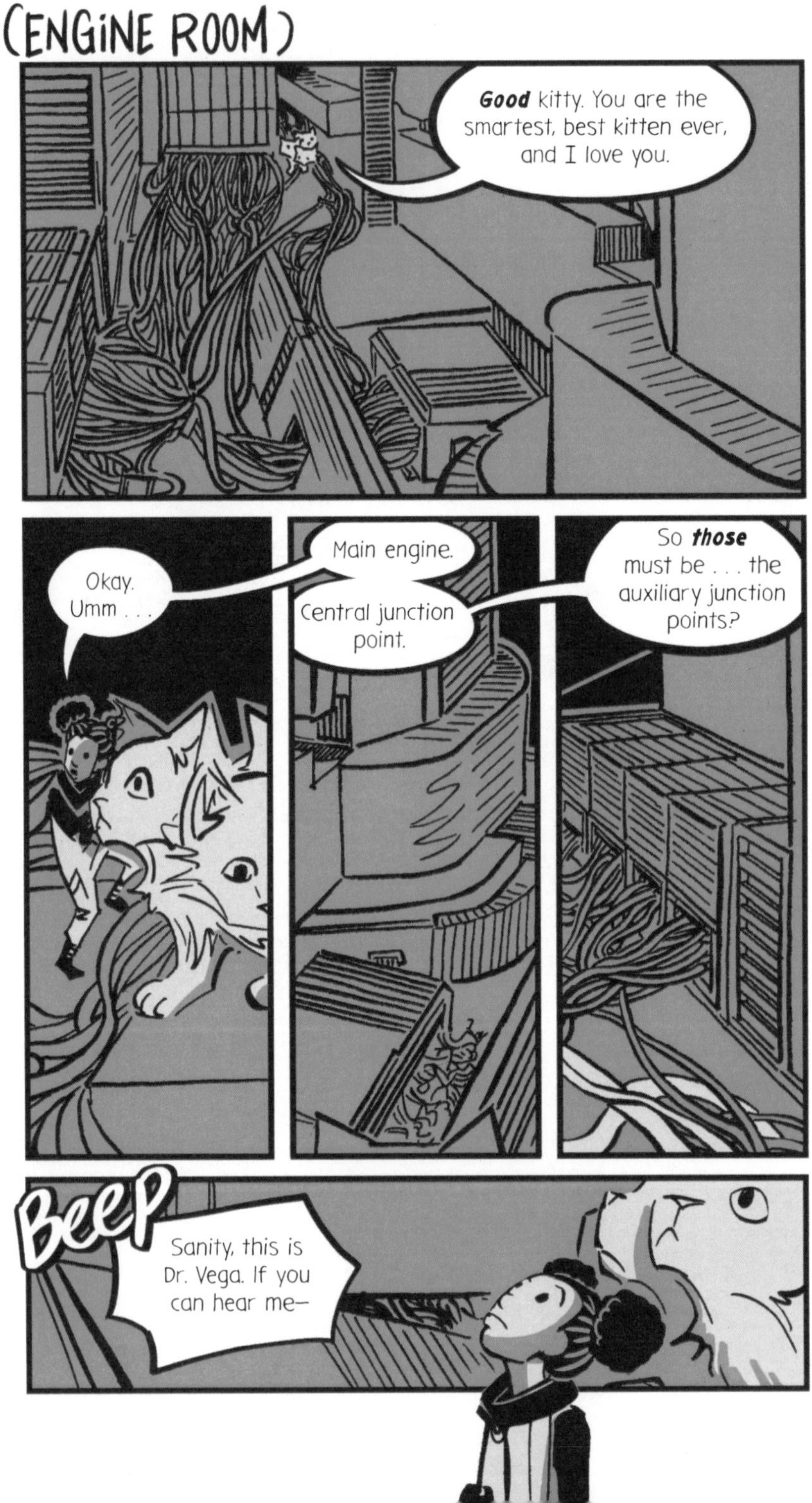
(ENGINE ROOM)
Good kitty. You are the smartest, best kitten ever, and I love you.
Okay. Umm . . .
Main engine.
Central junction point.
So ***those*** must be . . . the auxiliary junction points?
Beep
Sanity, this is Dr. Vega. If you can hear me—

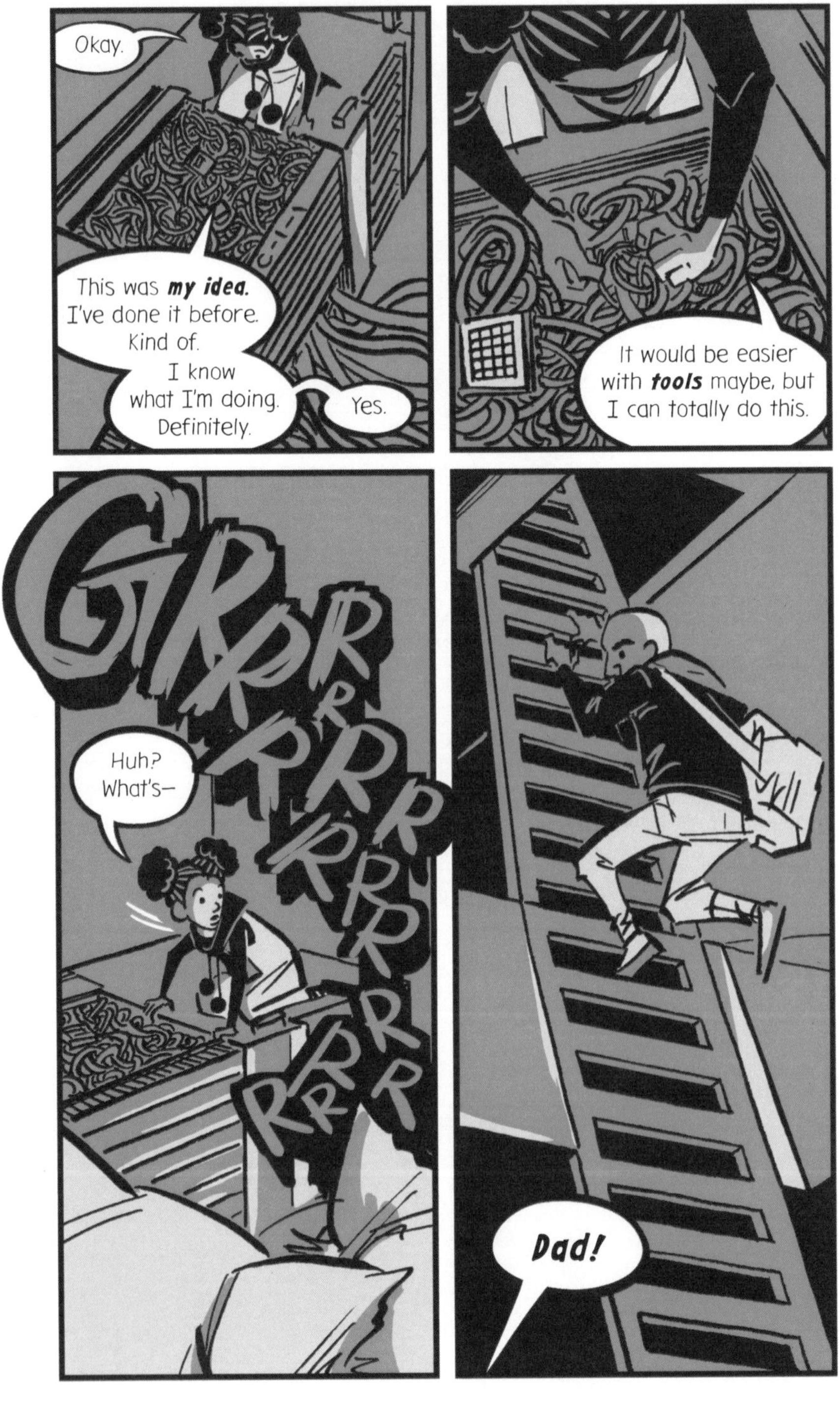
Okay.
This was **my idea.** I've done it before. Kind of.
I know what I'm doing. Definitely.
Yes.
It would be easier with **tools** maybe, but I can totally do this.
GRRRRRRRRRRRRRRRRR
Huh? What's—
Dad!

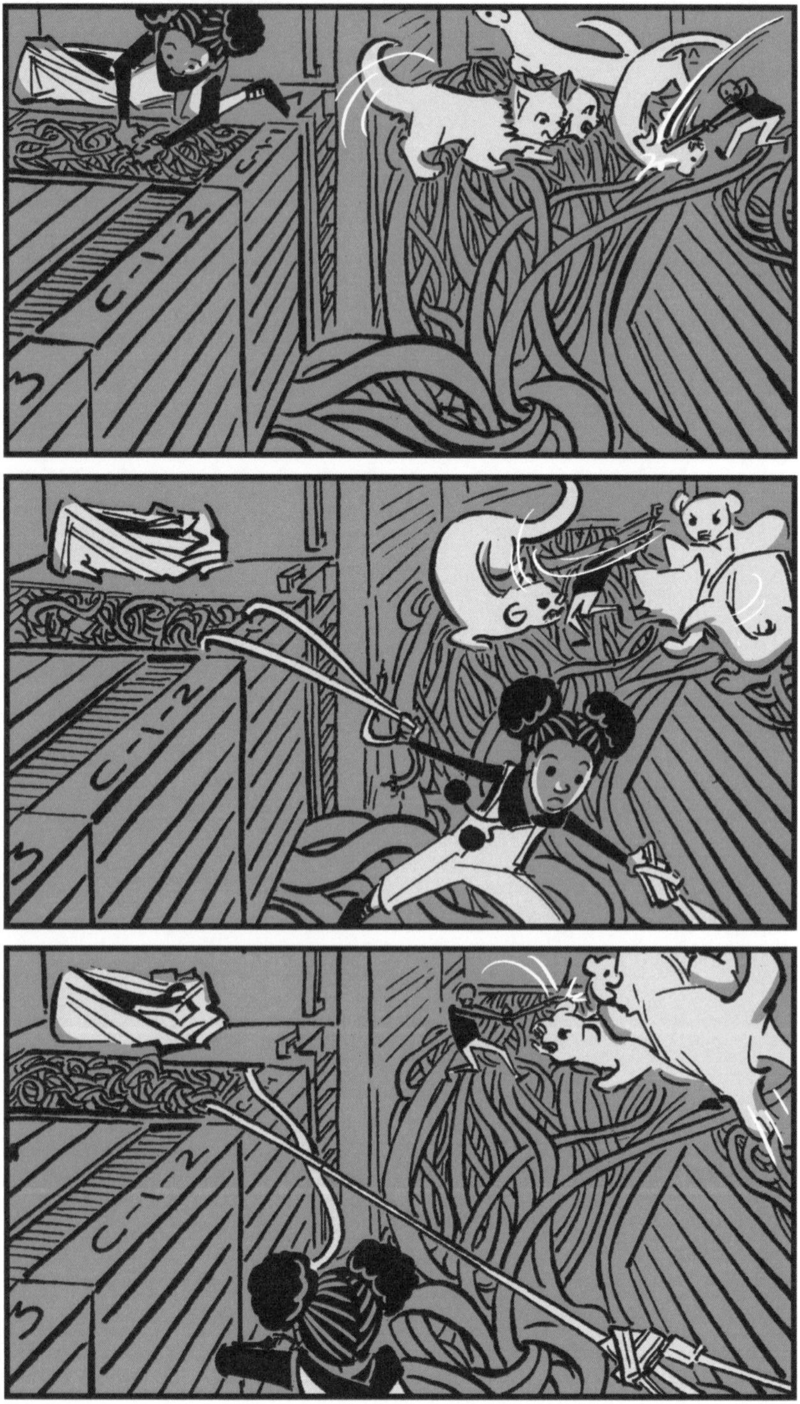
C-1-2
3
C-1-2
3
C-1-2
3

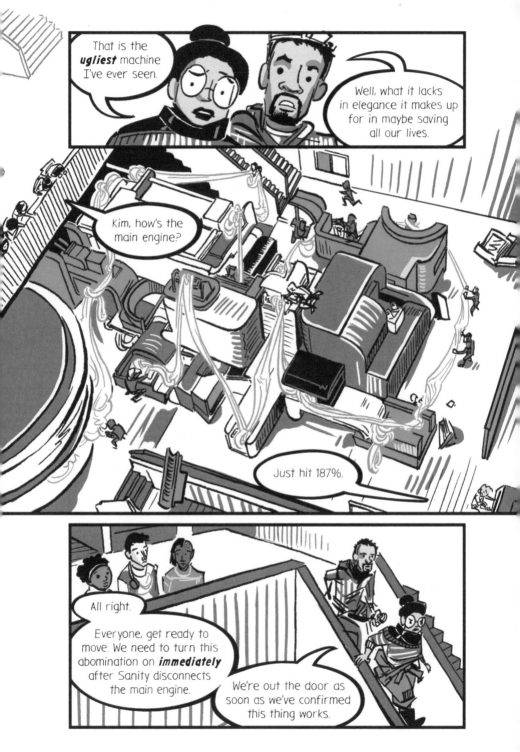

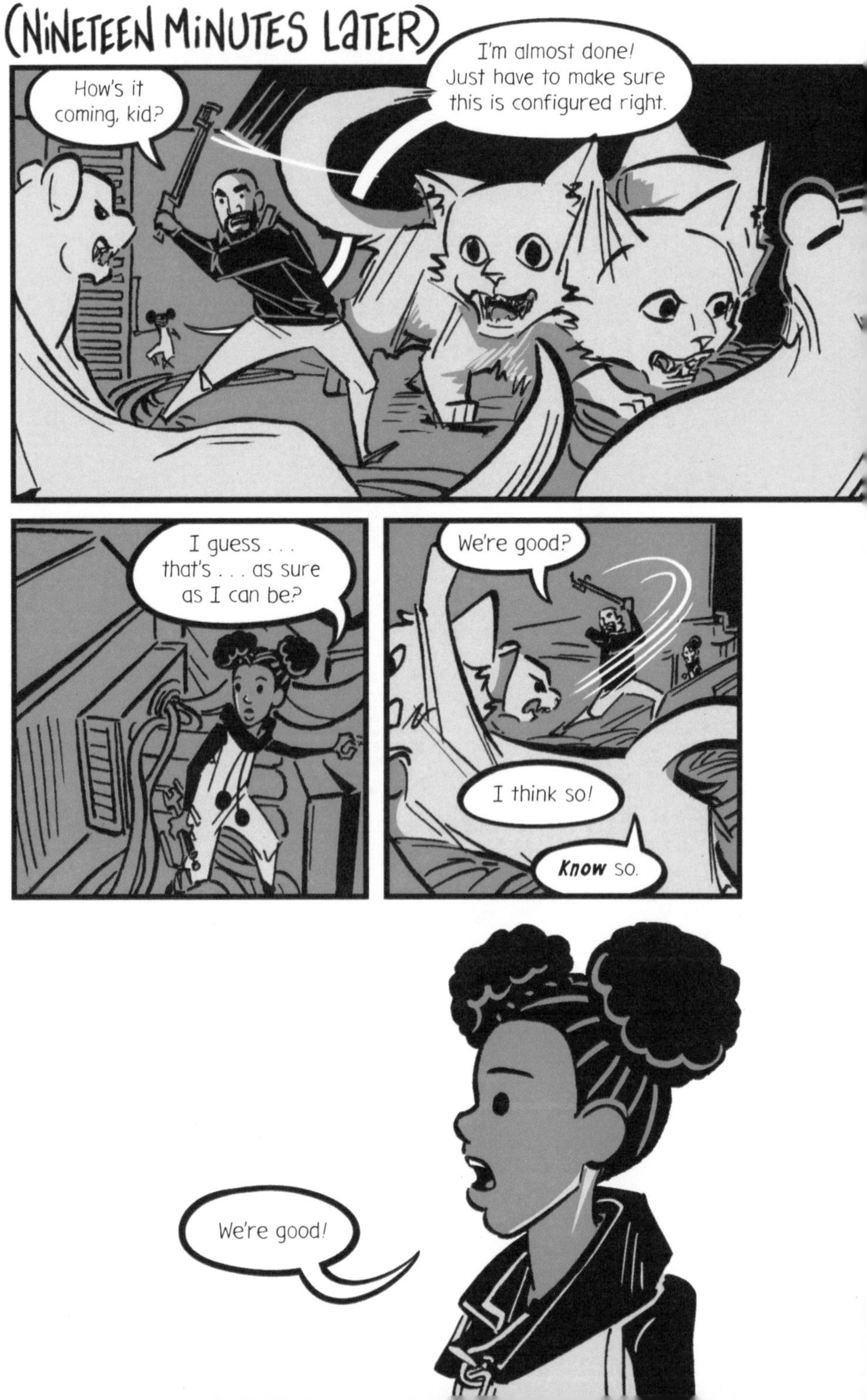

(NINETEEN MINUTES LATER)
How's it coming, kid?
I'm almost done! Just have to make sure this is configured right.
I guess . . . that's . . . as sure as I can be?
We're good?
I think so!
Know so.
We're good!

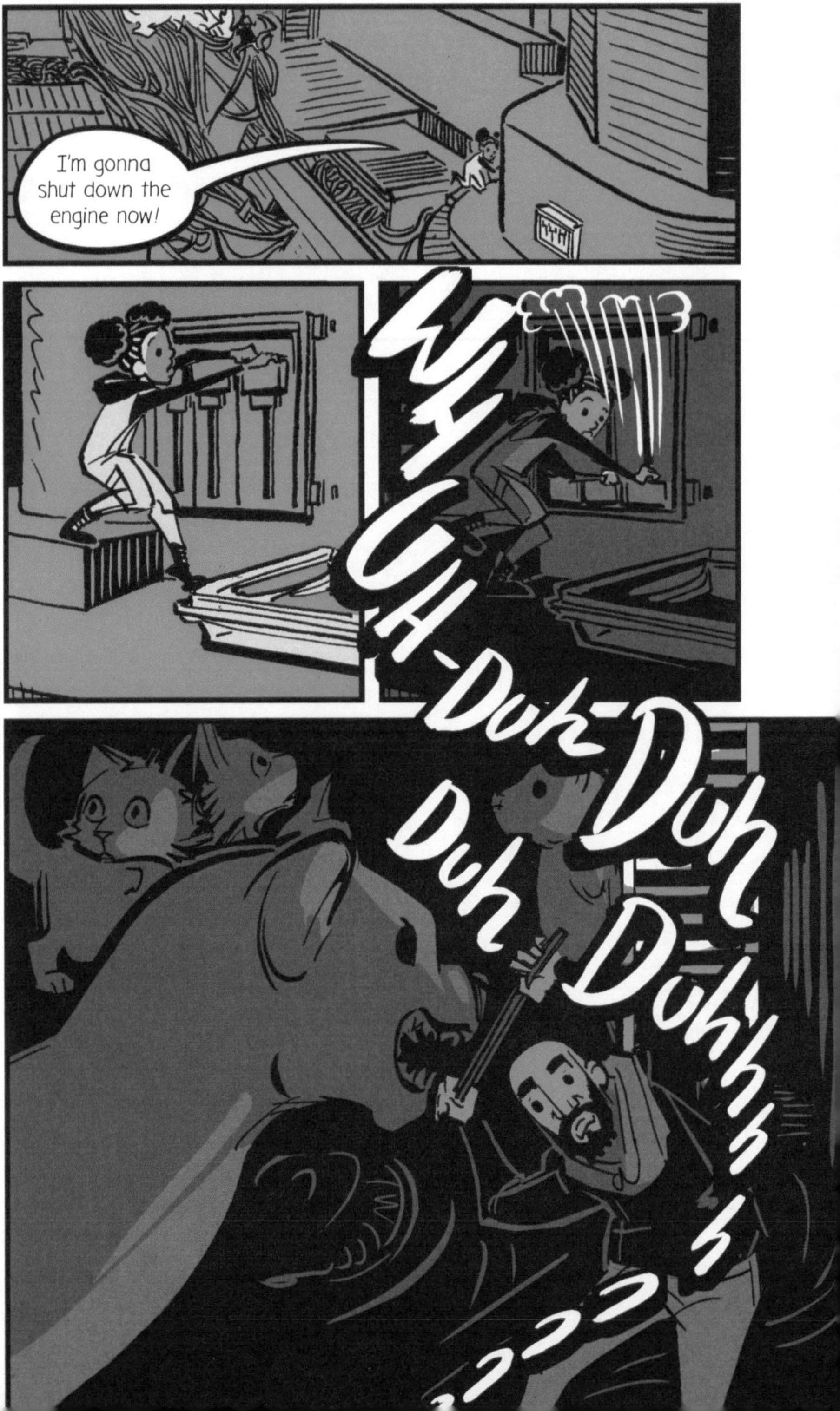
I'm gonna shut down the engine now!
WHUH-Duh Duh Duh Duhhhh

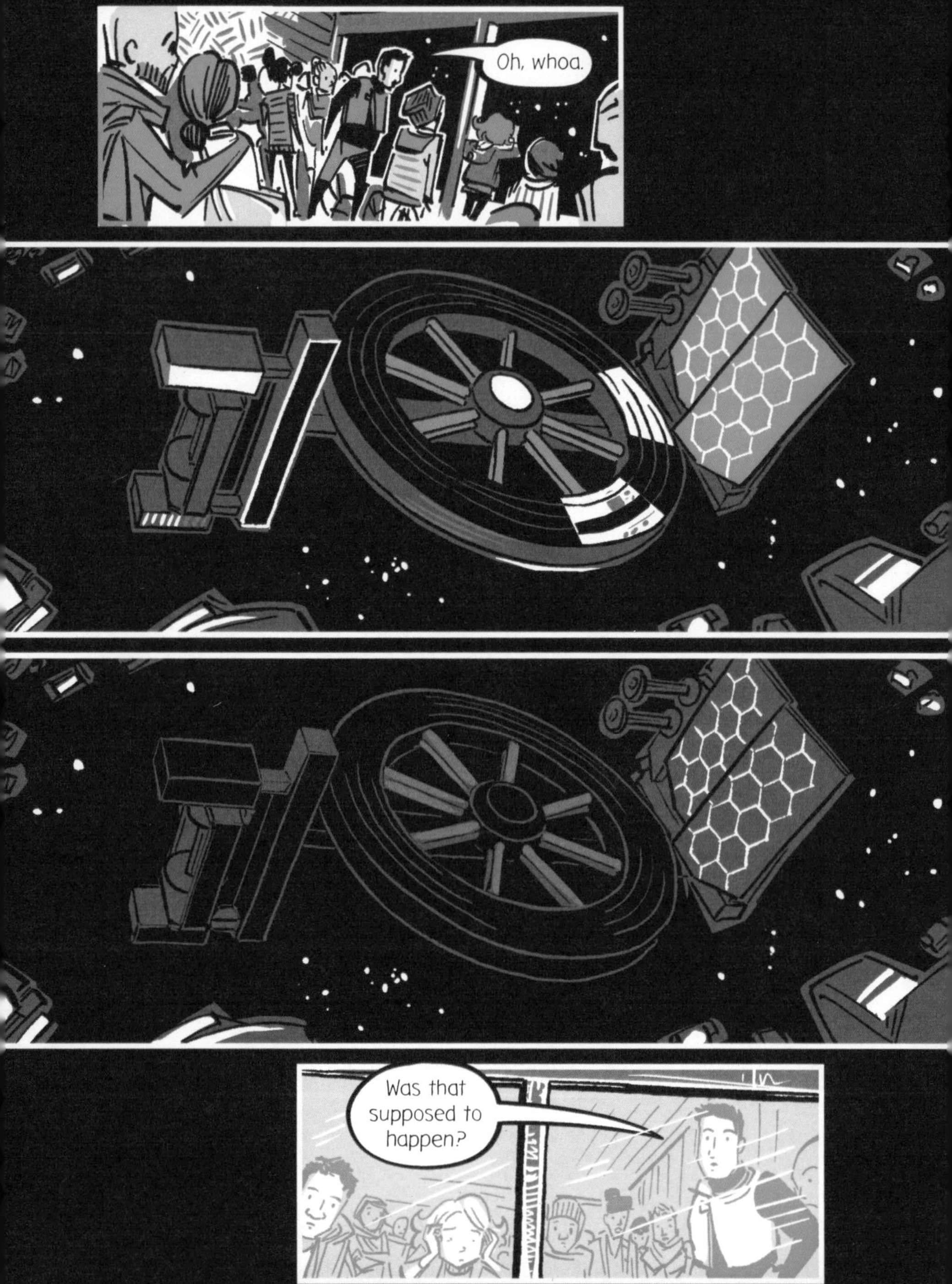
Oh, whoa.
Was that supposed to happen?

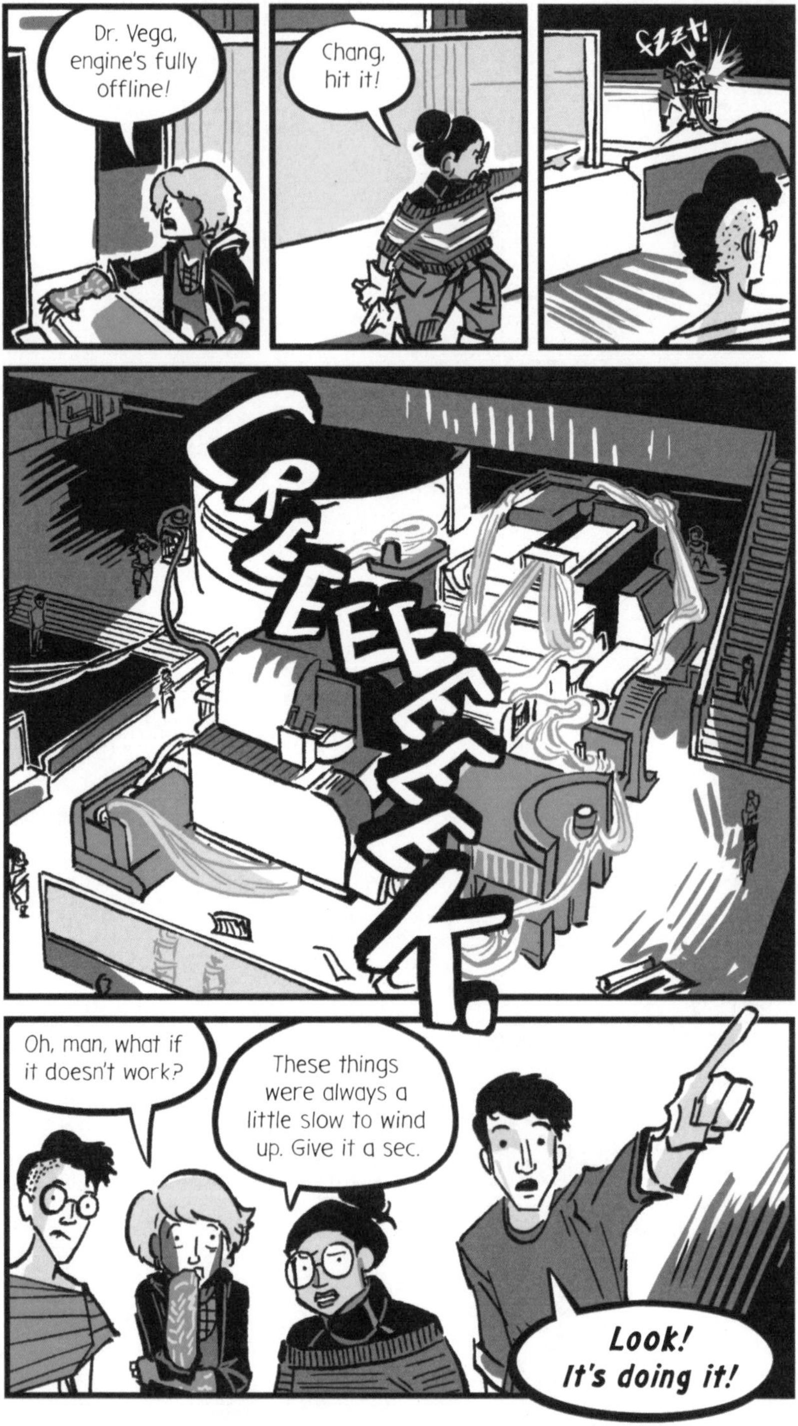
Dr. Vega, engine's fully offline!
Chang, hit it!
fzzt!
CREEEEEEEK.
Oh, man, what if it doesn't work?
These things were always a little slow to wind up. Give it a sec.
Look! It's doing it!

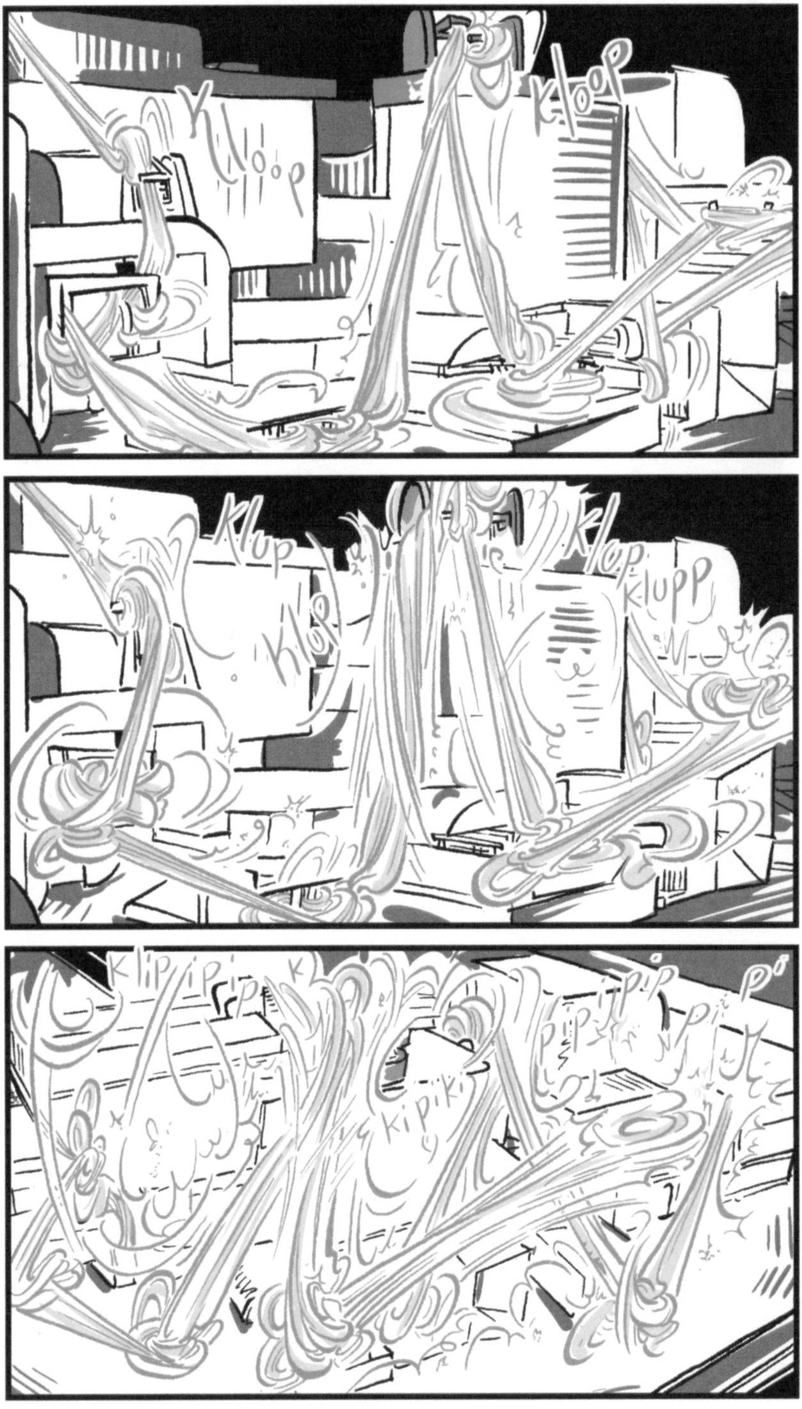
Kloop
Kloop
Klop
Klop
Klop
klupp
klipipi
kipiki

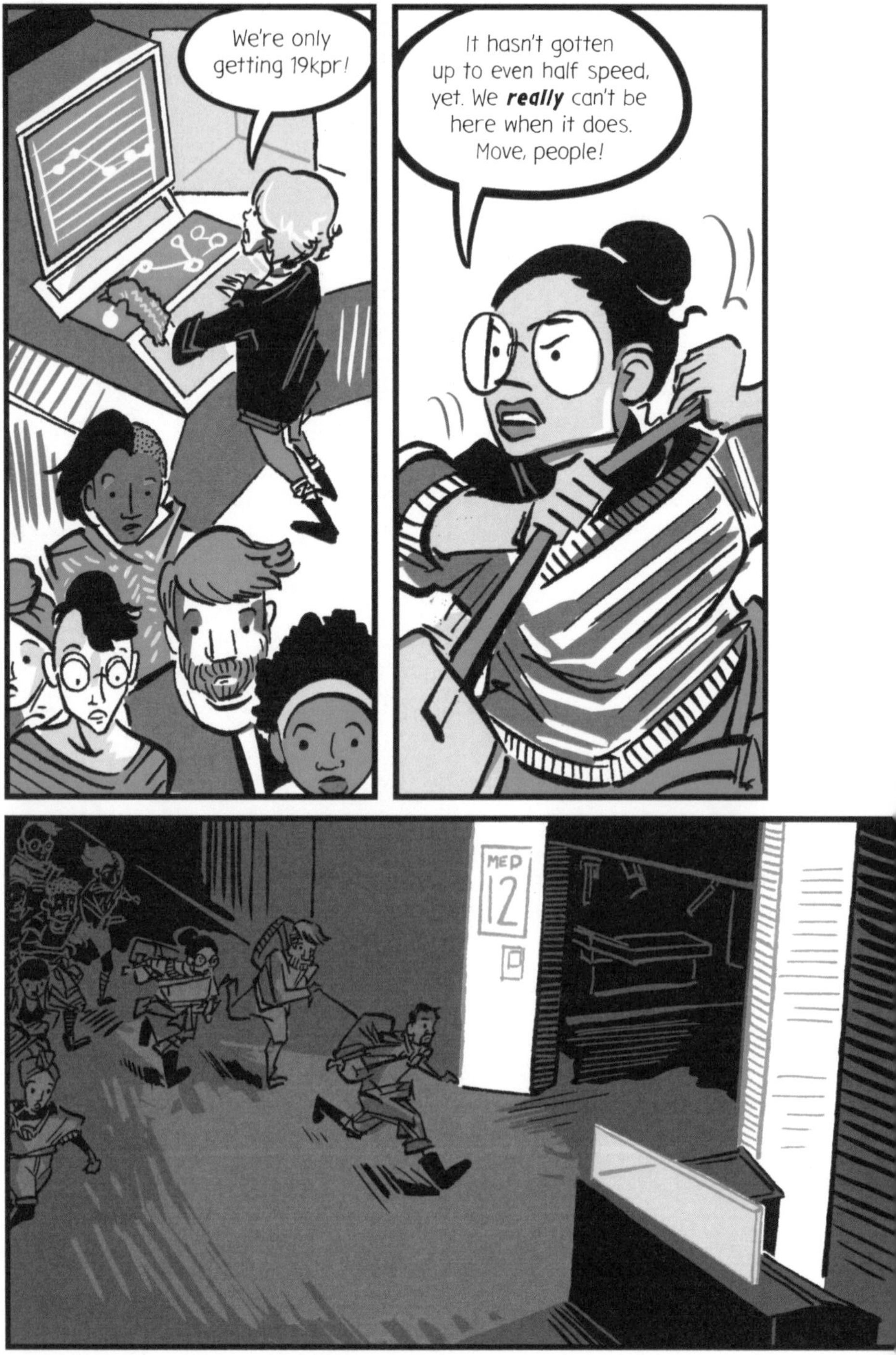
We're only getting 19kpr!
It hasn't gotten up to even half speed, yet. We *really* can't be here when it does. Move, people!
MED
12

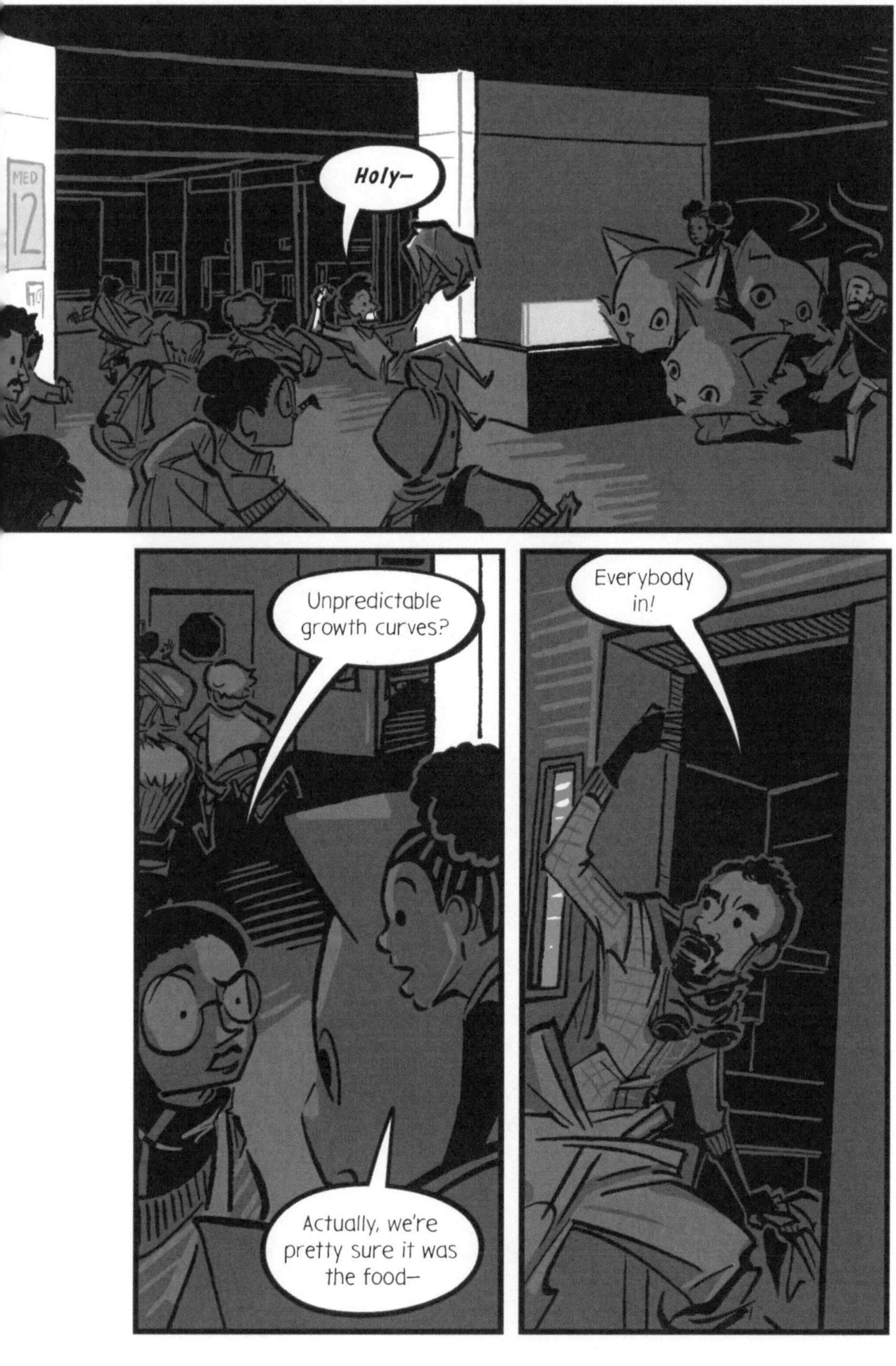
MED
12
Holy—
Unpredictable growth curves?
Actually, we're pretty sure it was the food—
Everybody in!

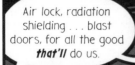

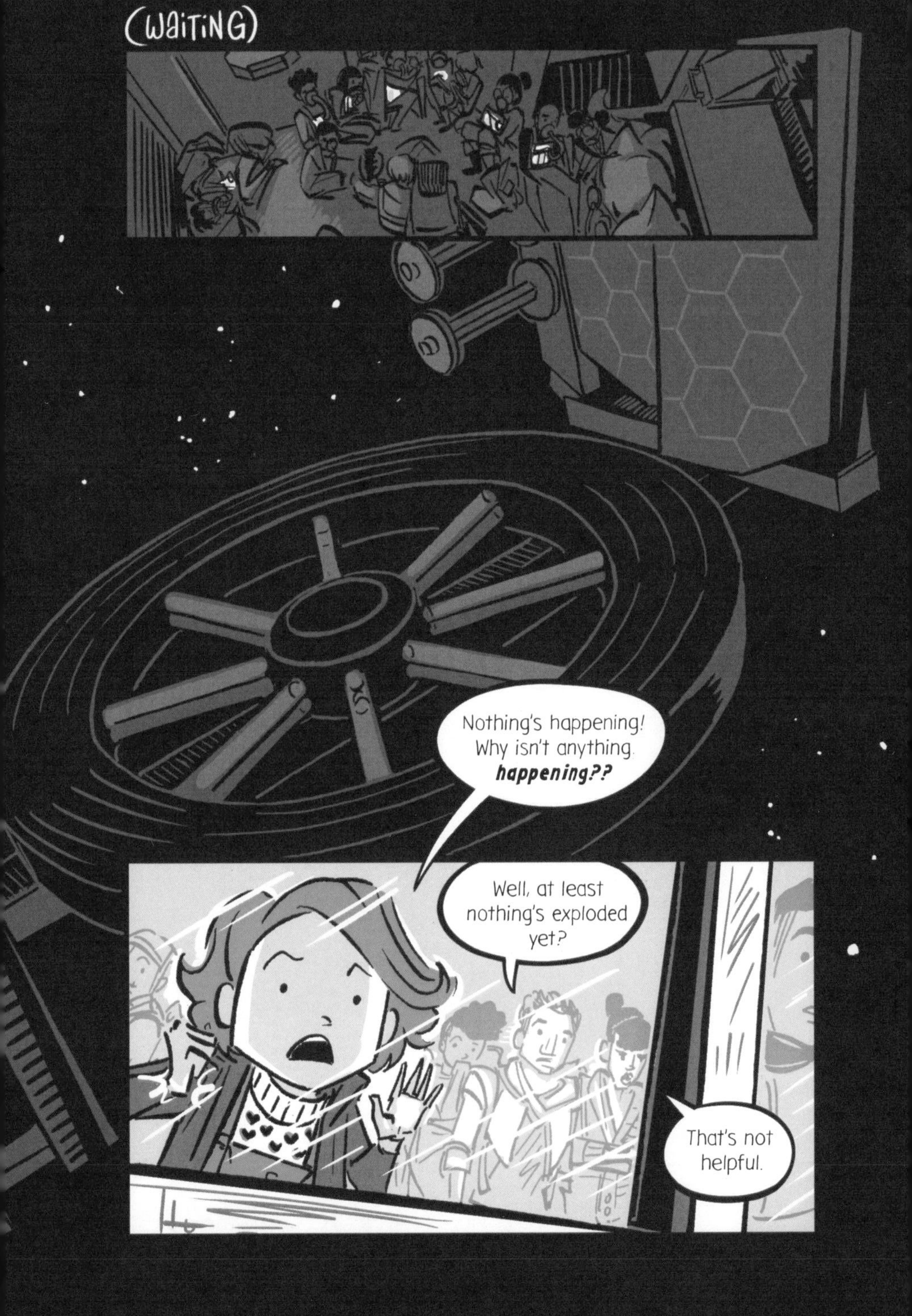
(WAITING)
Nothing's happening! Why isn't anything **happening??**
Well, at least nothing's exploded yet?
That's not helpful.

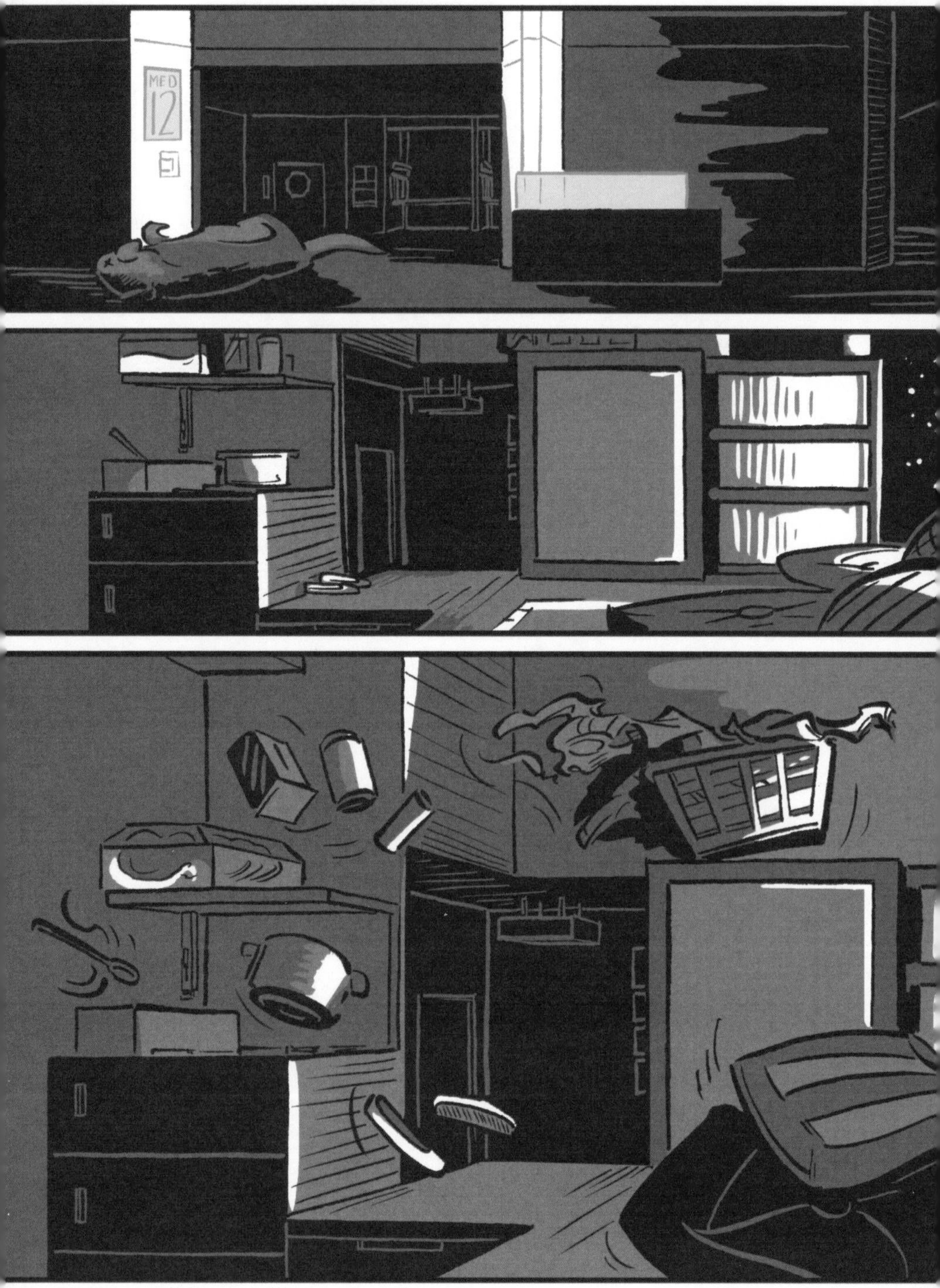
MED
12

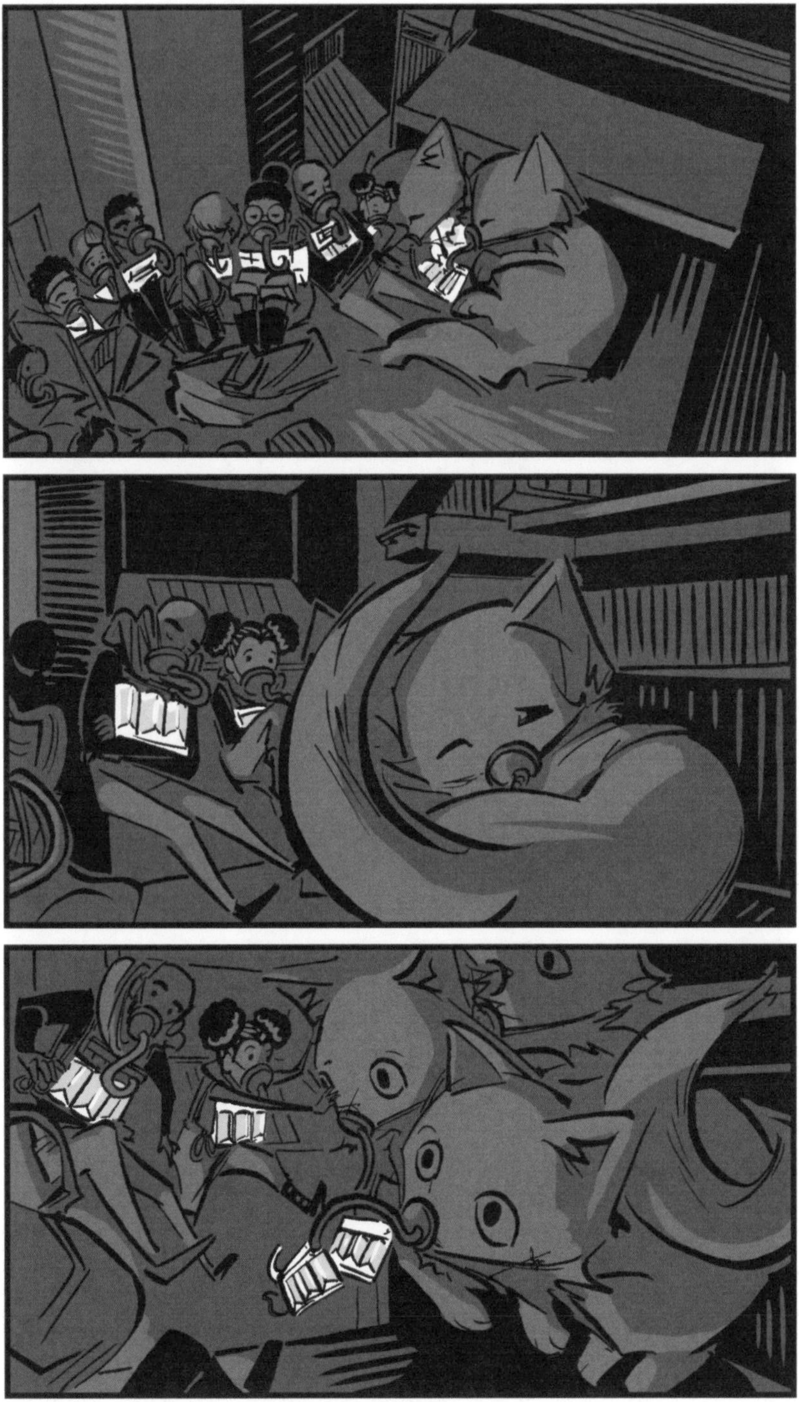

(EVENTUALLY)

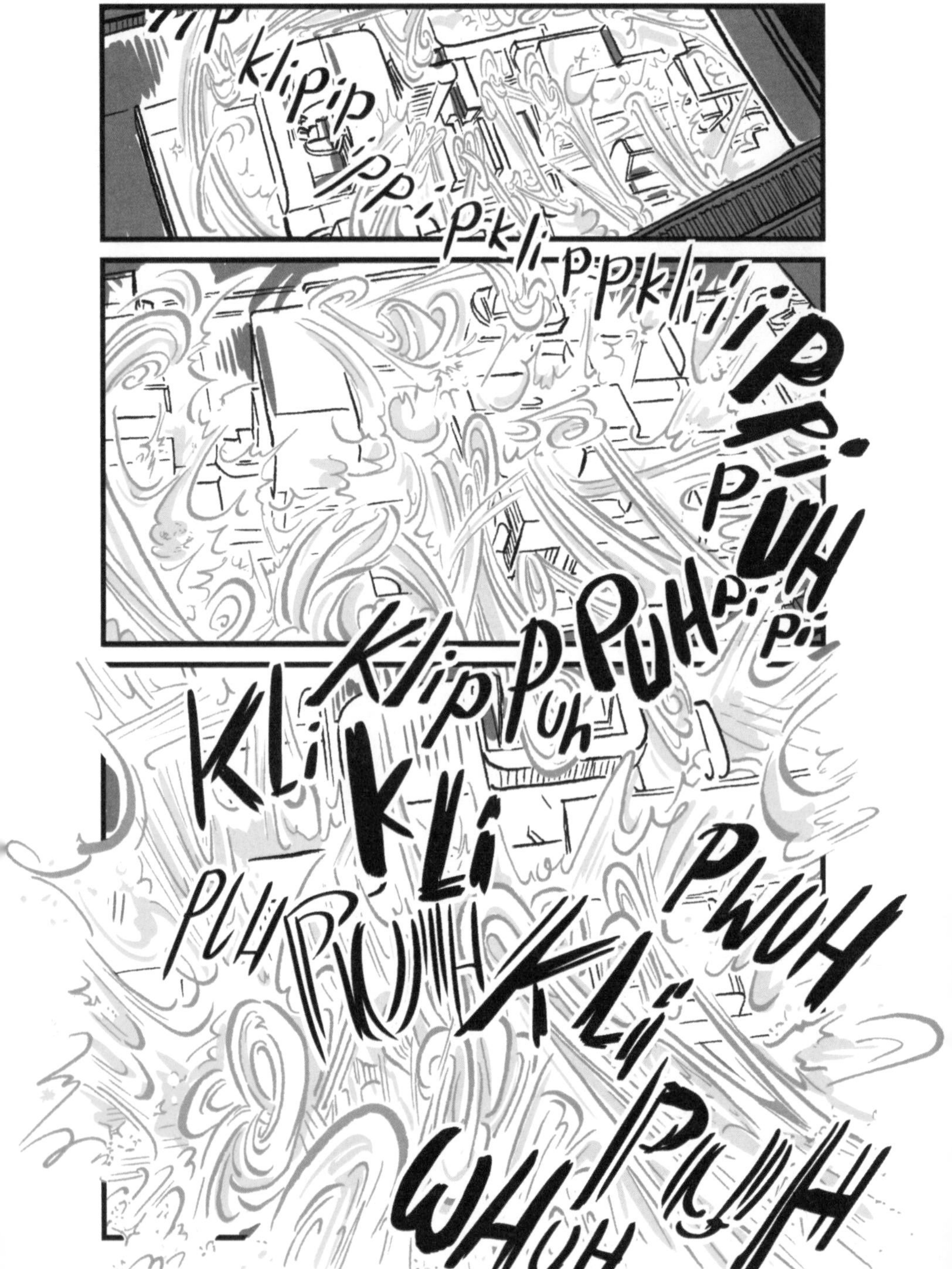
klipip
pkli
PPklii
KLI
Klip
PUH
KLI
PUH
PWUH
KLI
PUH
WHUH

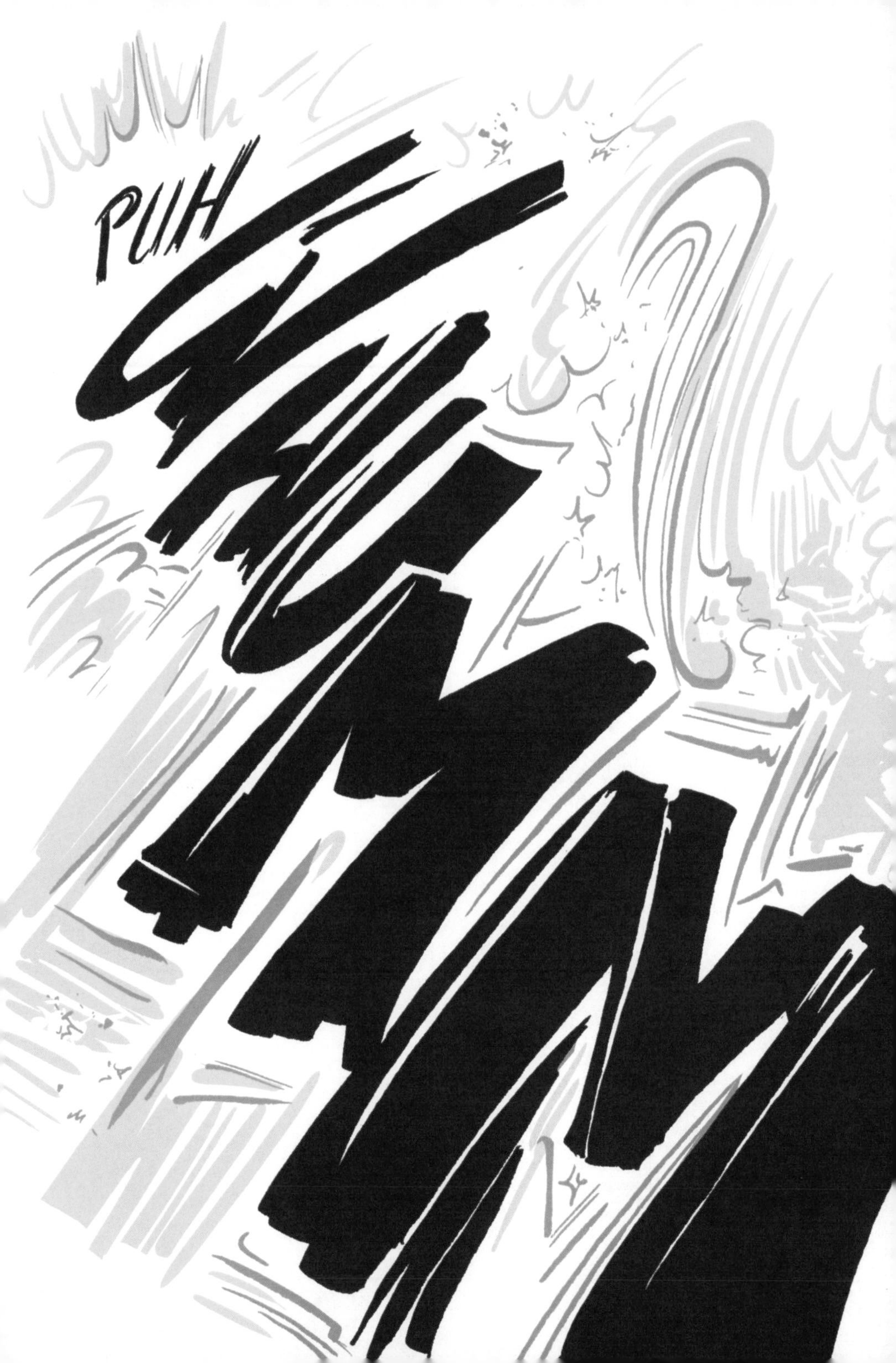
PUH

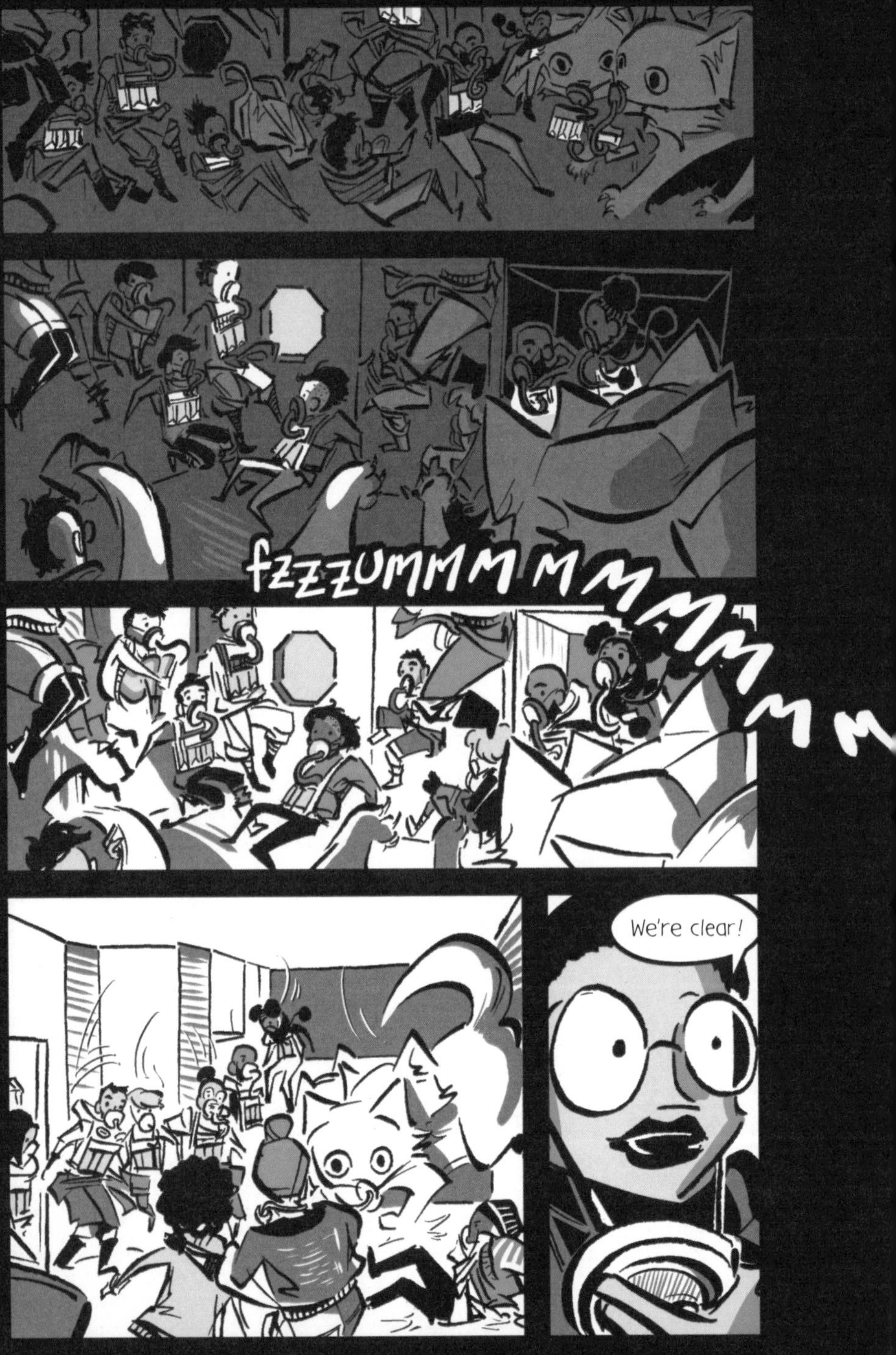
fzzzummmmmmmmmmm
We're clear!

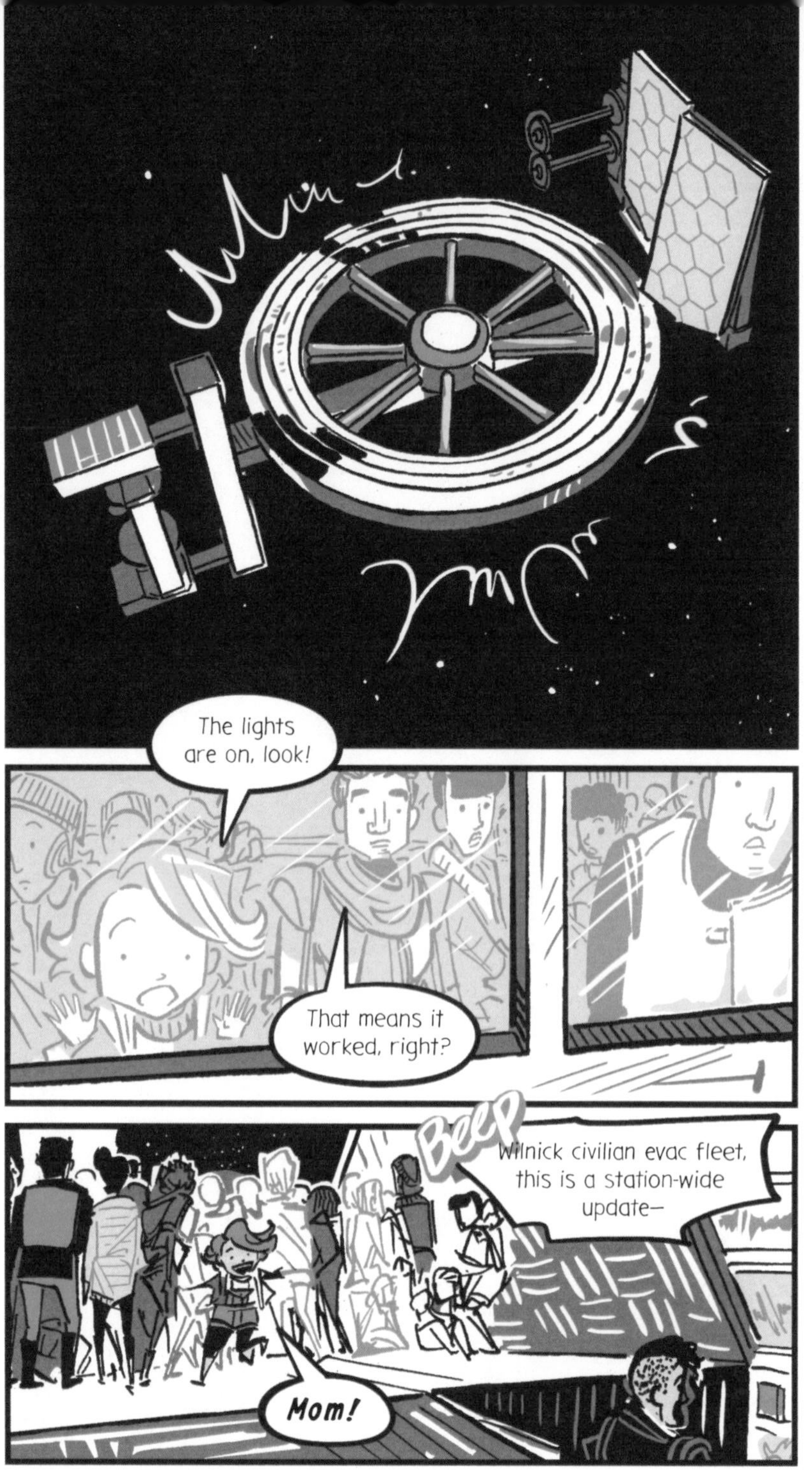
The lights are on, look!
That means it worked, right?
Beep
Wilnick civilian evac fleet, this is a station-wide update—
Mom!

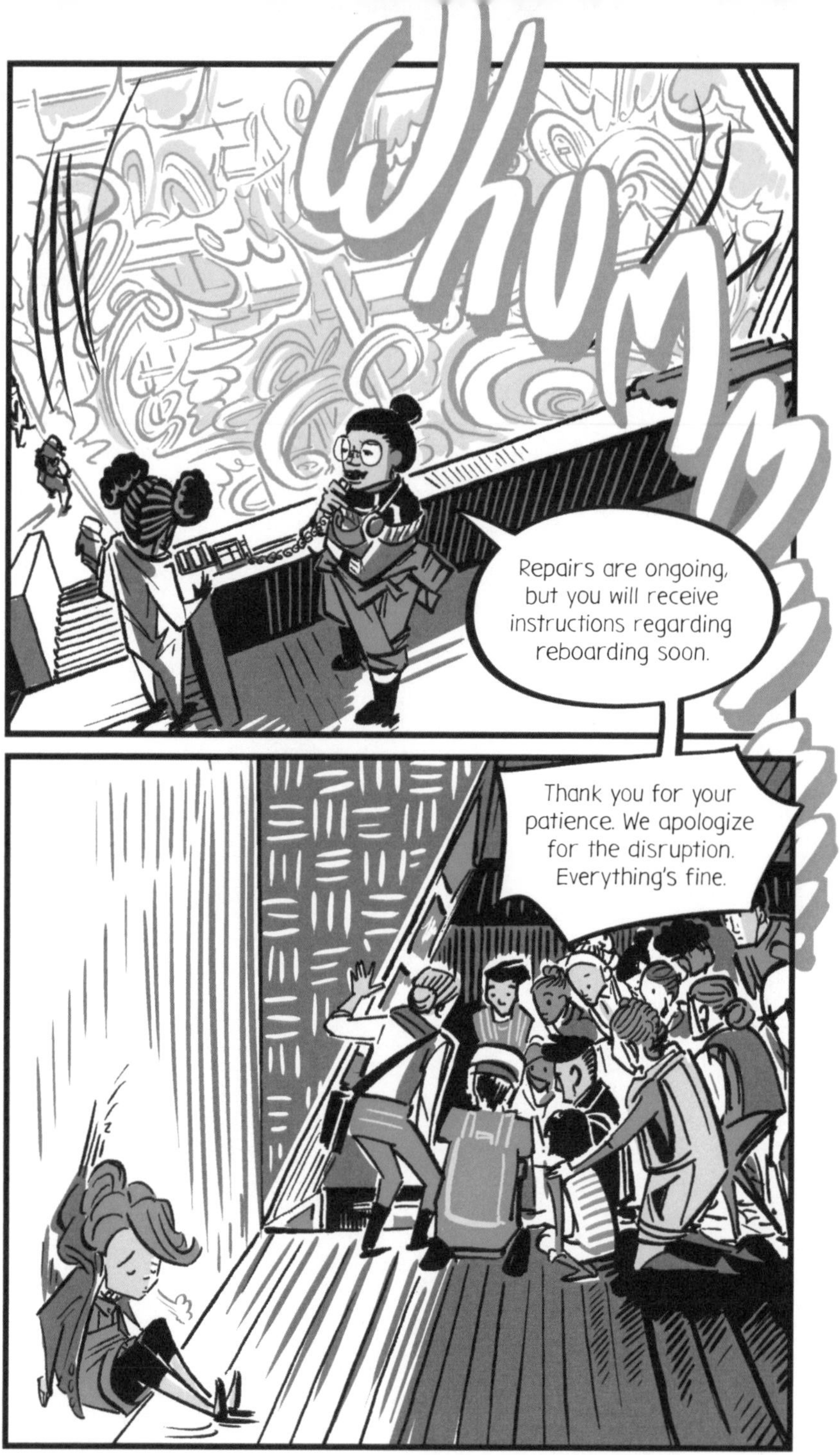
Repairs are ongoing, but you will receive instructions regarding reboarding soon.
Thank you for your patience. We apologize for the disruption. Everything's fine.

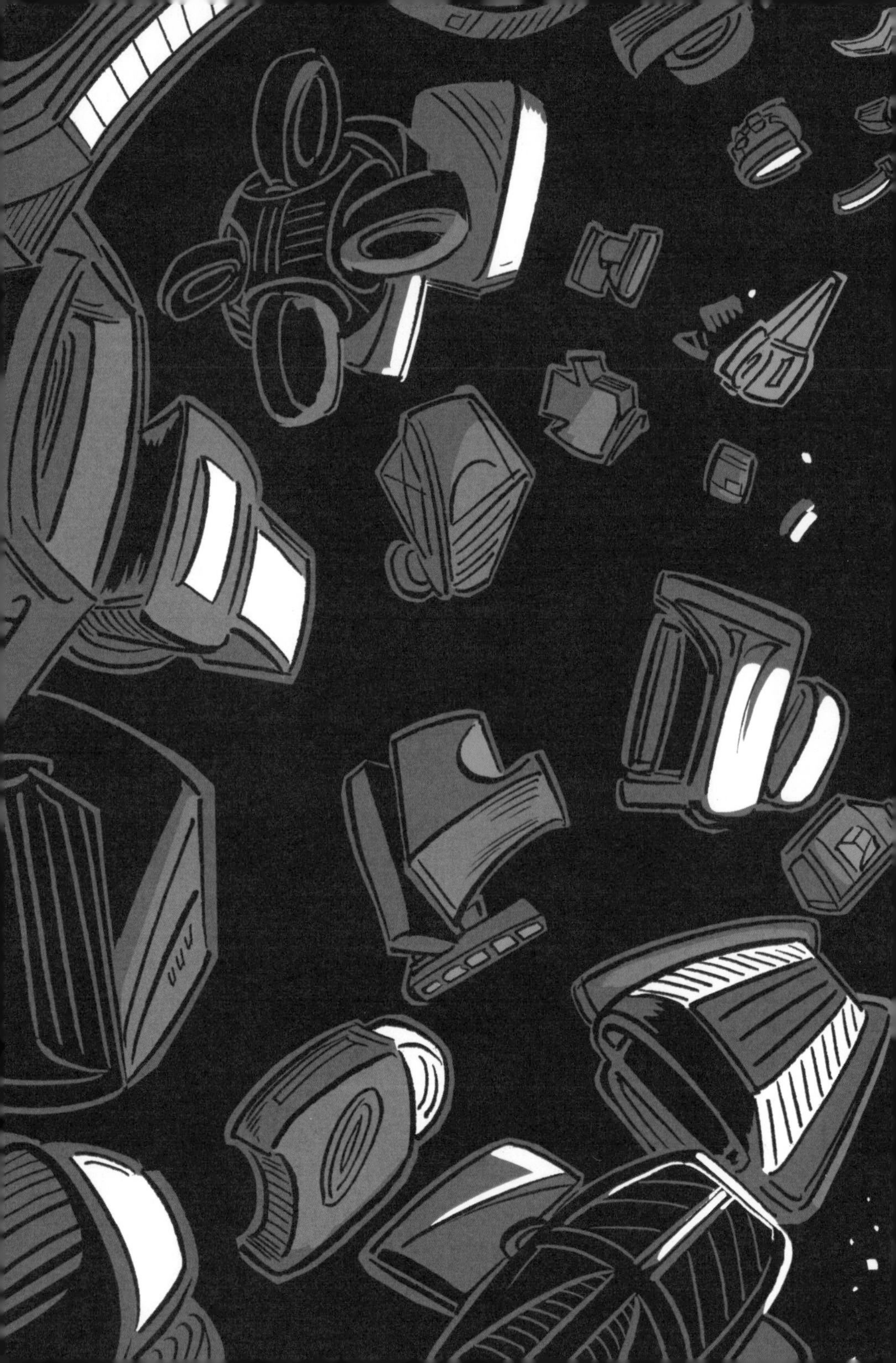

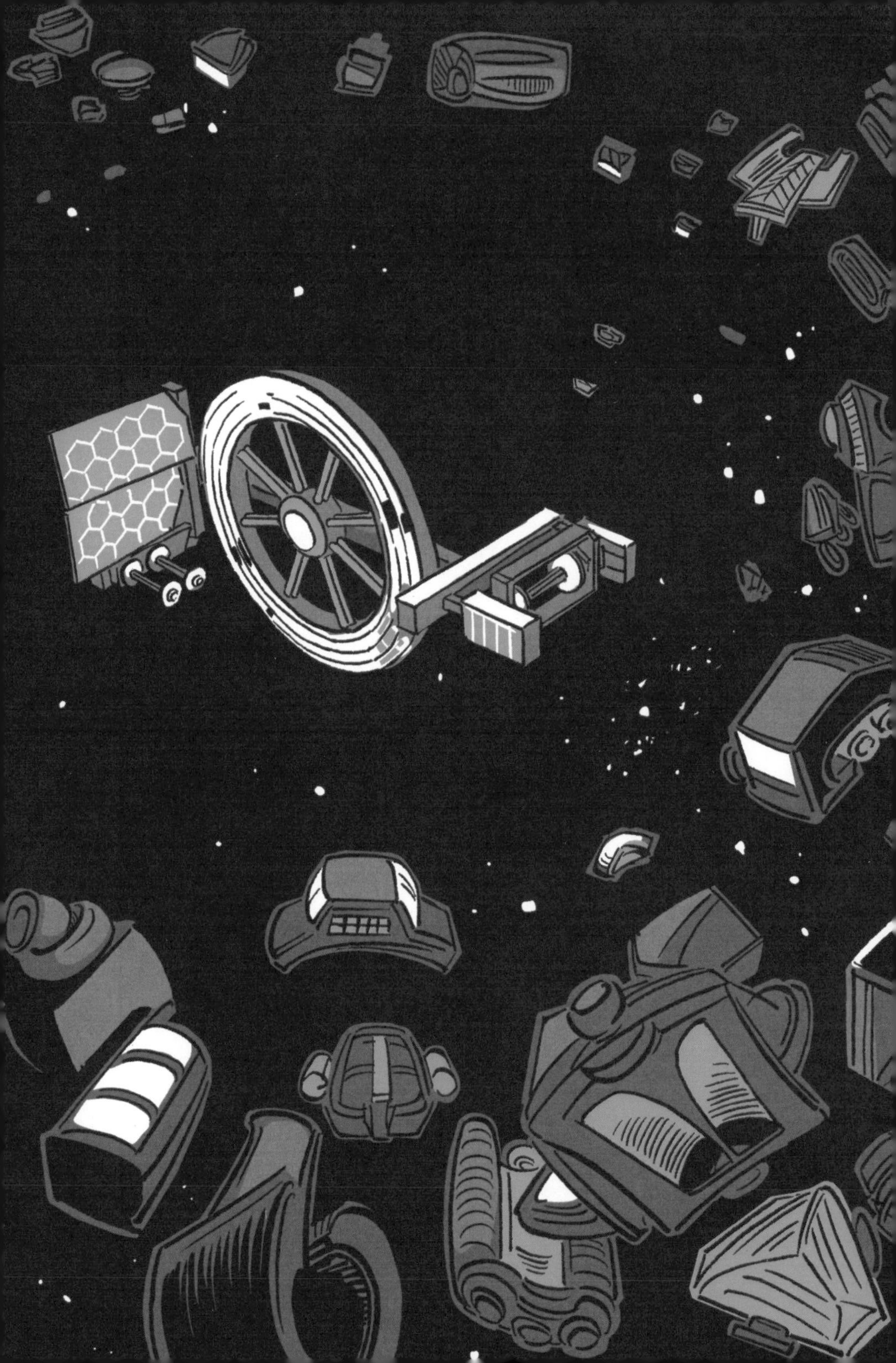

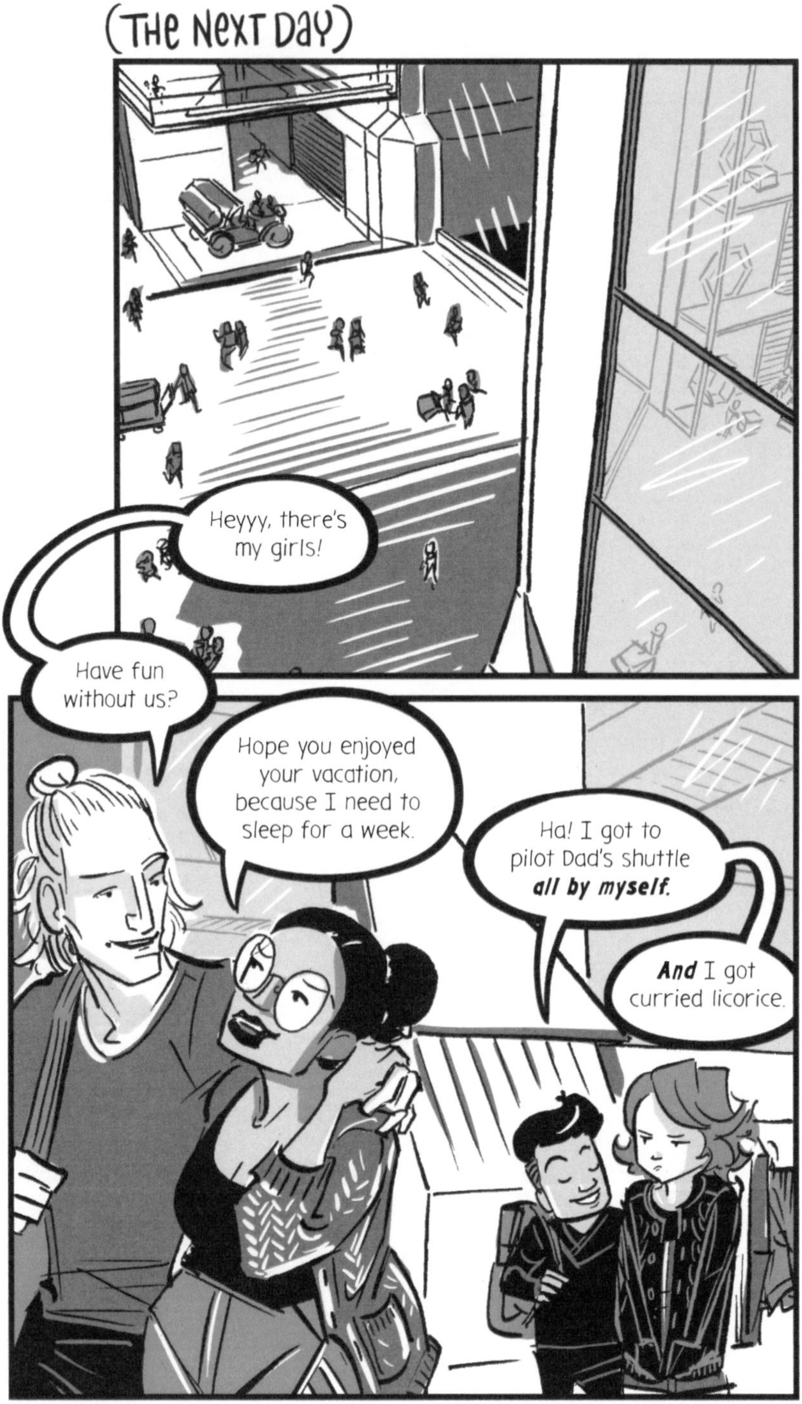
(THE NEXT DAY)
Heyyy, there's my girls!
Have fun without us?
Hope you enjoyed your vacation, because I need to sleep for a week.
Ha! I got to pilot Dad's shuttle ***all by myself.***
And I got curried licorice.

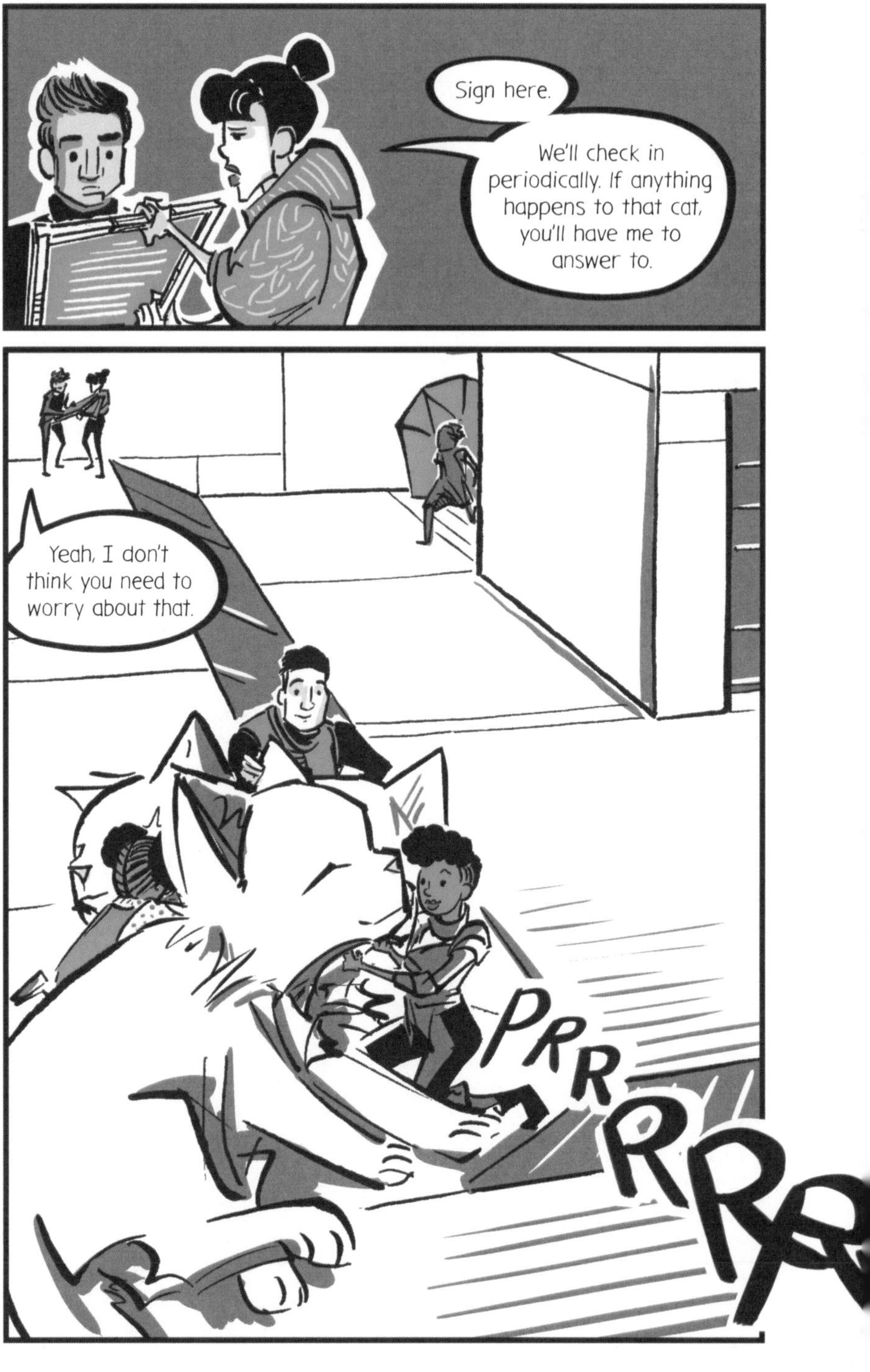
Sign here.
We'll check in periodically. If anything happens to that cat, you'll have me to answer to.
Yeah, I don't think you need to worry about that.
PRRRRR

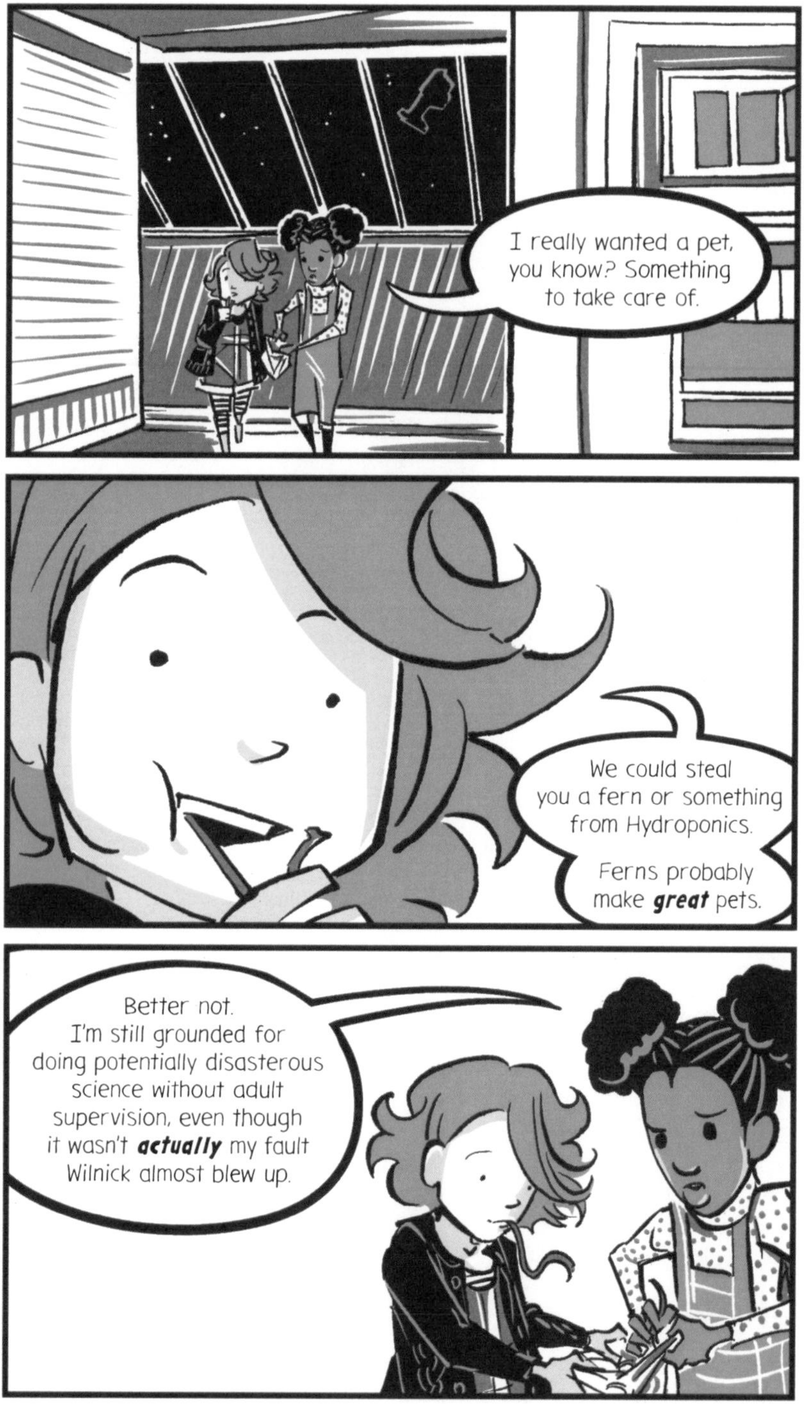
I really wanted a pet, you know? Something to take care of.
We could steal you a fern or something from Hydroponics.
Ferns probably make **great** pets.
Better not. I'm still grounded for doing potentially disasterous science without adult supervision, even though it wasn't **actually** my fault Wilnick almost blew up.

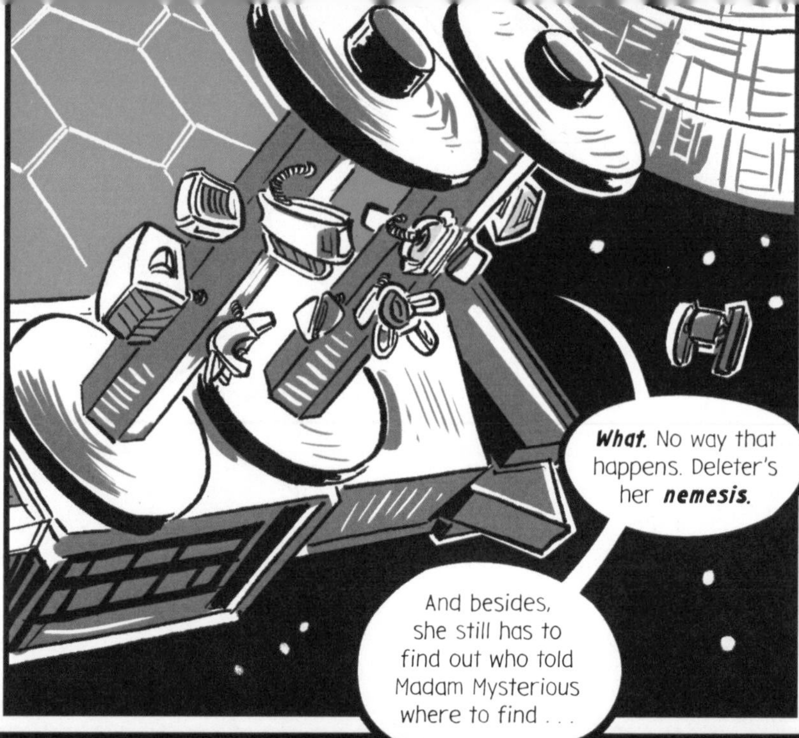
What. No way that happens. Deleter's her ***nemesis.***
And besides, she still has to find out who told Madam Mysterious where to find . . .

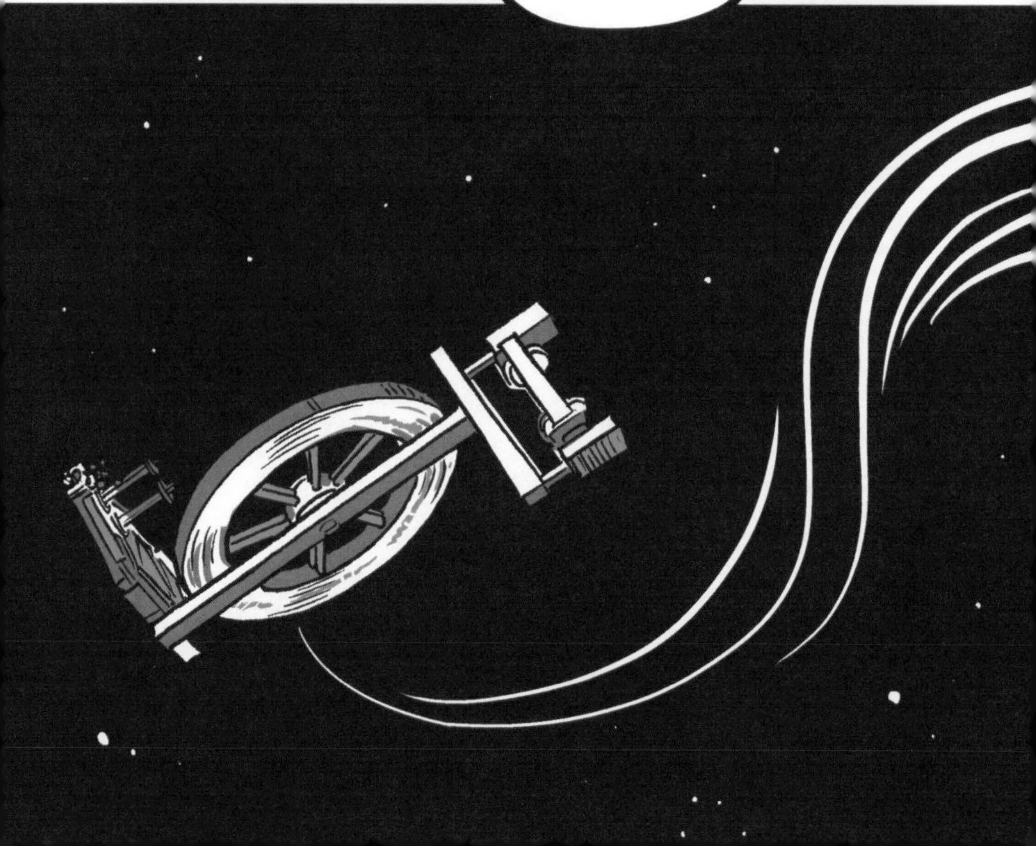

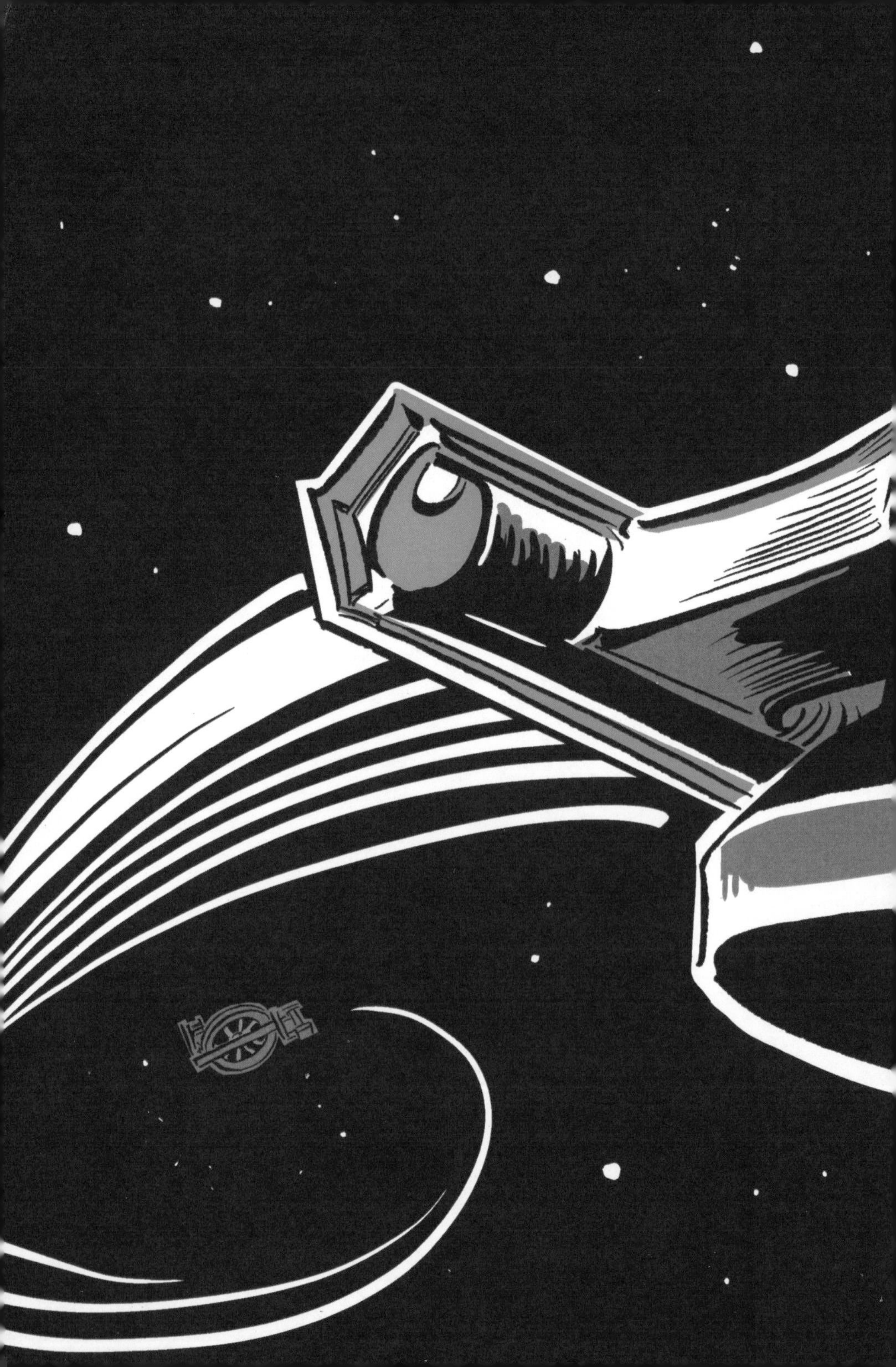

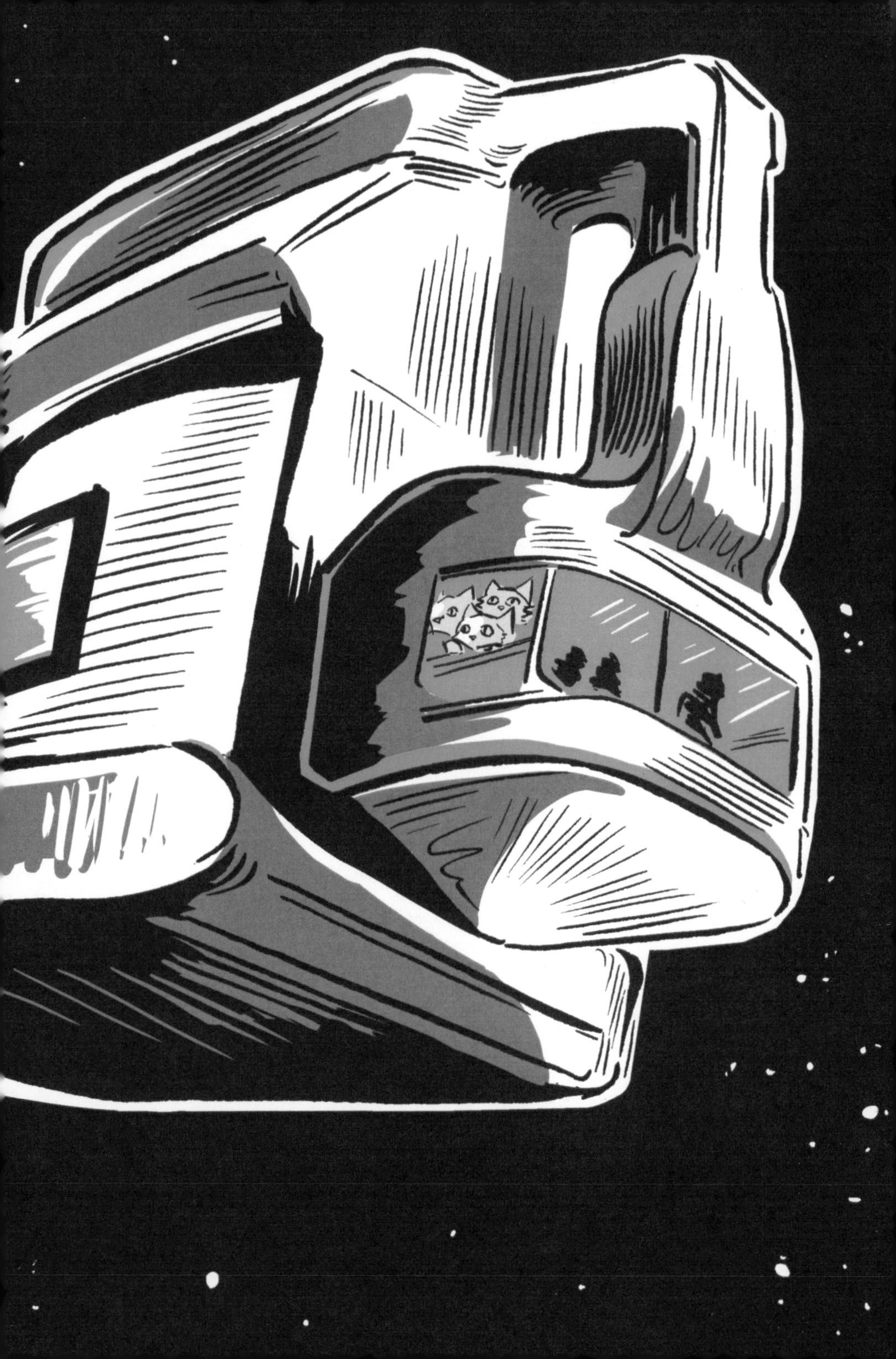

MOLLY BROOKS is the illustrator of *Flying Machines: How the Wright Brothers Soared* by Alison Wilgus, and the creator of many comics, which you can see on her website (mollybrooks.com). Her illustrations have appeared in the *Village Voice*, the *Guardian*, the *Boston Globe*, *Time Out New York*, the *Nashville Scene*, the *Riverfront Times*, the *Toast*, *BUST Magazine*, ESPN social, *Sports Illustrated* online, and others. She spends her spare time watching vintage buddy-cop shows and making comics about knitting, hockey, and/or feelings. Molly lives and works in Brooklyn.

Stay tuned for
more adventures with

Sanity &

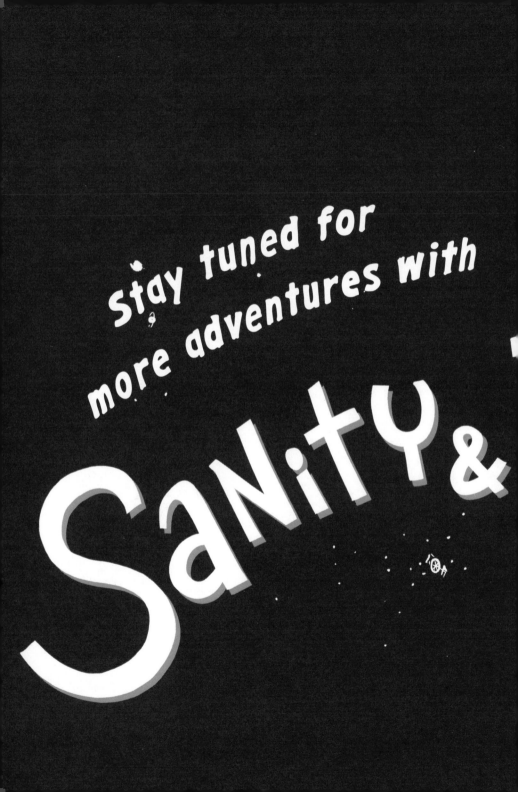

TALLULAH

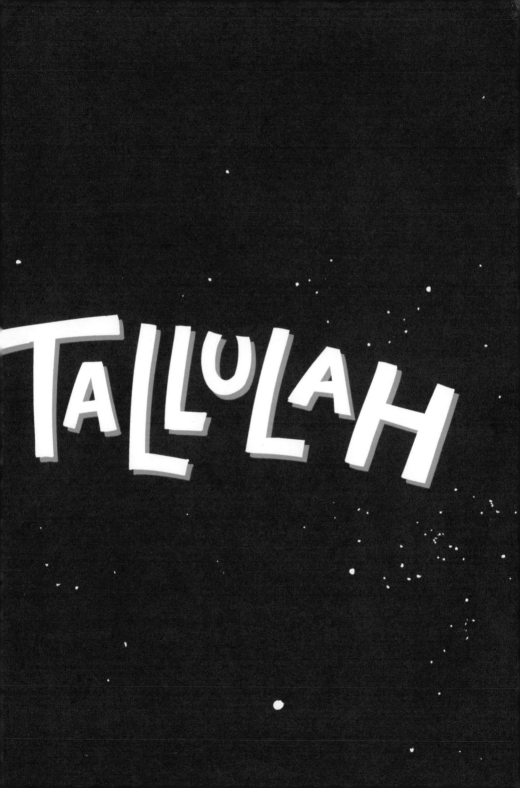